More Outstanding Praise for
WELCOME TO BRAGGSVILLE

"The most dazzling, most unsettling, most oh-my-God-listen-up novel you'll read this year is called *Welcome to Braggsville*. . . . T. Geronimo Johnson plays cultural criticism like it's acid jazz. His shockingly funny story pricks every nerve of the American body politic. . . . *Braggsville* lashes self-satisfied liberals in the academy and self-deluded Confederates in the attic. As we feign surprise at police brutality and our Twitter outrage flits from Ferguson to Staten Island to Cleveland, this is just the discomfiting book we need. . . . Johnson is better at mocking academia than anybody since David Lodge, and his narration has such athleticism that you feel energized just running alongside him—or even several strides behind. . . . Welcome to Braggsville. It's about time."

—Ron Charles, *Washington Post*

"Reading this novel is not unlike listening to an erudite satirist play the dozens in a marathon performance. . . . But the satire leaping off these pages is not hate, nor the dead-end cynical variety that withers with a sneer. Here, the observations have too much wit and knowing, the characters too much soul, for Johnson's story to feel trapped in callow hipster irony. Organic, plucky, smart, *Welcome to Braggsville* is the funniest sendup of identity politics, the academy and white racial anxiety to hit the scene in years." —*New York Times Book Review*

"A partial list of great American writers whose names came to mind as I was reading T. Geronimo Johnson's new novel, *Welcome to Braggsville*: Tom Wolfe, Mark Twain, Toni Morrison, H.L. Mencken, Don DeLillo, David Foster Wallace, Norman Mailer and Ralph Ellison, Ralph Ellison, Ralph Ellison. Johnson's timely novel is a tipsy social satire about race and the oh-so-fragile ties that bind disparate parts of this country into an imperfect and restless union. It's an ambitious book that not only wants to say something big about America, but aims to do so in a big American voice that contains multitudes. . . . [It's] *Confederates in the Attic* meets *A Confederacy of Dunces* . . . It's as American as chattel slavery and Lenny Bruce Lee."
—Maureen Corrigan, NPR's *Fresh Air*

"When was the last time you were shocked by a turn in a novel? Not merely surprised or astonished but actually stunned? T. Geronimo Johnson makes it happen twice in his second novel . . . *Welcome to Braggsville* is audacious, unpredictable, exuberant and even tragic, in the most classic meaning of the word. . . . A heady mix of satire and hyperbole . . . [it] reads like a literary hybrid of David Foster Wallace and Colson Whitehead: word-besotted, incorporating references that are, by turns, high and pop cultural, while piercing the pretensions of academia and the complacencies of small-town life. . . . Although Johnson's novel does not touch on [Eric Garner or Michael Brown], it is impossible to read without imagining them as context."
—David Ulin, *Los Angeles Times*

"A rollicking satire . . . Radical, hilarious, tragic, and all too relevant."
—*O, The Oprah Magazine*

"As daring a literary high-wire act as has come along in some time. . . . This is literary showmanship . . . at its most provocative and daring. And one of the most daring things about the novel is that it's frequently and unabashedly funny. . . . [Johnson] possesses a satirical gaze that is as merciless as it is meticulous: He misses nothing. . . . [A] volatile mix of stinging satire, linguistic pyrotechnics and heartbreaking narrative."
—*San Francisco Chronicle*

"'Contradiction is the lever to transcendence,' Simone Weil once said, and transcendence is what Geronimo Johnson achieves in this remarkable novel. Every racial assumption is both acknowledged and challenged in ways at times hilarious, at other times poignant. *Welcome to Braggsville* is ambitious, wise, and brave. Johnson is an exceptionally talented writer."
—Ron Rash, *New York Times* bestselling author of *Serena*

"Johnson dresses his social criticism in lively, colloquial writing . . . On one side he depicts a reactionary South unwilling to fully reckon with its history and terrified of the slightest outside scrutiny. But his sharpest elbows are reserved for left-wing academia, which, despite its air of moral superiority, leaves its charges haplessly unable to comprehend the world outside the cloister of the classroom."   —*Wall Street Journal*

"Johnson turns this tale of a misbegotten college student protest of a Civil War reenactment into a subtle exploration of identity, personal narrative, collective narrative, racism, academic elitism and far more. . . . [B]y turns silly, somber and sharply satirical . . . *Welcome to Braggsville* doesn't offer easy polemic or easier sentimentality, but a deep dive into the American race problem as muddled, terrifying, and absurd as the reality."   —Huffington Post

"*Welcome to Braggsville* is a radical book in every sense of the word—thoroughgoing and extreme, ghastly and funny and gloriously provocative, a gauntlet thrown. And an inherent challenge to anyone who thinks they know the conventions of the American bildungsroman, or of a contemporary 'race and identity' novel. 'Bezerkely and Braggsville were two worlds on opposite sides of the sun,' explains D'aron/Daron, whose uneasy peregrinations between these two planets power this really shocking story. Its laugh-out-loud humor always underscores the pain of exile; the punchlines form an index of the sickening cost of D'aron's journey from Georgia to Berkeley, with all the requisite betrayals, the tolls exacted in both landscapes as D'aron/Daron crosses borders and must amphibiously reconstitute himself in order to survive. Johnson's prose is by turns scathing dark humor, soaring lyricism, and a quietly devastating analysis of every species of injustice. The result is a kind of mind-melting poetry—a linguistic electroconvulsive therapy for the reader. This book will wake you up! *Welcome to Braggsville* toggles brilliantly between tragedy and comedy and never lets the reader off the hook."

—Karen Russell, *New York Times*
bestselling author of *Swamplandia!*

"Amusing . . . unpredictable. An ambitious book, and [Johnson] handles with aplomb the complexities of growing-up, with its cumbrous transitions. . . . Despite the story's dark turn, there's humor in the wonder of oracular pronouncements."   —*Atlanta Journal-Constitution*

"[Johnson] is a fearless writer, and *Welcome to Braggsville* is one of the most provocative, daring novels we've seen in a while. . . . An unsettling story that forces us to examine our own prejudices and what, if anything, we're doing to make America more tolerant." —*Chicago Tribune*

"Both funny and frightful . . . Johnson deftly pokes dark fun at a wide swath of culture, high and low. . . . But as 21st-century American culture crisscrosses with the nation's history, Johnson's story evokes more than satirical humor. A sense of conscience and moral purpose takes shape at the heart of the book." —Associated Press

"Southern Gothic meets West Coast political correctness with hilarious results in Johnson's new satirical novel. . . . An odyssey through Waffle Houses, evangelical churches and backyard barbecue's ensues, with attitudes about everything from race to social media getting skewered." —*New York Post*

"Madcap, satirical, sometimes profane and uncanny in his descriptions, whether he's portraying self-conscious academia or a backyard barbecue, T. Geronimo Johnson is both a relentless social critic and a compassionate bystander. . . . *Welcome to Braggsville* is a deeply pleasurable read for the sheer wonder of Johnson's prose, but a deeply disturbing read for the truth it reveals about us." —*BookPage*

"Combines Ben Fountain's steely political eye, Junot Diaz's pop-infused dogma, and Toni Morrison's sense of social justice through historical reckoning. All that to say this: *Welcome to Braggsville* is the best and most powerful form of satire; it sets fire to your brain while expanding your heart. Big, shiny literary prizes were created for books like this one."

—Wiley Cash, bestselling author of *This Dark Road to Mercy*

"[A] 'performative intervention' gone wrong in Ol' Dixie. Race and class only top the list Johnson takes on in this satire."

—*Daily News* (New York)

"Stunning and poignant . . . Johnson's novel may not have the answer to the problems he's addressing, [but] it's clear that he's asking the right questions." —*LA Review of Books*

"A coming-of-age tale filled to the brim with amazing ideas and finely honed characters, this novel is both funny and sad and reads like a work of modern art." —Bookreporter.com

"There are not many novels that you crack open and find reminiscent of William Faulkner, but T. Geronimo Johnson's *Welcome to Braggsville* is such a novel. . . . T. Geronimo Johnson can write rings around this world . . . a biting, satirical take on much of what plagues today's society."

—*Free Lance-Star* (Fredericksburg, VA)

"Tyrone Geronimo Johnson is a fearless and driven young writer of dazzling gifts, a cosmopolitan of hick towns as well as university enclaves, savvy in many tongues—those of law, art, and academia as well as of the ghetto and the city streets, of country grocery stores and ruined churches lost in the kudzu, and of decent, hapless folks on both sides of the tracks. *Welcome to Braggsville* plunks four engaging but naive young ideologues from Berkeley into the middle of the

Civil War reenactment of a small town in the contemporary South, with results that are surprising, heartbreaking, tragicomic, and deeply disturbing."

—Jaimy Gordon, National Book Award–
winning author of *Lord of Misrule*

"*Welcome to Braggsville* is that rare book so highly charged with both comedy and tragedy, and so nimble in its storytelling that it seems to understand the world of its characters down to the smallest particle. This is one of the most invigorating and least predictable novels of the year."

—Kevin Brockmeier, award-winning
author of *The Brief History of the Dead*

"Johnson spares no faction in his biting indictment of American society, a sprawling tapestry of different styles as complex as the issues he explores. . . . Funny and wrenching, this coming-of-age story leaves one reeling but satisfied."

—Shelf Awareness (starred review)

"DeLilloesque for its orgiastic pop-culture roiling, *Welcome to Braggsville* deconstructs race, class, and gender, leaving the human heart wholly intact. This is a virtuoso performance by one of our strongest new voices."

—Richard Katrovas, award-winning
poet and author of *Scorpio Rising*

"In exuberant prose, Johnson takes aim at a host of issues, gleefully satirizing political opportunists, social media, and cultural mores. . . . A provocative exploration of contemporary America."   —*Booklist*

"Geronimo Johnson's powerful second novel combines the intellectual urgency of a satire with the emotional resonance of a tragedy. *Welcome to Braggsville* is as smart as it is subversive, and as bleakly hilarious as it is deeply necessary."

—Jennifer duBois, award-winning author
of *A Partial History of Lost Causes*

WELCOME
TO
BRAGGSVILLE

Also by T. Geronimo Johnson

Hold It 'Til It Hurts

WELCOME TO BRAGGSVILLE

T. GERONIMO JOHNSON

WM

WILLIAM MORROW
An Imprint of HarperCollinsPublishers

P.S.™ is a trademark of HarperCollins Publishers.

HarperCollins books may be purchased for educational, business, or sales promotional use. For information please e-mail the Special Markets Department at SPsales@HarperCollins.com.

A hardcover edition of this book was published in 2015 by William Morrow, an imprint of HarperCollins Publishers.

FIRST WILLIAM MORROW PAPERBACK EDITION PUBLISHED 2015.

Designed by Diahann Sturge

Library of Congress Cataloging-in-Publication Data has been applied for.

ISBN 978-0-06-230213-7

16 17 18 19   OV/RRD   10 9 8 7 6 5 4

For all the Louis Changs,
from my parents

Meet the New World, same as the Old World.

Contents

To be likened? The moon'll tell. Might not a listen, might not a like it, but it'll tell if you can. Give yourself in a jar. Cleave a tomato. Pick the seeds clean. With your mouth, now. Leave it sit for three days behind that rank of elfinwood yon. A palm of milk and enough honey to feel right and rub it back up in there real good. Sleep on your left side. The moon'll tell you, in sooth, but you might not like it, even if you be likened. You can bathe at the river, can't you? But dam it? Tell me, now, what good be a pond with no fish? You seen Bragg. Recollect.

—Nanny Tag

D'aron the Daring, Derring, Derring-do, stealing base, christened D'aron Little May Davenport, DD to Nana, initials smothered in Southern-fried kisses, dat Wigga D who like Jay Z aw-ite, who's down, Scots-Irish it is, D'aron because you're brave says Dad, No, D'aron because your daddy's daddy was David and then there was mines who was named Aaron, Doo-doo after cousin Quint blew thirty-six months in vo-tech on a straight-arm bid and they cruised out to Little Gorge glugging Green Grenades and read three years' worth of birthday cards, Little Mays when he hit those three homers in the Pee Wee playoff, Dookie according to his aunt Boo (spiteful she was, misery indeed loves company), Mr. Hanky when they discovered he TIVOed *Battlestar Galactica,* Faggot when he hugged John Meer in third grade, Faggot again when he drew hearts on everyone's Valentine's Day cards in fourth grade, Dim Ding-Dong when he undressed in the wrong dressing room because he daren't venture into the dark end of the gym, Philadelphia Freedom when he was caught clicking heels to that song (Tony thought he was clever with that one), Mr. Davenport when he won the school's debate contest in eighth grade, Faggot again when he won the school's debate contest in eighth grade, Faggot again more times than he cared to remember, especially the summer he returned from

Chicago sporting a new Midwest accent, harder on the vowels and consonants alike, but sociable, played well with others that accent did, Faggot again when he cried at the end of *WALL-E,* Donut Hole when he started to swell in ninth grade, Donut Black Hole when he continued to put on weight in tenth grade (Tony thought he was really clever with that one), Buttercup when they caught him gardening, Hippie when he stopped hunting, Faggot again when he became a vegetarian and started wearing a MEAT IS MURDER pin (Oh yeah, why you craving mine then?), Faggot again when he broke down in class over being called Faggot, Sissy after that, whispered, smothered in sniggers almost hidden, Ron-Ron by the high school debate team coach because he danced like a cross between Morrissey and some fat old black guy (WTF?) in some old-ass show called *What's Happening!!,* Brainiac when he aced the PSATs for his region, Turd Nerd when he aced the PSATs for his region, Turd Nerd when he hung with Jo-Jo and the Black Bruiser, D'ron Da'ron, D'aron, sweet simple Daron the first few minutes of the first class of the first day of college. Am I pronouncing that correctly? Yes, ma'am, Daron it is. What about this apostrophe, this light-headed comma? Feel free to correct me. Oh no, ma'am. Ignore that. It's all one word, ma'am. No need to call me ma'am. Yes, ma'am.

AS WAS EXPECTED OF VALEDICTORIANS, he had spoken of choices, though not his personal choices. His desk *was* stuffed tighter than a turducken with acceptance letters, but to list those would have been smug and boastful when most classmates were going to State or to stay. He instead pontificated on abstract opportunities to be grabbed, snatched out of the air like so many feathers, of the choices life extended to those who dared dream, of new worlds awaiting, of hopes to be fulfilled and expectations met, of how they would go forth and put B-ville, GA, squarely on the map. Never mind that it was ninety-two degrees, never mind that they could drink the air, never mind that, as Nana used to say, it was so greatly humid a cat wouldn't stretch its neck to lick its own juniors, he carried on about wishing over dandelions, and their delicate floating spores, and how they multiplied, superstitions taking seed even without belief—where he had heard that he couldn't recall—and explained that our eyes move when we dream, and, lastly, with a smile, advised the audience to, Always use sunscreen. His parting blow: an open invitation to visit him at *My future alma mater,* until then unknown to his father. Teachers applauded vigorously; peers clapped listlessly, more with relief than appreciation, but they didn't understand, and that was why he was glad to be leaving. He stepped from the podium a free man, at long last deaf to their tongues, and later thanked with aplomb the classmate who sidled up to the smoking steel drum and congratulated him on his engagement.

Chapter Two

Of course there were the Bulldogs or the Yellow Jackets or the Panthers, or even the Tigers. And after a week as a Golden Bear, he wondered if one of those might have been a better choice. Long accustomed to the teacher calling on him after his classmates proffered their feeble responses, D'aron sat in the front row but never raised his hand. He was not called on to moderate disputes, to weigh in on disagreements, to sagely settle debates. He was not called on at all, even when the subject in American History turned to the South, a topic on which he considered himself an expert, being the only Southerner in the class. (Not even when D'aron resorted to what the prof called a Horshack show.) The professor rationalized his reluctance to call on D'aron on such occasions as a resistance to *essentializing*. Said resistance D'aron found puzzling, and said affliction he apparently had developed no resistance to, constantly provoking the professor to ask, Am I the only Jew? Mika the only black? You the only Southerner? If the professor said he was Jewish, well, D'aron would take his word for it. Mika, though, was obviously the only black in class, and D'aron the only Southerner. Wasn't he essentially Southern? Wasn't that the core of his being, his essence, as it were? At least that was how he felt now that he was in California.

He held doors for the tender gender and all elders. *Thank you* and

Please and *May I* adorned every conversation. *Ma'am* was an escape artist extraordinaire, often slipping out midsentence. Professors wagged their fingers, but even the one who claimed it aged her, Only slightly less subtly but just as permanently as gravity, appeared at moments to relish this memento of a bygone era, this sole American who, like foreign students and athletes, recognized the instructors as ultimate authorities, approaching their bunkers as shrines bearing cookies and other gifts in outstretched hands, like a farmer leaving a peck of apples or a pair of just-plucked broilers at his lawyer's back door. *Sir* he could utter without censure.

Yet this inbred politeness was not what set him apart. Every student at Berkeley—all 36,142, he believed—played an instrument or a sport or volunteered for a social justice venture or possessed some obscure and rare talent. Or all four. Students raised in tents in Zimbabwe by field anthropologists and twin sisters who earned pilot's licenses at age fifteen and Olympians from as far afield as Norway. One student athlete, a track star, upon being asked, Are you considered fast in your country? smiled charitably, I am the fastest.

And the Asian students, he'd once confessed awe-stricken during a phone conversation with his mother, Some of the Asians, well, I shouldn't say some when they are a majority, but some of the Asian students speak multiple languages—more than a Holy Roller—languages I didn't even know existed. Kaya, in Calc Two, for example, is half-Korean but raised in Malaysia. She speaks Korean like her mom, Chinese like her dad, Malay like her cousins at home, and is already in French Two and Spanish Three. Does she even speak English? He sighed. Don't fret, honey. You earned the right to be there and you'll do fine DD baby. Don't fret. He murmured his thanks, reluctant to admit, let alone explain, that his distressed aspiration bespoke not lamentation but yearning. Kaya! Kaya mesmerized him, sitting in the basement commons study sessions twirling her hair around her pen as she wrote notes in Korean and IMed in English and tweeted in Malay, all while conjugating the subjonctif, her bare knees pressed together to balance a laptop surely hot to the touch.

DON'T FRET, HIS MOM WOULD REPEAT after his long silences. He didn't.

He didn't *fret*. Nor did he *reckon*. Or *figure*. Or *git*. Or study. Having followed his favorite cousin Quint's advice and picked a school more than a day's drive from home, he found the freedom intoxicating. If his parents could see him Monday mornings: tongue a rabbit's tail, stiff and bristly, D'aron not knowing whether to feel pride or shame. They guessed at it, though, after reading his midterm report. His mother, Are you sick, honey? His father, in the background, With alcohol poisoning maybe. (Following that call, D'aron changed his mailing address to the dorm.) But he didn't yet regret his decision to go westward-ho!

When he'd left home back in August to start school, Quint warned, Don't go ABBA or Tiny Dancer! Huh? Don't get gay. Don't get roofied and get made gay, either. Or, ho-mo-sex-u-al.

When he returned home for Thanksgiving, Quint squinted, You got AIDS? D'aron gave a lick and checked his reflection in his spoon, as if he hadn't only hours before, and every morning for that matter, paraded at length before the bathroom mirror in his skivvies. I can see your fucking ribs. You need a one-eight-hundred number. D'aron smiled. Without grits and waffles and hash browns and toast all at the same breakfast, and with walking everywhere, the famous fresh-man fifteen had gone the other way, but it looked and felt like fifty. Without the extra weight, he could finally confirm that his relatives weren't lying when they insisted he'd inherited his father's shoulders and forehead, and his mother's eyes and nose, and from them both a decent height.

And when he went home for Christmas, his aunt Boo teased,

So you do have cheekbones. What are they feeding you, grass? You spent that money I sent you on crack?

Hey, hey, c'mon Auntie B.! Don't essentialize. All crackheads aren't skinny.

Is that a joke, Dookie? I got one for you. Hay is for horses!

He loved his family, but God was he glad they now lived so far away. Quint was at least right about that.

During those three years in special ed, I only missed the food. Quint paused. And tits. And of course my mom, she's mom, you know. And you, number one cuz. Exclamation point by way of a punch. But sure didn't miss all the yappity yip-yappity yap. And hunting. I missed hunting.

At least Jo-Jo, D'aron's best friend from high school, was happy for him. Jo-Jo patted his belly, I oughta go to college. That was a lot from him.

CHRISTMAS BREAK DIDN'T END SOON ENOUGH. The morning the dorms opened, D'aron was on the ground in Cali three time zones away. It wasn't even the same country. By then he understood the geo-lingo. San Francisco was *The City*, Oakland was *O-town*, to be avoided at night—that was where the blacks lived—and the city of Berkeley was *Berzerkeley*, while Berkeley the school was *Cal*. The East Bay, where Berzerkeley was located, supposedly suburban, felt plenty busy. Collectively, it was the Bay Area, a megalopolis—oh how that word polished his tongue—where the elsewhere unimaginable was mere mundanity.

Across the bay, The City convened in costume to race from bay to breakers. Happy meal toys and plastic bags were long outlawed and voters threatened circumcision and goldfish with the same fate. They'd once had a mayoral candidate named Jello. A roving band of Rollerbladers performed the *Thriller* zombie dance—that pop nativity—Friday nights in Union Square. And fuck, it was China in the airport. Yet The City thought Berzerkeley was weird. D'aron thought it beautiful, never mind the nag champa, never mind the crusty hippies and gutter punks in greasy jackets stiff as shells lined up on Telegraph Ave hawking tie-dye and patchouli and palming for change. On clear days, a pageantry of wind and water under sun, the bay a sea of gently wriggling silver ribbons, and the Golden Gate hovering in the distance like a mystical portal. East of campus lazed tawny hills. On foggy days blinding bales of cotton candy strolled the avenues dandy while in the distance the tips of the bridge towers peeked through the mist like shy, gossamered nipples. The Bay Area was a beautiful woman who looked good in everything she wore.

What had intimidated him those early weeks of his freshman fall semester felt like home during his second semester—freshman spring. The clock tower known as the Campanile rose from the center of campus with the confidence of the Washington Monument, marking time in style, and on the hour, music students sounded melodies on the carillon. He often lunched alone at the base of that monolith, on the cool stone steps, facing the water due west, attention drifting with the lazing waves and the steady stream of Asian students moving—no, migrating—between the library and the engineering buildings. As he worked up the courage to wander farther from Sather Gate, the symbolic campus border, he discovered Indian, Vietnamese, Mexican, Thai: tastes luring him deeper and deeper into a town of Priuses and pedalers, both of which yielded patiently to pedestrians. Laid back, liberal, loose. The locals' mantra, No worries; the transplants' motto, It looks like a peninsula but feels like an island.

Chapter Three

His second semester, freshman spring, also brought a life-altering move to a new dorm. His first-semester six-man suite had been too rowdy, excepting D'aron, of course, so the RA dispersed them across campus like parolees. D'aron's new roommate wanted to be the next Lenny Bruce Lee, kung fu comedian. Asked who the first one was, he answered, See?

Chang, aka *Louis Chang,* aka *Loose Chang,* was none too pleased to have a D'aron Davenport aboard. After Louis's former roommate dropped out midway through the first semester, he'd grown accustomed to living single in a double. The room was barely fifteen by fifteen, with a bed, desk, and chair on each side, and on the wall opposite the door a window overlooking the courtyard. The day D'aron arrived clothes smothered both beds and books tottered on both chairs: chemistry, botany, zoology on one side; George Carlin, Steve Martin, Paul Mooney on the other; and atop each pile several well-worn *National Geographic*s. Had Res Life double-booked the room?

Chang crossed his arms, Which side do you want?

He was slight, dark-skinned, narrow of eye, and like so many other California Asians, he spoke with no accent, a phenomenon to which D'aron was still growing accustomed. At home, all the Chinese people (seven) had thick, nearly impenetrable accents, incomprehensible unless pronouncing dinner items; numbers and directions were plain fudruckers. Shrimp-fry-rice. Yes. Fie-dolrah-fitty. Huh?

Well? Chang repeated his question.

The right side?

Chang nodded, Good, we'll get along.

They did. Not only because Louis was possibly the only Asian male who hadn't mastered that damned twirling trick—pen mawashi—and not only because they had, surprisingly, so many common interests—porn, the Premier League, Arcade Fire, Tyler the Creator, Kanye, Kreayshawn—but because Louis was hilarious and possessed of an enviable irreverence. Strolling along Telegraph Ave, Chang responded to the gutter punks' outstretched palms with, No, it's *Chang . . . Chang.* And once to a black bum in People's Park he shrugged, You got Obama, what more do you want? Then he gave him a dollar.

Louis also didn't flinch when D'aron slept with his head to the window the night before tests so that he would wake up on the right side of the bed. Pointing at the little mirrors—which D'aron hadn't before noticed—Louis admitted, Mom's feng shui–zee crazy.

Loose Chang was a refreshing antidote to the somber, tense mood sweeping campus. Old folks gathered year-round at the West Gate hoisting nuclear disarmament signs with surprising gusto, and young folks huddled on Sproul Plaza extolling the virtues of the tree people—Ewoks, according to Chang—who had lived like monkeys for more than a year, occupying old oaks to prevent the university from cutting the trees down, all of which D'aron found odd, being from a town where they flew flags high, carried guns with pride (no matter how much they cost, they're cheaper than dirt), and everyone worked for the same hot air factory (though they called it a mill). As of late, though, there were also rumors about tuition hikes and budget cuts and the threat that the school would accept more out-of-state fart sniffers to collect more out-of-state tuition. Those out-ofstaters who protested that they'd earned their scholarships, as D'aron felt he surely had, were eyed with even greater disdain. By the middle of his freshman spring semester, helicopters were hovering over campus more days than not, buildings were regularly occupied by designer-sneaker Zapatistas—rappers for some—and students were on hunger strikes. Five days couldn't get together without his mother calling to remind him that he was there to learn, not cause disorder, and that he was to study and be respectful and mindful of the professors. And always say please and thank you, and sir and ma'am. You'll be amazed.

Louis routinely received the same directives in person. His family lived in the Richmond district of The City and thought nothing of showing up unannounced and en masse—parents, twin little brothers, and two great-uncles—to deliver healthy snacks, inspect living quarters, and shoot D'aron the hairy eyeball. We were in the neighborhood, they'd say, though according to Chang, before his acceptance to Cal his parents hadn't driven farther east than the downtown San Francisco Embarcadero for fifteen years. Sometimes they'd offer no greeting, just sit on D'aron's bed and wag their mysterious tongue. (Was this what Prof. Kensmith meant by cultural relativity? Louis's grandmother insisting that D'aron sample her homemade candied fruit under her watchful cloudy eye, tapping the bottom of his chin with two fingers to assist mastication. He knew a hex when he tasted one, and packed the sour green resin away with the deft touch of one long accustomed to surreptitiously enjoying Bandits only feet from the chalkboard. Later, he would slip into the bathroom and send the waxy balls to the bay, but not before his tongue grew numb and resentful.) After his family left, Chang would apologize for the stares. They're just old-fashioned, just old-fashioned, just old-fashioned, he chanted for weeks before admitting that his parents thought the messy half of the room was D'aron's.

The real disappointment, though, was that Chang did not know

Kaya, and so couldn't broker an introduction. D'aron was certain that if an Asian introduced him to Kaya, or she saw him with an Asian, she would be more likely to consider him datable. This wasn't mercenary but pragmatic. At home, whites identified the blacks who would date them by watching who their friends were, and vice versa. He went everywhere with Louis, but the campus was quite large.

The perfect opportunity arose only a couple weeks into the semester. Some students in his old dorm were hosting a dot party, and Kaya would certainly be there. Per the tweet, one rule: Wear a dot where you want to be touched. Chang affirmed his attendance before being asked.

Chapter Four

Under black lights installed in the basement commons for the occasion, Day-Glo stickers radiated warmth from cheeks left and right, aft and fore, knees and elbows for the shy, and hearts for many, though more than one person complained vigorously that they meant breast not heart. Golden Bears milled, glowing smiles, drinking sodas, though some clearly had other substances. Golden Bears clotted in pairs and groups of three, laughing too loudly, though some were obviously looking for a better conversation. Golden Bears kicked it in dark corners, though some wore poses of cool disaffection that were indistinguishable from anxiety. Four people wore dots in the middle of their foreheads, which, oddly, some found offensive. D'aron meant only that he wanted to provoke, in the words of his lit professor, A raging storm of violent thoughts, an explosive torrent that demands channeling lest it destroy you by driving you mad, making you whom the gods would have. Whatever that meant. That was often his answer when asked, but really he thought it subtle reverse psychology. No one seemed to believe that either, unfortunately, and about an hour into the party, he found himself in the sunken courtyard with Louis and the two other dot heads, as he thought of them: a blond female with weepy eyes and a black guy with pig-iron arms, obviously an athlete, like most of theyselves at Cal.

Louis looked at each of them and made a show of counting on his fingers, One little, two little, three little Indians.

The blonde groaned with understanding. Shit!

The black guy shrugged. Fuck them if they can't take a joke. He pointed to Louis's forehead. Make that four. Or are you really Indian?

This happened to Louis on occasion, him being Malaysian. He also caught hell at the airport from the devil in the blue uniform. Yes, he told them in his best Bollywood accent. I am Indian, naturally, not through adhesive like you. How feel would you if I wear Afro wig and gold teeth, and carry pit bull puppy naming Takesha?

The black guy laughed. You're funny, dude.

Hella funny, thank you. And you, he turned to the blonde, you, madam, how would you like when you come to my country and I wear a blond wig like valley girl, speak, you know, you know, you know, it was like. He paused to suck his teeth. You are not liking very much that?

The blonde went crimson and pursed her lips, clutching her neck as though cut, slashed, hacked even, spewing tearful, spittled apologies through the air.

Louis reached for her shoulder, which surprised D'aron because it seemed an apologetic overture when Louis himself always insisted that the comic's job was to wake people up—with a full five-finger slap when necessary. She jerked away, her ponytail splitting the night. It was too late. The tears were in full-court press. She hadn't meant anything by the dot, only that she wanted a good conversation, and she was from Iowa, and even if she had meant something by it, no one in Iowa would have gotten so upset about it. What is it with Berkeley that you can't make any kind of joke, even accidentally?

D'aron hadn't really noticed her until she began crying. (Louis would argue, The reptilian brain is like a Japanese tourist armed with a digital camera with infinite memory; therefore D'aron had noticed her, but hadn't yet noticed that he had noticed her.) Now he looked again. She was average height for a woman, her chin at his shoulder, and average build, at least for D'aron, because her physique was not that of the desiccated, squirrely girls who foraged at the co-op, standing in the center of the aisle as still as Lady Justice with a container in each hand while deliberating the benefits of garbanzo miso versus soy miso. No. Hers was a figure forged in the same furnace as the girls he'd grown up with, with full legs and arms, and long straight hair, past the neck, that at night glowed like butter on burned toast. She sniffled and her cheek twitched, tickled by a tear, and he felt compelled to protect her.

He's just joking, he's Malaysian, not Indian, explained D'aron. To Louis, You'll cut your tongue talking that way.

Really? The blonde sniffed. Screw you! She flipped off Louis, though she didn't thank D'aron. But she did look him over.

What's the difference, asked the black guy. Welcome to the club.

The difference, Louis explained, is miles and miles, but that's about all.

D'aron laughed and removed his dot. They all followed suit, except Louis, who pantomimed looking in a mirror, dusting his lapels and arranging his hair. How do I look?

They replaced their dots.

The Prayer, an old Bloc Party song, played in the background, the band's prerecorded clapping in rhythm with the strobe light. Their faces flashed in unison as the lyrics drifted out to D'aron, one line catching his ear: *Is it wrong to want more than is given to you, than is given to you?* For the first time at Berkeley, he felt at ease. He half hummed, half sang the lyrics. *Is it wrong to want more than is given to you, than is given to you?* No, it's not.

Excuse me? hissed the blonde.

My, you're sensitive . . .

The blonde glared at him. You mean a mite sensitive? She drawled out *mite.*

How's that?

How?

How, Tonto!

The blonde cranked her middle finger up for Louis. I resent that, especially coming from you. I'm part Native American.

Aren't we all?

Thus they became the 4 Little Indians. D'aron, Louis, Charlie, and Candice. It mattered not that Louis swapped statistics for film studies only to be near Candice, and she swapped theater for rhetoric only to be near Charlie. D'aron was just glad to be close to her, and to have friends who were also uncertain about their place at Berkeley, and who were nerds, not that anyone could be a nerd at Berkeley. Besides, he had heard that it was easier to get a girlfriend when you had a girlfriend, so being seen with Candice could only further his cause with Kaya (who that night was nowhere to be seen). When D'aron muttered his frustration, Charlie confirmed his theory: The most important lesson I learned in high school was that banks loan quickest to those who don't need money.

But first they reentered the party, and, as Indians are wont to do, were promptly relocated. One by one, D'aron, Candice, and Charlie were tapped on the shoulder. One by one they were beckoned outside by strangers mouthing entreaties in tones too polite to be heard over the music. One by one, one little, two little, three little Indians followed their interlocutors—new friends, they thought—to the exit, where they could be better heard. Once reassembled at the outer door to the basement commons, in the sunken courtyard where they'd first met, the 3 Little Indians faced a brave detachment of revelers—a cobbler's dozen threatening to give them the boot—a hodgepodge of both upper- and lowerclassmen, both humanities and science majors, both athletes and scholars, both males and females, students tall and short, brunette and blond, stout and slim, sober and drunk-it.

Their leader? A feisty blonde who wielded her index fingers like a two-gun cowperson, a blonde who stood offended by, Your savage insensitivity, who exclaimed in a voice inflated by indignation, Only freshmen could disgrace a simple dot, a blonde who had the decency to wear her own ornament politely left of center, Where the heart is actually located, a blonde who suggested that they do the same and, Show some empathy for other people. Some respect, too.

There, in that umpteenth year of our Lord, at Dormitory Door, a historic treaty was proposed: Remove the dots and you can stay.

During the blonde's speech a cluster grew, not chanting Fight! Fight! Fight!, but listening intently, as in a lecture, cupping ears and shushing and frowning as each new outflux burped though the dorm doors with the sonic aftertaste of thumping bass. The cluster was soon a crowd, and the crowd soon a congregation constellating in concentric circles around the 3 Little Indians: In the buildings students at their dorm room windows watched like wary settlers wondering how their wagon circle had been breached; within the ring of buildings, passersby perhaps expecting a juggling show or puppetry performance milled at the outer edges of the courtyard, popcorning on tiptoe; within them was a ring of polka-dotted partiers; within them were the blonde's foot soldiers (that cobbler's dozen Louis later referred to as Satan's Anal Army). Our Tribe in the center, fidgeting, with the exception of Charlie, who stood lock-kneed a couple feet apart, and whom no one directly addressed or approached, as if he both was and wasn't there, a secret at a family reunion, in the same way that no Braggsvillian ever mentioned how Slater Jones was born near the end of his father's uninterrupted fifteen-month tour of duty. (Everyone just lamented how he was a preemie, and that's why he was shorter than a Georgia snow day and so Old Testament angry at math.) Yes, Charlie stood there like a secret, if such a thing was possible, which obviously it was. Candice, for her part, was as beet colored as a real red man.

The offer was repeated: Remove the dots and you can stay.

Around this time Louis wandered out, with his collar prepped up and pop-star sunglasses on, and stood next to D'aron.

The blonde pointed to Louis. Except for you! Looking puzzled, she asked, Why are you even out here?

I'm with them. Louis tipped his sunglasses up and mirrored her puzzled expression. The better question is why are you wearing yoga pants?

The blonde blinked as if rebooting. Why are you even out here?

I'm with them, repeated Louis. He again mirrored her puzzled expression. The doors belched two stumbling students and a few bars of a tricky beat. The even better question is why are you blasting that Jay Z and Punjabi MC joint?

Blink. Reboot. Repeat: Remove the dots and you can stay.

Louis began speaking. Candice interrupted him. I'm Candice Marianne Chelsea. I am part Indian. She tapped her forehead. Not the kind you were looking for, but the kind you found. One-eighth to be exact. And I'll be damned if you get to tell me what to do anymore. She shouldered past the blonde and the foot soldiers and walked in the direction of the door. The crowd parted like the Lord was drawing her finger through water. Charlie followed. The crowd parted wider, eyes to feet. D'aron and Louis followed, but were rebuffed, drowned in the confusion like the Pharaoh's men after Moses.

When Candice looked back and saw D'aron and Charlie floundering, she huffed and shook her head like a disgusted parent. She pointed to the nearest courtyard exit, put her hands to her mouth like a megaphone: Let's go. Where I'm from, women don't need to wear stickers for guys to know where to touch us.

She huffed and marched in the direction of Bancroft Avenue. The other three followed, and 4 Little Indians laughed hee-hee-hee all the way home, never more so than when Candice again claimed to be part Native American. For real!

AFTER HIS ABYSMAL FIRST SEMESTER, D'aron's academic advisor suggested a meeting, her e-mail as disconcerting as Quint blasting Dio in that stolen ice cream truck. (When Sheriff appeared at his door worn by rue, Quint told him, Grand theft audible: possibly six months. Selling Good Humor wherever the fuck I want, including the Gully: priceless. Sheriff handed him the cuffs. You know how these work.) The good humor of the advisor's letter, sprinkled with words like *informal* and *independent,* was offset by underlying chords of words like *probation* and *tête-à-tête* and *self-directed learning* (all of which had for D'aron become slang for watching Oprah, itself slang for porn, itself slang for the visiting German professor's stats class, itself slang for beer, itself slang for a few drinks, itself slang for bar crawl, itself slang for . . . You get the point). When he finally summoned the nerve to meet her, it was nearly spring break, nearly midterms, and at every desk in the César Chávez Center students turtled over laptops. He had applied himself with determination in the few weeks since meeting the other Little Indians, and carried to the meeting those few recent assignments on which he had earned a B or better.

Mrs. Brooks occupied a small inside office whose only window was the sidelight beside the door. On her desk, family photos greeted all who entered. D'aron always found it hard to imagine people in authority with a family, arguing over Netflix and ice cream. She sat with her back to the hall, boxes of tissues piled high on her credenza, her face only inches from the computer screen displaying . . . was it MS-DOS?! When D'aron knocked she spun around and waved him in with a smile and a How-do-ya-do. Seeing that she was black, he turned to leave. Sorry, I'll make an appointment. He wasn't in the mood for an ass-chewing. No, no, no, no. Come in. He thought he detected a faint accent, but couldn't be sure because once he gave his name, her expression grew stern and officious. I've been busy and stressed and am trying to do better, ma'am. She softened a bit, leaning back in her chair and sighing as if there was a big decision weighing on her, one she regretted being charged with making, like a soccer ref giving a red card to a favored player.

Let's start at the beginning, D'aron. Is it Daron or *Da*ron or Da*ron*?

Daron, ma'am.

What about this apostrophe?

The name's . . . Irish, he started to say before catching himself . . . The name's misspelled. I never figured why it's like that or how to git 'em to change it.

Where are you from, Daron?

He told her and she smiled. I'll bet Berkeley has more students than there are people in your entire town.

Yes'm.

It was the same for me when I first came here from Tennessee, too long ago to tell you. I'll just admit that when I was an undergrad here, twittering was for the birds. Even now, back home anyone who tweets too loudly is likely to end up plucked, stuffed with spicy pork sausage, and served with cornbread.

They both laughed.

She leaned forward and whispered, I'm from a holler.

My backyard backs right up to one. Daron settled into his seat. It was the first time he'd met anyone in California who was from a holler. Most people didn't even know what it meant, and he'd stopped explaining because too often they'd ask why he couldn't be like everyone else and call it a valley.

Look, Daron, it's a big school. It's an achievement and an honor for you to have made it this far, so don't sabotage yourself. If you need help, ask. There are too many students in some of these classes, and it's only going to get worse; however, the school is committed to seeing first-generation college students succeed. But you have to ask for help. No one is going to offer it.

Yes'm.

And you have to stay on top of your work. It's not high school.

It sure ain't. I didn't even have to study much in high school. I could show up for the test and—

—A lot of students fall prey to that mistake. It's not as easy as you thought, so then you kind of check out. You start asking yourself crazy questions about your intellectual abilities.

Daron's face burned and he looked away.

Then your grades plummet, and you start to wonder if you even belong here, or if it's a mistake, or if you were a sympathy admit.

Daron looked at his shoes, unable to hold her gaze. He had wandered up to that idea on many occasions, but never explored it at length, treating it like a street he mustn't cross. Why had Berkeley accepted him? Candice had gone to a small public school in Iowa, but her parents were professors. Louis was Asian, so he possessed the magic membership card. Charlie was black, but he went to some fancy boarding school on a football scholarship. Then there was Daron.

If you were accepted, you deserve to be here.

At that, Daron started to cry, and as he did so, he admitted that he sloughed off for the first couple months of each semester, planning to pull it out of the bag at the last minute, but also thinking that if he failed at least he couldn't be blamed because he hadn't studied. He knew it was crazy, and couldn't explain how he knew, but he knew nonetheless that somehow his ego had tricked him into adopting this strategy so he wouldn't be disappointed. He had seen this as clearly as a drive-in movie screen against a starless sky, the insight cruelly ambushing a fine Friday-night buzz, and so he refrained from sharing with Mrs. Brooks the specific circumstances surrounding a revelation she deemed preternatural. He told her about high school, which he had burned in effigy shortly after graduation but now missed terribly because he had been on top, at least academically, while here he

was average at best. She handed him a tissue. How his entire high
school graduating class would jeer—Faggot!—if they saw him all
snotty-nosed in California in this black lady's office, except Jo-Jo,
who wouldn't have laughed at all, who woulda told D'aron, in that
regretful tone he used for both bad and good news, I warned you,
they ain't like us. And if Daron didn't succeed, after flaunting UCB
back home, after defying his father's wish that he become a Bulldog,
after applying to Cal in secret, he would never be able to return home
to B-ville, and would end up like those homeless kids on Telegraph—
wouldn't he?—with only other homeless kids and mangy dogs for
friends, and he saw how people looked at them. He felt idiotic admitting this, especially when she chuckled.

Mrs. Brooks stifled her laugh. Daron, honey, those are not ex-
students. Those are people getting an early start on an unusual career.
Don't you worry; no matter what, you'll never end up like that. You
come from a good family.

A line had formed in the hall while they were talking. Mrs. Brooks
pushed the box of tissues across the desk. Take a minute to get yourself together. I know it's hard, sugar, I know it's hard.

I just want to fit in.

I know, dear. You said they spelled your name wrong?

Yes, ma'am. All wrong.

I'll take care of that for you. You just focus on your work and let
Mrs. Brooks know if you need anything, and remember, you deserve
to be here as much, if not more, than everyone else. Repeat that.

I deserve to be here.

That's right. You come back and see me every day if you need to.
In the meantime, there are over one hundred student organizations
here at Cal. Whatever your interests or beliefs, you can find a like-
minded group.

He left relieved to have learned he was not alone in his anxi-
eties, feeling unburdened of a load he had not fully comprehended

the enormity of, much as he had felt after his first real sex ed class
(not that makeshift tutorial Quint choreographed wherein a hot dog
rousted an unsuspecting chicken). He also found himself wishing,
he noted with puzzlement, that more professors were black. He understood them, it seemed, and they him. All the way back to Unit 2,
he repeated Mrs. Brooks's mantra. I deserve to be here. I deserve to
be here. I deserve to be here. He also resolved to find a like-minded
group. All of this he did while wearing empty headphones so as to
appear to be singing.

BACK HOME IN B-VILLE, GA, the 4 Little Indians would stand
out like J. Crew rejects, but in Berkeley they were just four friends,
four inseparable friends, four constant companions, so close that he
wondered if siblings could be closer. No, explained Charlie when the
subject was raised. I love my brother and all, but it's not like we actually talk. We didn't even do that after my dad died.

That was Charlie, wise beyond his years. But they were all savvier
than Daron. Louis taught him hard-learned lessons like the wisdom
of avoiding edibles after drinking. Candice taught him that one must
never follow white with red. Once a month they did medicinal 420
and communally fashioned quotes such as, How do we know stars
aren't just holes and God hasn't just thrown a curtain over a cage?
Their jointly constructed code word for weed aka grass aka Mary
Jane: *alien technology*. Technology because it made them smarter.
Alien just because. (Alien because it make my May-he-can real good,
hombre, Louis liked to say.) On their languorous strolls the percus-
sion of Daron's flip-flops calmed him, and air running between his
toes formed fins that climbed his back and combed his hair into
lightning rods. And when they sprawled along the water at Berkeley's Aquatic Park—lungs bursting between breaths, counting ducks
as day hushed and short gusts soughed the bobbing grass along the
bank, the longer stalks arcing over to nose the lake—passing head-

lights might brush Candice's hair, the ponytail resting across one shoulder like a small animal while she absentmindedly stroked it, or sketch Charlie's profile, his regal nose, his broad back exaggerated in shadow, or highlight Louis's sneakers worn like slippers, his habit, when in thought, of axing the thin edge of his hand against his forehead, his hand in profile resembling a cockscomb. Daron (and not only at those moments, to be honest) desperately wanted to hug them all, and instead would settle for the huddles between bursts of Frisbee football.

It wasn't all parties and drugs. There was also sex, or at least the promise of it, which led Daron to hang around the protests. With the exception of the lesbians, and who knew what they did, the women who engaged in protests were said to be the most sexually liberal, their politics freeing them to celebrate their sexuality without shame, supposedly. Daron, though, could never work up the nerve to start a conversation with somebody holding a banner that read EDUCATION IS AN INALIENABLE HUMAN RIGHT or chanting, Harvard had a Moor; we expect more of Cal, and so that second semester, his freshman spring semester, was all fits and starts, and he ended it as he began it, as he had ended his high school career, uninitiated into the mysteries of intimacy, though in the late-night cobalt glow of the bathroom stall he observed scores of demonstrations on his laptop, loading many to his hard drive. He was probably better off, having heard somewhere that herpes traveled swifter than Hermes, or at least that's what he said to himself, but that's not how he told it when he went home that summer.

IT'S NOT THAT DARON LIED, or intentionally misled anyone. The confusion was preordained; he didn't even know it was happening. The other Little Indians tweeted and Facebooked all summer (or tagged and twitted, as Daron's parents said anytime he was on the hall computer, that old tower that whined and whirred like even powering down was a burden). They begged him for photos, so he sent a few, of the quarry, of a fish his cousin Quint caught, of one of his mom's cookouts, all, as he knew with tactical embarrassment, much less exotic than his friends' snapshots, no matter how much they *liked* the images, *liked* the way Pickett Rock was frog-shaped unless you approached it from the south, from which angle it resembled an eagle, *liked* the shimmering bass curled in retreat from the sun, *liked* the squat sausages nestled on the grill like chubby kids at their first sleepover, huddled against the dark. Charlie was filing cleats at some fancy upstate New York university football camp, followed by an Airstream to Scottsdale with his high school friends. Louis was visiting family in Kuala Lumpur, and had been to the tallest twin towers in the world (Daron skipped that photo). Candice was in Provence with her parents, trying to dread her hair, from the looks of it. It was these pictures he showed his friends at home, and several from the school year: All 4 Little Indians under Berkeley's famous Sather Gate, in line at Memorial Stadium before the big game against Stanford, in The City at the Golden Gate Bridge. Always places where there were plenty of bystanders to take their picture. Always with Candice standing between Daron and Charlie while Louis crouches in his prison pose. He'd never considered the implications of those group shots until Jo-Jo, whom Daron still considered his best friend, asked him about the juniors.

What?

You prinking? Don't get shy on me now.

They were at the edge of unincorporated Braggsville at Point Pen Dry Bluff, a granite scarp—dubbed The Balcony—from which they'd often Geronimoed into the cool blue twenty feet below, much to the horror of more than one shrieking mother. Earlier that morning, Jo-Jo had asked him to take a ride, which they did in silence, which meant that Jo-Jo wouldn't admit what was on his mind until he'd cracked at least three High Lifes. Jo-Jo was one of those guys who would snap his fingers and complain—Look here, Cochise, I'm trying to talk to you—even when he wasn't saying anything. Unlike Quint, who'd inherited from his mother a tongue that could talk a gray sky dry, Jo-Jo measured his words like he was underwater. Matter of fact, with that short, perpetually wrinkled brow, he always looked like he was holding his breath. When Jo-Jo said nothing after the fourth can, except to ask about the juniors, Daron felt a guilty rush of relief and repositioned himself to better appreciate the view. It wasn't called The Balcony for nothing. Mayor Buchanan, who owned the land, years ago had his earthmovers carve the best-lit ledge into a shallow, beach-like slope lined with smooth pebbles, all at his own expense. Now all four Rhiner girls—woman-sized by middle school to the one—lay splayed head to head, spread-eagle, as if to catch more sun. The Rhiners were there when Daron arrived, so maybe Jo-Jo knew this and planned to hang out and enjoy the natural scenery.

Like a snowflake. Jo-Jo pointed.

Or dream catcher. Or, thought Daron, a tête-à-tête, at last recalling the word.

Or semen catcher.

That, too. Daron adjusted his trunks. The youngest sister had been Chinese skinny when he left for college, but now cut quite the figure. She had a split in her bib damn near deep enough to hide a baby.

So, she ever put a finger up in the juniors? asked Jo-Jo.

What?

Don't get shy on me now.

Daron shrugged.

Ever got that velvet rabbit when she was on the warpath?

Huh?

Miss Iowa. When she's scalping.

Yeah.

When Jo-Jo first saw the pictures of the 4 Little Indians, he'd tweaked Daron's titty as if to say, Good job, hoss. The suggestion had indeed pinched Daron at the time, but he had ignored it. He now regretted not correcting Jo-Jo, but at the same time considered this scenario kin to noticing before anyone else that his own fly was undone. Why call it to everyone's attention? Yeah, Daron repeated.

You crack those juniors and get up in that wormhole yet?

Yeah.

She ever swallow your Johnny Appleseed?

Yeah.

Ever blew dice so hard she fell off?

Yeah.

Jo-Jo laughed. Hmmm. Might be I ought get outta Draggsville. Go to college.

Don't see why not.

Might could, but won't, 'cause it costs, and I mean to be paid.

Yeah.

Old man say I can make foreman in two years. Tells me he seen it happen that quick. Get out of the oven, get over to the saw.

Yeah.

Hmmph. Jo-Jo pointed. Through the pines the mill could be seen in parts: the circuit board of ducts and compressors atop the big brick hotbox where it always felt about ninety million degrees and some distance away the sawtooth roof of the shipping warehouse where the greatest hazards were paper cuts and losing hair to packing tape. From where they sat on The Balcony, they couldn't see the building that connected the two—the rib—a low-windowed, narrow block structure where the air-conditioned offices were located. Everyone Daron knew spoke of the saw like Canaan. None aspired to the rib, almost as if it was cursed, almost as if it didn't exist for them, almost as if they went outside and walked around it to get from one end of the compound to the other. Jo-Jo elbowed Daron. The Rhiner girls were peeling themselves off the ground with arched backs, yawns, outstretched arms, and then took to the water with a battle caw, cutting air fifty yards out to Pickett Rock, giggling off the warm sting as they settled on the boulder's edge, juniors rocking, feet exciting the water, legs exciting the boys, especially where the stringy denim rode high thighs like fine blond hairs.

My father's at it again.

Sorry, muttered Daron after a moment during which, even after a year at Berkeley—including a special student-led DCal class on interpersonal communication—he could think of nothing else to say.

Daron brushed the rocks from his bottom as he scooted back out of the sun and onto a smoother shelf of granite. The heat wasn't hearing it, though, and like Georgia humidity was wont to do, the mugginess shadowed him. No one sunned at Berkeley's Aquatic Park, and the reservoir was polluted, but what it lacked in bikinis, it made up for with decriminalized alien technology and near-perfect Mediterranean weather. Unlike the gorge. Never mind the chain links of light reflecting onto Pickett Rock or gliding metallic along the sandy bed where the lake was shallow, or the buff scent of pine resin, or the empties whistling green and gold as the workers on the far side buckled shut their lunch buckets, he knew what Jo-Jo meant by his father being at it again.

Jo-Jo's father could be up to any Old Scratch tack, from moonraking, to knocking noggins around the yard, to putting the shine on old Martha Redding down at the Pik-n-Pak, to trying to creep a peek at June Tucker's butterfly. It was Jo-Jo's father, in fact, who had told both boys about his infamous and eponymous courtship kung fu move: Just let me stick the tip in, baby. Daron's own father had told him nothing about sex except to use protection because, Loose lips really do sink ships, and nothing will sink your ship faster than a kid or a disease. Daron's grandfather, Old Hitch—whom Nana called, in sooth, My right minder—offered the only sober advice: Remember, ripe fruit is always marked down. Gotta see something in 'em they can't see for 'emselves. Don't lie, but you gotta be a real generous mirror. (Back in ninth grade, Slater Jones from 4-H said only: I don't have sex, I make babies. Remarkable prescience for a fourteen-year-old, hence this parenthetical.)

The water clapped below as the girls abandoned their perch. Pickett Rock was chalky where dry and black where wet, so that the wet parts, once the last Rhiner slapped water, were like the shadows of dancing figures, and Daron was reminded of a tenth-grade lesson on Nagasaki, after which the teacher had been transferred out faster than a mad cow. She had read to the class a first-person account by a survivor who was lucky enough to be not only swimming, but also submerged when the blast passed over him. After seeing the flash reflected in the pool, he surfaced to discover that where his friends had once stood only their twisted silhouettes remained, draped on the ground like shadows, forgotten clothes, except white not black. With no frame of reference for such a phenomenon, he could only imagine a bizarre prank, so bizarre that he didn't immediately notice the damage to the pool house or that the water he trod now felt near boiling. The survivor said he could take no credit for it, that it was preordained that he would live and his friends would die, and he would never understand why. All he knew was who. Who is who? asked the teacher, closing the book with a resolute thump and letting her readers jangle from their rattling beaded-glass tether. It's us. Japan was ready to surrender as early as the defeat at Midway.

Jo-Jo dragged a heavy hand across his eyes. Now what about those juniors?

Yeah, Daron repeated, nodding, certain that it couldn't matter because Berzerkeley and Braggsville were two worlds always on opposite sides of the sun.

Chapter Five

His sophomore fall was without incident, but halfway through his sophomore spring, everything changed. As Quint would say, his pancake got flipped. The class was American History X, Y, and Z: Alternative Perspectives. The course reader, peopled with notables such as Freire and Marx, was book-ended by Chomsky and Zinn. The 4 Little Indians had taken the class together to satisfy a core requirement and because they heard it was fun, or at least that's what they told each other. The professor wore a monocle and resembled Mark Twain, and, better yet, video projects were accepted as capstones.

The first day of class the professor shepherded the students through the maze of Dwinelle Hall and down the front stairs, broad as a stage, across the plaza where Mondays through Wednesdays a man lay on his back all day with his bicycle across his chest like a security blanket, his arms and legs clawing the air in slow motion like an upturned turtle; and into the grand lobby of Wheeler Hall, where an elderly blond man wearing a kung fu gi and curly-toed shoes like a court jester practiced tai chi, his ragged braid gently sweeping his yellow belt: and ending in the Grinnell Grove, where upon a fallen blue gum eucalyptus a bearded man lunched each day wearing Indian dress and twelve multicolored berets stacked on top

of his head like a Dr. Seuss character. The point? By the end of the
semester, the professor hoped they would be able to tell him.

On Fridays, the professor hosted Salon de Chat, an informal class
with the tagline: People who don't know their history are doomed
to eat it! The desks were arranged as four-tops covered with butcher
paper and a sandwich board was installed in the hallway. Their bistro,
like all classrooms on the south side of Dwinelle Hall, overlooked a
thin creek spanned by a wooden footbridge and straddled by a tree
shed that blocked the worst of sound and sun. The first few weeks
of class, Daron arrived early to ensure a seat near the window from
which he could observe the world four stories below—the students
eating along Strawberry Creek, rushing to and from the Bear's Lair
café, hustling through the breezeway leading to the bookstore—and
imagine himself already a Berkeley graduate; a king of industry on
high appointment in his city club; a Carnegie, but a true philanthro-
pist. In his employ even the cafeteria worker who napped where the
roots had riven the retaining wall and the earth opened into alcove
would be warmed by his generosity. (He would never forget that
workingmen, like his father, carried this *litter,* as the prof called it.)
This fantasy lasted only so long as he was alone and soon gave way
to fancying that the students tromping in behind were assembling
to hear him speak. That whimsy he could retain only until hearing
chalk scrape, sometimes a screech as anguished as a balloon at the
edge of constraint.

He then was back in 512-A, a narrow classroom with chalkboards
on the long walls and, on the ceiling, cocked fluorescent fixtures
with those damned baffling fins, Candice never seated beside him.
Those fantasies lasted only the first few weeks because by then it was
apparent that the professor thought it impossible for a rich man to
be a good man. Salon de Chat, though, was always fun. After being
assigned to a table of three or four diners, each student received a
menu of conversations.

SALON DE CHAT
Starter
    Civil Disobedience
Entrée
    Tradition and Social Justice
Dessert
    Uncivil Disobedience and Protest

As usual, Daron and Charlie sat together, and Louis sat elsewhere with Candice. How Louis always managed to partner with Candice, Daron had not yet figured out. The prof lurched from table to table, ears out, eyes to the floor, finger to the ceiling, nodding, rarely talking, more a mascot than a teacher. Daron was still unaccustomed to this practice, most common among humanities professors, of mm-hmming more than speaking, which was the exact opposite of high school.

Laughter shot across the room. From Louis's table. His three partners were all doubled over, and Louis wore his famous face of fatuity, eyes wide, mouth straight and slightly open, head back like he'd narrowly missed a slap, an expression that asked, Did I say something?

At Daron's table, a junior from L.A. blathered about documentary filmmaking as the next social protest movement. Documenting protests, that is. A performative intervention, she explained, drawing the words out like a foreign term. Read Mark Tribe. She had hair blonder than Beyoncé's (her dyed coif quite unlike, he imagined, her Southern cousin's) and he doubted she could read anything through those sunglasses, maybe not even without.

Another volley of laughter from Louis's table. Candice was literally crying, her mascara fanning like Tammy Faye's. Why had she started wearing so much makeup? Last semester, she wore none, to honor her Native heritage.

L.A. continued her litany of the merits of documentaries.

Vous n'êtes pas sérieux? What is performative intervention? That could be sex, or shoplifting. Daron counted the options out on his fingers. Is sex or shoplifting going to change the world? Better yet, how 'bout shoplifting sex?

That would be rape. And that is not funny. That is very serious. Failing to believe the humor in that remark, I'm departing for another table. L.A. stood then, but not before daintily counting out three index cards on her seat. There are my notes for the next two courses. That should cover my portion of the bill.

She strutted off, shorts nibbling cheeks, perfectly painted legs tucked into huge furry boots, like she was wearing the feet of a baby wooly mammoth.

Daron clambered to his feet, but Charlie extended his arm like a parent coming to a sudden stop. She'll be back.

Daron muttered his agreement. He believed Charlie. There was never a shortage of girls volunteering to be in Charlie's group, and he wasn't even on the football team, he only looked like it.

She was here until the shoplifting sex part. You can recover as long as you don't apologize or follow her now. Saying sorry would be giving up the advantage.

Daron considered this. If that was the case, he should draft an official apology. Forget La-La Loosey, as they called her. He had forgotten about Kaya, his freshman obsession, it was now Candice who inflamed him. The way she laughed, like she had a big appetite.

Daron ignored the fun being had at Louis's table. Louis probably could have gotten away with a shoplifting sex comment.

The professor chose a replacement from the five coeds who volunteered and soon they were again picking at their appetizer, but they would not have room for dessert because for their entrée someone mentioned reenactments. A few people were surprised to hear that a professor at Brown was holding reenactments of famous civil rights demonstrations. The immediate consensus: It was a joke. It had to be ironic.

They have a reenactment every year in my hometown, announced Daron.

That can't be serious, piped La-La from her new table. Vous n'êtes pas cereal.

Pull, Daron mumbled, borrowing Louis's skeet-inspired euphemism for shooting the bird. They're real cereal.

A reenactment? ¿Por qué? ¿Por qué? Candice groaned as if someone had run a fat baby up a flagpole. ¿Por qué? ¿Por qué? was her way of saying: Why? . . . No! That's not why. Have a seat. I'll tell you the real reason, whether you want to know or not. Worse yet, her conversations had astral bodies, as Louis joked. They'd be hearing about this for weeks (as they had been about Ishi).

And she was not the only one. The table was shocked. The entire class in fact. They'd heard tell of Civil War reenactments, but they were still occurring? The War Between the States was another time and another country. As was the South. Are barbers still surgeons? Is there still sharecropping? What about indoor plumbing? Like an old Looney Tunes skit, Tex Avery tag ensued. Charlie gawked at Louis, who gawped at Candice, who generously suggested it as a capstone project to the professor, who Googled the event and announced that it coincided with spring break, Serendipity has spoken.

Candice's eyes were still pinwheeling as they had when she'd learned about Ishi, last of the Yahi. In 1911, that wild Indian wandered into Oroville, CA, where he was caught stealing meat. ¿Por qué? Because, according to Candice, Ishi was driven to desperation by California's Gold Rush–financed Indian removal campaign. Seeing as how the locals didn't take neatly to theft, the sheriff took Ishi into custody for Ishi's own protection. ¿Por qué? Because, according to Candice, Ishi's scalp alone was worth $5 U.S. After reading about Ishi in the paper, a kind UC anthropologist named Alfred Kroeber became Ishi's benefactor, and installed Ishi in a comfortable apartment in the Museum of Anthropology at UC Berkeley. ¿Por qué?

Because, according to Candice, Ishi wasn't considered fully human. This was institutionalization, no different from being imprisoned or placed in a zoo. And, according to Candice, a Civil War reenactment was little better. She insisted they spend the break in Georgia recording the reenactment. Because!

About this idea Daron felt as he had during that first face-off with sushi. No matter what Candice said, mixing boiled eggs into chicken salad was not the same as dropping a dollop of roe on raw tuna! Not at all! Not when eating, not the next morning. And wasabi? That word sounded like a scourge for the soul as well as a torment for the tongue. But, because they were enthusiastic, and Candice suddenly so interested in him, and the entire class chanting, *Go for it;* because at that moment seventeen students were hunger striking in response to the reduction in funding for Ethnic Studies, Gender and Women's Studies, and African American Studies; because it was Berzerkeley, dammit to Hades, Daron couldn't say no. He didn't say yes, but couldn't yet say no. Never mind that at home, his friends would have half considered—briefly—a hunger strike only if it meant getting classes canceled, not added. Never mind that he had never actually ventured onto Old Man Donner's grounds while the reenactment was being staged. Never mind that the notion of recording morphed into participation.

But mind he did when Candice suggested a performative intervention, or, in Louis's words, a staged lynching. Daron protested that lynching never happened in his town.

That's even better! The prof clapped his hands softly, his right eye red-rimmed from the monocle. You can force States' Rights to take a look in the mirror and they will not like what they see. Will this be safe? There won't be any danger, will there?

The class looked at Daron expectantly, all twenty-nine eyes.

He snorted. What did they think Georgia was like? Of course not! There's no danger at all. It's safe. The reenactment is open for public viewing. It was decided then, in the wink of a cat's eye. Next month, spring break, would not see him in Tijuana or Los Cabos or Guadalajara enjoying tacos, Tecate, and tequila with other Berkeley students, though perhaps there was still a chance of dissuading them. During the walk from Wheeler Hall to Foothill, he wasn't sure he wanted to dissuade them, not with Candice at his arm, Please-please-pretty-pleasing him to tell her all about Braggsville, which there was ample time to do because it was uphill all the way. He savored every step, every time she touched his elbow, every time she exclaimed with disbelief, every time she waved her hands like flippers, which she did when excited.

At first Candice had not seemed different from the girls he went to high school with, didn't look any different, but her enthusiasm distinguished her, and once committed, her zeal was of a predacious intensity. She would be, in Quint's words, Hard to wife.

If I were Southern, Candice whispered, I'd be real angry about that kind of history being celebrated. She repeated herself, the words again spoken softly, almost hummed.

Daron heard her as surely as if she had screamed. (What had Nana always said? The good Lord speaks with fire on tongue but man heeds man's counsel only when spoken softly, almost sung.)

I'd plan something big, really big, she added, just as quiet as the first time.

Their plan: Three of them would dress as slaves, one wearing a harness under his clothes. One would act as the master, cracking a whip and issuing random, absurd orders. They assumed there would be enough rocks or branches nearby to form a pile for the slaves to carry back and forth. While this was happening, they would run a hidden camera and record the reenactors' reactions and ask them a few questions about the war, local history, and the reenactments. Then the slave wearing the hidden harness would get uppity, maybe make some untoward comment about the lady of the plantation or try to run off or just complain that there wasn't enough salt in the food. Then the party would get started. That slave would be hoisted from a low limb as if lynched. They debated whether or not to hang Charlie. Louis argued that using the Veil of Ignorance as a guide meant lynching a white person, ideally a white female, pretty, blond, because they were the most treasured people in the whole, wide world, if not the entire known and unknown universe, in this life and the next, in this dimension—Charlie cut him off, worried that might provoke gunfire, that most people were ignorant of the Veil of Ignorance, so it wouldn't work. Candice had said (parroted Charlie, really), It is what it is. They should call a *spade a spade*. At that the debate came to a halt.

Maybe we should do a practice run? Remember that quote from the Gold Rush? From that Pierson Reading guy? "The Indians of California make as obedient and humble slaves as the Negro in the south. For a mere trifle you can secure their services for life."

Daron remembered it all right, but didn't think it had anything to do with Braggsville. He felt indignation rising as one of Nana's sayings came to ear: Don't curse a child for doing childish things, but don't 'courage him none neither.

Chapter Six

¿Por qué? ¿Por qué? ¿Por qué? Porque it was her idea to ride Medusa—Because! Because! Because! Nonetheless! Understandably!—it was her idea to ride Medusa; because when she whispered in your ear that foggy A.M. in that class that only you two share, that morning after—OR but days after—that party when YOU dressed in vintage polyester and pleather like the cast of the *Rocky Horror Picture Show* and paraded down Bancroft Ave á la *East Bay Story,* a new itch stitched YOUR ribs; because when she whispered, beeswax binding her riotous golden dreadlocks, bundled solid, squat enough to pinch you with envy, of course you thought FUCK calculus, FUCK history, FUCK ethnic studies, and not at all metaphorically; because when she whispered, voice riding up from her gut, wearing the sun like a saint, hair riding the air as she turned to you, you envisioned *Legend of the Overfiend,* bukkake, that fifth-grade slide on conception, now most immodest; nonetheless, YOU are forgiven because she routinely refers to herself in the third person by her First Peoples name or her Tibetan name or her Burner name; understandably forgiven by even the sardonic professor who, midmarker, raised only his left eyebrow when you pressed cracked lips to hand after Goldilocks whispered, Haven't you ever wanted to ride Medusa?

Then THEY texted you. Couldn't back out then, even if you wanted to—Because! Because! Because! Nonetheless! Understandably!—your heart exploded like a watermelon being eaten by an elephant.

And so YOU are at Six Flags in Vallejo. Va-yay-ho! Screams overhead; fluorescent math problems ride the sky. Vallejo was once the home of the Miwok, Suisunes, and the Patwin, a Wintun people, according to her. In 1850, the government drafted plans to build a new city within the city, a well-appointed capital district complete with a university and botanical garden, according to her. This gilt municipal zone was to be called Eureka, according to her. The irony is lost on you. The irony is not lost on you, but neither is it found. And you, Ferric, you say. A wink your reward. A tickle in your gut, shame, because that's how it always is, Banks loan quickest to those who least need money. Celaka!! Fuucked up, you say. You don't know what a ferret has to do with anything, but you'll, Ferret it out, you promise, you'll have that *vayay-ho*, that *va-jello*, that earthy gash, your own Eureka.

But first you tried to eat, Charlie and his Macho Nachos, Candice and her Paddle Handle Corn Dog (could the universe be more unfair?), Daron and his Smokehouse burger, and Louis and his Totally Kickin' Chicken, which he pushed away after two bites, I'm throwing in the chopsticks. Was it nerves, or was it that centered on the picnic table marred with initials carved, etched, and drawn, and stained with mustard and food scraps, sat a fluttering stack of memorial brochures doctored by Candice—*Adbusters*-style complete with new photos—to extol the virtues of the Six Flags Graveyard, and one box of ashes. The remains of Ishi, if asked.

Chapter Seven

Was this what Mrs. Brooks meant by a like-minded group? How did he get into Berkeley anyway? Professors, students, Miss Lucille—that dining hall attendant who always complimented his manners—even Daron himself. They all wondered, he knew, especially hearing his Friday-night accent, *you*—fermented—becoming a long *y'all*, and *ain't* rearing its ugly head before, worse yet, being distilled into *'ant*. He could reckon the direction of the wheels turning in their heads: budget cuts plus more out-of-state fart-sniffer students equals lower standards. They were wrong, and if they dared ask, he'd say so. Unlike some of them, he'd done it on his own. No college counselor, no private consultant to groom and polish his applicant profile, no practice admissions interviews. Hard work, summer school, and all the AP he could eat were his salvation, the price of his admission. That, and he wrote a damned fine application letter.

He had revised for weeks, reading every Wikipedia entry on writing, watching every YouTube video on the application process, some links provided by the school, others he found on his own, checking out every book of cover letters from the library. He even ordered online, with his lunch money, a book entitled *100 of the Best Application Essays Ever!* He consulted, at their insistence, his father and his

AP English teacher. His father's advice: Tell the truth. A man's word is his only honor, and honor is the only currency that never needs exchanging. His English teacher's advice: Teachers spend most of their lives reading piss-rich attempts at mind reading. Distinguish yourself in writing by being completely yourself and speaking your piece, even if your opinion runs contrary to the popular position, in fact, more so in those instances. D'aron had done just that, at the end, working in secret.

Freshman applicant prompt:

Describe the world you come from—for example, your family, community or school—and tell us how your world has shaped your dreams and aspirations.

Dear _____ Application Committee,

I am submitting respectfully this essay written for your perusal.

If we were a TV show, we'd be a soap opera. If we were a musical, we'd be a rock opera. But, in real life, we're a Shakespeare play, Romeo and Juliet.

I was born into a working-class family in the heart of Georgia. My mother's family was Irish and my father's family was descended from coal miners. They never had much, but we worked hard and made our way up. Mostly everyone works for the Kenny Hot Air factory where they make motors for the hand dryers used all across our great United States of America. The Davenports and the McCormicks never got along until my folks were married. We believe in diversity and multi-cultural-ism.

My father wanted to go to college, but after coming back from Honorably serving his country in the First Gulf War, the

GI Bills weren't any use because he had to work and couldn't commute seventy-five miles each way to the nearest community college. Now he is a floor manager and enrolled to earn an online degree in business because capitalism is the future of the world and even China realizes that now, after what Reagan did to Russia and Germany.

My community is working class. When we get together each summer for the annual town picnic, we all share food and really we're like one big community. We have the most Special Forces soldiers in all of the state per capita. We don't have a school in town or a college nearby. The nearest community college is 75 miles away and the high school is in the next town.

My town is small, only 700 people, so I had to be bused to school. I integrated well and managed to get along with everybody. I was captain of the debate team and I once saved my grandmother after she was lost in the woods for three days with cancer. It was a scary time.

We're blue collar, but proud and my family supports the American spirit and the freedom we're bringing to the middle east, and our town has that same kind of spirit. We're all red, white, and blue underneath.

I want to major in political science, bio-engineering, and bio-technology because people require peace, parsimonious food, and hygienic water. We also need to protect the earth. Ecology is the future. Not a day goes by when we don't see a volcano erupting or an earthquake. Global warming is debasing the atmosphere and only we can prohibit it.

I am also interested in education because we need better schools and no child should be left behind. The children are the future. After I graduate, I will also teach. My town needs a summer camp that doesn't involve hunting and camping *and whittling. Trees have rights, too. It should involve things to prepare you for the real world, like math and science and computers.*

That is why I am applying to _____.
_____ has the best programs in these majors. Every time I read the paper, I see someone from _____ being quoted in the news and giving scientific evidence and explanations for how we can make the world a better place for everybody. That's how I know that _____ is the school for me.

Prompt for all applicants:

Tell us about a personal quality, talent, accomplishment, contribution or experience that is important to you. What about this quality or accomplishment makes you proud and how does it relate to the person you are?

One day I was down at Lou Davis's Cash-n-Carry Bait Shop and Copy Center, where the slogan is "You Want Credit, Come Back Tomorrow."

I was after gum, but killing time. It's dim in there, the only light comes off the iceboxes. Ever since I was little I liked to stand there in the blue glow and pretend I was on a spaceship. That day it was hot, so hot I had to walk to cool down. I walked along the big fridge and freezer, feeling the chill, and saw all the venison sausage and souse and Georgia hash, which was all pretty cheap, cheaper than Jimmy Dean, but more than it would really cost to hunt. I added up the cost of the shells, and the gun, and the time, and the deer lick, and the beer, and whatever else. They'd just built a Super Walmart two towns over, and I thought about how you could track out all day after a deer, or you could shoot up to Super Walmart or Lou's and be back in a couple hours with all you needed for a week.

So I decided I didn't need to hunt anymore. It didn't make sense.

Now understand that my hometown has produced more Special Forces soldiers per capita than any other town in America.

And when the season opens there's more hunters out than trees can shake a leaf at. When the season closes, there's still more hunters out than trees can shake sticks at. Everyone has trophies mounted over their mantels or the front porch and the first buck is a bigger occasion than the 13th birthday.

You got to understand we're proud, and we respect prey drive. We put down dogs that don't hunt.

So, I got more hell for this than for being a Battlestar Galactica fan or complaining that Lost was stupid. But I argued that we didn't sew our own clothes even though there were still patches of wild cotton at the edge of the old Southerby Plantation and that we didn't make our own shoes even though there was a dairy two exits up, and a hemp farm in the next county so we could make laces.

I'd been a scout all my life, all the way up to Eagle Scout, but hunting just didn't make sense. I stuck with my guns and am proud of that decision to this day, even though everyone still teases me about it. I won't repeat here the names they call me.

My father took it hard because that was the one thing we did together that my mom just wouldn't go for. But he hasn't given up on me, right now he's snoring soundly, thinking that I'm pecking away at a letter to UGA.

Freshman applicant prompt:
(Revision)

Describe the world you come from—for example, your family, community, or school—and tell us how your world has shaped your dreams and aspirations.

Dear Sir of [sic] Madam,

My mother helped me write several previous drafts of this personal statement. In them, we listed accomplishments such as the Eagle scouts, the volunteer work for the local Red Cross, and my membership (for one day) in the Braggsville Historical Preservation and Dissemination Society. We also listed my participation in several school organizations and the time I saved my cousin from drowning, saved a cat from a bird, and saved my grandmother from certain starvation when she wandered off into the Holler and got lost. I also claimed a long-term interest in about a dozen majors that aren't even related.

I learned a good word in the process: logorrhea. Not only were those letters too long, and had too many fancy words, the biggest problem was I didn't remember many of these things. I will not dare to question their veracity. It was my mother who spoke those words, mind you. But the fact that I could neither remember these renowned events with which my extended family regaled each other around the Green Egg, nor supply my own memories, explains exactly how my world has shaped my dreams and aspirations. As my cousin Quint would say, I've been worked over by a one-armed potter.

It is not a college admission board who I write at this late hour, long after the parental units have retired because I need to write this on my own, it is to a parole board that I write.

I love my family and my town. My parents never went to college, but have done right by me all their lives. They didn't take my schooling for granted and they made me study and take summer classes, and made me read all those test-taking books because they wanted me to go to college, but neither could tell me what for, other than that I have to. And for years I never understood why I have to, especially when they want me to go right up the road. But I need to get out of shouting distance of this place where everyone secretly calls school, Juvie!, and openly calls prison, School!

So in addressing the parole board in this hearing I feel I must demonstrate that I have changed, that I have atoned for whatever sin caused me to be born in this partially dry county, that I have learned my lesson. And I have.

I have learned that no matter where you go to school, it's what you do after school that counts. But, we don't have an afterschool program. I have learned that kids from all different areas can get along if given a chance, but our schools rarely meet and have only limited contact with other schools. I have learned that sports can bring people of different races and colors together to work for a common goal, but I don't play sports and we only have one team, and it has only one race on it. I have learned that with access to public health care people avoid dying unnecessarily painful and lonely deaths, but the nearest hospital is over 100 miles away.

I have learned all this from reading books and watching the History Channel and Discovery because my town is tiny. It isn't even on most maps, and we never had a representative. All our lives we wanted to matter, and we've applied for the Special Olympics, the Georgia Games, and the Capital Seat, all to no luck. We've tried, but our resources are limited until someone invests something in us, like time and a little money and a little outside influence.

So I guess what I'm saying is that I'm like my hometown, and I need someone to take a chance on me so I can prove my worth. And, I also would really like the chance to experience in person what I so far learned only on TV.

In regarding my major. There are over three hundred at Berkeley, and it's hard to choose one when the most popular extracurricular activities here are 4-H, hunting, and Xbox. I like food and I observe that most people do as well. When the whistle blows at the mill the blacks go back to the Gully, the Mexicans to Ridgetown, and the Whites back here. But they all meet at the markets and after they talk about the weather, they exchange recipes. My parents are now making burritos and the Mexicans are eating headcheese, and for the best barbecue, Old Lou Davis has the biggest smoker and makes good pulled pork, but I've heard the Gully is where they have the best beef ribs. I think nutritional science and anthropology are my interests. To meet other people and learn how food can bring us together.

Thank you for considering my humble application.

I read on the YouTube advice link connected to the application page that we're not supposed to end with a quote, especially from a book called "The Road Less Traveled." Well, I guess I just did that anyway, but only to remind you that to get to some of my relatives we drive partway and walk the rest because they don't have roads leading to where they live. (I hope you liked that.)

I gave up hunting and I'm a vegetarian and I think I'm ready to be released into society.

On another note, YouTube also said to be honest, so I must

admit that the other reason I like UC Berkeley is because the only way I could get farther from home is to learn how to swim.

Sincerely,
Hopefully,
Daron Little May Davenport
Class of ??!!

Daron stumbled across those letters shortly before Operation Confederation, as the 4 Little Indians had begun to call it. Rereading them he prickled with guilt.

I gave up hunting? I'm a vegetarian? I'm ready to be released into society? What was he thinking? Community? He'd never used that word so much in his life. Dear parole board! It was as though he had begged to be released from a cage of savage animals. What was wrong with hunting or eating meat? Nothing. Had he felt differently back then, or had he written what he thought they'd want to hear? He feared the worst. Even if it had felt honest at the time, he now recognized a shameful pleading, a palpable desperation, the stench of superiority.

Anxiety redoubled as self-reproach. Spring break was fast approaching, and he had better warn his mother. On the phone he asked her to request that Uncle Roy not use the N-word. His mother paused.

An word? she mused. Oh, in-words? Is that slang?

You know. Nigger.

Oh. Then louder, Oh! So you mean you are bringing friends. Okay, dear. I'll make all the preparations.

And, ask, no, tell Quint not to make that Chinese joke.

What Chinese joke?

That thing he says that isn't even funny. When Quint disagrees with something or someone, he says, Hell naw! Start that shit and next thing you know you're Chinese. Not to mention—most definitely not to his mom—that to Quint, getting Chinese means getting high, and ordering Chinese means ordering dope.

Oh! You're bringing home company. Don't fret, D-dear.

Thanks, Mom. I owe you.

No charge, son, no charge. The full cost is no charge. She hummed for a moment her favorite Melba Montgomery song, *No Charge*. Don't fret, dear, everyone will be on their best behavior.

And they would be. No one messed with his mother, who could stare a stone into sand. Could you also ask Dad to . . . well . . .

Yes, dear. We'll move The Charlies.

The Charlies were what his father and grandfather called their black lawn jockeys, those two statues flanking the driveway, Serving with a smile. When referring to only one statue, they called it Tom, but together, and collectively, they were The Charlies. As in: Damned tractor went off the shoulder and took out my favorite Tom, they don't make that size no more so I got to buy two new Charlies. As in: When are we lighting up The Charlies this year, Black Friday or December first? As in: Two Wongs don't make a wang between 'em, but two Toms make The Charlies. He'd read both the Wikipedia and Uncyclopedia entries on *Uncle Tom's Cabin* and found no connection. He knew it was supposed to be funny, but he never understood the joke, and didn't think he wanted Candice or Louis or—good Lord, goodness, no—Charlie asking for an explanation about The Charlies. Charlie would take it in stride and Louis would say something funny, but Candice would go astral as she had after learning that Ishi meant man, that it was against Yahi custom to tell outsiders your name, that Ishi had no formal Yahi name because there were no surviving members of Ishi's tribe to name Ishi, that Ishi therefore meant Ishi. She had, as Quint would say, gotten a red-eyed bull up her ass about Ishi, and Ishi wasn't even alive.

Chapter Eight

¿Por qué? ¿Por qué no?

Porque, as she explained it, Ishi is Yahi for man, Ishi is Yahi for Ishi.

Porque, as she explained it, there was a difference between apologizing and anthropologizing, and neither excuse the desecration of a body.

Porque, as she explained it, they were Ishi's remains. They *are* Ishi's remains. If a picture was a captured soul, what the fuck was a book of them, what the fuck was a history of one people written by another, except an imaginary menagerie, a colonial shadowbox, a little foot warmer for those cold-existential evenings, an amulet against those starless, soulless nights?

You understood none of it, except the part about the foot warmer, which you knew was a myth of Northern aggression, though you daren't interrupt when the spirit combed her tongue.

Mengapa? Mengapa tidak?

Is that Malay? Uh, you know I don't actually speak Malay, except for curse words, right?

Mengapa? Mengapa tidak?

Kerana, as she explained it, if everything's symbolic, then everything's real. Then when we spread these ashes in Vallejo, people will know. They will know that UC Berkeley, supposedly the best public university in the world, took a man and made him live in a museum like an Epcot Center attraction, that we're all in prison. That this is what public schools are. People will ask questions. People will demand answers. They will find there are none, and that will be the beginning of a reckoning . . . (A nod at you.)

What you talking 'bout, Willis?

What I'm talking 'bout, Willis, she explained, is how could any decent human force the last living member of a tribe to live in a museum? Ishi, how Ishi must have dreamed at night, how Ishi must have dreamed. How Ishi must dream even now. Though the museum and Kroeber both promised that Ishi's body would not be desecrated, Ishi was autopsied in defiance of Native custom, Ishi's body cremated, and Ishi's brain wrapped in deerskin and shipped by mechanical conveyance to the Smithsonian. Ishi! How Ishi must dream.

Candice was not reassured to learn that the Smithsonian repatriated the body. Would we commend a stock market swindler for repaying stolen funds? Plan A: We're taking Ishi to Six Flags and we're riding Medusa and we're releasing Ishi at the summit, and . . .

¿Cómo? Bagaimana? How? A padded bra! With three pounds of ashes double-packed in eight lucky-ass Ziploc bags, duct-taped like Styrofoam padding lining a bike helmet inside a Victoria's Secret triple-D underwire, she'd put the pied piper out of a job, or at least off of it: the Six Flags guard checking her bag didn't see anything in that shadow, not the collapsed box that would be the urn, not the clutch of feathers, not the half pint of Old Grand-Dad, none of it. She had borrowed Charlie's rugby jersey, and damned if a spontaneous folk etymology didn't cleave your brain as *scrum* took on a whole new meaning.

(Is it that . . . could you be . . . are you . . . might you be predisposed to objectify women, to remain stunted in what one prof called abject masculinity? Are you unfit for the university, the universe where no one has a body? A shame you cannot name scores you. For one class last fall, you read Andrea Dworkin, Akasha Gloria Hull, Martha Nussbaum, and at least a dozen other feminist authors, including Naomi Wolf and John Stoltenberg, both of whom argue that even the idea of physical attraction is socially constructed, argue that no one is innately beautiful, argue that society just told you so— about certain people. You found, though, that the more you tried looking at Candice and not thinking about her as a body, but as a person, the more you thought about her body. And now this!)

So there you are. At the picnic table. The air at last out of Candice's balloons; and right before lunch, YOU made extended trips to the bathroom and let some pressure out of yours. But your palms are sweaty, and your feet, and you avoid looking at the guards—who all stare at you—and the ride attendants, too, and you get it. You know what he means. You want to tell him you understand how it feels, but he will say for you this is only today, for me this is everyday, every day—watched, followed, harassed—everyday. But, still, you get it. You wish you knew what to say to him, how to begin the conversation. Instead, you let him sit next to her, which he does in silence, as do the rest of you until the agreed-upon time, eyes on hands, feet, legs, neck, everything but Candice, until show time, when YOU learn that nothing, no purses, no hats, and certainly no glossy cardboard boxes can accompany riders on the Medusa. Because. The attendant Pearl pointed to the sign overhead, a periodic chart of pictograms among which, Candice insisted, she saw no cardboard boxes. One hand on her hip, rocking heel-to-toe in her thick-soled grudge-green Doc Martens, Pearl lectured them on the many perils of high-speed travel in unpiloted vehicles. Ever seen a pair of AA batteries fly out of a camera and slam into someone's face at 110 kilometers an hour? Know what a can of Mountain Dew can do at those speeds? A book? A Big Mac?

To Daron's amazement, Candice didn't try to persuade the attendant to change her mind. As the 4 Little Indians retreated, Candice snorted. All she had to say of Pearl was, She'd wear black nail polish if they let her.

COULD A BEAK BE TOO PINK? Daron wondered as they instituted a hasty plan B. After having been turned away from Medusa and discovering that the highest point in the park, the Volcano, was inaccessible to pedestrians, Candice swiveled her scope toward the heart, the center of the park, the fountain, a circular basin finished in stucco and slate and surrounded by tiny red flowers, a fount from which surged a curtain of mist shaped like an inverted Bundt pan and ribbed by a dozen sprouts of water, and from the center of that erupted three bronze dolphins imprisoned eternally in the hazy bell jar, their bowed bodies predicting long arcs, their eyes on points distant.

The sculptures had appeared to piss Candice off more than anything else. She had rounded the fountain twice, tracing a larger circle with her feet, her backpack clopping loudly whenever she stopped to stomp on the three spots where the dolphins would land were the miraculous to occur. Even the fucking statues want to be free! Hungry, and so tired, Louis and Charlie had taken a seat on a nearby wrought-iron bench. Daron stood midway between Candice and his buddies, between the bench and the fountain, feeling as he had all morning—like an emissary, an ambassador, the diplomatic hotline between squabbling republics. He had encouraged Candice not to give up, if it was important to her. He had encouraged Louis and Charlie to have patience when waiting in line, though he hadn't expected Louis to interpret that as license to hold a conversation with Candice's breasts (which she adjusted far, far too often for Daron's liking). Lastly, he had waved them all together once Candice decided on a spot. Charlie and Louis staggered over with the enthusiasm of teen relations visiting Seventh-Day Adventists on a Saturday morning, taking stilted, robotic steps as if they had no ankles.

Candice arranged them in a semicircle around the cardboard urn, armed them each with ceremonial feathers, furs, and ornaments (all made of red paper, which Louis assured them was okay because Chinese people did that for funerals). Charlie had a Native bracelet he'd received as a gift. Louis donned a Burger King crown, the paper plumes willowed with gaudy jewels, glass trinkets he'd bought at one of Berkeley's many bead stores. Candice wore a dream catcher around her neck right where her oversize crumb catchers had been earlier. She laid out an arc of smooth rocks between the three of them and Ishi's urn, and two larger concentric arcs between Ishi and what she called, The Outside World. Atop Ishi she placed a paper tomahawk. I'll read something I've found online. She waggled her phone. It will take maybe two minutes tops. On her cue they held hands and began to hum. Her only instruction being, Hum!, Daron was surprised that they quickly fell into harmony as surely as if they had rehearsed for weeks, and he felt a nervous thrill whenever someone glanced in their direction. She restarted reading her passage at least four times because every fifteen fucking seconds a kid dragged his mommy or his nanny or his daddy or sometimes, because it was California, his mommies, or more rarely, his daddies over to see, Oooooohhhh powwow. Candice always wanted the kid to hear the whole thing. She was like the teacher he'd had in eighth grade who believed, You can only combat absenteeism and truancy with love. If you were late, no matter how late, she'd catch you up on what had happened so far, stopping the entire class to greet every tardy student like the prodigal son. The only reason she wasn't fired was because, Methuselah be damned, she could trick the sun into oversleeping, as Daron overheard a teacher say one afternoon at Lou's.

Mrs. Price. That was her name. Eighth-grade D'aron—aka Mr. Davenport, aka Dim Ding-Dong, bka (*better known as*) Faggot—

had always wanted to come in late enough so that for just a minute or two, Mrs. Price would devote all her attention to him and only him, and he would have a feeling all over that was a mix between a warm bath and rubbing his groin against the kitchen sink, which was unavoidable when reaching for the tap. Mrs. Price, smells so nice, Mrs. Price, let me taste your spice, Mrs. Price, let me juggle your dice—always snake eyes, must have come to Daron's mind because he stood between Candice and Charlie, and the hand Candice's held—and that hand only—was clammy, that entire arm warm and tingling as if it had fallen asleep and been violently awoken.

Like criminals, kids attract each other, and soon eight children sat in a row before them, clapping at the end of Candice's every sentence. Fortunately, their parents appreciated the break and relaxed on nearby benches—close enough to watch their children, but not close enough to get a good look at our 4 Little Indians. One of the kids stared like Daron was somebody important, and he had to admit the kid was cute. From a passing first aid attendant—Whassup? From a short black kid pushing a broom—a nod. From a cute brunette driving the handicapped golf cart—a wave. From the fountain—Dribble dribble. Briefly, it all felt very natural. Then came Tweety Bird, whom Daron had never seen up close. Then came a Latina who stopped at the insistence of her two blond charges, twin boys about waist-years-old. The crowd had grown. The kids hummed along as best they could, harmonic as a holiday hymnody. Candice chanted:

> You are the sparrow's song, the crow's caw
> The rose's fragrance, the spring thaw
> In our hearts you live forever,
> Children will celebrate your brave endeavors
> And we'll take strength from your resolve
> Until we meet again in heaven above

Charlie squeezed Daron's hand, motioning at the nearby twin boys. One twin did cartwheels while the other coyly reached for a paper feather. Candice hissed him away. The Latina in charge of the twins made an apologetic face, more so, it seemed, for her powerlessness than for the twins' behavior.

But Tweety deserved the attention, now only yards to their left, her fluffy finger dragging through the air like that of a director shadowed in the stage wings, resigned to her cast's tendency toward insurgency. But this Tweety, as Louis pointed out in an inching whisper, has a clitoris-colored tongue—a hot one—a clitoris-colored tongue with a soft groove as inviting as a warm hot dog bun. Behold the blessed velvety furrow! And this Tweety, much to Daron's surprise, is too pink in the beak, too pink for him to be at the same time holding Candice's hand, too pink for him to be at the same time having random memories of Mrs. Price, such as a vivid image of the scrumptious freckle centered in the cleft of her chin, peeking down the split in her bib, pink enough to threaten a hot and perhaps soon not-so-private bristling, and about this he feels that confusion, that particular confusion he felt after the first time he knew himself in the biblical sense and lay there for some long, huffing minutes, afraid to look down because he thought he'd peed in his hand. It was a particular confusion that provided the only reliable refuge against shame.

Again, Candice hissed away the twins, but these two Willy Wonka rejects were professionals and used their similarity to great advantage. One would dance, try walking on his hands, mime—anything to distract, while the other wreaked havoc, stealing other kids' toys, poking children, both of them acting all around like midget assholes. Louis tried motioning to the nanny, and Candice shushed him. But I didn't say anything. Shushed again. One twin danced wild in a scuba mask while the other snuck behind them again and grabbed the paper tomahawk, upsetting Ishi.

Was Daron the only one to notice that Tweety Bird's eyelashes

were too, too long, fine strokes tapering gently up and across the forehead, framing blue eyes almost as big as Candice's? And again, that
particular confusion; he couldn't bear to look down, the hot bristling
now a full-on shadow box, noun and verb, so he dropped to one knee
right as the wind scooped Ishi up and along the sidewalk and to the
wider world.

Ishi, Candice yelled, Ishi, we commend you to the wind.

Tweety, hand to her temple as if compressing a wound, cater-
wauled as if she tawt she taw a putty cat, stirring the crowd out of
their enchantment. The audience politely danced the ashes off their
feet and applauded. Tweety, hand still to mouth, scurried off as best
she could, knees cycling as if pushing pedals, those canary clodhop-
pers working the ground like snowshoes.

Chapter Nine

At the San Francisco airport Charlie discreetly pulled Daron aside and asked if there was anything he needed to know, if he should expect more crazy-Colonel-Sanders types of people in Braggsville. After the Ishi Incident, the 4 Little Indians had been invited to eat with a charming Southern couple who, as promised, made the best fried chicken west of the Mississippi. The couple, by Daron's mind, had exemplified Southern hospitality by sharing with the hungry Indians what food they had, by making space at their dining table for strangers. Was Charlie offended because that table had been plastic and they'd sat on metal folding chairs? Daron hoped Charlie wouldn't be so particular when meeting his relations. My mother, warned Daron, despises people who wear shoes without socks, and anyone who eats non-finger-foods with their fingers, like picking up the last pea. They had a good laugh over that, at least Charlie did.

While Charlie, Candice, and Louis were fastening seat belts and returning chair trays to the upright and locked position, it dawned on Daron that though he'd asked his mom to move The Charlies, he'd neglected to mention the mammies from New Orleans, Salt and Pepper Climb on Cucumber, as well as the Bibinba, Zwarte Pieten, and Hajji Firuz dolls his cousins had picked up while stationed abroad, not to mention the Blackface Soap and Watermelon Whistler tins. And that strange guy with the big grin dressed in only a loincloth and turban. That they were antiques, that they were valuable, that they were gifts wasn't going to make Candice feel any better about them.

It's not that the Davenports had never had black people around their house before, or even a Chinese guy once, but never a Malaysian who looked Chinese to some and Indian to others, fancied himself black at times, and wanted to be the next Lenny Bruce Lee; a preppy black football player who sounded like the president and read Plato in Latin; and a white woman who occasionally claimed to be Native American. They were like an overconstructed novel, each representative of some cul-de-sac of idiolect and stereotype, missing only a handicapped person—No! At Berkeley we say handi-*capable* person—and a Jew and a Hispanic, and an Asian not of the subcontinent, Louis always said. He had once placed a personals ad on Craigslist to recruit for those positions: Diverse social club seeking to make quota requires the services of East Asian, Jew, Hispanic, and handicapable individuals to round out the Multicultural Brady Bunch Troupe. All applicants must be visibly identifiable as members of said group. Reform Jews and ADHDers need not apply. Daron felt now as he had when people had started responding to that ad, that he couldn't help but expect a spectacular disaster.

HARTSFIELD-JACKSON ATLANTA INTERNATIONAL AIRPORT was among the most active transportation hubs in the world, in some years ranked the busiest. Daron never claimed Atlanta as his own, nor did anyone at home, but when they landed, he acted as tour guide, sharing all he had read online, and there was much to tell, see, and do on the long journey from Terminal E to baggage claim. Modern art graced the terminals and African sculptures lined the underground walkway. Any kind of food could be found, or movies rented, or prayers proffered, but that's not what captivated them, not what had Candice shy, Charlie bright-eyed, Louis agape, and Daron feigning indifference, affecting an at-home swagger.

Theyselves were porters, skycaps, desk agents. TSA and armed officers. Businessmen, mothers, families. Teens traveling alone. Clerks and janitors, not to mention the pianist entertaining diners in the international terminal food court. Waitresses, waiters. Flight attendants. Was that Waka and Gucci? A pilot even! Tall short fat. Pretty ugly glamorous. Theyselves were flamboyant and poised. Rambunctious and composed. Svelte and slovenly. But mostly middle class and well-to-do, from the looks of them. Atlanta's nickname was well earned; a Chocolate City indeed it was.

Beyond baggage claim, the 4 Little Indians were equally mesmerized. Daron was reminded again how different Atlanta was from most of Georgia, and from Berkeley or San Francisco even. It was impossible not to notice when theyselves comprised more than 50 percent of the population (especially when they were only 3 percent of Berkeley). Circling the concourse in vehicles ranging from beaters to Beemers, but mostly the latter, their significant middle class was outdone only by their extensive upper-middle class. Charlie, Candice, and Louis stared in awe as an elegant middle-aged woman clicked past them, the fox staring back as she flung her stole over her shoulder while wheeling a Tumi to a red convertible Aston Martin, the engine idling like Lord of Misrule nuzzling the gate before that famous derby. The driver, of average height and build, greeted her with a kiss on both cheeks, leaning back between each one as if to get a look at her. It was impossible not to feel pleasure at their reunion.

Candice nudged Daron, Famous?

Who they were, Daron didn't know; the driver was obviously no athlete and too old to be a rapper. This was normal for Atlanta. He'd even heard that southwest of the city was a vast tract of million-dollar-plus homes all owned by blacks, a fact he proudly shared. Welcome to the new South.

It's like being Asian in SF, or it must be, Charlie mused aloud.

Daron was glad it was Charlie who'd said it.

Except it looks like they have more money here.

Daron's mother nosed her boxy white Ford Bronco into the space behind the Aston Martin. She clapped with glee and skipped to greet her D'aron, smothering him in kisses. Don't be embarrassed, they have parents, too. She affectionately greeted each of his friends with a kiss on the cheek.

Actually, Charlie doesn't. Daron regretted how that sounded when Candice glared at him.

Is that so? She tilted her head and turned on her heels to face Charlie.

It's my dad, ma'am.

So sad. She kissed him again, squeezing his arms. You're a big boy.

Yes, ma'am.

See! She elbowed Daron. He didn't wipe his off. Charlie is a young man with good home training. She turned to Charlie, You play football? Cutting her eyes at Daron, she added, Forgive me if I'm *essentializing*.

Whatever! Daron began loading the luggage into the car, starting with Candice's Hello Kitty bag, which momentarily reminded him of Kaya, and he wondered what Kaya would make of this Atlanta place, as she liked to phrase things. More importantly, though, what would Candice make of Braggsville? Straining to heft an oversize duffel with Fu Manchu mustache patches sewn onto either end, he was surprised again that the distinction of having the largest bag went not to Candice, but to Louis, whose only explanation was, Stuff.

Your mom's so friendly, Louis added.

Daron nodded glumly; handlebar-headed was more like it. She's not normally so saccharine.

Before leaving Cali, they had agreed to speak French or Spanish as necessary for security, but Daron knew his mother wouldn't know that word anyway, at least not as an adjective. Nonetheless, a hurt look passed across her face.

Play what you like on the radio, she offered in a grim voice, jerking the seat belt as if closing a coat against the cold.

With Louis cooking up a story about every trucker they passed, and Charlie explaining to Daron's mom what life was like as a poor kid in a rich boarding school, something he'd never even mentioned to Daron, the two-hour drive passed pleasantly enough, and before he knew it, Candice, who read every single printed letter and punctuation mark along the highway (emphasizing the many Indian names)—a fact Daron was glad to have learned before they went on an extended road trip—yelled, Welcome to Braggsville, The City That Love Built in the Heart of Georgia, Population 712. Was there a Bragg? Candice asked.

Sure was.

Signs for the reenactment adorned every corner, each one a line drawing of a Civil War soldier superimposed over the Confederate battle flag. The signs promised THRILLING HISTORY AND HERITAGE, BREATHTAKING SCENERY AND SOUND EFFECTS, and the EDUCATIONAL EXPERIENCE OF A LIFETIME all at the Pride Week Patriot Days Festival. Red, white, and blue lights strung across Main Street blinked, illuminating the matching streamers wrapped around the light poles. Enormous Confederate flags dressed the watchtower—strung high enough to ensure passersby a clear view of the memorial plaques dotting each of the walls. Four men in full Confederate regalia stepped into the crosswalk, spaced like the Beatles on the *Abbey Road* album cover, one even barefoot. Candice fumbled over her iPhone.

Dear, don't you ask people before taking their photograph? asked Daron's mom as she steered the car into the parking lot of Lou Davis's Cash-n-Carry Bait Shop and Copy Center.

Excuse me, ma'am. Candice, surprisingly chagrined, powered off
her phone and slipped it into her pocket.

Lou's? asked Daron.

They're expanding, she explained. To Candice, she smiled. No
need to apologize.

Lou's? asked Daron.

Look at it. They're expanding.

Lou Davis's was designed in the style of an old general store with a
faux plank face. Old Man Davis had torn down the original dovetail
chink log cabin and replaced it with this cinder-block structure back
in the forties. For a long time, it was the town's central landmark.
(Everything was measured by its distance from Lou's, the watchtower,
or the tree known as Miss Keen, even though that old sweet gum had
long ago been debilitated by canker and had succumbed, at last, to a
careening Walmart rig driven by a Mexican barely tall enough to see
over the instrument panel and so when the stewing citizens arrived
at the scene to find only one slight young man no taller than a three-
year-old Christmas tree, they assumed that the operator had run off
and took pity on the young Latino. The state trooper had called him,
One lucky jumping bean. No one likes Walmart. They tolerate it
because it's cheap, but no one likes it.) When the reenactments were
reinstated back in the 1950s in response to mandated integration,
Lou installed the fake wood front, For the sake of authentic-nessity.
(Lou used -nessity the way Gulls used Texas Pete hot sauce.) A room
that doubled the size of the store was now being added to the right,
jutting out into the parking lot. A handmade sign with a border of
roses drawn with a highlighter promised that dine-in seating was
coming soon, though obviously not in time for this year's reenactment. Daron recognized Lee Anne's writing and wondered if she'd
be working. The exposed cinder blocks contrasted with the wooden
front, reminding Daron that the store wasn't historic, only dirty and
cluttered. Inside, though, was cleaned up significantly. It was brightly

lit, the new tile floor shiny, and, the biggest surprise, central air had replaced the dusty old black fan. (I love the sound of a compressor in the summer, a line the locals often intoned in the manner of Robert Duvall in *Apocalypse Now*.) Rheanne Davis, Lou's youngest grand-daughter and one of Daron's early hitches, and with whom he had shared many a milk shake for one summer in high school, sat behind the register reading *People*. Behind her was the updated copy center, an all-in-one inkjet printer and scanner. Back then he'd been heart-broken by her decision to take time apart, and wrote her every night for a month, though he never mailed the letters. He wasn't that fool-ish. He did, however, relish this moment to introduce her to his new friends, but hoped she wouldn't mention their previous relationship, not with those bleached bangs and the T-shirt dress.

Welcome back, Little D.

Hi, Rheanne. These are my friends from—

Hi, Little D's friends.

He rattled off their names, but she'd already returned her atten-tion to her magazine. No handshaking and hugging here.

At the back of the store Lou had installed a new deli counter, behind which stood his oldest granddaughter and Rheanne's older sister, Lee Anne, who waved politely from her folding chair, posi-tioned so that she could watch *The Voice* on the television in the corner.

Welcome back, Little D.

Hi, Lee Anne, these are my friends—

Hi, Little D's friends. What are all y'allses names?

His mom rushed through the introductions. They were in a hurry, she explained as she gave her order.

Three pounds of three kinds of meat? Sliced? Lee Anne groaned. You coulda called that in, Miss Janice.

I realize that, Lee Anne, that's why it's an emergency order, be-cause I wasn't able to plan ahead, and pick up my son and his wonderful friends, who flew clear across the country to see our little festival. I had a lot to do to prepare for this trip, and now that I have an emergency, I knew I had to come here, and not up the road to that big cold box.

Of course. Lee Anne's voice softened at the mention of the big cold box, the mart that was to remain unmentioned, but apparently appreciation wasn't ample motivation. Lee Anne had graduated only two years before Daron, but she already moved like her grandfather Lou himself, and five minutes surely passed while she shuffled to the deli case, turned over several slabs of meat before finding the right one, peeled the plastic back, adjusted the slicer, washed her hands, and, finally ready to begin—no, not yet, it seemed—brushed aside a few stray hairs with her bare hands, made a face of intense concentration, flipped the switch on the machine, and guided the meat across. Lee Anne took a deep breath. A single slice of ham fainted across the wax paper like a Southern belle in sight of a chaise lounge. She exhaled dramatically. One!

Louis and Candice snuck a glance at each other that said, No fucking way this can be serious.

Just joking. I like to do that for the tourists.

Daron's relief was physical.

A young girl of no more than seven came in walking on her heels and stood beside Daron's mother. He recognized her as Irene's daughter Ingrid.

Hello, dear. Daron's mother raised her voice to be heard over the slicer. How are you today?

Fine, ma'am.

Doing some shopping for your mommy?

For myself, ma'am.

Lee Anne stopped slicing. The whirring blade slowed and the sound of the motor faded. Do you need something from this here counter, Ingrid? I done told you this here AC ain't free.

Yes, ma'am, Lee Anne. Two slices of bologna and two slices of cheese.

Lee Anne glared at her, holding the stare while picking up a microphone, unnecessarily as it turned out, and yelling, We need backup at the deli counter. Rheanne slammed her *People* down like last week's *TV Guide* and stomped to the back of the store. Candice approached the deli counter with a handmade doll in her outstretched hands. How much is this?

Rheanne shook her head and picked up the microphone, We need a price check.

Those two were still fighting like it was high school. Daron walked off in frustration, leaving Charlie chatting with his mom. He hadn't wanted to come in here anyway. They'd made a stop for gas as well, which really irked him. Why couldn't his mom have done all this before picking them up? She knew how far away the airport was. But she didn't plan and they had ended up in a gas station with Candice and Louis gasping and pulling out their phones to snap photos of little jigaboo dolls and bumper stickers with slogans like ARIZONA: DOING THE JOB THE FEDS WON'T DO . . . BLIND JUSTICE IS EQUAL / SOCIAL JUSTICE IS RACIST . . . GUNS DON'T KILL PEOPLE, DANGEROUS MINORITIES DO . . . I DON'T LIKE HIS WHITE HALF EITHER . . . IF YOU'RE ANY 'CAN, EXCEPT AMERI-CAN—GO HOME . . . IF I'D KNOWN IT WOULD BE LIKE THIS, I WOULD HAVE PICKED MY OWN COTTON. By tomorrow this time, the slogans would be all over Facebook and Instagram. Worse yet, Louis might method tweet, which was his form of method acting. He certainly had enough inspiration.

When Lou rearranged the store, he'd tucked away the bumper stickers in the back corner, but after the last stop, Candice knew what to look for. AMERICAN BY BIRTH, SOUTHERN BY THE GRACE OF GOD announced the one Louis and Candice were reading aloud, working over the words like kids sounding out the list of puzzling ingredients on the side panel of their favorite sugary cereal.

Rheanne was on the phone now. Was she staring at them? He couldn't tell, but suspected it. She must have been because for just a moment her eyes met his, and they both quickly looked away.

Louis and Candice read the rest of the stickers, each of which bore the Confederate flag and a slogan: THESE COLORS DON'T RUN . . . HUNTING IS THE BEST ANGER MANAGEMENT . . . THE SOUTH SHALL RISE AGAIN . . . KEEP HONKING—I'M RELOADING. Lou's selection, fortunately, was not as obnoxious as the gas station's. Daron had never thought much about them, his attention from a young age drawn to the sign over the register: YOU WANT CREDIT, COME BACK TOMORROW.

What's tomorrow? asked Candice when they were checking out.

The reenactment. Rheanne blinked once, slowly, as if in disbelief, as if the question were an affront.

You get credit for the reenactment?

That's only if you come tomorrow.

Wednesdays?

On Wednesday, tomorrow will be Thursday.

Oh. That's funny. She gave a frenzied, feverish laugh, so unrestrained that Daron worried she was mocking Rheanne, but Rheanne joined in, too. Candice picked up a pamphlet entitled *History of Braggsville.* How much is this? Rheanne shrugged and picked up the microphone, We need a price check.

Lou's was a few blocks from the edge of town, and from there it was barely a ten-minute drive to Daron's house. The rest of the way home, it seemed that everyone was on their front porch. If they didn't have a porch, they were in the window. Daron called out their names and waved as they passed. There was Mary Jo, Bobby, Kevin, Dennis, Raymond, Lucille, Frankie, Coddles, Lyle, John, Andy, Miss

Ursula, Jim, Lonnie, Postmaster Jones, William, Travis, Todd, Tony, Dennis M. . . . They all waved back.

Will there be a quiz? You know, it's hella creepy, all those waving bingo wings, Louis slapped his triceps.

We drive everywhere here. It's too hot for old people to walk. Daron went back to listing names, hoping to distract them from The Charlies—a legion theyselves—guarding driveways, gracing lawns, standing sentinel on porches with wide-eyed accusation. Not to mention the Hobarts, who were shoe-footing it in the single lane ahead of them with I DON'T LIKE HIS WHITE HALF EITHER pasted dead center below their license plate.

Candice leaned over and whispered to Daron, Where do all the black people live?

In the front yards. Louis pointed randomly.

Charlie laughed, followed by Daron's mom.

Daron slapped Louis's hand. No, in the Gully.

The gutter!

No, the Gully, the Gully, repeated Daron, flushed from Candice's whisper, her arm against his, her strawberry breath at his ear. Their neighborhood is called the Gully. It's right behind my house, on the other side of the hill, on the other side of the Holler, then walk a little ways. My nana—grandma—nearly got lost back there and she was from the woods.

Can we walk there?

I don't exactly know how to get there on foot.

Isn't it behind your house?

Sort of. I know how to get there. It's just you don't walk it. After you cross the hill, the Gully is still behind the Holler, but no one actually walks through the Holler. To get to the Gully, you drive back to the highway and around.

She made her life-is-unfair face, angry and sad all at once, like a child who had paid her quarter but received no bubble gum ball from the globe, a look he hated because it made him feel protective but powerless and swelled a sudden urge to cup her breasts. He tried explaining that the Gully wasn't worse off or hidden. They had it good for work because they were actually closer to the mill, and upwind. They had their own houses and their own store and their own mechanic. It was just that no one walked through the Holler. Nobody. You didn't have to be Methuselah to know that.

Chapter Ten

His mom's backyard rivaled Berkeley's best. The entire plot was five acres, as were most along their road, but his father was one of the few who'd cordoned off a portion of his land, erecting a solid six-foot wood dog-ear fence behind the house to create a sizable yard, almost the dimensions of a basketball court, in which over the years his mother had planted a small herb garden, ivy to dress the gazebo, a flower bed along the house, and several rows of dwarf pear trees. She planned well. When all the planting was finally finished, bounded on each side by colorful flowers or edible fruit was a neatly cropped, lush lawn in the center of which the gazebo sat like a paperweight.

When they entered the backyard, his mom gesturing as though announcing dignitaries to the royal court, a cheer sounded across the crowd. Daron cringed when he heard *Jungle Boogie* playing. His family was dangerously drunk when they started playing soul, and it was only eight P.M. Almost thirty people danced, sang, chatted, smoked, or swapped stories in various corners of the yard, all waiting to ambush him with embarrassment. His fifty-seven-year-old aunt Boo would soon be dropping it like it was hot, his uncle Lance would soon be doing the funky chicken clogging routine, and his seven-year-old cousin Ashley would soon be doing her Beyoncé

Single Ladies impersonation, complete with a body suit, stockings, and high heels.

Then there were his older female cousins—the stripper, the trucker, and the elementary school teacher—referred to as no-count because they'd never married. The stripper and teacher were twins, and rumor had it they occasionally played switcheroo. At most gatherings, one started a fire and the other a fight. But there was no telling who because they switched roles for each party.

Of course there was Uncle Roy, who resembled Don Knotts and chanted nigger like it would cure his pancreatic cancer. His wife, Aunt Chester, never knew where to put the needle down in the conversation and couldn't meet people without making fun of their names, if she liked them. Daron couldn't blame her. Her Christian name was Anna, but Uncle Roy always introduced her as his wife, Chester, and often added, nodding at her bosom, You'll never guess how she got that nickname or why I married her. Quint, more a brother than a cousin, had the Confederate flag tattooed on his left forearm, in case you didn't see the one on his right, Balance, his only explanation.

Daron led his friends around the yard, introducing them to everybody more for his own benefit than for theirs, wondering what he would do and whom he would talk to when the niceties were over. Since college started, these get-togethers felt more stressful. His young cousin's dancing was evidence of the media's deleterious influence on her definition of beauty and her self-image. (He had written a paper proudly entitled *The Story of Oh: Hypersexualization and Young Girls,* and e-mailed it to one cousin, who e-mailed it to another cousin, who e-mailed it to another, who posted it on Facebook with a request for help interpreting the, Journalism of my little cousin who I always knew was going to be a genius. Another cousin had it bound and shelved.) She would never look like Beyoncé; even most *black* women didn't look like Beyoncé. Though when young he had admired their sarcasm and sharp wit, his older female cousins—the misanthrope, the pyromaniac, and the exhibitionist—all obviously hated their lives, lives that would never recover the hope of their youth, lives now defined by their status as old maids, though barely thirty. They were stuck here, and the finality of that sentence pained him. It was impossible to have a conversation with one of them and not feel like he was addressing a ghost. He should have warned his friends it would be BYOC—Bring Your Own Conversation.

Yet, every few encounters one of the Indians fell happy captive. Charlie was the first to go. Uncle Roy asked if he had folks 'round the way in the Gully. When Charlie shook his head, No, Roy offered to tell him about it. A few minutes later, the crazy cousins, avoiding Daron's eyes, sheepishly asked Candice about medical marijuana, and the four of them huddled like old friends under the umbrella his mother had borrowed from Lou's for the occasion.

And Quint waited at the end of the circuit the entire time, grinning, stroking his thin chin, sharp elbow propped, pinned to a stumpy forearm thick as a pig's knee; he'd recently spent another thirty days on chopping down a tree to steal a bike. (He blew time like he had it to spare, like it grew on clocks instead of died there.) His favorite top, when he wore one, was any T-shirt with writing because, It's like you can say something without saying anything. Today's slogan: I MAKE IT LOOK EASY.

Quint hugged Daron so tightly pain passed immediately into nostalgia. Six years older, Quint was forever bigger and stronger, and always squeezing or thumping or noodling Daron, as he did now, slipping Daron into an arm-bar and a full nelson and then a headlock to give him a noogie. Their entangled limbs did not resemble those of wrestlers at work so much as modern dancers in choreographed chaos. Daron had long since stopped resisting and accepted that Quint had to thump his chest at least once in front of all new folks. There were two types of people, as Daron learned in Anthro 101:

tree climbers and tree pissers. His older, stronger, and quicker cousin Quint, unfortunately, was of the latter variety. (And no Twitter rants would suffice; Q was analog as a motherfucker.) On the other hand, at least he was a cousin. Threat of Quint was enough to limit the high school bullying to name-calling (Donut Black Hole beat big black eye). No one wanted Quint on their back, the very position in which Daron now found himself.

Louis raised his hands in surrender. I'd help, but I'd only end up in the same position as you.

Don't worry 'bout him none. Quint tightened his grip. Ya'tta know by now. Oysters up under pressure, but he'll come back later and deliver a pearl. Quint plucked him on the head one last time before releasing him, Won't ya?

Daron stretched his neck, rotated his head in one direction, then the other. Quint, this is Louis, my roommate. Louis, Quint, first cousin.

Loose Chang. Louis extended his hand. Friends call me Loose.

He never told me you was so cute. Y'all live together?

Not by choice, not by choice. After a moment of silence, Louis added, For one thing he's messy.

Just fuckin' with ya. You eat? He pointed to the folding table against the house where the awning would protect the food from the sun. That there is the best potato salad, cold cut dip, and cobbler you're going to find.

Cold cut dip, repeated Louis haltingly.

Quint wrapped a massive arm around Louis's neck and steered him away, winking over his shoulder at Daron, who wondered if he was supposed to know what that meant.

Smoke wafted over to him and his mouth watered, even though he hadn't eaten meat for five years. Berkeley and its gas grills, expensive gas grills, expensive shiny stainless steel gas grills, with casters and more attachments than Inspector Gadget and price tags that made him gag, yielded a result no better than poking a coat hanger through a hot dog and holding it over the range, as he did when a kid. Fire isn't flavor, but the Big Green Egg, that ingenious ceramic capsule of goodness, that Reese's Peanut Butter Cup of cookout equipment, both grill and smoker—God bless!—was guaranteed to give even the veggie burgers and tofu dogs a cheek-smacking hickory finish, except there weren't any veggie burgers in the coolers, nor were any in the backyard refrigerator.

He found his mother in the kitchen, which betrayed no evidence she was hosting a party for more than thirty two-fisted, high-livered Davenports, McCormicks, and their miscellaneous miscellanies. It was a spotless white room, surgically so, the only color coming from the piglets. Pink piglets on dish towels, placemats, plaques: all from Daron and his father, her little piglets. She was leaning over the sink, scraping a nonstick baking sheet with a red rubber spatula. When he asked her about the vegetarian items, she stood, groaned and slapped the sink. I knew I forgot something.

It was typical that she was so busy cleaning she'd forgotten the most important items. She couldn't forget meat because there was always a year's supply in the freezer. Shit, Mom, that was the most important thing, Daron's voice went high.

Is something the matter?

Everything's the matter. You know they have dietary restrictions. Candice and Charlie don't eat red meat. If you weren't being all extra nice and going out of your way like, you know, to be like, all, you know . . .

Saccharine?

Yeah, saccharine.

I was going to wait until later, but since you're bringing this up now. I assume you mean artificial. I am not artificial, and I'm right appalled and embarrassed that you would say that about me, and suggest it in front of your friends.

I'm embarrassed that you flirted with Charlie.

She slapped him on the cheek with the spatula. You know better. Don't get highfalutin in front of folk. You told me you were bringing home friends, and gave me specific instructions that made me think . . . Never mind. One day when I'm not here, you'll appreciate me.

Daron walked out, stomping down the hallway to the foyer, where he stopped short of slamming the front door because his father was across the yard, leaving the garage and walking toward the backyard. Daron waited in the doorway until he disappeared, not wanting his father to tear into him about the temporary tattoo on his cheek, as he would call it, before lecturing him on respecting his mother.

Ruts ran from the small squares of dead lawn on either side of the driveway entrance to the detached garage. His father had remembered to put away The Charlies. They were passed down from his grandfather, Old Hitch, who counted them creepier than bankers, he said, with those watermelon-red lips, but who kept them because his father had given them to him. Daron's own father had the same complaint, and had promised to put them up when Old Hitch passed, but after the funeral, when the first thing Daron thought to do was move them, because from his bedroom window he could see them leering at night, wild-eyed, his father took to Daron's neck with a shuddering reminder that, This is my house. I make the rules about who goes where, when, why, and how.

Laughter erupted from the backyard while Daron was toeing one of the squares of dead grass where The Charlies had stood, and he looked up to see his mother kicking the other. He had not heard her come out.

Those were heavy. She flexed her arms.

That explained the ruts. Daron muttered his thanks.

Does our deal still stand, D'aron?

Yes'm.

Don't *Yes'm* me. Does our deal still stand?

Yeah, Mom, it does.

Okay. She pinched his cheek and it burned even more than the slap. He flinched. Trying to disfigure me?

They laughed. She kissed him.

You don't really think I forgot about your girlfriend, did you?

She's not exactly my girlfriend, and she does eat meat, just not beef.

Oh. Well. Anyway, what I was going to say was I forgot to take those veggie thingamabobs out of the freezer. And who knows, after she gets to see you in your home environment that might change. Hmmm?

Daron tore the blade of grass he was holding.

His mother chucked his chin. I love you, hon.

Me too.

She went, as she always did, Thank you, honey. You know that's my favorite band.

WHEN HE RETURNED TO THE BACKYARD, Quint and Louis were sitting on the red beer cooler, thumb wrestling, Candice and his stripper cousin—at least he thought it was her—were in the gazebo in deep conversation, and Charlie was talking to Daron's father. The Davenports were big men and women. Two generations in the mill. Before that, three generations of farming, his father liked to say, Yeoman. Yo-man! His uncles would kite their arms like they were steering a bullwhip and declare, We're the original Georgia Crackers. But next to Charlie, his father looked puny. He never thought of Charlie as large until he saw him next to other people, or recognized the look of closeted alarm some people wore as they tried to avoid being next to him. In The City, rarely did anyone sit beside him on the subway, even during rush hour. At night, women clutched purses, crossed streets; guys steered wide. Charlie would occasionally whistle Vivaldi to reassure bystanders because, No one expects to be mugged by a dude who knows classical music. More than once he claimed he enjoyed the extra space. Daron never believed that. Today, no one behaved like that. But then again, they knew if anyone was going to gladly handle their possessions, it would be Quint. His father waved him over.

D'aron, is there something you want to say?

Daron stuttered, giving Charlie a quizzical look.

Tell me again what D'aron told you about us, Charlie.

Charlie looked confused.

His father laughed. I'm just teasing you. I wouldn't want to know what you said, especially if you didn't say anything. I thought my mom was old-fashioned for scaring us off the radio, D'aron thinks we're old-fashioned, and your kids—he rested a hand on Charlie's shoulder—will think you're old-fashioned.

Just a cycle, sir.

That's right, sir.

They went back to talking about the playoffs, and Daron quickly excused himself. The smoke rising from the Green Egg swayed lazy in the wind, the bright coolers were lined up beside the house like Legos. Candice was now moving through the crowd, snapping pictures of everybody. Daron would have to ask her about that later. He didn't want his family to be featured in the final project, the object of academic scrutiny, their every cough subject to diagnosis by his professor and classmates. But he couldn't say, No, no he couldn't, not while she was hugging up next to his uncle and aunt, teetering, extending her arm before her to capture what she called her Paparazzi shot. Last year she'd cut her hair short a few days after they first met. He remembered because the week after the dot party, she waved him over to her bench on Lower Sproul Plaza and he felt a momentary thrill at being hailed by an unknown female. With the cropped hair, she looked tomboyish, which he liked. In profile tonight, with her dreadlocks pulled back, he saw that again, the slight nose, the promi-

nent forehead, and the smile, always a smile like she knew you. Over
the sound of the breakers at César Chávez Park, she'd once admitted
that her family wasn't close; that her father expressed a greater affinity for moths and fruit liqueurs and her mother a keen interest in civil
rights. She dubbed them emotionally abusive. Taking it to mean that
she wasn't as spoiled as she would have preferred, Daron had laughed
so hard he hadn't even seen her walk off, vanish into the grassy hill,
footsteps light as a squirrel. But as she shared more about her parents, he wasn't so sure, and now prided himself on the fact that in
his family, no one had ever been interested in anything other than
someone else's business. Candice remained between Roy and Chester
for several minutes, showing them photos, or who knew what else, on
her phone. With Aunt Chester gasping in amazement and Uncle Roy
squinting with disbelief and Candice grinning proudly, they looked
like a family. Daron took a picture. He had anticipated protecting his
friends, running interference, but everything was going smoothly.
Even Quint and Louis were still getting along. They stood at the
table, deep in conversation, eating directly off the serving dishes,
Louis gnawing a rib and Quint a piece of chicken, both ignoring
Daron when he walked up.

Louis's fingers and face oozed, gooey as those of a zombie at a
fresh coffin trough. He sucked the knuckle of one hand so hard it
looked like he might take the skin off. This is the shit! Someone put
their foot in the sauce.

Oh. Is that a—Chinese—saying, too? asked Quint.

Simple math. Everything Chinese saying, if you add accent and
subtract words. You put foot in sauce!

Quint guffawed, spraying flecks of chicken across the table. Daron
made a mental note of the dishes seasoned thusly.

You oughta be a comedian. Chinese people are funny and all, but
you got some jokes.

Louis beamed like he'd found a buttered Olsen twin in his bed.

Quint kept talking, all the while pouring a shot from a bottle of Jack, which he handed to Louis while taking an impressive draw himself, enough to bob his apple a few times. Louis continued bobbleheading. About ten minutes later Quint called for everyone's attention.

Hey, hey! he yelled, tapping a fork against a beer bottle. Before they all could hush up, Quint escalated to bottle-on-bottle action, head-butting two fallen soldiers, which he did until one broke, at which point everyone fell silent and looked at Janice, who stood in the kitchen doorway, one hand holding open the screen door, the red spatula at her side.

What the heck are you doing, Quintillion Lee Jackson?

I'm gettin' y'allses attention. The stony grit in his voice ground down a measure, he continued, I see you're armed, so I sure ain't aiming to get on your short side, Aunty J. They all laughed. No, ma'am, not when you standing there looking knotted like Sheriff when he come 'round to see me the odd Friday. Used to be he came only after something went wrong. Now he rolls by every couple weeks, asks me if I got anything to confess. I always say, No. Quint winked. But y'all knows I always do. More laughter. I'm just the opener. Just the opener, not the beer, so sit back. We're fixing to have a show. It's the first performance in the South of the famous California comic Lenny Bruce Lee! Clap, y'all! Let's hear it. Make him welcome, dammit.

Quint set a white plastic chair in front of the food table. Louis sat down and Quint grabbed his arm. After a moment of drunken pantomime, Louis understood and stood on the chair, at which point Daron's family applauded as if a trick had been performed.

Louis cleared his throat and appeared to be reciting something to himself. Okay, let's get started.

Hello, Braggsville! You don't know me. I'm Chinese, but I had a typical American upbringing. I was also beaten by the Vietnamese. At that, a few people shared sympathetic chuckles. Only Charlie and

Candice laughed heartily. Daron was disappointed. Louis was Malaysian, and claimed to be Chinese only when it was the easiest explanation. As he put it, It's like saying you live in Unit 2 at Berkeley. No one knows that, so you go, San Fran, and people go, Oh.

I have the same relationship problems. Sometimes my girlfriend is like, Why don't we go dancing? I'm thinking this is like if I opened the fridge and the steaks were like, Why don't we go hunting? They liked that one. Louis stood a little straighter. The chair wobbled. Did he glance at Candice when he mentioned girlfriend? Daron hoped not.

See, this points to the differences between the sexes. I asked her, Seriously, do you think men really like to dance? If we could pay admission, give a chick the same amount of cash it would take to buy ten drinks, and take her home, we would. But that would be a brothel, or a sorority house.

When the crowd responded less than enthusiastically, Louis explained, See, we have this thing in some colleges known as sorostitution. It means rich girls . . . never mind. So then, my girl is like, But dancing is how you tell who's good in bed. Maybe so, I told her, but that's another difference between the sexes. You think we care about that.

She was like, All men care about is sex.

I was like, Yeah, that's true, but not whether you're good at it.

They liked that one. Uncle Roy pointed to Aunt Chester, who smacked his hand away.

Okay. My friend Charlie is here. Let's hear it for Charlie. Chinese people and black people have a lot in common. Charlie clapped politely.

The Wu-Tang Clan. Quint spit out his drink laughing.

Tiger Woods? The black part was cheating, and the Chinese part was driving when he hit the tree. Charlie shook his head regretfully.

We each give our children funny names. There was silence, until he added, That white people can't pronounce. It's a conspiracy.

White people can't cook our food, but they love to eat it. Though someone here makes good-ass ribs. He hiccuped. Excuse me. Good ribs. That was my black joke. I gotta represent. He gave Charlie a thumbs-up.

Oh yeah. Chinese people got some things in common with Southerners, too. You ready for this, Braggsville? I was at this store—he pointed over his shoulder, Lou's Bait and Cash and Copy.

A few people in the crowd pointed in the other direction.

It's in the other direction!

It's called Lou Davis's Cash-n-Carry Bait Shop and Copy Center!

Yeah! the stripper yelled.

The crowd all gestured toward town until Louis, too, was pointing in the right direction.

Yeah, so Chinese people are big into directions, too. He paused, collecting himself. But, I was at this store, Lou Davis's, and it was like a Chinese store, you had everything: meat, bumper stickers, everything. In Chinatown, it's like that. You can buy fruit and bread and get your teeth pulled in the back. Anyway, at Lou Davis's I saw some strange stuff, like headcheese and all, and thought, hmmm, *headcheese*. Maybe these people are weird. Then I had an image of my grandma eating, guess what, chicken feet!

I thought, Okay, Southerners are like Chinese. We have pig's feet and ears, and even the ovaries. A collective groan issued forth. Louis raised his hands. I don't write the news. I just deliver the paper. Whole point is if we even got the ovaries, you know we don't waste nothing. We eat everything but the oink or, sometimes in our case, the bark.

A hush fell over the crowd. That's a joke, you all, Louis added, and the crowd went into an uproar, clapping and stomping their feet.

Louis paused, savoring the moment. He was much better than Daron expected.

Louis began speaking, but in the corner, Uncle Roy whispered in Aunt Chester's ear, a mite too loudly, *I think he mean they eat dogs. See!* and the crowd went wild again.

Daron's father was red in the face, as was his mother, who clapped both hands over her mouth as she often did when laughing against her will. His cousins held their sides as if in pain, and tears streamed down Quint's face. After the crowd finally settled down, Louis continued.

And vegetarians? Who would willingly give up meat? I saw a menu in Cali with vegetarian beef stew. That's going too far. If it's vegetarian, why does it need a meat name? It just can't be good. It's got to be like sexing a blow-up doll. It'll do the trick for a minute, but you won't feel good about it afterwards, and you keep it to yourself, and you hide it when company comes over. He bowed to thunderous applause.

For the rest of the night, Louis was the star. Daron had wanted to invite Jo-Jo but knew he wouldn't fit in. The last time he'd seen Jo-Jo was over winter break. They'd spent the afternoon on the hill above Old Man Donner's land drinking Old Grand-Dad, sitting Indian-style on a ledge of rock that gun-sighted dead right over downtown, a meager allotment of buildings cupped in a gentle swale, Main Street stitching through like a scar. Once more, Jo-Jo had called him early, asked him to take a ride. Once more, they had ridden in silence.

The Rhiners, the Foldercaps, the Gull prom, some new shirt-sleeves at the Hot Air factory, that Mr. Buchanan, the debate coach and eleventh- and twelfth-grade English teacher, had finally been fired, were topics of discussion, but all Jo-Jo had admitted that day was, Thinks she won't find out. But he cain't figure shit. Up at Dougy's every night, tits riding the well with the rest of 'em, telling lies. He cain't figure shit.

Sure can't, Daron had said, after a moment during which, even after three semesters at Berkeley—including an Intro to Social Linguistics class where the professor spent hours lecturing them on prestige and speech communities and attuning them to class inflection in language—he could think of nothing else to say. He had wondered, for the amount of time it takes to crush a can, if school itself was making it hard for him to talk. The prof always said, Learning Spanish doesn't mean forgetting English, but learning English often means forgetting Spanish. Think about that! Daron had laughed it off at the time. He and Louis spent hours in parodic paralysis: Eating pussy doesn't mean cannibalism, but cannibalism means eating pussy. Tink about that, holmes. An oral exam isn't a blowjob, but a blowjob is an oral exam. Tink about that, amigo. Daron had tinked about it a lot since, and knew what the professor meant by *language is power* because the more he learned at school, the more he understood, the less he understood. Maybe language was power, but not his to harness.

And not Jo-Jo's either, not with all his comma-averse posts about the second coming, the first of which Daron had clicked on expecting anything but an animated video on the return of OUR LORD, and after which Daron had read every Facebook FAQ and forum to learn how to adjust his privacy settings to ensure that his two worlds remained just that.

Watching Louis's routine made him wish it were otherwise. Jo-Jo would have found it funny, and they all would have gotten along. He had emailed Jo-Jo that he would be in town soon and would call once he arrived. But Daron hadn't, he knew that Jo-Jo still thought Candice was his girl, and he couldn't face him seeing that she wasn't. Maybe if Jo-Jo saw them all together, if he met Louis and Charlie, he would understand. Daron doubted it. Not to mention Jo-Jo's mullet. Even Iran knew to outlaw that hairstyle.

By the end of the night, Daron relaxed. Over the course of the evening several people asked Charlie if he was from the Gully or had folks there, but each time he said, No, they answered brightly, Well, welcome to Braggsville! And better yet, when Quint put on David Allen Coe's *You Never Even Call Me by My Name,* Charlie and Louis knew the lyrics word for word, trilling operatic the verses about mama, trains, trucks, prisons, and getting drunk.

It was nearly midnight when Daron sat down next to his friends again. They looked pleasantly tired. He was about to ask them if they were enjoying themselves when his father opened the back door and whistled for him. His parents were alone in the kitchen. His father studied his face, his mother was straightening the canisters, her back to them, but her posture belied where her attention lay.

Call it off, son.

How do you mean?

D'aron, I don't want to keep you from your friends or have a big discussion about this. Whatever you was planning, call it off.

On the way from the airport, his mother had inquired about their plans for the week. As previously agreed, Daron said they would visit Atlanta a few times, and Savannah, and some Indian burial ground. They needed only to keep their secret until the next morning, at which point phase two would begin. The lynching wouldn't get far because someone would stop it, someone would give a fit as soon as rope one got tossed over a branch. Louis and Candice insisted on secrecy because if the townspeople were warned, the spectacle wouldn't have the same effect. There would be no control group, and the post-maim interviews, as Louis called them, would be pointless. Charlie, lastly, insisted this was a situation where it was best to act first and ask permission later. Seemed he was right.

For the first time, Daron felt motivated to do it, to act. He was not one to directly disobey his father. But they had planned this for weeks, and had Professor Pearlstein's permission to do ethnography, like Zora Neale Hurston or Franz Boas. Daron blurted out, It's field-work. A school project, for Christ's sake.

I knew it. His father set his jaw like he'd been swindled.

His mom shuddered, apparently at the notion of fieldwork, not the invocation of Christ, because all she had to say was, Why can't you just read books and write papers, like we used to do in school?

Daron knew that Mr. Davenport would make the final decision, and judging by his silence, it had been made. This was not how Daron would have planned to ask, had he developed a mind to do so. He would have taken his father aside to talk man-to-man, like the adult he was, to explain that times had changed and that direct action was big again, that the South had to catch up with California, and the rest of the world, and stop wading in the sandpit licking its wounds like an old, toothless dog. Yes, reason and rhetoric would have been his strategy.

You best do as I say, hear me, son, or it's me 'n' you.

Chapter Eleven

Centered on Daron's dresser was an oversize Styrofoam light-bulb graced with an Afro wig. Magnifying glass in hand, Louis alternated between examining the wig and Charlie's scalp. With her hands clasped behind her back, maintaining a respectful distance as though guided by tape on the floor, Candice studied the walls as if some brilliant curator had assembled these posters of Jay Z, MGMT, James Franco in *Pineapple Express*—which his parents still thought was a fruit drink—Miley Cyrus, *BSG,* Jessica Alba, Outkast, and Tool, the latter of which made him terribly sentimental because when he was young, it was his father's mulling music, under the stars, in the backyard, the only sounds *Aenima* and the bug zapper, the first a eulogy, the second what his father called life's biggest lesson.

Quint bounced on the edge of the bed rambling about how they all were coming to his place the next night for another cookout. Chez Quint—Quint's Pub? Louis agreed, but Daron didn't like the idea. Quint's friends liked to wrassle and slapbox and shit like that when they got drunk, though some didn't wait that long. He imagined them fucking up Louis and yelling, Don't you know karate or Hong-Kong-Fooey?

Every few minutes, Quint's girlfriend, Maylene, called him, triggering his *Knight Rider* ringtone, at which point Louis and Charlie would pop-lock, their performance prompting Quint to ignore the call.

Candice stopped before the poster of Michael Jackson in a scene from *Smooth Criminal,* leaning forward at an impossibly acute angle, covering that halfway was a Harry Potter poster. She traced the outline of Harry's face. Somehow these two belong together, don't they?

Believe in magic. Don't want to grow up. High voices. Not bad, girl, not bad. Quint sucked his teeth as though chuffed, like he did whenever they drove past an ATV/four-wheeler dealer.

Candice blushed like she'd been goosed.

With an orchestral flourish, Daron turned to study the posters. They both represent forbidden desires. Each of them seems uncertain of how to manage the power they have acquired, and confused about whether it resides within them, or requires external agents to activate. MJ felt it was outside of him, but his life was a hero's journey . . . He faded out, not because they were all staring at him, which he expected to see when he dramatically turned to face them, but because they were all ignoring him. Candice had moved on to Jessica Alba. Louis was holding the magnifying glass to his nose, Look, Charlie, could I be black now? Quint was laying a mighty eye on Candice.

Knight Rider played. Sine and cosine, bitches! Louis did the wave and transferred the power to Charlie, who leaned back in a slow-motion *Matrix*-style pop-locking maneuver.

Quint raised his hands like an emcee, Go Loose! Go Loose! Go Chuck! Go Chuck!

Earlier in the evening, Quint had insisted that Candice liked Daron. Break out Oscar, Quint had instructed. Daron thought his cousin was putting him on, setting him up for embarrassment, but sometimes Quint just knew things about women: if they were single, if not, if they were open to exploration, when they were packing the shark's tooth, if they were a pulsing vessel or a dry vein. As he put it, Trust me. I know these things, almost like I can remember when we had gills, when we rode scales out of the sea. Swore he could smell it, too, and that made Daron nervous, especially when Candice was all blush and blustering and even she was dancing now, watching Quint out of the corner of her eye. She couldn't like Quint. How could someone as smart and beautiful as Candice even like Daron? And what about Charlie, with his sullen gravity and size fifteens? Everyone knew about those rumors (One Louis punch line: If I was named Tyrell and had a ten-inch dick, I wouldn't go to school, either). And Louis liked her. A year ago, he would never have imagined Candice with someone like Louis, but anything could happen in California.

Quint's girlfriend hung up. Louis sat down. Charlie opened the window, fingered the sweat behind his ears, Shit, that's worse.

Let's go for a walk in the woods, suggested Candice.

Quint jumped to his feet. All right.

Daron glared at Quint. Not at night.

What do you mean, not at night?

C'mon, Quint.

Who shot you?

You don't have to be Methuselah to know.

Damn, your juniors is bounced tight. Methuselah and 'em, now? Didn't you learn nothin' in college? Besides, the Holler don't start for almost a quarter mile back there.

Technically, Quint was right. You had to climb the hill to go down into the Holler, but they were the same in Daron's mind, and always had been. All's I'm saying is everybody knows 'bout the Holler at night. She's thinking about a cornfield in Iowa, and it ain't like that here. It's too easy to get lost. Even Nana got lost back there once.

Quint stared at him so hard that Daron tensed for the blow. The others must have felt the air cool because Candice was, On second thought, I'm too tired. They sat there in silence for a few more minutes. Louis plunked into the desk chair. When Quint's phone next rang, Charlie and Louis stood silent.

Oughten you answer that? Daron pointed to the phone. I mean, she might be worried, is all. She might be worried.

Worry's good for 'em. Ain't it, fellas? Louis and Charlie nodded. Candice, you don't respect no man who don't worry you none, ain't that right, girl?

Candice bit her lips, a thoughtful look on her face. Sometimes women are like wild horses. You have to earn the right to saddle them. She finished with her nose in the air and excused herself to prepare for bed.

Couldn't have said it better. The *A-Team* theme song sounded from Quint's waist. He jumped to his feet. Shit! Mad cow on the move. I'll be heading out, too. Catch y'all tomorrow night. My place, right? An evening of guns with occasional music. Chez Quint.

Daron bet he spelled it with an *s,* judging by his pronunciation.

Hell yeah. You got some Vince Gill? Louis juked his neck like he could already hear Gill, Paisley, and Co. performing *Cluster Pluck*.

No. Ain't playing no new shit. Merle Haggard. Bocephus. Ted Nugent.

Just checking. Gotta make sure you're keeping it real . . . country.

You a funny motherfucker, he told Louis. Loose Chang. I like that. That shit makes you sound Bangkok. Like you could smite a mother.

Louis leaned back in his chair and stroked the thin beard he'd been struggling to grow for the last two years. Smite. That's Old Testament. With a glint in his eye, he added, Like I know kung fu and shit?

No. Like you just motherfuckin' crazy, like a Coke that's all shook up and waiting for a sucker to pop the top.

Quint tousled Daron's hair. Get some rest. Tomorrow's a big day.

After he left, Daron listened closely for Candice's voice, fighting the urge to go see if Quint was in the hall close-talking her.

Your cuz is the shit.

Charlie nodded his agreement.

That hung in the air for a few minutes. Charlie and Louis sat on the end of the bed, Daron settled into his beanbag, still on Cali time.

Louis was fidgety, Did they like me?

Oh yeah, they were laughing. Daron nodded.

You were awesome, fucking rocking, dude!

I hope I didn't offend anyone.

Maybe my mom when you stood on the furniture, but don't you always say it's the comic's job to offend? The full five-finger slap, right?

It's your family.

Isn't that the first shell to crack? Like Zeus killing the Titans?

It's your fam, and they're good peeps. Comics want to offend assholes.

I don't think anyone was offended. One of my cousins wants you to hang at his bachelor party in a couple of days.

Ice, ice, baby! If you can play off a black or Southern audience, you're killing it like a real comic. Now I need to perform for a black audience. A real one, like Oakland or Atlanta, not like a school student group.

Charlie, who had been fiddling with his phone, tapped the screen. Here's your chance. This weekend in Atlanta there's an open mic. Two-minute first round. Kill that, you get a five-minute second round. Kill that, the final is three people at ten minutes each next weekend. Want in? All you need is a two-minute audition video. He pointed to his phone.

How far away is Atlanta?

Does it matter? It can't be far. It's in the same state.

Three hours.

Sign me up.

Louis stood in the chair, Ladies and gentlemen, hailing from the West Coast, also known as the Left Coast, which is the Best Coast.

From the heart of the Bay straight to you in *A* . . . TL. It's Loose Chang, also known as Lenny Bruce Lee. If you don't laugh, you better duck. With a grand sweep of the arm, he gestured at Charlie, You got that?

Charlie waved his phone. I recorded you earlier. I'll edit it down and shoot it to them later.

What was that wild horses shit? asked Louis, putting on the Afro wig.

If you must ask—Charlie smirked—there's no use explaining. What was that Methuselah shit?

It means everybody knows something, like it's common knowledge. Look, serious question again. Who told my parents?

We told you already.

Daron had asked them earlier and they'd both denied it. Who told them what we're planning? he asked again.

Louis and Charlie shook their heads.

My father was all like, Call it off, son. Call it off. Someone had to tell him.

What does it matter anyway?

We had an agreement. It was supposed to go better if no one knew what we were planning, then it would be more of a surprise and we would catch their real reactions. If everyone knows, then they'll ignore it as a joke, and you all will say they're fucked up. That's not fair.

I think they might be a little fucked up any way you grate it, D.

The whole town is a Confederate museum, replied Louis, holding his hands up palm out. I'm not saying your whole town is housist or anything!

Housist! *Housist* was Louis-speak for racist, invoked after Daron tried explaining that just because someone preferred a mansion didn't mean they'd torch a ranch. Housist, Loose?

Charlie nodded his agreement. You ask Candice yet? Maybe she said something.

Housist, Loose?

This is damn near the only house without a Confederate battle flag and those creepy statues in the front yards. He elbowed Daron, and added, You know what I mean, the ones that look like Charlie.

DARON FOUND CANDICE IN THE LIVING ROOM on the couch next to Quint, almost head-to-head, leafing through a photo album balanced on Candice's knees so that Quint had to reach across her lap to turn a page, which he did at that moment, grazing Candice's shoulder as he did so, her face turning to his when he pulled back. Daron gently removed the album from Candice's hands.

Come on, man, I thought *The A-Team* was your emergency signal. He helped his cousin to his feet.

Can he drive? whispered Candice as Quint stumbled toward the door. Daron waved the question off.

I showed her the baby pictures, drunk-whispered Quint, so no matter what, your Oscar'll look giant. He held his hands far apart, as if describing a mythical fish. Fucking foot long!

When Daron didn't respond, Quint added, C'mon, D, shit. He eyed Candice. Lotion look out! I'm investing in tissues and lotion. There's also liquid soap, your mom's got a ton of that. You have to use more and it makes more of a mess, but it smells nicer. On the other foot, it'll make you scaly as a snake. Quint leaned on Daron for support. You got yourself a love square.

You mean quadrangle. I don't think so.

She likes you, my main man Loose likes her, and if it was 1990 the black dude would be twirling a phone cord around his index every time he talked to you. He counted on his fingers. Four makes a square.

Twirling a phone cord around his index? Once Daron understood, he laughed it off, even as he ran through a mental list of Charlie's female friends, and they were many, never mind that he never referred to them as girlfriends. Whatever Charlie had done that made Quint think he was gay, Daron didn't want to hear about it tonight. He guided a stumbling Quint outside before he could expound on his ridiculous love square theory. Quint's last words: Be real. As he peeled out of the driveway, Candice called out from the living room, asking again if Quint would be all right.

Daron swaggered back into the room before answering. That's how he always drives. What's he gonna do, kill a tree? You can't tell, but he's at his best. NASCAR? We own that shit. *Dukes of Hazzard*? That, too. Daron didn't ask Candice if she had mentioned anything to his parents. She was too smart to do that.

Oscar? Isn't that what Quint called . . . it? Too cute. She tucked her legs under her chin.

It? Shit. Daron sat next to her, and explained that his first sex ed lesson had starred a hot dog, a frozen chicken, two marbles, and a baseball. Just thinking about it sent flames crawling up his face. He wondered for a moment if that explained his reaction to Tweety, but dismissed the thought as too Freudian, and he and Louis avoided all things Freudian, going so far as to threaten lapses with, I'll slap your dick with this psychology textbook. All I remember is being terrified after that sex ed lesson because Chamber, our German shepherd, ate the expectant mother. I didn't eat chicken for weeks.

Candice laughed heartily. How he had missed that.

You gobbled up the Sanders' fried chicken without complaint. This she delivered without so much humor. The Sanders were the family that had fed them at Six Flags. From the sound of it, Candice had liked the Southerners no more than Charlie had.

Louis and Charlie must have powered up his PSP because Daron heard the *Grand Theft Auto IV* theme song, tinny and distant, as it always sounded on those little speakers. They were occupied. Good.

I'm sorry the Ishi thing didn't work out. He had wanted to say it for weeks. Candice had been glum ever since the performative intervention at Six Flags went haywire. He should have said nothing, apparently, because Candice stiffened then stood.

They regarded each other—warily, it felt to Daron.

It was my fault, Daron, not anyone else's. I should have planned better. As she said this, she turned away and inspected the pictures on the mantel: reunions, school photos, Quint in his perennial Halloween costume—a policeman, D'aron and his father standing over a buck.

You shot this?

No.

Really?

That's the last year I went hunting with him.

Bet he didn't like that.

Nope. Not at all, he answered, pride apparent even to him. Want another beer?

No thanks. She sat down again and he followed suit. It was their first time alone together in a while. There had been a cooling-down period after Six Flags—almost like they were embarrassed for each other, a three-week stretch when everyone was studying a lot. He thought he'd follow Quint's advice to be real. I've missed you.

I've missed hanging out, too. She said it as if she knew what he meant and wanted him to know that she meant something different.

Really, Candice. I miss you.

She stared ahead as if he hadn't said it. He stared ahead as well, afraid to move. After about ten minutes, she fell asleep. Daron was wide awake, watching out of the corner of his eye as her chin dropped lower and lower, as she snored and sniffled, as she slumped until her head rested against his shoulder, as her arms uncrossed and one hand tumbled to his lap, and as she jerked awake thirty minutes later when a door slammed somewhere in the house, followed by clumsy footsteps and the chunky clatter of drunken discretion. They stared expectantly at the maw of the dark hall, listening to breathy giggles, hands raking the wall, hale hearty lusty hushing, until at last his Uncle Roy and Aunt Chester emerged, flat-backed and hugging the perimeter of the room like two cartoon spies, the latter's blouse a tell-all, each button crashing at its downstairs neighbor's place.

Uncle Roy feigned a toast as he and Aunt Chester backed out the front door, bidding their adieu to, The couple of the witching hour.

Excuse me. Candice withdrew her hand from Daron's lap to wave good night. When they were gone: Why do they think we're dating?

I have no idea.

She stared at him, leaning closer as if an inspection might reveal the truth. Are you sure?

He leaned forward to hide his erection. I'm sure. Ask them.

What are you pissed about?

Nothing. I'm not pissed.

She rubbed his arm. Nervous about tomorrow?

No. It'll be fine. Probably funny. When he thought about it, though, he was nervous about tomorrow. What if Jo-Jo was there, and asked after Candice in front of everyone else?

It's all right to be nervous.

Daron leaned farther forward. He wanted to tell her now that his father forbade him to go, wanted to stand to do it, but couldn't stand and face her. Maybe if he told her again how much he'd missed her, maybe if she believed it, that would make it easier. He couldn't see a way to say that again, either. When he said nothing for a few minutes, she asked, Would you mind if I stretched out and slept a little? She held up the blanket, like he needed that to aid comprehension.

Sure. Why don't you turn on the lamp and I'll turn off the big light. As soon as she reached for the lamp he stood and left the room, keeping his back to her the entire way.

On the way to his bedroom, he stopped in the bathroom to relieve himself. Earlier that evening he had walked in on Candice in there and froze with embarrassment, I just needed a towel. She waved him in, grunting her reassurance that it was okay. Leafing through the towels, he glanced at her as she perfunctorily wiped the toothpaste from her chin, spitting at the same time, and saw the woman in her eyes. She was fully dressed, but the proximity felt intimate nonetheless. He imagined couples doing the same, sharing small spaces while attending to separate tasks. After a time, they hardly noticed each other. But he would never grow weary of watching Candice. Each day would mean a new observation or revelation, such as how she attended to her teeth like she was angry at them, those big white teeth, bright and shiny, brushed so vigorously he imagined them smooth as marble, but warm instead of cold, inviting, even in their sharpness, one to lick them. Inviting—no—daring even, like a blade. Of course Louis liked her. Quint as well. Everyone did. Aunt Chester had called her, As soft-nosed and sweet as she can be. Daron was sure Charlie liked her, too, though he never admitted it. But Charlie had more women trying to park in his lot than Walmart on Black Friday. He couldn't cross campus without girls waving to him, and not the shy, polishing-a-bowling-ball motion they reserved for coincidental classmates, but full-bodied hails, sometimes with two arms even.

IN THE MIDDLE OF THE NIGHT, Daron woke thirsty, stepping over Charlie and Louis, bypassing his midnight oasis in the bathroom, and stopping in the living room, where his mother had left a night light on for Candice, who snored softly on the couch, curled up like a cat, her lips parted, eyes still, chest rising and falling, his breathing, for a moment, matching hers. He had seen her passed out, often facedown, once slumped in a closet corner like a discarded snowsuit, but never sleeping so peacefully. It was hard to believe they were all in his house. He was an ambassador, the cat who dropped a thrasher or mole skink on the kitchen tile as if to say, You have no more to fear from them. It is safe. It was as if he had brokered a great peace. He watched her for a moment, listened to the humming refrigerator, the ticking clock, the creaking noises the house made only at night, the shifting of the attic beams, the settling of the floor, the sway in the walls, all slowly adjusting itself to the earth.

LATER, DARON AWOKE TO CHARLIE'S FACE only inches from his own, his friend's breath heavy on his chin. Charlie was hyperventilating, his eyes hovering in the dark like some kind of magic trick. Daron led him outside in silence, knowing, hoping, that he would back out, too. Daron hadn't yet told his friends that his father expressly forbade him to go.

In the backyard with the door safely shut, Charlie asked, Are you sure about this? I don't remember ever being this frightened before. I can't do it. I can't. I can't pretend . . . not this. I can't pretend this. His forehead gleamed and his hands shook worse than his voice.

Was Quint right about Charlie? No. Daron recalled the sensation that had swept over him at Six Flags, the feeling that everyone was watching him, waiting for him to fuck up so they could swoop in. He'd felt under so much pressure that he'd wanted to scream, Stop staring at me. He should never have asked Charlie. Charlie shouldn't dress as a slave and pretend to be lynched any more than Daron should dress as a Grand Dragon and pretend to burn a cross. Charlie had nothing to fear from Braggsville, but they shouldn't have asked him anyway.

Charlie and Daron were still sitting in the backyard at five thirty, the appointed hour, when they heard Candice being quiet in the kitchen, which was clean as a chemistry lab. The canisters, spices, and condiments all put away. Everything out was labeled. There was no way they could return it to that condition before they left, so he suggested Waffle House, Right up the road a spell.

They packed into the Bronco.

WAFFLE HOUSE, A SOUTHERN ICON, the black lettering on a yellow background a beacon of gastronomical joy to the road-weary traveler, the Chapel of Carbohydrates where the high priest dispensed waffles to salve the soul, to satisfy every spiritual desire, even with chocolate chips. Then there were the hash browns, which could be ordered as a double portion, scattered, covered, smothered, and spiced. In Yankee-ese that meant with onion, cheese, chili, and jalapeños. Not quite home cooking, but a welcome treat because each location was locally owned and operated, and so felt like part of the family. The Braggsville kids traveled distances to circle BK or McD's on Friday nights, but when munchies took over the wheel, it was here they came. In this Awful Waffle, as it was affectionately known, Daron had broken up, made up, and broken up again with Rheanne. In high school, Daron often stopped here for midnight meals on his way home from parties as far as fifty miles away. It was fifteen miles from home, twice the width of San Fran, a short jaunt to Daron.

That country mile shit is true, complained Louis as they sat in a *Goodfellas* seat, as he called corner booths. Up the road my peach ass.

Peach ass?

Like that? I'm adding it to my routine. If you're Asian but act black, you're a peach. It's like the opposite of a Twinkie. The peach pit is reddish brown, though. So if you look Asian generally, but you're Indian specifically, does that make you double Asian? Or maybe if you look Asian, but you're Indian like, How, on the inside? That's Asian-Indian, which we already have. All right, all right. Wait, wait, wait. He waggled his finger. Malcolm X was reddish-ish. So, peach means you're Asian, but you're angry inside. Switching to his best black voice, Louis asked, Can you spell peach ass? Up the road my peach ass.

Everything is bigger in the country, Daron explained.

Hmmph. Charlie eyed the waitress and cook, leaning back as if at the base of a monument.

It sure is, Louis agreed. Even the parking spaces.

Please, hushed Candice.

They're fat. And I can say that. We're in the South. We're free to talk. Daron waved his fork like a magic wand. The muzzle was lifted. What had his mom told his uncle? Forget about unbuckling your pants, eat another bite and you won't fit your coffin.

Charlie studied the menu, mouthing out the options as if he had only recently learned to read.

After taking their order, the waitress stood at the end of the prep line and called out to the cook in a code only part of which they understood.

That's it? asked Candice.

Daron nodded. That's it. He remembers it all just like that.

They watched as the cook laid out plates and bowls in a mnemonic arrangement. Charlie continued to read the menu until Candice snatched it from his hands. Well?

It's one thing to talk about it. It's another to do it, answered Charlie.

We agreed, Louis reminded him.

Yeah. Candice's voice was both low and sharp. Remember. Make a difference. We'll have better luck in the real world, where people actually listen, not an amusement park.

It's different for me. Charlie held up his hands.

You think you're the only one? asked Candice. Okay, back to me on the tree and Louis issuing orders and you two asking questions.

Charlie cut his eyes at Daron and Candice banged the table, scowling as she realized that both Charlie and Daron were backing out.

Louis placed his hand over Candice's clenched fist, so tiny. I got this. Think about this a minute. Come on, Candy—

—*Candy!* thought Daron. When did that start?—

—Think about it a second. We're asking a lot of him. Besides, if anyone sees Daron, they might think it's a joke anyway. So this is better. I'm surprised Charlie ever agreed to this. For all we know, we could show up and they could shoot him for sport, just for the hell of it. They could have a past life flashback and try to hog-tie him and sell him; they could think he's a runaway and try to collect a bounty. They might eat him. Or maybe they'll only ask him to pump their gas or bag their groceries—

—Wait now, Loose, protested Daron. You're out of hand and making it sound—

—Like something that you two don't want to do, and for good reason. Right?

I live here.

Candice asked, So that makes it okay? Look around. We're raising the diversity level by one thousand percent everywhere we show up. You don't even know how to get to that black neighborhood, the Gutter.

I do. It's just you don't walk there. It's like, like, like, you fly over the ocean because it's quicker than swimming. And, it's the Gully, the Gully, like—he thought a moment—Like a gully, which is not a gutter.

Louis adopted his Indian, the other Indian accent. Me on your side, Kemosabe, but that no pearl. Maybe you should 'splain self later.

I only mean that as the crow flies isn't the quickest way. But I know how to get there. We could go there right now.

Nice try. Candice wriggled her fingers as if beckoning him to try again. This was your idea.

No, it wasn't. I mentioned it in class, and—

Charlie cut him off. Cut it. He's not backing out. His father asked him not to do it. He has to respect his family's wishes.

—It wasn't my idea, Daron insisted.

Candice was no longer listening to him. She'd turned to face Charlie as if he were the last man in the world. Charlie, Charlie, please don't back out now. There was real pleading in her voice. Remember what you said? Remember. You wanted in. We wanted to put this BS to rest and you said we can't dig a grave without a spade. You said that. You. I was like, whoa, right on, that's my friend. We do need the right tools. Performance is a tool. Intervention is a tool.

Charlie hung his head at half-mast. The food came. Charlie, Daron, and Candice picked at theirs. Louis wolfed his down like a dog on death row.

Southerners. Candice snorted. Louis and I will go, and Daron and Charlie can do some interviews, okay? But you must do the interviews while we're there. Go to that weird store or wherever and ask people on the street what the war was about. You can't ask them after. If you do it afterwards, it's too late. Will your daddy let you go downtown? she asked, her tone saccharine.

My family came over as farmers. Then they worked the mill. They never owned slaves. If my uncle Roy said anything about crackers, he meant the sound of the whip cracking over cattle. No slaves.

Okay, Herr Vandenburg. And Ishi never lived at Six Flags Vallejo with Tweety Bird, but the Miwoks did, and they were massacred for gold.

That didn't work. He laughed at us. Vandenburg was the Six Flags park director in whose office they had spent, to Daron's mind, far too much time after their demonstration, or, as Candice called it, their performative intervention.

So you can go downtown? Can you go to the Gully? Why not ask them what they think?

D, can you at least drive Charlie downtown? asked Louis. We have to complete some interviews while the event is going on, before news of the performative intervention spreads.

That sounded fair enough to Daron. He wanted to contribute more, but Louis was right. If anyone saw him, they would think it was a joke, and their efforts would be wasted. He only wished he had thought of that sooner.

Charlie hadn't spoken for some time, and just sat there before his nearly full plate, his lips pulled into a sneer, tapping his incisor with his fingernail, which he often did during tests, and which Daron only now associated with nervousness.

I still can't believe this. We flew all the way out here. We had a plan, insisted Candice, making her hurt face.

But that morning it wasn't working on Daron, who was thinking, If you hadn't been fucking around interviewing and taking photos, you wouldn't have tipped off my parents.

Can we pay now?

Daron left a larger tip than usual, and covered his plate with his napkin to hide that he hadn't eaten the food.

THEY DROVE BACK IN SILENCE. Charlie suggested they only do interviews, but no one responded. Daron said they didn't have to prove anything to anyone, to which Candice replied, We sure don't. You're proving it to us.

I told you, just because we're from Georgia doesn't mean we had slaves. My family never had slaves.

Neither did mine.

Even if we did, Harvard had that Moor, and no one complains about him.

I wish my family had slaves. In fact, I want them to bring that shit back. Maybe I'll convince some people of that today.

When they reached the south side of Old Man Donner's field, Charlie remained in the Bronco staring at the floorboards. Louis got out, tossed his oversize duffel decorated with Fu Manchu mustache patches on his shoulders like a drunken friend, and started walking without a word up the hill. After a moment, Candice turned and followed him. Daron and Charlie would return to the Davenports' home and wait for full sun before driving downtown to do the interviews. It was early yet, and they had at least two hours before the detachment reached the nearest ridge, the point from which the troops would be able to see the tree planted by Bragg himself to commemorate his 1864 speech on freedom, the giant poplar under which Louis and Candice would stand dressed as slaves.

Chapter Twelve

¿**P**or qué?
    Why did YOU go along with it? Because she spoke Spanish to the guard at the Mt. Olivet cemetery who, once informed of her plans, mucho gustoed all the brochures she wanted plus one plaque that danced between your spooked fingers like a shekel that still smelled of the mint. Because her great-grandfather was from near here, and could have been Ishi. Because to be one-eighth anything is to be one-eighth everything.

Because she spent three weeks ex-libris-ing the Doe Library, the Morrison noncirculating collection, the Gardner stacks, Moe's Books, et al., reappropriating Alfred Kroeber anthropology tomes until her shallow-bellied, two-burger hibachi sat ripe with enough ash to satisfy an urn (and she was nearly ticketed for that final cookout on the dorm balcony, all 448 pages of *The Nature of Culture* and all 243 pages of Mrs. Kroeber's *Ishi in Two Worlds,* but let off with a warning after she explained to Officer Hernandez, again in Spanish, what she planned to do).

You lounged on the beanbag, amused. You surreptitiously recorded the contact—as you called it—on your phone. But, you, you tried backing out then, packing while watching Hernandez whistle down Haste Street, miraculously absent that common cop accoutrement, you. And you, you who had spent Officer Hernandez's entire visit seated on the tub lip or the toilet or listening at the door or inspecting the medicine cabinet, packed your bag even as she explained there was no crime, no law, no injunction against conspiring to dispose of simulated human remains. You and you said nothing, both equally skeptical of the possibility of success. You later relented because, truth be known not even to you, she also cried a little, expressed regret for her insensitivity, for forgetting that they all, except you, had very different relationships with cops (which you did, because, more than anything else, you were polite). And you, whose mom cried you a river that floated you right out of going to Howard, had no levee system, locks, canals, or channels to rout or reroute people in distress, your father had always warned you not to let your heart become, A bay for broken-down boats.

But on that day, the day Hernandez arrested no one, when Candice informed you that you could not walk out, you answered by way of tightening the straps on your pack. You added, Candyland, he can moonwalk out, and we're his backup dancers. And YOU left. At the corner, YOU parted, ostensibly for campus points distant. Thirty minutes later you returned, Just in case. YOU collided in the elevator. You told them you knew they were going back, and you couldn't let them go alone. You told them you knew they were going back, and you couldn't let them go alone. And you told them you knew they were going back, and you couldn't let them go alone.

Besides, she had a plan, and compelling raisons d'état, and, The First Peoples did, like, get kinda screwed, you know.

For nearly 300 years white Americans, in our zeal to carve out a nation made to order, have dealt with the Indians on the *erroneous,* yet *tragic,* assumption that the Indians were a dying race—to be liquidated. We took away their best lands; broke treaties, promises; tossed them the most nearly worthless scraps of a continent that had once been wholly theirs. But we did not liquidate their spirit. The vital spark which kept them alive was hardy.

—Hon. John Collier, Commisioner, Bureau of Indian Affairs
Annual Report of the Secretary of the Interior
for the Fiscal Year Ended June 30, 1938

FOUR YEARS LATER

Our job is to work with you toward making this place a truly happy place where individuals and families will be giving themselves utterly to the community and winning a reward of inward power and inward joy—Greater than anything external in the whole world.

. . . I am satisfied in my own mind, and we of the Government are satisfied that this colony, as the months go on, is going to provide a democracy of efficiency and the splendor of cooperative living.

—Hon. John Collier, Director, Poston Japanese internment camp,
Colorado River Indian Reservation, Arizona, June 27, 1942

Chapter Fourteen

S he was the last of the colonies—Lucky Thirteen, founded in 1733 by social reformer John Oglethorpe [with the intent to resettle imprisoned debtors] as a buffer zone of stalwart British farmers with which to stave off invasion from the Spaniards to the south. Slavery therefore was outlawed as a threat to civic morale and military readiness. Nor were Roman Catholics allowed: too many already polluted Florida (with their pagan rituals, though legitimated by biblical text, only one remove from native bloodlust). Nor could homesteaders claim more than five hundred acres. Nor was alcohol allowed (until 1742), being as it was a source of sloth. (Most grumbling was in response to the involuntary abstinence, and, of course, the absence of slavery, because it so clearly bestowed unexampled economic grace upon the other Southern colonies.)

The capital was to be Savannah, formerly known as Yamacraw Bluff, where Oglethorpe and his men planted stakes with the blessings of Chief Tomochichi. According to the standing agreement, there were to be no further settlements south of the Carolina border; however, in the chief's eyes, there was more than enough land for the one hundred Yamacraw Indians and the one hundred and fourteen settlers.

After the Salzburgers' and Scots' antislavery petitions drowned in the wake of Oglethorpe's return to England; after the royal decree legalizing slavery (1751); after the first American Revolution, the land rush, the Pine Barrens Speculation (1789–1796), the Combined Society, and the Yazoo land fiasco (1794), a spectacular disaster; after Indian agent Col. Benjamin Hawkins's patient negotiations with the Creek and Cherokee and Muscogee Nations were compromised by the Red Stick Revolt, which saw Andrew Jackson's near spontaneous ascension by saber; one Raymond Bragg pushed north to make his fortune in the heart of the state, complaining at every turn to any who would listen that he didn't understand why such hard-won independence hadn't earned a new name for the growing state whose every legal document echoed the colonial past, bearing across the masthead the name of a long-deceased monarch. Bragg traced his heritage back to the original Oglethorpe one hundred and thirteen who braved the dangerous crossing aboard the *Ann,* and considered it his duty, honor bound, to do proud that Georgia lineage. And he had, as a young man fighting alongside Old Hickory himself, as Jackson would soon be known, in the battle of Negro Fort (1816) and again in the First Seminole War (1817–1818).

Savannah ('77–'78, '82, '84, '85) and Augusta ('79–'80, '81–'82, '83, '84, '86–'96) had between them freely shared the honor on several occasions, like a toffee stick growing shorter by the minute (had not Augusta been the epicenter of the Yazoo fiasco?), then Louisville (named after a Frenchman and populated by only 550, half of whom were slaves?), and finally Milledgeville (where they hadn't even the foresight to complete construction in time to hold the first assembly?). It was August 1830. The natives were peacefully relocated to Oklahoma, and the land prices once more stable, in no small part because of the valor of men like Bragg and Jackson. If the shifting winds could be caught just right, like that moment when fish school, why then—why, why, why—couldn't this very spot where Bragg laid claim, these fecund twenty-five thousand acres of sweet-smelling pine and clover, ripe for cotton and timber harvesting and a mill, be the next capital?

BECAUSE ALONG ITS SOUTHERNMOST BORDER LAY an inexplicable depression some called the Devil's Footprint and others Pasco Holler, and all agreed was haunted. For proof they needed only regard their own history: Bragg's caravan lost there for days like a schooner listless, adrift without anchor or sail—while his missus, gripped in a stupor by the nameless illness that befell her, the old folk claimed, the very second the very first Pasco tree dropped shadow on them—lay wasting away in the carriage, quarantined from even her three young sons, giving up the ghost just as they escaped the cruciferous canopy that had played day for night the better part of a week. Murmurs about a curse, a murder, a lone Indian left behind to guard the wood, an enchanted elm, but these were never mentioned out loud. The widower's gray face cast doubt on all unfavorable speculation. Himself sick with grief, Bragg ventured little farther than the hill beyond that tree line. There where the Oconee forked in sight of the Holler, he laid his wife to rest in the center of what would become known as Braggsville, the city that love built in the heart of Georgia.

He erected a watchtower on that spot, and there strode imperial, overseeing the construction of his lumber mill, pacing the platform. The moon was always full in Braggsville. Shine during Prohibition, cotton when it was king, real estate and livestock during the Great Depression, hemp during the bull scare, an ordnance mill during the First World War: the town never fell prey to the capricious economic tides buffeting the rest of the country, and the colored folks liked it, too. They even had their own quarter, the Gully, and their own currency. (Except Nanny Tag, who wet-nursed Bragg's three boys, and so was given room and board by Bragg, and was paid in cash by the superstitious townfolk for whom she performed certain favors.)

The currency was called Nigger-head, and it couldn't be traded for a real penny, but it had value nonetheless. All services a colored man rendered in good faith to a white man to whom he was not legally bound were rewarded with a Nigger-head that could be exchanged for various goods at the side window of Mrs. Lee's General and Feed.

Bragg never failed to share this fact with the state legislature when petitioning for Braggsville's rightful recognition as the political center of the state. He redoubled his efforts after the Civil War, that second revolution, which saw Atlanta deservedly burned to her curbs, while Braggsville, where they had the foresight to dismantle their machinery, remained largely untouched because it appeared to the Union detachments to be, for all intents and purposes, decrepit. Inspecting the mill, the machinery in shambles and scattered about the floor, one Union general was reported to have said, They ought to stick to farming.

The drums and handlers and frame saws all tucked away in the Holler, the mill was back in service within two weeks after the shameful incident at Appomattox and was for several months one of the few operational industrial centers in the South. Bragg again petitioned the state, inviting the Milledgeville legislators to Braggsville to tour the mill, admire the town square centered around the watchtower, itself ringed with smiling azaleas, and enjoy a brief reenactment of the decisive battle in which the local men had figured prominently in *humiliating* the Yankee forces. He greeted the envoy wearing the boots he'd worn in campaigns with Old Hickory himself, by then known more roundly as the Hero of New Orleans for his instrumental role in suppressing a coup. A new courthouse was constructed (now a Circle K convenience store), the main streets widened, and the railroad station expanded to become the first two-story in the state, complete with a sitting room from which gentlemen could view the incoming trains. The government responded by selecting as capital a town once known merely as Terminus because it was there that the railway ended, then Marthasville—in honor of the governor's daughter—and finally Atlanta, because the tracks would eventually run from the Atlantic (east 364 miles) to the Pacific (west 2,180 miles). Raymond Bragg redoubled his efforts by redoubling the reenactment in size and frequency, but he died in 1885, childless (his three sons killed in the Battle of Atlanta), without seeing Braggsville accorded the honor it deserved, and before, Fortunately, said all, seeing the mill eaten to ash when a rogue boll weevil broke ranks and ate the insulation out of an already faulty circuit breaker. The reenactments ended soon after. They started once more, unfortunately, when Georgia again raised the Confederate battle flag in 1956, the same year the state legislature passed bills rejecting *Brown v. Board of Education*. But they have nothing to do with slavery, secession, or segregation. It's only civic pride.

DARON HAD HEARD IT ALL BEFORE, except the part about the Nigger-head and the reenactments coming back with the flag. He'd thought they'd always been part of the town. His mother told the story for Charlie's benefit (as they picked at his mom's famous *French* toast, finally removed from the No Fly List), explaining that Charlie was wise not to get involved because it didn't have anything to do with him. Daron listened patiently, and though the currency issue deserved further investigation, he asked no questions so as not to encourage her. She was already angry, as was his father, who was at that moment driving out to Old Man Donner's land.

As long as Daron could remember, the mill ran at half capacity on the day of the reenactment, operated mostly by folks from the Gully and the few townies who picked short straws. His father, though, worked that day every year. To his family, he explained it as time-and-a-half. To his coworkers he said, It's not good and smoky until nearly four, when the battle climaxes. Strange thing was his father never was at the field by four, or at all, as a matter of fact. This morning, though, when Daron and Charlie returned from dropping off Louis and Candice, he was sitting in the living room, and wasn't even dressed for work. He'd taken the day off because his son was in town, had planned to surprise him, but he quickly turned woeful, as he had before they put down Chamber, their old German shepherd, his face bunched up at hearing that Daron let his friends go and do alone what he was forbidden to do. Son, I would have preferred you defy me than abandon your friends, which no man should do. Daron tried explaining that they were only planning to remain at the house those few hours until the parade started, at which point they would conduct their interviews. Mr. Davenport didn't want to hear it, and before leaving to find Candice and Louis, he stopped at the front door and took one last look at his son that made Daron feel like his balls had retracted completely into the cold corner pocket of his stomach. Daron had wanted to go with him, but his father said he'd better do it alone, Besides, you had your chance to go tits up.

THEY'D ALL BEEN TO LOUIS'S HOUSE on several occasions, taking the ninety-minute bus ride to the Richmond district for family dinners with Louis's parents, grandparents, two great-uncles, and younger twin brothers. Lasagna for the first visit, after that, authentic Malaysian food such as chicken curry, roti canai, nasi lemak. Candice adored the twins and often spent the afternoon with them across the street in the Argonne Playground. Louis's mother in the kitchen working her magic while keeping an eye on Candice, Candy Can-Can from the land of Candistan, as she called her, and the twins. Candy Can-Can and the boys at the swing set, each one competing for her attention, swinging higher and higher yet, their squeals reaching a crescendo at the zenith where they momentarily vanished into sunlight on noon-bright days. Charlie and Louis shooting hoops. Nonstop bantering. Louis's secret weapon? The well-timed punch line. Daron reading or sometimes playing hoops—if they were in the mood to take it easy on him—but mostly watching Candice and how natural she was, how she fit right into the family, how even Louis's mom had noticed, joking once that her sons would do anything for a blonde. They have big blonde spots! So, I fight fire with wood. No, really! Once—Louis hates homework—once I bought blond wig, and said I was teacher now. Do it! He says only if I promise to take off wig. Still worked. Bad report card, he knows I'll pick him up in the blond wig. And she wasn't even the funny one. The uncles were.

On their visit to Braggsville, Daron hoped, Candice would play with his little cousins, Uncle Roy wouldn't tell his racist jokes, and Aunt Boo wouldn't pass out drunk. Mostly, he prayed that no one would use any of his nicknames. He wanted Candice to fit in, to think of the Davenports' as the Changs', another home, but more so. It was more . . . familiar. Maybe even one of his older cousins would give Candice a new nickname (that wasn't seventeen syllables long). What he had not anticipated was that Candice might hobble up to the back door about an hour after he'd dropped her and Louis off at Old Man Donner's, shaking, arms clawed by thorn and bramble, rooted to the back patio, shivering, refusing to come in because, Don't want to get blood on the floor. Don't want to get blood on the floor. Her clothes torn, shredded hems wavering around her pale ankles, zipper broken. Daron averted his eyes, but not before seeing a flash of cleavage, a triangle of tiger-striped panties. She had thistles in her hair, and she clutched her blouse desperately across her breasts, her white knuckles scraped and bruised, eyes swollen dark with fear.

Daron yelled for his mom as he and Charlie helped Candice to the nearest chair, but even as her legs shook she stiffened, again because, Don't want to bleed all over it.

Charlie and Daron stood on either side of her, Charlie holding her arm, Daron the white plastic chair, insistent. Shit, Candice. It's plastic!

At last she sat, hunched head to knees with her legs pressed tight together, her frenzied hands pawing her face as if she'd been contaminated with pepper spray, and silently wept, more shivers than sobs, her cries barely audible but her body everywhere shuddering in unmistakable grief. Daron felt the trembling in her arms traveling through the chair legs and the sand-set patio stone and into his feet with the insistence of electricity. Charlie felt it too, judging by his mournful expression. He looked on the verge of tears and was breathing steadily through his mouth to fight them back.

Candice, Candice, they whispered. Candice, tell us what happened. Can you tell us what happened?

She shook her head with a low moan and, without looking up, pointed in the direction from which she had come, the direction of the Holler. For some moments this was all she was able to communicate. Then she was still for a few minutes, during which time both Daron and Charlie tried calling Louis, but got no answer. When she did speak, it was in wet bursts between breaths. All of them . . . Barely got away . . . All of them were after me.

Louis? Where is he? Charlie looked over his shoulder toward the back fence. Is Louis back there?

Candice, where's Louis? Daron spoke slowly, nearly slow enough to spell it out. Louis? Where is Louis?

Candice shrieked and stomped. Looking at her feet Daron winced. The ankles and insteps red clay encrusted. The left little toenail ripped off. Muddy blood caulked the cuticle and the nail bed was red as a blister. They . . . took . . . him! They . . . took . . . him!

They who? They who?

Candice was sitting upright now, no longer clutching her blouse. Her bra, also tiger-striped, poked through the hole where the breast pocket would be. Charlie reached over and gingerly adjusted her shirt, but there wasn't enough fabric to cover everything.

She looked up at Daron, and her eyes, always a little sleepy in a cute way, were inflamed, and her stare so fixed and piercing, her expression so numb, that Daron turned away, afraid that otherwise she would communicate with that gaze all that she had seen and he simply could not bear it, not in his town, not in his house. All of them, he heard her repeat, but he didn't look back, instead continuing the course he was charting through the yard away from her.

Charlie called 911 while Daron traced Candice's footsteps through the begonia bed and to the fence, on which she'd left a bit of her shins. In the distance he saw a feather of smoke—someone was burning trash. He had thought he smelled something burning. He hoisted himself up to the fence top. Footsteps in the dewy grass ran between the edge of the Davenport property and the wood line, forging a path that would cut through the Holler and into the Gully. He was thankful she had made it back. He'd heard tell of people lost to themselves in the Holler for years.

Charlie said something. Candice shrieked again, and yelled, I don't know! I don't know! I don't know! I don't know!

Daron cursed to himself. Last summer they had walked all the way from downtown Berkeley to downtown Oakland, because Candice wanted to see how black people really lived. (*Really lived,* she stressed. How they teased her. Will they have iron lungs and barometric chambers? Do they hang from the ceiling like bats?) Another time they high-stepped over every drunken cripple in the Tenderloin to see Little Saigon. She drove through Hunter's Point blasting Kreayshawn, and registered to tutor at San Quentin, where she already had a pen pal. Candice, with all her questions about where the black people lived and the Gully, had wandered off on a crusade and gotten herself raped by a nigger. Louis got hisself shanked or shot or Jehovah knew what trying to stop it. Daron was sure of it.

No wonder she was in such shock. She had come to Braggsville only to help. Candice must have felt terribly betrayed to be attacked by the very people she so often advocated for. Daron could not imagine a deception of similar magnitude, except maybe learning much, much too late that you were adopted.

His next thought was to retrieve the shotgun in the hall closet. What if they came looking for her, chasing after her to get rid of the evidence? He had to go back for Louis, too. At the patio door he paused at Candice's side, unsure whether to touch her, unsure whether he wanted to. She twitched like she was possessed. Charlie squatted beside her, holding her hands, speaking in a soothing voice. She still refused to enter the house. Daron ran inside, calling for his mom again as he went. As he slid the patio door shut, out of habit—Were you raised by jackals, young man?—the cool, conditioned air gave him goose bumps and the smell of bacon made him want to vomit. It felt unreal. How could Candice be out there in that state, just inches away, when inside it was so safe?

From the kitchen, he dialed 911 for an ETA, and was quickly frustrated by the operator's request for more details, because details would only improve the possibility of a positive outcome. That's exactly how the operator said it. Positive outcome. Daron wasn't certain there could be a positive outcome after rape, but he told what he knew: she was attacked in the woods near the Gully. He tried calling Louis again. No answer.

He then retrieved the gun and walked back outside. Candice sat with her face hidden in the crook of her arm. Charlie knelt beside her, stroking her hair. His hand was large enough to cover almost half her face, and yet his every touch was gentle and controlled, like Chamber had been with children. Daron thought Candice's self-control was commendable. She didn't flinch, even though only moments ago she'd been pawed and clouted by hands much-too-much like Charlie's. Then again, soothing looked to come natural to him. When he saw the gun in Daron's hand, he turned ashen.

Are you up for this? asked Daron, pulling him to his feet and out of earshot.

What are you planning, D? I don't think you can take them all.

How many were there?

She says it was all of them, Charlie whispered. It must have been the whole town.

All of them. They were all around. In every direction. They took Louis. They were everywhere. It was like a riot, said Candice, or at least that's what Daron thought he heard. He was not sure because her face was still tucked into her arm. When he said that he couldn't hear her, asked her to tell him again, she lifted her head only enough to pull her shirt collar up to her eyebrows and declared, All of them.

All of them?

Daron waited a few moments, but all she had to say was: All of them.

Are you up for this? Daron again asked Charlie, gesturing with the gun.

Charlie's regretful expression was answer enough.

Daron stepped around him. He could do this on his own. Hunting was one thing, but Daron could do this. It had been hard not to feel a smug pride when he brought home this menagerie. It was, of course, mixed (one part anxiety—one part pride—one part concern they'd think his family nuts), but it was hard not to have considered himself urbane, sophisticated with Charlie in the front with his mom, Daron himself volunteering to ride bitch in the back so that he would be between Louis and Candice, feel her leg against his, and at the same time showcase them all, but now he felt as if he had driven through town with a fourteen-point buck strapped across his hood. Of course by nightfall everyone would be cold-nosing the back door after a slice.

Chapter Fifteen

Mr. Davenport drove Daron and Charlie in the white Bronco. Candice and Mrs. Davenport had gone ahead in an ambulance. County General was a squat, meagerly windowed seventies brick building that resembled a school more than a hospital, which meant that it looked like a prison. Smelled like one, too. The emergency room was fit to bust with reenactors, so many that they overflowed into the waiting area, and then the smoking lounge outside, most still wearing their heavy wool Confederate uniforms. Daron had half expected to find Louis among them, doing his version of a USO standup routine for the troops. But he wasn't. And he still wasn't answering his phone.

Daron's father led the way from the parking lot, followed by Daron, and Charlie several steps behind, out of anger or to avoid family frictions, Daron didn't know. Whenever he looked back at his friend dragging the toes on his classic high-tops, Charlie avoided his gaze.

The porter directed them to reception directed them to emergency directed them back to reception directed them to triage; all the clogs knew who, but none knew where. While his father talked to the triage supervisor, an embarrassed Daron meandered over to Charlie, who picked up a retirement magazine and busied himself reading. They had not shared a sentence since the paramedics arrived at the Davenport home and Daron's mom informed them there was no rape (cutting her eyes at Daron), though the EMTs wanted to bring Candice in for X-rays and to let a doctor look at her feet. By that point, Candice was calm enough to explain that Louis had not been taken by Gulls but carried off by Confederate soldiers after passing out. But, when Daron thought about it, Charlie had stopped speaking before then, before the ambulance, before Daron charged into the wood only to be recalled by sirens. Charlie had stopped talking when he saw the gun. Daron extended his hand. Charlie flipped the magazine page with a snap.

I'm sorry. I just freaked out.

I know, answered Charlie. I was there.

You know I'm not . . . I just panicked.

I know, answered Charlie. I was there. I heard you.

You were there? You heard me? That's it?

Don't get hot with me, no suh. Please don't shoot me suh, no suh. I's sorry, Mr. Security Guard suh. Mr. Neighborhood Watch suh.

You sound like a white dude trying to do a black dude.

Daron! His father gave him the hairy eyeball.

Daron repeated himself in a hushed tone, adding, Louis does a better black voice than you.

Hopefully, that means you won't shoot me, whispered Charlie. Suh.

I never said I was going to . . . I never meant . . . You saw her. Her pants. The zipper. His hands fanned the air before his groin. Her underwear was showing through. He pressed his hands to his chest. Her shirt all out of sorts. What else could I think?

I don't know, Daron. She wasn't in the same outfit she was wearing when we dropped her off. Maybe she was dressed like a slave? Did you think about that? You stupid motherfucker. Charlie sat back and crossed his arms, head cocked to the side. Dressed like a slave. Think of that? Did you?

Daron hadn't. He had jumped to a conclusion, or as Nana always accused him of doing, jumped to a confusion. Deep shame blood-hounded him, not because he had thought Candice was raped. He still contended he had good reason to suspect that. What troubled him, though, was a moment of faint suspicion, too faint, tenuous even in hindsight, when he had doubted Charlie, when he wondered if Charlie's reluctance to enter the Holler was a twisted allegiance to his race. Daron didn't even know why he would think such a thing about his friend, and for that reason accepted Charlie's scorn as deserved. He expected Charlie to calm down in a few hours. Louis, on the other foot, was never going to let Daron live this down. Don't tell Loose, okay? Do you have to tell Loose?

Daron's father finished his conversation with the triage supervisor and came and stood near the boys, which was just as well. The crumpled magazine like a bow tie in his fist, Charlie was now sitting with his chin to his chest like a bull ready to charge, tapping his incisor with his fingernail. According to Daron's father, no Chang had been checked in, but who knew with all the chaos. Fortunately, one of the Braggsville deputies recognized them and waved them through the confusion.

Real sorry 'bout your friend there, Daron. He put a hand on Daron's shoulder. Didn't get checked in up here. He's downstairs. You want to see him?

Which way?

The order reversed. His father lagged behind while Daron and Charlie walked abreast of the deputy, nearly ahead of him, and would have run had they known the way. After taking the elevator down one floor, traveling through a wide service passage with multicolored pipes lining the wall on either side, they climbed stairs back to a ground-level hallway and found themselves facing a wooden door with a green pebbled window across which was written: CORONER.

Charlie patted his face with his open hands, audibly.

Confused, Daron looked at his father, and then at the deputy.

We came around to avoid the crowd up there. You didn't know what I meant by downstairs? The deputy looked distressed. Shit, Daron. I thought you knew what I meant, but just not how to get here. No one told you? The deputy looked at Mr. Davenport for help.

Mr. Davenport offered his hand. Thank you, Tom. Let me get a minute with the boys.

Of course. I'll just inform the coroner now that y'all here. The deputy opened the door a crack and whispered to someone on the other side, listened a moment. And whispered again, louder, It's his friends. That wouldn't be right. He gently closed the door, nodded to Daron's father, and leaned against the far wall.

Daron. Charlie. Mr. Davenport. All three stood facing the door. As if trying to make out the meaning of the letters etched in the glass. C-O-R-O-N-E-R. Certainly a misunderstanding, a case of mistaken identity. Certainly. No one died in Braggsville unexpectedly. Not because of a joke. Unless it was a sick joke on Louis's part. Daron'd heard the deputy, heard his father, heard the coroner, but Daron knew it was a mistake—certainly—until his father turned so that he was between Daron and Charlie and the door, turned with a certain determination, as if to shield them, turned with the resolution of the sentenced, faced Daron and Charlie, palmed their necks, squeezed once, swallowed, nodded as if he had rehearsed this speech, as if he knew beforehand what to expect, and Daron rolled his shoulder back and pulled away from his father, away from the unwelcome awareness that his father *had* rehearsed this speech, performed this speech in Iraq, oh how many times, Daron didn't know, but often enough to have an expression on his face that Daron had never before seen but knew with certainty meant this is no mistake, that meant, Son, your friend is dead. That much is certain. Now you must go through that door there and identify his body. You invited him here and you owe him that much. That much is certain, as unthinkable as it is, that much is certain.

Daron had felt his legs shaking ever so slightly at the sight of the door; at the thought of going in, both legs now shook uncontrollably. I can't do it, Dad.

His father hugged him close, cradling his head in his hand. It's your friend. You owe it to him. Here might be your only chance to be alone with him again.

Charlie, looking at the floor, whispered, I'm going in. Could have been me.

At that, Daron cried aloud, sobbing fully now. The deputy moved farther away, kindly taking a seat on the stairs at the opposite end of the hall, his back to them.

Charlie knocked, and the door swung open. A few minutes later, he came back out, pulling the door shut silently behind him with a restrained twist of the knob, sniffing, eyes red, lips quivering, breath in sharp bursts.

You come in with me, Dad, please. I can't go alone, Daron whispered. Bail bondsmen's and undertakers' and attorneys' business cards were affixed by straight pins to a small cork board. On the wall beside it, flyers for bereavement support groups, grief counselors, a local pizza parlor. He studied them all, staring away, away, away from the door, from the deputy, who was turning to leave, away from Charlie, now weeping, and away from his father, whose gaze remained locked on Daron even as he inched closer to pat Charlie on the back, flinching away from his face reflected in his father's eyes. Please, Dad, he mouthed. Don't make me.

His father said nothing, but Daron felt his eyes on him. Charlie's weeping increased in volume. The deputy returned with a cup of water, which he handed to Charlie along with a fistful of paper towels. Charlie drank the water in one gulp.

Asked if he wanted more, Charlie nodded affirmatively but crumpled the cup, regarding his hand as if it were alien to him, then the other hand, then both, turning them back and forth like a baby who has discovered how unimaginably far the body extends beyond the self.

As Daron prepared to knock, the sound of a saw shrieked through the thin door, and he shrank back.

Sorry, muttered the deputy as he squeezed by Daron and into the morgue, the shrill of the saw rising strident as he opened the door enough to stick his head into the room. A moment later it was silent again. The deputy stepped back from the door and nodded at Daron.

Though it was ajar, Daron knocked softly on the door. He thought he heard someone say come in, but waited to be sure. He didn't want to walk in on people in a place like this. The coroner who leaned into the threshold to motion him in looked familiar. That was a strange sensation. On campus he often saw people who reminded him of other people he knew—especially the Asians—but the campus was so large he rarely ran into people he knew unless he was in the dorm or at one of the buildings where their classes met. But back in Braggsville, everyone knew him, and he had forgotten that feeling of never being anonymous.

You JT's uncle?

That's right. You Janice's boy.

Yes, sir.

My condolences. I don't know what all the scheme was, but it's a sad ending.

Louis was on a gurney with the sheet still over him. The coroner paused. You ready, young man?

Daron shook his head, No, even as he mouthed, Yes. The coroner peeled back the sheet.

Sorry he ain't been cleaned up yet.

Louis lay on his back, his open eyes staring straight ahead, like when he was drunk or playing possum. His legs were knotted and twisted. Black polish stained his face, starting in a neat line halfway down his forehead where the wig had once been and spreading in a web of rivulets under his eyes. On his chin was one quarter-sized spot where the makeup was wiped clean and Daron could see a few hairs of that thin, patchy beard. Adding to the surrealism was the wig cocked like a baseball cap. It had managed to stay on even as they removed the noose, but it was pushed back the way one pushed back a ball cap at the end of a long day, or when taking a moment to think. That's how Louis appeared, like he was in deep thought. Daron looked closely at Louis's legs and saw that he was wearing the pants of a muscle suit. Louis's bag was on a nearby gurney. Daron picked it up. It was now so light, unlike the day they'd arrived in Atlanta.

Don't think you can take that. Evidence. The rest of the muscle suit is in there. The EMT cut him out of the top. They tried, but seems he'd been gone for a while before they got there. What was he doing out there anyhow? What were the lot of them up to?

Protesting the reenactment.

The coroner gave a humorless guffaw. Protest? Isn't the reenactment already a protest? No one pays them two cents. Can't get a buffalo nickel out of a donkey hide. Guess that's gonna change, now. Y'all stirred up a mess for Braggsville. Real Wile E. Coyote move, pissing on your own shoes there. Won't be able to call it Draggsville no more. With a quick nod he replaced the sheet, jerked it straight so that it gently settled over Louis's body, the big lump of the wig first, then the legs, the torso last.

Replacing the sheet did nothing to abate Daron's terror, to fade the horrid image floating still before his eyes, transforming the set of Louis's mouth into a macabre grin. Louis rarely grinned. Laughed a lot, but rarely grinned. Daron once asked, How can you be a comedian if you never smile? Exactly! Louis had answered.

You know how to contact his family? Phone number, anything?

Daron silently backed away from the gurney and through the door.

In the hall, the deputy asked Daron if he wouldn't mind stopping off to see Sheriff on the way home. Charlie, too, if possible. He then repeated the coroner's question: You know how to contact his family? The girl's already down there, but apparently ain't talking none. The deputy stared closely, searching, like he was looking to see if Daron was going to lie, the look the cops would give him when they pulled them over on weekends in high school, the looks teachers sometimes gave him as they handed back his papers. It asked, Are you really one of us?

Chapter Sixteen

—Miss, please, miss—

—I am Candice Marianne Chelsea. My identification number is 20A30185. My date of birth is July third, 1992. I'm a sophomore. At UC Berkeley. I'm majoring in anthropology, with a minor in public health. I am—

—Young miss, once again, you are not being interrogated—

—I'm . . . I'm Candice Chelsea, a sophomore at Berkeley. My ID number is 20A30185. I'm an anthropology major minoring in public health—

—Young lady, please—

—I'm Candice Marianne Chelsea. My identification number is 20A30185. I'm a sophomore. At UC Berkeley—

—Young miss, please. I'm only recording this to aid the old noggin. It'll be the same when I meet with the other two. This is informal, miss. Tell me a little about yourself. That always helps to relax. Just talk about what you know.

[long pause]

We were curious about how people would react. There's Epcot Center or Williamsburg, Virginia, but no one reenacts the Tet Offensive or dresses like Kim Phuc. So why the Civil War? Like Charlie says, let's call a spade a spade. You don't think it's weird to reenact an ancient war?

Yes. Sir. My name is Charles Roger Cole, born January fifteenth, 1994, Sir. I am originally from New York, but was raised in Chicago, specifically Chicago-Bronzeville. I currently reside at 45A Addison Way in Berkeley, California. I'm a sophomore at UC Berkeley. My major is business administration and my minor is accounting. My friends' names are Candice Chelsea, Daron Davenport, and Louis Chang, the latter now deceased. I understand, Sir, that this statement is voluntary and I am not being charged with a crime, Sir.

You can't be serious. [pause] I'm D'aron Little May Davenport and I *reside* about five miles up the way at Gearheart Lane, about four and a half miles north of Lou Davis's. I was born November thirtieth, 1992, in Braggsville, Georgia. You drove Ma to County 'cause Pa was stationed in Germany.

How about telling me what all you can about this morning's incident?

We planned it a month or two ago, but everything changed when the troops arrived.

It wasn't supposed to go like this. Sir.

This wasn't what I reckoned on.

How 'bout that. So you planned this out in advance?

Yes.

Yes. Sir.

Kinda sorta. I didn't think on it none a long time.

How 'bout that. Call that a plan, do you? Whose idea was it?

I don't remember. We were all curious.

I don't remember? Everyone was curious, Sir.

They was all curious about the reenactment. I shouldna said nothing. They just got curiouser and curiouser.

How 'bout that. Curious? That's curious. What was your plan?

It was supposed to be a performative intervention. When Daron told us about the reenactment, what else could we do? At first, even Charlie thought it was a good idea. The first plan was that three of us would dress as slaves. One would be the master, cracking a whip and issuing random absurd orders. Whatever they used to do. We hoped there would be enough rocks or sticks to form a pile that the slaves could move back and forth. You know, like work. While this was happening, we would use a hidden camera to record the reenactors' reactions and ask a few questions about the war, local history, and the reenactments.

The action is known as a performative intervention, Sir. According to the initial plan, I was supposed to dress like a slave. Then Louis said that would be too obvious, and therefore too easy, Sir.

I figured we would just dress like slaves, horse around a bit, and videotape it. I didn't think anything could go wrong at home. Not like this.

Mr. Chicago, you're young for a sophomore. About two years younger than the others, it looks.

I graduated early.

That's right. You went to one of them fancy stay-away schools. So you're a smart one?

No. I've mastered adaptive testing, which transforms the examination into an assessment of strategy more than knowledge.

[long pause]

[muffled]

No, Sir. I'm good at taking tests, Sir.

Gotta be a little smart for that, don't you? Don't you?

Yes, Sir. I guess you do, Sir.

But it never occurred to a smart fellow like you that this was a bad idea?

Well, Sir, I did reverse my earlier decision, Sir.

But you let the young lady go off on her own with the Chinese boy.

No, Sir, well, yes, Sir. I didn't want her to, though, Sir. He's . . . was . . . Malaysian, though, Sir . . . In case you need that for the records, Sir.

Says here your major is business administration and accounting. You topping that sundae with criminal justice?

Understood, Sir.

As I was readying to say, a big, strong fellow like you couldn't stop them? So you sent that little girl and poor boy off to do this alone? Was that your original plan, Chicago? Do you hate the South?

No, Sir. I'm quite unfamiliar with the South, Sir, except for the last twenty-four hours. And what I read in that brochure. But there's no stopping Candice once her mind is set.

So it's the lady's fault, now? You deserted her, and it's her fault. That's how you do things where you're from?

[Pause] No, Sir.

So it's not her fault?

No, Sir. I do not hold Candice accountable, Sir.

So, college boy, you want to explain how this performance protest procedure is supposed to work?

Performative intervention, Sir?

[muffled]

Today's change agents perform instead of picket, Sir, though a picket line is itself a performance, as any scholar will tell you. Some change agents play the role of pickets, others scabs, others managers, et cetera. These various roles are all enactments of concretized ideologies. Judith Butler, for example, says gender is a performance, Sir.

But how is it supposed to work? What's supposed to happen afterwards?

I don't know, Sir.

Miss, where is that hidden camera you mentioned?

We forgot it.

Where?

At Daron's house.

You don't mind me looking none at it, do you, miss?

We didn't bring it. We forgot it at the Davenports' house.

All the same, you don't mind me looking, do you now, miss?

I guess not.

Your phone, too.

Okay. I guess.

D, why did you back out?

I wasn't going to disobey my father. You know how he gets.

Guess he hasn't gotten it enough lately. So if it wasn't for your father acting as the voice of God-given reason, you'da been out there, too? Was you scheming to string yourself up like the other one?

Hadn't reckoned to, Sheriff.

D, what I still cannot understand is how this performative intervention is supposed to work.

Me neither, Sheriff.

So you went out there to California and got your . . . Never mind. You don't know nothing about it, do you?

Not really, Sheriff. I never really got a good sight on it.

How about y'alles other plans? You said first—no, initial—plans. Tell me about the others.

The second plan was more provocative. It was Louis's idea to use Charlie as the master. Louis said we should use the Veil of Ignorance, which meant lynching a white person, ideally a white female. Charlie was like, It's highly possible that might provoke gunfire, and most people . . . How'd he say? . . . would be caught in a double-bind because they're ignorant about the Veil of Ignorance, so it wouldn't work. Charlie was like, It is what it is, they should call a spade a spade.

Well, Sir, Louis wanted to fabricate replicas of the discipline instruments he'd read about in *Beloved,* such as the spiked punishment collar. Louis wanted me to be the master because the irony would deepen the experience, but I couldn't do that either, Sir. I backed out at the last minute.

I don't know not all 'bout no complete second and third plans. We had considered some field modifications, but it weren't like we were plotting a revolution. We ain't a terrorist cell, Sheriff.

How about explaining that performance of inter-what again? Is that some private school high-jinking? You done any others?

It's not our idea. We learned about performative interventions in school. It's the theater of the real. Like holding a magnifying glass to life. It can be critical remixes, too. Someone in our class took a scene from *Seinfeld* and the dialogue from *All in the Family* and mixed them to prove that the shows were not much different. *All in the Family Seinfeld*. I think they call it that. Someone else updated *Peter Pan*. You know how Peter Pan flies? That's where we got the harness. [Pause] It was a mash-up of Brit-kid-lit—Peter Pan leads the Hobbits on a revolt in Narnia, but he is captured, and while he's imprisoned, rumors about his sexuality are spread, like Sir Roger David Casement in the Tower of London, and the Hobbits desert him. They call it *The Killer Mockingbird*. Another group did a project called Frankenmime, and acted out how Big Pharma creates and feeds addictions. One performance artist lined up ten kids in white suits with red dots on their butts to truck through communion. Sometimes it's the only way to expose how accepted wisdom reinforces normative middle-class Christian values and sexual mores to our common detriment. According to Judith Butler, even gender is a performance, a real prison for us women. You have to call a spade a spade.

Well, Sir, the concept is not our creation. It's a form of 4-D art. It's activism. It's the way of the future. No one writes letters anymore. Mass marches are inherently exclusive because access is restricted by geography and mobility, thereby fortifying the enduring social asymmetry they seek to undo. Instead, imagine a thousand performative interventions wherever injustice occurs, whenever it occurs. Social justice meets vaudeville. Or the troubadour. It's the poetry of performance. Me, you, black, white. It's all an act, Sir. Vershawn Ashanti Young says even race is a performance, Sir.

I didn't make it up, Sheriff. It's a theory. It means we're all made up. There's other words for it—big ones I don't recollect right atop this moment—but in the end, it means to say we're all made up. All of us.

How 'bout that. All made up? I still can't figure out the sense in any of it. Whose idea was this again?

After Daron told us about it in class, everyone wanted to come here. We all did. We don't do this in Iowa or California. Reenact, that is.

Well, Sir, the professor was extraordinarily enthusiastic, Sir.

They were talking about reenactments in class, and I mentioned our Patriot Days Festival. All I did was mention it, though. Like to defend the idea. We done reenactments since I don't know when.

Young miss, are you telling me it was Daron's idea?

No. He just mentioned it. We immediately thought about You-Tubeing live to compare it to Mark Tribe's Port Huron Project. But Louis had a good point—if we broadcasted it and left it at that, that would be too hipster-cool, just finger pointing.

How 'bout that! It's the dead boy's fault, now. That's convenient.

No. Daron told us about it. He was a cub scout or junior ranger or ROTC or something, didn't look like it when I first met him, but he was something like that and bragged about knowing knots and how he could make it look real. But it wasn't supposed to be real. First, we're not even black, right? We don't even have real slave outfits. All I had were Uggs, which would make me look like a Flintstone, so I went barefoot. It wasn't supposed to be real. If Charlie was the master, how could it be real? The irony, right? You see what I mean?

Not sure I do.

Before Daron backed out at Waffle House—

—Waffle House? How about telling me what . . . transpired at Waffle House?

We ate breakfast there. When Daron backed out, I kind of got pissed and decided to go with my original plan. Louis carried our costumes in the duffel bag. We took turns changing behind the tree. Then Louis showed me the shoe polish. Louis asked me to help, made me, really. I didn't want to, but when he started smearing it on himself and trying to use the inside of the lid for a mirror, I had to do something, otherwise it was going to look like war paint instead of blackface. I don't know why I agreed. I told him that every college student who uses blackface regrets it. He was so stubborn. A Virgo that acted like a Taurus, he always joked. [pause] I helped him put it on, and then he was like, Loose Chang in the big house! Who's the realest? Who's old school, now? [wet laugh] [sigh] He was always making a joke. [pause] By this time it was getting windy and the sun was coming up and I was disgusted already, but it was only a performance, like Frankenmime. Louis put on the wig, and that was it. He told me the night before it might be just the two of us. He sensed it somehow.

Well, Sir, way before the restaurant, I'd already changed my mind, Sir.

Part of me was hoping they'd back out, too. But I never figured anything could go wrong, least not these ways, Sheriff.

Go on, miss.

After he put on the wig and we hooked up the harness . . . What? . . . Okay. It looks like a dog harness because it has two straps that cross your torso and a middle strap that runs along the spine, with a hook at the top, just below the back of the neck.

[long pause]

Go on, miss.

Yes. I tied his hands, but loo— [pause] loose— [pause] not tight.

Go ahead, miss.

When I was seven, I chased my jacks ball into the street and looked up to see cars coming right at me. I froze. One of the drivers had to get out of his car and walk me back to the sidewalk and up to my porch. This was the same, but worse. Worse because I knew they were far enough away and walking slowly enough that I could run. This time I wasn't frozen, I knew I could run, but I couldn't leave Louis. Louis started braying and kicking and yelling, Sorry massuh, please don't whip me.

I yelled for him to shut up because we had to get out of there. I tried to unhook the pulley cable, but I couldn't. [Long Pause] That's the only reason I yelled like that. I couldn't concentrate.

So, you were the first to adjust the pulley?

Yes.

Before anyone else even got up close, you'd already tinkered with the pulley?

Yes.

And what was the deceased saying at the time?

I don't remember.

You don't remember what he said, or you don't remember if he said anything?

Both.

[Long Pause]

You didn't have no help with that pulley, getting it up or over or nothing? He didn't help you hoist his weight?

Maybe. I'm not sure.

[pause]

Go on, young miss.

I tried to run. I felt myself backing away without wanting to, and by the time they were fifty yards away, I was, too. There were just so many of them, and all the guns and everything. And this one guy, the captain maybe, asks what's going on here. We had practiced what to say. It's 1865, what do you think is going on here? This negro tried to run away. I couldn't say the other word. This negro says he don't want to work for free anymore. So, we got to make a lesson out of him.

—Don't worry, I can focus. Not thirsty, thanks.—

Loose was supposed to wiggle and yell that he was sorry, and he wasn't human, and he couldn't think real good on account of his being black. He wrote that line out, and rehearsed until he was satisfied that it sounded right. I was dressed like a man. We didn't think women did much of the whipping back then. That might make it too erotic.

But the captain guy was like, What in hell's tarnation is this getup here 'bout? And I'm like, It's 1865, right, dude, wassup? For a moment, I felt like we'd already won, like we were having a dialogue. That's all we wanted. Discourse. It was all going so well, or seemed to be then. I was thinking about how jealous Daron and Charlie would be to miss it all. The captain was so mad, I could tell he knew what we were doing, and we were doing just the one thing he hoped no one would ever do, the one thing that each and every fucking—excuse me—damn year they probably hoped no one would do. But, having a Civil War reenactment without slaves is like setting a love story during a bubonic plague outbreak and never having anyone get sick. Gabriel García Márquez never wrote a novel called *Love in the Time of Cold and Flu Season*.

The captain was a short guy, stocky, with a beard so thick I thought it was part of his costume until I saw him here later in uniform. He asks what the heck we're doing and asks about a permit. I was like, We don't need a permit in 1865. The men had grouped behind him until they had us surrounded. And one of them yelled, He ain't even black.

That's when they all started laughing, even the captain, kind of, and one of them stepped up and took the whip from my hand. I tried to snatch it back, but he was like, If it's 1865 then a woman got no rights. You could see he was proud to have thought of that.

Miss, I thought you were some distance away?

I was. I think I was. [pause] I'm not sure. There was so much confusion. It felt like they were far away but they were close enough to take the whip from my hand. But before that, when they were just coming over the hill, and were far away, they felt close. [sigh] [PAUSE] After they realized he wasn't black, they relaxed a little, and the whole thing seemed funny. They were laughing, the captain was laughing, Louis was kicking so I thought he was laughing, and I was laughing, too. It was like a moment in a film where everyone finally connects, and I thought it was okay, our work had been accomplished and we'd been successful. We were having discourse. Then the other one started whipping Louis. I just remember he had a cross tattooed on his hand. By the thumb and index finger. Next they were grabbing Louis's feet to lift him up, but he just sort of flopped to the side and I turned away. Someone said something about cutting him down and then I heard a terrible thud. I knew they'd dropped him . . . Someone threw up, I could smell it. There were big waffle chunks on the ground. I thought, Oh. Someone else went to Waffle House, too. Maybe they were there when we were. [pause] I didn't connect it to Louis at the time.

You're saying that these men helped you? They cut him down, which you couldn't have managed on your own. Looks to me like they helped you.

Yes. I suppose so.

And that could mean the man with the tattoo as well, couldn't it?

He had the whip.

How many of them were there?

All of them. It was all of them.

But you said you turned away. So there's a chance you might not be one hundred percent sure this guy might not have helped when you was turned away?

I guess he could have been.

Maybe the whip didn't even connect. He could have been cracking it just for y'allses show.

My show?

My show, Sir?

My show, Sheriff?

Yes. Your show. Just a few more questions, young miss. When did you dial 911? At Donner field with the deceased? Or after?

I didn't.

I'm sorry, I didn't hear that.

I didn't.

What happened at the end there, young miss?

I got scared. [Pause] I ran. When they cut him down, and were wrestling with him, I called for him to come on. I heard something going on and thought [long pause] I thought they were arresting him, maybe. I wanted to get to the Davenports', so we could go bail him out.

You didn't call 911 and report a rape?

No. [pause] Daron was mistaken.

You didn't tell him you were raped.

No.

Did you suggest it?

No.

Did you imply it?

No.

Did one of your . . . ah . . . friends take advantage of the confusion?

[long pause]

Miss, I can help you, but only if you tell me the truth.

I wasn't raped. That's the truth.

Why'd Daron think it?

I don't know.

And after you tied your friend's hands behind his back, and after you hoisted him up in the tree with your homemade noose Charlie-rigged around his neck, these men in uniform helped cut him down?

Yes. I suppose it appears that way.

Chicago, why'd you report a rape?

I didn't, Sir.

D, why'd you report a rape?

She looked like she'd been in a dogfight. Her clothes were all torn up, with her private wear sticking through. She was panicked.

[Long pause]

Tell me again whose idea was it?

I don't know.

I don't remember, Sir.

I should have never mentioned the reenactment. But all I did was mention it. I was only showing spirit.

Young miss, do you know what a spade is?

Of course.

Would you have done this in your hometown?

No.

No, Sir.

[pause] I get it, Sheriff. Cast iron's cracklin', Sheriff.

You done anything like this before?

No, sir.

No, Sir.

No way, Sheriff. No way. You'd know.

Mr. Chicago, what do you know about knots?

Nothing, Sir.

How did you decide what rope and pulley to use?

I never saw the rope or pulley, Sir.

And the noose?

Never saw it, Sir. I never handled any of it, Sir.

Not once?

No, Sir. I never saw the rope or harness until the morgue, Sir.

D, we contacted the Changs. They're on the way. Do we need to contact Mrs. Judith Butler?

No, Sheriff.

D, do you know this Mrs. Judith Butler?

Not personally, Sheriff.

GO AHEAD, MR. CHANG.

When we arrived, I knew Daron wouldn't be able to do it. I wasn't mad at him. I understood and I saw it before he did. Charlie and Candice couldn't see it, but I could. It was his father, the way he was, the way he looked at us. Not mean, not even wary, but measured, the way my elder uncle is. I imagined telling my elder uncle we were going to reenact building the railroad or the burning of Chinatown. Truth was, at that point I would have been disappointed if Daron had showed up because it seemed more important to honor his father's wishes than to needle a bunch of pinheaded white dudes with no fashion sense. Besides, there was always the chance they would like it, and where would that leave us? Oppression porn.

I got up early and asked Daron to show me the knots, just in case, I said. He was outside with Charlie. I knew what was happening. I couldn't blame Charlie. If I were black, I wouldn't swing any more than I'd dress like a ten-year-old Chinese virgin at a reenactment of Nanking. At sunup, I put on the blackface. I mentioned it to Charlie once. He didn't like it. Candice liked it even less, and was reluctant to help me put it on. It smelled oily and was cold on your skin. For the first few minutes it keeps feeling like a cool wind is blowing on your face.

The wig? Mine was part of last year's Disco Ronald McDonald Reagan Halloween costume. I liked Daron's more. I put on the harness and then a torn shirt over it. We flung the noose over the highest branch and looped it around my neck. The noose rope was pretty thick. The harness was ballistic nylon and we used a cable for that. The cable was thin enough to hide behind the rope, and we threw the cable and a pulley over the lowest branch. She hoisted me up with the pulley, and at the same time, pulled on the rope, so it looked like I was being lifted by the neck.

I always wanted to be taller. It was a beautiful view. From about four feet higher than usual, I could see across the valley to where the Union soldiers were camped and I could see the center of town, which the Confederacy hoped to defend and make the new capital. I read that somewhere. I knew when they were coming. That many people you hear before you see. They came over the ridge with the sun striking those canteens and tin cups, making them glow like scales, like it was a massive, slithering creature. You're never completely prepared for that. Candice was frantic. I felt kinda bad for her. And for a moment, I was scared.

But as they grew close, I thought, How could they hurt a hanged man? Then the big one snatched the whip from Candice and started cracking it in the air. He laughed and cracked it again. Another one grabbed the whip and did the same thing. We went on like this for several minutes, until another one grabbed it, and not being content to slap the air, started to whip me.

In the struggle to avoid the lashes, I must have snapped the hook, leaving all my weight to be supported by the noose, or maybe the harness caught my neck. What did I think as those troops continued to stream down that hill—their crushed gray hats so similar to the hipster style now popular in San Fran and New York? This would be a hit in the Castro.

Chapter Seventeen

A relationship is like a road trip: You get bugs splattered on the windshield. By the time you see them, it's too late, but you still keep going. It's like starting out on patrol: once you strap on the battle rattle and mount up, you ride until it's tits up, Daron's father often said. Under Daron's mother's scowl, he would then bluster through an explanation of—and cobble together a synonym for—Tango Uniform, in other words, Tits Up, in other words, Toes Up, in other words, On Its Back, in other words, You stay in the transport unless absolutely necessary to leave, and even then you seek nearby cover and concentrate on protecting your squadmates in the vehicle. But after his mom left, he would say, Son, ride till it's tits up and you'll do all right.

He'd first offered this wisdom after the Davenports once again made the long September school shopping trip to and from the outlet mall in aggressive silence. He'd gassed the shocks on the driveway curb, and terminated the journey not with his usual request—Permission to dock, Commander—which D'aron always granted, but instead ended with the strained plastic ratcheting of the emergency brake. On that trip, D'aron realized what he'd long suspected: He was the source of his father's stress, as was the another-one his mother was apparently crazy to even mention. What he'd done wrong D'aron could not say, and it was years before he understood that, A credit card is not the same as money, or, Women work all the time now, or, A part-time job can't carry a full-time life. Until those ragged perceptions coalesced into a nameable fear, the uncertainty kept D'aron in the car at every rest stop, afraid to be left behind—with the another-one his mother was apparently crazy to even mention. (The only thing missing on those trips, he once joked while possessed by alien technology, was the wet throstle sound of the compressor pumping its Freon-filled, single-chambered heart.)

That deepest of fears, being left behind, even amplified as it had been in the mind of his child self—aka Little Mays—took new form on the return drive from the hospital morgue to Sheriff's and Sheriff's to the house, a journey during which neither the Davenports nor Daron's friends even cut eyes at each other, scanning their respective sides of the road like grunts on security detail. Except Daron, again riding bitch, had no place to look except down, or at the backs of his parents' heads, or at the gearshift, where his mother's satiny hand lay draped over his father's own fine diamond wrinkles, a reminder it was not their quarrel. They'd spoken only when necessary—not at all—angling over knees and elbows to retrieve ultimately unneeded items from the glove box, center console, seat pocket. Candice shrunk herself into the corner, as did Charlie, only their legs touched, and even that felt a reluctant concession to a need Daron couldn't name, a need that nettled his chest as it desperately uncoiled, a need that also shamed them into contracting, shamed them into withdrawing that contact when they passed Lou's and Candice gasped, or when the wire-haired pizza delivery driver pulled abreast of them on Main Street, or when they turned the corner where Louis had made the bingo wings comment on the way home from Lou's—only yesterday!—a comment that Daron at last understood, watching Miss Ursula tax her rickety aluminum glider, hands interlaced behind her head like a stoic coach, the sagging skin under her triceps wavering like a bag of goldfish, but offering no wave. His mind flitted between Louis, mostly the first day they had met, how long it had taken to crack code word Lenny Bruce Lee, and his father, whom he expected to strike him at any moment. His father, though, was acting strange, tres bizarre: each time he caught Daron's eye in the rearview mirror, he looked away, which he never did, but not before registering a certain surprise and relief—was it?—to see Daron still there.

Once more Mary Jo, Bobby, Kevin, Dennis, Raymond, Lucille, Frankie, Coddles, Lyle, John, Andy, Miss Ursula, Jim, Lonnie, Postmaster Jones, William, Travis, Todd, Tony, Dennis M. . . . On the ride home from Sheriff's office, everyone was again on porches or at windows. Daron didn't call out their names this time, and this time no one waved. Where do the black people live? In the front yards! It was funny. (I guess that's better than the back of the bus, Louis had later added. Daron had thought that funny, too.) Louis's absence was always noticeable. Though skinny, he'd filled space like a fat man on a crowded elevator, except a welcome addition, not someone who provoked strangers to regard each other with situational solidarity. He had, in fact, induced people to regard each other with suspicion, to question the known. Louis would have made this funny—no, not funny but comic, and in doing so would have made it real, would have made it possible to express what they felt—aloud. When anxiety threatened to smother them, when the 4 Little Indians had nearly succumbed to the block and tackle of cluck and cackle in the entry line at Six Flags, Louis spurred them on, and relieved the tension of waiting forty-five minutes to enter the park (just to wait what they knew would be another fifty-five to ride Medusa) by interviewing Mary-Kate and Ashley, the honorifics he'd bestowed upon Candice's prosthetic protestants.

As soon as his father eased up the driveway, Candice was out of the car and limping toward the house. Charlie, always more patient and self-controlled, waited for the car to come to a complete stop and called after her, carrying her crutches. Before Daron could chase after them, both his father and mother twisted around to face him. In the space between their heads, he could see Charlie helping Candice into the house; he could only watch as Candice shambled along with one hand on a crutch and the other on Charlie's shoulder, only watch as she took slow steps steadied by Charlie's arm around her waist, only watch as Charlie's fingers grazed that slice of honeydew between her belt and her shirt. He wanted to be the one to help her.

It's a terrible thing that's happened, son. It's terrible to lose your friend like that. It wasn't a good idea, either. It was dumb as shitting on your own shoe, to be sure, but that's for later.

I know you must feel terrible, baby. His mother's face, like his father's, was a mixture of grief and something else—relief?—two looks that stung his cheeks and fell Daron ill, queasy, as had the smell in the coroner's office, as had the smell of bacon in the kitchen that morning. It opened a space in him that he didn't want to explore, so he continued scooting toward the car door.

What we need you to understand today—his father reached into the backseat to take a good handful of Daron's jaw and swung it to face him—what you have to know is that you are alive and you need to keep on trucking, and you couldn't have saved him. Maybe if you woulda went along to Old Man Donner's things woulda gone differently because people would recognize you, but maybe not. And unless you plan to be everywhere for everybody, you can't save everyone. That's the first thing you learn under fire. And you are fixing to be under fire, son. Stay strong. Don't give me that look. I know what you're feeling, D'aron. I know it too well. That's why I was glad when you went to school. Got it?

Daron nodded, Yes, sir, and followed after his friends. When only a few feet from the car, he slipped in mud slick as oil where one of The Charlies had once stood and landed with his feet in the air. Hobbling through the front door, he found that inside felt like those afternoons when his parents fought in silence, everyone dispersed through the house like rival gangs, each spraying their territory not with graffiti, but with music. Tool on the living room stereo. Dixie Chicks on the under-cabinet receiver. Their dialogue a call-and-response of banging doors, slamming cabinets; stomping feet, scraping chairs; drill and vacuum. Today everyone wore headphones, but Daron knew Charlie was looping *There for You* by Flyleaf and Candice was listening to *Cute Without the E* on repeat. Candice vanished in the direction of Daron's bedroom. Charlie went outside. Daron sat in the kitchen scrolling through pictures of Louis on his phone until it was unbearable. Then forced himself to start over again.

In between, he watched the activity in the backyard. He focused only on what he could see through one vinyl mullion, as if confining perception meant controlling emotion. He couldn't see where Candice had climbed the fence, or where Louis had delivered his routine. He could see the six-pillared gazebo, built of wood, not the more durable synthetic lumber because, The doctor's office and schools are the only places to sit on plastic. Charlie was drinking a glass of boxed wine with his mother, who had sparked the grill. She hoped it didn't seem festive, but, he heard her say, People still have to eat, and it just doesn't feel like a night for cooking. When she'd poured the wine, she and Charlie had held it to the sky like connoisseurs, and it occurred to Daron that his mom might be joking, but Charlie probably did know a thing or three about wine. His mother gave a sweet wave in the direction of the house. Daron returned the gesture, and was disappointed when his response didn't spark an enthusiastic uptick in his mom's flutter. The back door slammed, and he understood that she had not been waving to him. He expected to see Candice, but it was his father's legs stamping grass across the yard.

The three—Charlie and his parents—sat like friends, like three old friends at a wake, his mother running her fingernails along his father's jeans seam, Charlie across from them, where Daron usually sat, shielding his eyes from the sun whenever he tilted in to hear Daron's mother. They looked to be giving advice. Each time they spoke, Charlie leaned in, listened silently, sat back and bowed his head with understanding, two fingers anchoring the foot of his wineglass to the table.

When his parents fought, after a half hour to an hour of baking, tinkering, adjusting hinges, and other cacophonous domestic penitence, they would reconvene in the bedroom (Bang! Click! Listen up!), and start all over: muffled exclamations, roars, yellow bawling, silence. Next, rhythmic quaking pulsed optimistically, eagerly into shameless and squeaky clamor, followed by giddy, barefoot reemergence (and cigarette smoking). That was the enigma: argument fired hearts into crucibles of flesh. That was the mystery that drew Daron into the shadowed hall and kept him there watching Candice, kept him standing there even after working up the nerve to talk, even after taking several mental dry runs, even after he heard her shuffling toward the hall and he saw Charlie loping toward the house, even after he knew he had to talk to her before Charlie did, to have it out with her before Charlie did, even after he felt certain that having it out was part of adulthood, having it out strengthened bonds, having it out was his performative intervention. He was glad it was Sheriff who'd contacted the Changs. He couldn't even start this conversation.

From his bedroom doorway he watched her work. Half of Louis's stuff was still strewn across the corner he had claimed as his own, the other half across Charlie's corner. Candice was trying to clean it up. Her foot propped on Daron's chair, she sat perched on the edge of the bed, turned three-quarters away from him, the soft line of her cheek and bend of her breast wavering in and out of visibility as she worked. At the hospital they had outfitted her with a fracture boot for her right foot, and with her sweats and tank top and faint tan, she resembled a skier reluctant to disrobe. So meticulous. Socks she sausaged like everyone else, but T-shirts she folded and stacked like a factory worker. She laid each one out on the bed, smoothed it gently, tucked the arms in first, then the collar, then the bottom, and flipped it over so the logo was framed in the center and no seams were visible. Louis's DonkeyPunchLove shirt was thrown over the bed. Another one read, MY MOM WORKS AT WALMART, SO ALL I GET FOR XMAS IS THIS T-SHIRT, AGAIN. After folding each garment, she straightened and drew in her chin as if admiring her handiwork, patting each one like baby clothes.

Charlie's shadow plunged into the hallway. Not now, Charlie.

Not now what?

I need the bedroom.

I'm going to the bathroom. He paused, obviously expecting Daron to explain himself, but wore so exasperated an expression as to appear wary of the same. When Daron said nothing, he walked on with a loud sigh.

Okay. Daron slammed the door behind him. Locked it. Yelled.

(Bang! Click! Listen up!)

This isn't time to clean.

This isn't time to barbecue, either. Candice didn't bother turning to look at him.

At every funeral or wake he could remember there was a grill burning, and it had never occurred to him as strange until today. After a moment's thought, still didn't. Daron snatched the shirt from her hand. She snatched it back.

You can't fix this. *You* can't fix this. Not even *you*.

How about you tell me something I don't know. How about we let his stuff lie all around and get stepped on and messed up? That's your plan? What's happened isn't enough? Your mom shouldn't have to do it. Or are you going to fix it with a gun? The hillbilly cure?

Fuck you.

She turned to face him fully, to stare her challenge. Her lids were raw, but her face was swept smooth by grief, giving her a dignity. Her fingernails were chocked with black crescents of shoe polish. Do you mean You? Or You People?

The thing about women, his father always said, is that what they say they're upset about is never what they are really upset about.

Just get out.

You get out.

It's my room, and my house.

That's why you should leave. She turned back to her work, facing fully away from him.

Daron said nothing.

I know they let you see him.

Daron said nothing. She peeked back at him while saying it, as if to see if he would tell the truth.

Who identified him?

Daron said nothing.

Candice clutched the shirt she held to her stomach. Charlie told me. I know you saw him. They wouldn't let me see him. And they were the same people who took him. Her voice rose at the end.

What do you mean?

The soldiers who took him and the deputies who said I couldn't see him are the same people.

Everyone in town is part of the reenactment.

I know.

So you know it's just what they do.

They wouldn't let me see him, she screamed, burying her face in the shirt.

As much as he wanted to go to her, he seethed at the implication that Sheriff or the deputies had somehow caused Louis's death, enraged because it was an absurd notion, a mockery of logic, so far-fetched and ridiculous as to only reinforce Daron's own sense of culpability. It was as if she blamed them to avoid stating the obvious:

Louis's death was Daron's fault. The thing about women to under-stand, his father always said, is that they never directly tell you what they're upset about.

Did his parents also look at each other with resentment born of intimacy; did they want more than anything else to reach out to each other, to close cold space; did they say things to hurt each other first intentionally and then again, without meaning to, in the midst of apologizing? Did they inventory their intimacies? How did you look at someone and care so much for them and hate them at the same time, be so angry that you didn't even trust yourself to have a valid emotion, so angry it couldn't be real?

Had they asked themselves if they really knew each other at all, or too much? Had they wondered how can you despise someone who'll share anything but cookies; who makes every fight her own; who is creeped out by penguins (they strike her as crippled, and crippled things distress her), who asks you to read certain books only so that you'll hate them with her? Or did this anger itself illuminate the other person; did anger crystallize your affections; in a moment of alienation, did you see her anew? Admiring again the way she stood against challenge, even in the fracture boot, erect and long of limb, leaned forward when thinking as if her thoughts could support her, how her eyes sought yours and held them?

Did his parents also want more than anything else to shake their heavy pride, their cursed vanity, to splinter the malediction, squeeze it between them like a crying child transformed by tender affection? Had they not wanted, more than anything else, more badly than anything else—to say, I love you? Would that stop it? Daron was afraid to try. How did you tell someone your feelings? Did you just say it? That wasn't clever.

What did her parents, the professors, do? His parents were always happier after. And socked. Daron felt worse. Socked, shoed, shitty.

THREE TIMES SHE TOLD THE STORY, each version different. They would have asked for a fourth, but couldn't bear again the unexpected detail, such as how a soldier smeared with dirt smelled like fabric softener, or how the rebounding branch pitched a quivering green cloud, or how the sound of a regiment adorned with canteens and tin mess kits, scampering in confusion, could not mask the thump of his body knocking against the earth. Each version felt an account by a different eyewitness. In the first, she was initially approached by the captain, who incited the men. In the second, the captain was barely mentioned. In the third, the captain directed the cutting down. In all three versions, a man with a cross tattooed on his hand snatched the whip from Candice, brandishing it with zeal before whipping him.

Of the rape she said nothing.

The three of them sat in the gazebo. The box of wine his mother had left earlier remained on the table, now empty. The only light was the bug zapper, sleeved in a cyclone of gnats. His father had always called that life's biggest lesson. D'aron first assumed he meant, Moths to flame. For years D'aron prided himself on having perceived the answer without posing the question, but in high school he learned that platitudes were venial sins—easily forgiven, even if not easily fixed—and then at Berzerkeley he discovered that they were mortal sins, evidence of a corrupted soul and lazy mind, that clichés were an order of unsanitary intellectual musing akin to wearing someone else's crumbs on your own mustache. So the last time his father made the comment, Life's biggest lesson, Daron shrugged it off. His father smiled, So you get it? Moths to flame, moths to flame, Daron muttered. His father scoffed, and after repeated inquiries refused to share the meaning. When Daron ventured to ask his cousin about it, Quint replied, There's some shit you don't want to know, Li'l D, some shit you don't want to know, and then nearly broke a rib laughing at the wisps of exasperation wafting from Daron's ears.

He had delight in his eyes, she added after a long silence.

Light in his eyes?

Delight. The guy with the whip.

Fuck. I don't need to hear that. I really don't need to hear that. Charlie hunkered as he had for the last hour, elbows on knees, head on hands.

You mean he looked happy? Daron asked. Really?

My memory . . . maybe you should have . . . whatever.

Daron grunted.

I thought he was okay. It looked like he was laughing. When he was kicking, it looked like he was having fun.

Please. Fuck! Charlie rapped his fingers against his head. Enough. It's not our fault they wouldn't let you see him at the hospital.

Candice stood and walked to the edge of the yard. At the hospital, she had asked to see him. Demanded to see him. Said that she more than they deserved at least a final silent moment with him. It was forbidden. It was against the rules, the cops had told her. You're not family, their answer sounding, according to her, rehearsed. She seemed to think there was a conspiracy against her.

We should have gone, D.

I showed him how to tie the knots. I showed him three times. Over Charlie's head, Daron could see Candice sit on the hard ground next to the pagoda and turn her back to them.

We should have gone, Daron. People would have recognized you.

Daron knew they should have gone, but every time someone said it, his body rejected it like a toxic organ. He saw this happening to himself, yet was unable to stop it. Unable to stop himself from saying, Maybe you should have, but then you would feel like Candice. Louder: Maybe I would feel like Candice. Louder even: Maybe that's why she's angry. Because she was there and couldn't stop it. She was there and he is still dead.

Candice's head dipped lower with each sentence, until he couldn't see it at all, only her one hand ripping up grass, the opposite elbow cocked as if she were covering her mouth.

Charlie curled with rage. If this weren't your home, I'd light your ass six ways to Sunday. You think you're a man because you have some guns, because you wanted to shoot some—what are they called here—Gulls? Do you know what it's like to shoot someone? Have you ever seen someone shot? Have you ever seen a dead body?

Daron choked on his answer; Charlie on his apology.

Finally Candice asked, Why won't they let me see him? Because I'm a woman?

No answer.

Cut the bullshit. You know why.

Candice looked as if she had been slapped, her right cheek running crimson up to her temple and down to her neck.

Don't get cryatica and dramatica about that, really, Candy. I know you feel like shit because you were there and still couldn't prevent it, so your only choice is to jump on everyone else. Us for not being there, anyone who uses the wrong word, whatever. But that's not going to guarantee justice. It's only now getting started, so we've got to get our shit together, and get fucking serious, or what's going to happen when the real accusations fly? Charlie raised his brow in challenge. What's going to happen when they accuse you, Candyland, of being a clueless white girl who watched her friend asphyxiate because she was too frightened to move, or act, or call for help? That's what they're going to say. That . . . that you're making this up and you're an atheist liberal nutcase. The pressure is going to be on Daron's folks, too.

My folks aren't involved.

Charlie continued as if he hadn't heard him. They might get laid off, anything. It's going to get pretty ugly, and maybe the most we can hope for is that there is no civil suit. The Changs could get this house. Yours too, Candice.

Daron hadn't thought of that.

But we were being ironic when we posted those bumper stickers, protested Candice. Everyone knows we were joking.

Everyone who is our age, probably white, and a college student at a hella liberal school. Don't you get it? This never made any fucking sense to anyone but us, and there aren't as many of us as we fucking thought.

Everyone knows we were joking. They could even ask the girls in that Lou Davis's Cash and Copy store.

Of course! Charlie yelled. Independent verification by associate agents of the white girl brigade. It's always sunny in Candyland. You walked into an RV parking lot, without a word, expecting someone to let you into their home, on wheels, but a home, to use the bathroom. And they did, and they fed us. Because of you. Don't you get it? Both of you are playing games that you can't lose. I should have stayed out of this from the beginning. I should have listened to my father. When he sent me off to that school he said, Do your best, be your best, ignore the ignorant. Sometimes ignorance goes into remission and can be cured. Often it's metastasized, like my cancer, and nothing can be done about it. So that's why you have to ignore it, no matter what anyone says to you. Racism is white peoples' problem. They made it and they'll have to fix it.

I'm sorry.

Me, too.

Me, too.

They carried the somber mood to the bedroom, where they argued again. Candice still upset that she had not seen him one last time, Charlie repeating that they should have gone, Daron yelling that he would have gone had Charlie gone and then the knots would have been tied correctly. So Louis's death is my fault, stammered Charlie, ending the discussion, for at last they had said aloud their friend's name.

Chapter Eighteen

Adam Turing Hirschfield III moved like a ninja, light and quiet on his toes, on which he often stood. Daron would not have been surprised had Hirschfield opened his leather briefcase to reveal a collection of sparkling silver shuriken carefully nestled in fitted Styrofoam. He was diminutive, but when he spoke, his voice filled the room like a perfect gas, and he dressed impeccably. His suits must have been expensive, the sleeves seeming to anticipate his every move, the cuffs and collar starched so white, bleached to blind. If a superhero wore a suit, he would dress like Hirschfield. And he hit the courthouse like a superhero, at least in voice. His exact physical manner there was harder to describe. How he had confronted Sheriff in a matter-of-fact way—offering only half his attention, offering Sheriff the *opportunity* to *share* the transcripts or find himself buried under some arcane laws he would get a hernia lifting. And, were a superhero subpoenaed, he would retain a Hirschfield to represent him. His firm was a marquee name in Los Angeles and New York, that breed of old-school attorney that rarely appeared on television because they represented studios more frequently than stars.

When Charlie was in ninth grade, and that school offered him that academic scholarship with the matching tie and helmet, his father said, This is the end zone, son. This may be as far as football takes you. Your friends now are good kids, a few of them, that is. But most of them won't amount to shit. I know that. You know that. His father had then steered him by the elbow to the window, where he pointed at Charlie's friends, who had appeared as if on his father's payroll: Rock and T-bone were posted up on the corner spitting free-style, each with one thumb hooked on his belt loops, behind them the busted windows and the barbed wire around the school. Hell, they know that. But your friends at this new school, well, they'll be somebodies. One might even be president one day. (Charlie had been scouted, courted, but felt like Rumpelstiltskin. When the recruiter made that home visit, he felt like a daughter being married off, like a bride-to-be who, in sight of three aunts, two grandparents, and in-laws, had agreed to marry her high school beau with whom she hadn't even slept, not for love but only because a tour of duty felt impossibly long and probably terminal. What would he do in a school of white people? Plenty, as it turned out. As he admitted to Daron, Chase and Hunter and Preston were quick to befriend, slow to know, in short, the opposite of Cassius and Hovante and Tyrone. Charlie soon grew to like companionship without the burdens of intimacy, to no longer wonder whether to tease Hovante to cheer him up when his father was bending corners again, or to avoid teasing Cassius because it was his mother this time. And his teachers, Christ. They knew, how he didn't know, but they knew that his father was wasting away, swarmed him with compliments, one had even said, You're not going to be a statistic.)

It was too soon to know if a classmate would be president, but one of them, Alexander, the starting quarterback for three years, was the son of the third generation of Golds in Hoffman, Gold, and Sons. He was also the great-nephew of the original Hoffman. This was no accident, and Alexander's father, who wore that same school tie, never neglected to remind his son and his son's friends how lucky they were to grow up in the Midwest. The coast is good for some things, but a successful man must have values, and those start here, in the heartland.

Alexander heard about the Incident at Braggsville, as the media was referring to it the morning after, and next thing they knew, the now 3 Little Indians were seated at the Davenport kitchen table with a man whose tailored suit cost more than the refrigerator and who may have been the one to keep Lindsay Lohan and Robert Downey Jr. on the road for so long, on the studio's behalf, of course.

Here sat Daron in the same kitchen where he'd once made home-made costumes under his mother's tutelage: a knight, a crusader, an astronaut. On the side of the refrigerator hung one crayon pig wearing the blue Nikes D'aron so treasured in elementary school. That was the first pig he ever drew, and it had been in that same spot for years, protected by plastic wrap. The magnet that now held it was from a photo booth at the California State Fair: Daron, Candice, Charlie, and Louis wearing face paint and feathers costing ten dollars a go, but the money was for charity, and the opportunity too good to pass up. Beside that was a photo of Big Quint, his uncle who had died in Desert Storm, making two Vs with his hands. Beneath that was a photo of D'aron geared up for his first hunt, age eight, making the same Vs that his uncle, and, he realized, his roommate used to. Louis had only been there for a day, but the house already felt haunted by his absence, and the presence of the lawyer who filled the room, who—Daron at last figured out—had the manner not of a superhero, but of an undertaker, one possessing that rare and certain confidence in the inevitable necessity of his services.

Daron, his parents, and his friends sat at the table stirring cold coffee. Hirschfield had declined a beverage. Occasionally, Candice moaned and readjusted her position. Her foot kept falling asleep, and she couldn't scratch or flex it, poor thing.

Hirschfield paced the room, scanning the transcripts, running his finger along the page until he found what he was looking for.

Ah, here it is. He read slowly, Ten kids in white suits with red dots on their butts run through communion. No. Just, no. He looked at each of them in turn. I am charged with advising all of you until you secure individual representation. That comes from the top, so for efficiency's sake, we're holding this joint meeting. And Charlie, Mister-Race-Is-a-Performance, Mister-Sir-Every-Other-Minute? Adaptive testing transforms the examination into an assessment of strategy? Fortifies enduring social asymmetry? Enactments of concretized ideologies? That's a no-no. Open wide—let me see your teeth. Hirschfield enacted a dentist, continued speaking only when satisfied all enamel was present and accounted for. Charlie, your mom wanted you home if there was any uppity-Plessy, so you're flying out tomorrow with me. Daron, you better well figure out what this performative intervention is because whether you were there or not, you're the mastermind based on the *sole* fact that this is your hometown. Hirschfield paused, apparently waiting for Daron to indicate his understanding.

He reminded Daron of his professors who liked to hear themselves talk, the type who stopped midsentence to relish the sound of their voice. Daron nodded.

Candice, as the witness, the only witness here, you tried damned hard to do the right thing, but don't talk to anyone else without representation. This could be manslaughter, murder, or a hate crime, which is a federal offense. And it's definitely a hot mess as they say out your way, up in Norcal, that is. The papers are on it, the bloggers, and the news media will be here next. Candice, the town wants you to vindicate them for having rendered aid in an attempt to rescue you and the deceased from the ill-fated performative intervention being manipulated from offstage by this one here—he pointed to Daron. So, talk to no one else.

Louis.

Excuse me?

His name was Louis.

Of course, Louis.

Deceased makes him sound sick. He was murdered.

She's right. His father flashed him a look and Daron immediately regretted saying it, but she'd sounded so mournful, so true.

The attorney rubbed his hands together like he was washing them. I am sensitive to the issues at hand, but I will not abide some Left-Coast, hyperliberal deconstruction from a child who aided her good friend in hanging himself. I am here to help you. God has spoken. Not exactly God, but close—Gold, of Hoffman and Gold, has spoken, and I am here, in the South, which is actually a model for civil reform compared to the Bay Area, marked as it is by savagely persistent inequities amidst unimaginably abundant resources. You do not lecture me. He pointed at Candice. You do not know where you are. He pointed again, palm facing Candice, fingers curled, index and thumb up, like a Shaolin monk. This is not Berkeley, everyone does not have a voice, and in my informed opinion, you wouldn't be in trouble if you'd attended a school with a more traditional political climate, instead of a university that prides itself on being a hotbed of liberal activity and the center of free speech and progressive values, when, in actuality, their minority recruitment is abysmal as of late— excepting athletes—and what they have mostly given the world is an abundance of advancements in the sciences, most of which have been used for weapons. I know all about it. My brother attended Cal, until my father saved him from himself. Oppenheimer was at Berkeley, as were some of his other cronies. Keep up. Since 1943, a UC-managed weapons lab has overseen the design of every single nuclear weapon built for our national arsenal. I live in L.A., and I vote Democrat, but I pick my teeth with liberals after breakfast. So, you do not lecture me. May I continue?

Everyone nodded, Daron most vigorously, now aware that the senior citizens always protesting at the campus's West Gate had a legitimate complaint. Hirschfield certainly had some kung fu. Very strong.

Thank you. It's necessary to understand who is in charge. You need to work on these descriptions, especially of the man with the cross tattoo. Keep a notebook. Of course the entire town will render assistance, and necessarily so, when the entire town has convened on the site where said incident occurred. There is also the question of the bearded officer you mentioned, but he was off duty that day. I suspect, though, that had a crime, such as a robbery, happened to have occurred elsewhere, or perhaps a fire, or an automobile collision or other life-threatening medical emergency, there would have been a significant, perhaps life-altering delay, because the individuals in charge of providing the necessary services were all in costume, ardent adherents as they are to the cult of Southern victimization. The public safety officials were derelict in their responsibilities if they—and I suspect they had—indeed abandoned all public posts to participate in a role-playing game. He paused. Was mail delivered that day?

Daron's dad whistled long and low. Excuse me, but you're making it sound like a conspiracy. Do you want to know where I was? And my wife as well?

Forgive me, Mr. Davenport, if you took that to be a broad accusation of the entire town. Understand, though, that if firemen, local law enforcement, paramedics, and the rest were indeed present, they would be bound to intervene. If that is the case, it means that the sheriff's questions about who helped and who did what may be little more than an attempt to conceal an abject dereliction of duty. If they intend to put pressure on your son, you need to have something to come back with. Fire with fire, sir, you must understand that. This is like a boxing match, and the bell has sounded. The fight is under way and we may have lost the first round. If nothing else, we are against the ropes.

Daron looked at his father, who looked at his wife.

Janice, we get any mail yesterday?

She shook her head. I don't know. I don't think so.

One last piece of advice: the Internet is your enemy. Your Facebook pages can be introduced as evidence in court, as can your tweets. Even your e-mails can be subpoenaed. There is no privacy in the digital age, so type with caution.

Expect also to hear from the FBI, if you haven't already. They'll want to look into this lashing as a hate crime. It will be tough to prove because the muscle suit absorbed the force of the whip, meaning that the . . . Louis . . . alas . . . shows no sign of being beaten. I regret our meeting under these circumstances. Charlie, I'll pick you up at eight A.M. Good night.

THAT EVENING AFTER HIRSCHFIELD'S VISIT, when Candice called dinner their Last Supper, no one laughed, not even her. That evening after Hirschfield's visit, when Charlie called the front yard their Trail of Tears, no one laughed, not even him. Daron didn't even attempt a joke. In the hours since Charlie's departure was announced, their jokes were failed benedictions. After Charlie packed, they sat again in the backyard. For a long time, there were more fireflies than words between them. Daron counted. Doing so took his mind from the more disturbing question of why it was so hard to talk. At moments he felt the words pressing against his throat like sprinters neatly arranged at the starting block waiting only for him to fire the pistol. And when he didn't they would stand, stretch their legs, and cloud about in frustration as his thoughts went rogue, nebular. Again he would gather them together, line them up, but still couldn't even draw the starter, let alone fire it.

Candice's parents were professors. Was that like having an English teacher for a mother, but twice as bad? Did that make it impossible to talk about anything without being constantly corrected?

Louis was a natural. Charlie, though, was even more of an outsider than Daron. Why was it so easy for him to speak his piece, to share his mind? When they walked home after the dot party, Charlie had told Daron's life story, or may as well have. His mother wanted him to go to Howard or Morehouse or Tuskegee, he fled instead as far west as Greyhound traveled. And, like Daron, he also had what Mrs. Brooks called survivor's guilt, but Charlie's was more tangible, as Daron learned that evening under the gazebo.

I slept with many women, many women in Chicago, naturally. It's expected. But I'm still a virgin. My school had a Coming Out Day, and an LGBT club and student support group, but it was a collection of outcasts. Perhaps collectively their torments were lessened by being shared, but they continued nonetheless. Why join them if one wasn't even an outsider? In fact, to make it worse, I joined the football team in taunting and teasing the gay students, especially Tyler Ridges, the cherubic flutist. The band conductor would say, And now, our cherubic flutist. We kissed once in middle school summer camp, western Mass, snowy even in summer was my father's bad joke, never thought I'd see him again. But there he was when I got that scholarship, wearing the same tie. One day in the middle of gym class he broke down, crying out, He kissed me, but now he hates me! Dropped out soon after that. I mean, how could he live with those posters? Some guys put up posters of Chuck Norris with the slogan, I finger-fucked Tyler Ridges nka [now known as] the Colostomy King, and he's ruined for life. They scribbled his name and number on bathroom stalls and placed a personals ad in the local paper and on Craigslist in which he promoted himself as a cub in search of a bear, a puppy in search of a big dog, and a small pot looking for a tree to plant in itself to make it useful. There were hundreds of calls, not to mention the picture someone managed to shoot in the locker room of him in his undies bending over to pull off his sock. Out of context it did look like a weird boudoir shot. It was kind of funny and sexy at the same time, like a picture of a real fat lady in a bikini. Wasn't too funny though when Tyler hanged himself at his grandparents' home that summer, after his father put him out of the house, refusing to believe that anyone else would take the trouble to open an e-mail account listing themselves as TylerTheRiderRidges@gmail.com. It was too elaborate to be considered a hoax. Charlie paused. I'd thought only poor people were that homophobic. To be bullied into suicide. I think of it now as a lynching from a distance.

Candice reached across the table and took Charlie's hands between her own.

I told everyone I was going to Berkeley to try out for the team, but I just wanted to be near San Fran. It was only after the first year at Berkeley that I realized I could possibly be open about what I was, but I still wasn't ready. I'm not now. I am scared to do it and wanted to do it with someone who hadn't done it yet either. Look at me, do I look gay? He stood and extended his arms, a solid shadow. They would say that's why I didn't make the football team. He sat back down.

There are plenty of gay athletes now. Candice stroked his arm. Someone famous comes out every week.

Famous. Precisely. If you try to walk on gay, forget it.

Wait a minute, this does not mean you're gay, Daron whispered, looking around.

Does anyone know? asked Candice.

Weights, boxing, karate, football. My father suspected, which was why he was worried about the all-boys boarding school. My mother doesn't know. It would kill her. My father made me promise that even if I decide to get into that life, I must never tell her. Her brother, my uncle, died of AIDS.

It just sounds like you might be confused. That doesn't make you gay, argued Daron. I don't like guys in their underwear but that vampire movie dude is handsome. That doesn't make me gay. They had learned about this in school, about how not even gay sex makes you gay, like in prison, where it was merely situational sexual behavior. Prison sex, vo-technically speaking, was not homosexuality.

Louis would have come out, if he was gay. He would have done it. He would have. He would have.

Candice moved to sit beside Charlie. There, there. It was high school. We're never as liberal as we want to be then. I broke up with Darnell Jackson right before prom because my mom put pressure on me over the pictures. She said, Me and your dad laugh at our prom pictures sometimes, and it's such a joy to share them. You wouldn't want to have to hide them, would you? I told them I was going with someone else and spent the evening at Denny's. Louis wouldn't have done that. He would have stood up to her. He would have gone with whomever he wanted. My mom's funny. She's funny. She thought I was gay for a while. Remember how I dyed my hair the first year and cropped it, a few weeks after the dot party?

Charlie muttered affirmatively.

Daron nodded.

The day after I uploaded the photo to Facebook to show off my new hairstyle, I updated my status to Abstract but not Vague. Two hours later, my mother called under the pretext of catching me up on family business. At the end of the longest conversation we've had since I was eight years old and stumbled across her Internet porn bookmarks, she was like, Your aunt Carrie called and told your father not to be upset when he saw your new picture, but he was. I'm thinking, like, Aunt Carrie, who lived like Carrie Fisher, but without the fame or money? So, my mom's sounding all pained, like, Candy, it's okay to experiment, but don't advertise it. I grew it out, and haven't cut it since. They'd threatened to make me transfer to Temple.

With a sharp rock, Daron scratched lines into the wooden bench. He felt their expectant gaze, as if yesterday was really only the result of secrets coming out to die like poisoned rats. So, I should have never shoplifted or batted mailboxes, and then he'd be alive? he asked. And why was Candice growing her hair out only to let it get all dreaded anyway?

It's our fault. It's our fault, repeated Charlie. In school they teased me, in public school that was, for being Mr. Charlie. Mr. Charlie, especially if I did well on a test. What do you expect from Mr. Charlie? they would ask. Now, asked Charlie, who am I? I'm Judas, Iago, Nixon. Washington, Ellison, Obama. A great conciliator. But a part of me—his voice dropped to a whisper—is so glad to be alive. Before with Tyler, and even now. This sliver of myself, that part wind-thin, and just as sharp, as my own nana used to say, was relieved when Tyler killed himself. I know God hates me for it. He gave me that ulcer, for starters. It was like swallowing razors. I spent half the time in the nurses' station. He gripped Daron's arms, staring like a wild man. I know God hates me for it, I know he does, but I felt that way again when I saw Louis yesterday. I saw him there with that shoe polish on his face and that wig, and the muscle suit, and I knew that would have been me, and I was glad I didn't go. Glad to have been afraid.

Daron drew back from Charlie, shaking himself loose, brushing at his chest and arms as if to scatter the contamination. Charlie! Iago? Judas? Walking off, Daron thought conciliation was more his middle name than Charlie's, was it not? *Little May.* Hadn't he learned that much the first two years of college? Names were things, and things names, and both the stuff of thought, like stars, without which we wouldn't even see the night sky. What was the difference between *please,* and *can I,* and *yessuh,* and *may?* And Little May! *Little May?* Wasn't that a whisper, a faint inquiry, a question asked reluctantly? Crying in Mrs. Brooks's office like a bitch. How he wished she were here to talk to. She would understand. She would understand how he felt, how he wished so much he had defied his father's wishes and been there to stop it. She would understand how it felt to hear his father tell him, Son, I would have preferred you defy me than abandon your friends, which no real man would do. She would have understood that his sin wasn't any shameful act he'd hidden away, not even jumping to a confusion and thinking Candice had been raped by a Gull. His sin, if he had one, was no different from Alfred Kroeber's, the sin of being born in a particular time and place, and there was nothing he could do about that.

Chapter Nineteen

Hirschfield was right about the media. The next morning, two days after the Incident, regional news stations flashed a ticker-tape teaser: THE FIRST LYNCHING SINCE ALA 1981? When the anchors spoke, there was no question mark in their tone. The *Huffington Post* and NYT.com ran editorials. Facebook was on fire, the posts on Louis's wall growing by the minute, mostly from people who didn't know that he was dead. The day before Hirschfield's warning, Candice, always efficient with her 140 characters, had written a tweet heard around the Berkeley campus but impossible to contain there:

> Louis Chang hung from tree MURDERED in GA by
> Confederate pretenders whipped and teased—laughing
> paraded his body to town on car hood.

The ambulance battery was dead, or the paramedics couldn't get through the crowd, or there simply wasn't enough time. Excuses abounded, but one fact remained consistent in every newsflash: Someone had laid Louis across the hood and driven him into town for medical help. The news outlets didn't interpret it as quick thinking. Guided by Candice's tweet, they were enraged that someone had savagely paraded the poor young man through town on a car hood, a heinous and vicious act outdone only by the insurgents who had dragged dead U.S. contractors, naked, through the streets of Iraq. But that wasn't the worst of it. Moments before the Changs heard from Sheriff, Louis's cousin had read the tweet and called them.

Daron's mother had made up the guest bedroom (reserved for adults), fluffed the spare pillows, and inflated the air mattresses. There was no need. When the Changs arrived, they did not call the Davenports, let alone ask to stay in their home. As it was, the only reason his mom knew they were in town was because one of her knitting friends had called to report, A solemn Oriental family staying in the local Super 8. She'd heard from Quint that they had gone to the Gully, needing an undertaker skilled at adjusting necks just so. Daron learned of their arrival when he saw a photo of them on the local news.

From the moment he awoke, Daron knew it was going to be a day when two felt like four. He'd tried to ignore Charlie sniffling as he punched his clothes into his suitcase, but he couldn't ignore his mother calling Candice to the phone. He had been afraid of how his parents might behave once his friends left. His father's front seat speech after returning from County Morgue and Sheriff's made it very clear there was more to be discussed. But as Charlie zipped his bag, Daron knew that more than anything else he would miss the company. He'd never had friends stay with him. Relatives, yes, but never friends. The first few hours of the trip had been like finally having the family he wanted.

Candice and Daron saw Charlie off. Daron's parents stood in the doorway. As Hirschfield steered his oversize rental away, swaying on the shocks, Charlie waved, the attorney nodded. As if Charlie's departure wasn't enough, Candice said her parents would be there within hours, and that it would be better if Daron didn't go outside when they arrived because, My father . . . doesn't understand.

After passing the house three times, the Chelseas parked at the end of the drive. Mr. Chelsea popped the trunk and waited behind the car, stretching his calves, bouncing on the sloped curb. He was a large man, bigger than Daron had imagined, with heavy shoulders and arms, like he worked out more than most professors. He also stood differently, legs apart, arms crossed, as if in challenge. When Candice appeared at the door, which opened with a squeak, Mrs. Chelsea put her hands to her face in horror, and there they remained as Candice limped across the yard, her suitcase bumping along behind her. The wind stirred up her strappy yellow sundress and it looked like she would have been blown away without the boxy fracture boot to anchor her. Halfway across the yard, she dropped to one knee to adjust the Velcro strap on her bootie, hooking one elbow around her crutch for balance. Daron was reminded of an afternoon in Ohlone Park when he snuck up behind her to scare her, sticking a wet finger in her ear. She'd hugged him with relief as she now did her father—who was freed from whatever spell transfixed him and rushed to help her with the luggage. Next to him, she looked like a child.

The last thing she had done before exiting the house was kiss Daron's cheek and thank him for sticking up for her. If only she had stayed for a couple more days, Daron knew he could have helped her understand it all.

STARTING THE DAY HIS FRIENDS LEFT, a vigil gathered every evening at the giant poplar, lighting candles in Louis's name. Daron didn't see anyone he recognized. He didn't recognize the local Christian Fellowship Council leader, or the local Asian American Justice leader, or the NAACP local chapter president, nor had he known these organizations had local chapters, nor did he recognize the more assertive and outspoken protesters, the ones who carried picket signs with slogans such as BRAGGSVILLE, THE CITY HATE BUILT and

BRAGGSVILLE, THE CITY FOR JUST-US. He also didn't see the Changs, whom he'd stayed home to avoid, choosing to monitor the vigil on TV, even though his father said he couldn't escape the inevitable.

Braggsville had never been a town divided, but the news sure made it sound that way. They claimed that it was 99 percent white, and that the Mexicans and blacks who worked at the mill were denied promotions and refused the opportunity to buy newer housing in town. They claimed that Bragg built the Gully, and founded Bragg's Technical High over there across the Holler, just so the blacks wouldn't have to go to the white school. They claimed that the Gully wasn't part of incorporated Braggsville because they didn't want to provide any services. They claimed that according to the census, Braggsville hadn't had a registered black resident since the death of the midwife Nanny Tag, the Bragg family wetnurse, back in 1895. Daron knew that none of it was true, and whatever was fact was merely meaningless coincidence, but that didn't stop him from getting hot, especially seeing as how everyone blamed him, even Quint. As Quint said, You can't explain it away, D. You fucked the town up good. It was a jackass move. Your boy got done up like a nigger and hung hisself from a damned tree. What kind of shit is that? It's a shame. He was a funny fella, and your friend and all, but this is bad for all of us. They were at the Gorge, a twelve-pack of PBR on the console between them, and Daron found himself crying in front of Quint, which he hadn't done since fifth grade when Quint had tickled him until he peed himself. Like the deacon did that time in Nana's church, Quint grabbed his biceps and squeezed tight, once, then twice.

THEN, ALMOST THREE DAYS AFTER THE INCIDENT, the FBI arrived. If Hirschfield was a ninja, agent Philip Denver was a samurai, conservative in manner and armored always in a dark-blue windbreaker with the letters FBI on the back, regardless of the weather. He was a towering man with large hands and seventies sideburns, his eye in the peephole like he was trying to look *inside* the house. The visit was brief, and the agent returned repeatedly to one question, and that was one question Daron couldn't answer. And, unlike Hirschfield, Denver wanted to talk to Daron, and only Daron.

They were in the gazebo. Daron where he had sat the night after Louis's death, when Charlie shared a story that Daron still didn't quite believe. Denver sat across from him, where Candice had been, the same empty wine box on the table between them. When not repeating his favorite question, the agent lamented the media's treatment of Braggsville or shared personal information, as he did now.

I'm from Florida. Got out, went to school in New York, realized how redneck my home was, and never went back. He spoke with a measured tone, as if the silences between the words were more important than the words themselves. I had friends there growing up, but a few of them did some wicked stuff sometimes. One day I had to decide, was I them or was I me? It was hard, is real hard to leave what you know. Malcolm X did it, though, so anyone can, right? Right?

Right, Daron nodded, though he thought it an odd example because Malcolm X stood with his people, not against them.

You know why I wanted to talk to you alone?

Daron shrugged.

First off, is it *Da*ron or Da*ron*?

D'aron, with an apostrophe before the A.

Oh, why's that?

D'aron shrugged again.

Denver leaned back in his chair. You never asked?

Scots-Irish. Lot of that around here.

Denver slapped at a mosquito and leaned in closer, into the waning light, shielding his eyes with his hands as he did so. The back of his hand was hashed with scars. I'd like for us to get along, D'aron. I may be the only law enforcement officer on your side. Understand?

D'aron shrugged. Over Denver's shoulder, he could see that his father had returned to the kitchen window.

Look, D'aron. I'll ask again. Have you seen any militia activity in the area? Any military training, in or out of uniform? Men with guns who aren't hunting? Any unusual congregation in the woods?

D'aron laughed.

What?

My grandmother's church used to meet out there. That was one unusual congregation. He left it at that. There was no point in mentioning the snakes and anchors and all.

Denver stood and looked toward the hill. So, there's a church back in there?

It burned down long ago. I only went once, maybe was five or seven or something.

But no militia?

No, sir.

And you don't know this guy with the cross tattoo, either?

No, sir.

He noisily whipped through the pages of his notebook. Miss Chelsea mentioned this man a few times. Are you sure that doesn't ring a bell? He pinched the wedge of skin between his thumb and forefinger. A cross tattooed right here.

No, sir.

I'm having a hard time understanding why some kids from Berkeley would put on blackface and stage a lynching. Even as a performance. I have a hard time believing that was your idea.

It was my idea.

Has anyone threatened you?

No, sir.

One last question. What about this rape? Rescinded almost immediately after being reported. Tell me about that.

D'aron explained that he had seen her in costume and overreacted.

Denver then wrote in his notebook for so long that he could have been adding a chapter to the Bible. As he left, he shook D'aron's hand vigorously and thanked him profusely for his help. After he drove off, D'aron's father asked what he'd wanted.

He kept asking about militias.

And you told him?

I don't know nothing about a militia. We got no militia here. He's been watching too many movies. I told him that.

What was he thanking you for, then?

Probably saving him the time of walking all through those woods looking for a militia or an old church that's ate to ash.

We're getting you an attorney. I don't want you talking to no one else without an attorney, even that Hirschfield fella. He's a shark all right, we never know when he's gonna get hungry.

That's right, added his mom, stirring a pan of cocoa. She wore capris today, which she usually wore only on vacation. She had taken a few days off from the mill to keep D'aron company. He thought she'd irritate him, but he found her presence soothing.

I didn't trust him, she added. And I don't want you telling people about that old church. I told you that. I thought you forgot about it. Don't mention it anymore, you make us sound all—she waved the pot top like a fan—crazy!

What was that place anyway?

She gave him a stare, slamming the lid on the saucepan. Ha-ha. College makes you smart. It doesn't make other people stupid. I'm not so sure it makes you so smart, to have a second say. She wiped a spot off the stove and sucked on her finger.

Seriously, Mom.

You were sick, and I told your Nana. No one can ever say we have nothing against black people. Nana knew all that root stuff, learned it from the best, but even she couldn't lick this pickle. You had the colic so bad you didn't eat for three days in the winter, then you got the pleurisy, and old Tag took you out for a spell and you come back fine.

Old Tag? There were rumors about Tag. She was her own mother and grandmother. She never died. She was really the midwife Nanny Tag and still lived back in there. Whoever crossed her suffered unspeakably. She knew all them like that? asked D'aron. Nana went to the Holler that much?

Sometimes. This time she made a call, someone else makes a call and someone else raises a flag and someone else starts a fire and someone else lets a cat aloose, and all that stuff they did back then, and the next morning at sunup, tapping at the back door, is this old lady shiny as a black cherry and smelling of wax and vinegar. Old Tag. It was your Nana's doing and I raised hell about it, but it worked. So can't no one say we have anything against black people.

And that ain't the only reason, added his father.

D'aron considered that for a minute. He never thought his parents had anything against black people, but did they run that line on Charlie? Guilt a confession out of him? Who told you what we were doing? The night you called me in here. Who told you?

You were acting so strange. Every man is Sherlock Holmes to his son. His father laughed. That was a bluff. I had a pinch you were up to something.

That his father could so easily bluff him gave D'aron an unexpectedly sharp sense of security. Later, try as he might, he could remember nothing of the supposed early sojourn with Tag, though he did remember, and would always remember, the deacon there who chained himself to an anchor. How he dragged his burden along the aisle, splintering the floorboard, speaking in tongues for what felt like hours before collapsing in a heap, his sweaty suit shimmering like sharkskin, the heavy chain biting his ankle, tears streaming as he beat at his face with his fists, his hands finally going limp and the miniature crucifixes he held all that time tumbling to the floor, their tips red, all while his Nana gripped D'aron's sweaty neck muttering her Amens. He and Jo-Jo once went out there on a dare. The church was burned down, but the chain remained. D'aron walked it, arms outstretched like an acrobat, from one low singed wall to the other, but never admitted to Jo-Jo that he'd been there before.

Chapter Twenty-0

Grits and hash browns, bacon and sausage, eggs and toast. Two double portions scattered, smothered, and covered. No spice. Two cheesy egg breakfasts. Three waffles. Sheriff flipped over the ticket. Growing boys. Got the whole thing here. The waitress remembers y'all huddling like Comanches. Wasteful, too. Y'all shook Rick's seeds good, leaving most of the food uneaten as you done. D'aron was again in Sheriff's office, with the same gunmetal desk and same painted cinder-block walls and same sticky square-tube vinyl chairs and same photos of Chuck Norris and Buford Pusser sitting in judgment, exactly as they did when sixteen-year-old D'aron was brought in for driving like a choirboy who'd broken into the wine cabinet. The deputy made him sit in the cell for a few hours, where D'aron paced madly, as one did when fear and boredom peaked unendurable, and etched no less than seven hash marks in the wall, thinking at the time it was what hardened criminals did. It was the Friday before Thanksgiving vacation. Who was to say he hadn't spent a week in jail? Back then, after an interminable lecture in this very office, Sheriff released D'aron into his father's custody without booking him, expecting his father would do D'aron right. He'd since looked back on that occasion with laughter, but now felt the same again—terrified. Today, D'aron's father was outside in the waiting room because Sheriff said D'aron might want some privacy in light of possible delicate subjects.

After the welcome home barbecue, Candice had said, People here aren't that different, they just have accents. But if she could hear this, how their plan was being twisted, it would rock her little white-girl world, as Louis had always called it.

Everyone's entitled to be an idiot, but a few folks 'round here figure you is abusing the privilege. Sheriff sighed dramatically and finger-raked his comb-over. You done showed your ass at the Waffle House, it seems, Little D.

That surprised D'aron because, first, they were scared, if anything; second, they tipped well; and third, at every interaction they were polite. True, someone did comment on one server's alarming proportions, but mostly his friends found the place quaint. Charlie at one point nodded toward the waitress, a blue-haired Mabel with a charred-tip cigarette behind her ear, and said, She's so sweet you need to brush and floss after you talk to her. Whispering, Charlie leaned in to say it, and they all followed suit to hear. He added, My mom says that about people and usually means the opposite, but this lady is the real deal.

D'aron had been proud of the Southern hospitality that morning, and for a moment it had given him hope against hope that the day would go well. The service *could* give you a cavity—*Honey* this and *Sugar* that. You want coffee, hon? Toast, sweetie? Juice, honey? Now you know you gotta git a waffle, sugar. Read the signs.

Even Candice ordered a waffle after the cook echoed the order in a deep voice, almost threatening, That's right. Read the signs.

D'aron evidently had not read the signs, because Sheriff next mentioned the staff at Lou Davis's.

The staff? What staff?

Lee Anne and Rheanne.

Those are his grandkids. I went to school with Lee Anne for a spell. I dated Rheanne. They're crazy. Jealous. And they're not exactly staff.

You must think California made you slicker than snot. You're already in a bad odor with hell-all everybody else, so you best stop exercising me, D'aron Little May Davenport. Sheriff spun an old penny, the orb of flashing edges hummed across the blotter, lurching erratically off the desk before teetering to a stop on the industrial tile floor, camouflaged by grime. It wasn't a penny, but a dirty dime marked by verdigris. Sheriff raised his eyebrows at D'aron. Lee Anne said, They took pictures and acted suspicious. I repeat, They took pictures and acted suspicious. These's her words, Sheriff pointed. They looked mighty suspicious, like they were up to something, but I couldn't figure out what because I knew they wouldn't be shoplifting, not in front of Miss Janice, but they were scheming all right. He shuffled the papers. I also got reports from some of the festival participants.

Festival participants?

The local citizens who voluntarily participate in our annual celebration of our American heritage.

Lee Anne and Rheanne were informants? The reenactors were festival participants? The reenactment was our American heritage? Or was it: Our America? Daron stifled a laugh.

Sheriff planted his elbows on the desk, scowling, making the drill-sergeant face he used to intimidate them throughout their childhood. He was a big slice of cop, one of those people no one could imagine as anything else. Had never been anything else. You're in this up to the elbows, and you disgraced us, so I figure you best pay better attention. I'm trying to help you here, D. For your family's sake.

At that Daron straightened up.

I'ma need you to go around the way and meet with Otis, the mayor of Gully, and make a statement.

What?

This Nubian fella already met with Otis, and he's Twittering and Facebooking and Yahooing and YouTubeing and Googling and what all and what have you.

In the past few days, one protester had emerged from the crowd as the de facto leader, Francis Mohammed, a self-proclaimed high priest of the so-called Nubian Fellowship, which the followers called a spiritual liberation army and everyone else called a three-legged jackass black separatist cult. Mohammed issued a nightly statement on the status of the Braggsville Four. Yesterday, he said that this proved how dangerous it was to be a black male, a strong black male. Even impersonating one could get you killed. Mohammed didn't wear a kufi or dashiki, but he nevertheless struck Daron as violent and unpredictable, like the crazy guy in *Invisible Man,* the one that Ellison obviously despised.

You know this joker I'm talking about, Francis Mohammed?

Yessir.

Right now he's getting more press than anyone else in town. He can't be our spokesman. Listen up good now. I heard from the participants who saw the whole event and none of them recall seeing anyone get beaten. When these participants got there, your friend was already dead and the young lady was screaming. They cut him down and laid him out on a makeshift gurney, which they then placed on one of their personal vehicles, disregarding their paint job, mind you, and rushed into town where they met the ambulance. Are you with me? This is their report. He snapped the paper. Nod if you understand.

Daron nodded.

I also heard from people at the Git-n-Go gas station. Them and the crew at Lou's and everyone says the same thing. Y'all was acting funny.

Wait a minute, Sheriff, my friends were looking at bumper stickers.

Keep it buckled. Sheriff lifted one finger. If you would be patient,

I will be coming to that momentarily. As I was fixing to tell you, I done talked to everyone everyplace you stopped between Hartsfield and here. That Agent Denver has heard from them, too. Problem is Denver. Big problem. I'ma be straight with you, Little D. Between the festival witnesses, the Waffle House, Lou's staff, and all the rest . . . I'll just be honest here . . . With all those photos on Facebook and all of these bumper stickers and slogans your friends all tweeted and posted and whatnot, well, D'aron, I hate to say it, but I gotta be straight with you, D, I think this FBI fellow might have a case against you.

You found the guy with the tattoo?

You're not listening, D'aron. Ain't no tattoo. No one remembers no tattoo, and even Miss Candice says she wasn't sure. You got a bigger problem here. It appears to the United States federal government, and it would to me, if I didn't know you so well, but I remember when you wasn't but yea high—he held his hand out at desk level for emphasis—but it appears to the United States federal government that you orchestrated a hate crime. We're fixing to have paper airplanes flying in every direction in a New York minute, all the legal eagles, and the culture vultures, too. Everyone suing everyone. And judging by your black friend, y'all had a special relationship. Each of you liking the other. Some might say could be motives there. His voice dropped to a whisper. I know California's different. I'm not judging you. I'm just letting you know it's gonna get real ugly for everybody the longer it drags out, and this office, in an effort to keep the peace, and adhere to our duties, is obligated to recommend to the Feds that they escalate this hate crime investigation. That's an obligation, not a wish. If you make an appearance with Otis, and explain what you were doing, and that you didn't mean it, maybe you can beat them to the pass. You could win the public over, and it would be a good thing, 'cause, frankly, right now, most everyone is hot with you.

Those bumper stickers were a joke.

Hunting is the best anger management? Don't sound too funny to me. Sheriff handed him several pages of screen captures from Louis's and Candice's Facebook pages and a few Twitter feeds. Candice had tweeted several of the bumper sticker slogans, sans explanation.

They didn't write those. Daron pointed at the Facebook screen shots. This isn't serious. They don't mean this. Those tweets are slogans from the bumper stickers at Lou's. You can see right there in the photos. The tweets are from those bumper stickers in the photos.

Look closer. Look again at the Instant-gram one. If you're caught up in a cult, Little D, I might could help you, but only if you're honest.

A cult?

Look at that—he licked a pencil eraser and used it to thumb through his little yellow notebook—look at that old hashtag, that's what you call it, right? Hashtag? Way at the bottom.

Daron hadn't read the hashtags. Rather, he had read over them. There were three. #ZombieDick appeared once with a photo of a man in Hartsfield Airport getting his shoes shined. Of course the shiner was black and the shinee was white. When had Louis even taken that picture? #HomeOfTheKingKongZombieDickSlap appeared under a photo of the WELCOME TO BRAGGSVILLE sign. Daron checked the time stamp, and was relieved to see that the photo of the town's sign was posted after their visit to Waffle House. He took that to mean that at least Louis had thought about it first, and had spent some time in the town, and had some reason for writing that, even if it was known only to him. #ZombieDickSlap had been Louis's favorite. It graced photos of bumper stickers and The Charlies and a mammy doll (where had he seen that?) and tweets with only the text of the bumper stickers and rebel flags and rebel flag T-shirts and rebel flag hats and rebel flag bikinis and rebel flag bras and rebel flag pacifiers and Lou's Cash-n-Carry sign, the color scheme of which Daron only now realized, with great embarrassment, was Confederate inspired: red letters, blue background, and around the perimeter a regiment of white stars.

What's that mean? What's your friend into?

I don't know. I never seen it before. Daron had avoided Loose's Facebook page, Twitter feed, Instagram. What if he made one final post, uploaded his last vision? For a time, Louis and he'd shared a running dick slap joke, but those were threats about slapping the dick, not being slapped by the dick: Keep talking that Freud shit if you want! I'll slap your dick with this psychology book. I'll slap your dick with this remote control. I'll slap your dick with this skateboard. It had been funny. How, though, to explain that to this man with the scarped brow of a Neanderthal?

On the photo closest to Daron, Sheriff placed his hands, palms down and thumbs out, cropping it so that only Bragg Tower appeared. He did the same with a photo of Bragg's statue and again on a photo that needed no cropping because it was a fuzzy digital zoom close-up of the crotch of Bragg's statue. Sheriff tapped the hashtag with his eraser, word by word, as if that was the only way he could utter, Zombie dick slap. Got to mean something.

Daron answered, This isn't serious. They don't mean this. Never seen them before.

You don't friend your followers?

It's . . . No . . . It's . . . Well, yes, but they were all with me so I wasn't checking. But I know they didn't mean it. They were joking.

Well it's some real black comedy, that's for sure. Sheriff slid one of the sheets closer and read, If I'd known it would be like this I would have picked my own cotton. That's not funny, not now, not in these times.

Exactly. It's not funny. That's why they posted it. They were being ironic.

Sheriff spit into the coffee can he kept on the floor beside his desk.
He appeared to be chewing that over, literally, cheeks bellowing like
he had a mouthful of nails. I know sometimes things don't work out
like you mean 'em to. But it looks how it looks, and some will say
that's how it is. He gave Daron a wink like they were sharing a joke.
That, or his eye twitched. What did Miss Candice say? Call a spade
a something or other?

She didn't mean it like that.

Hmmph. Did you mean it when you reported her raped?

I thought she was.

There ain't never been a rape here. Last one even reported was
Mrs. Clark having the afterclap with her husband. And ain't no way
no Gull's gonna sneak over here and do nothing. They know better.
You live right back up on the Holler. You know it's safe. So seems
something else must be on your mind.

I really thought she was raped. She was messed up and bleeding
and her pants were torn and she was missing her shoes. She came
running from the direction of the Gully or the Holler—one of
them.

Chicago called in an incident before you, and didn't report a rape.
Ain't been a spit of polish out of the Gully since back in eighty-six
when Mabel and Kendrid got caught up in that likening business and
burned their luck trying to pass over in Doeville. Sheriff scratched
the back of his hand against the edge of the desk. Hard. Like he
was scraping something off. What about those hashtags? Don't know
nothing, huh? Sheriff cupped his hand to scratch behind his ear.
Talk about calling spades.

For years, Daron tried to hide that accent, even though more than
one professor said it was cute. Quaint he didn't mind, but cute was
unbearable. After a few drinks he would sometimes imitate Sheriff
(which was damn near as reckless as Louis playing at communion

with incredible edibles). Now, he imagined that Sheriff knew of his mockery and relished this moment, slowly pronouncing each word as if Daron didn't speak English.

Hear this. Hate crimes is Fed time, Little D, and Fed time is straight time. It's also inconvenient that the deceased was competing with you for a certain young lady's affections, according to other reports. It sounds like a complicated enough relationship to implicate you in a number of ways, none of them exactly funny. Or ironic.

Daron had never liked irony. He and Louis often argued about it, Daron insisting that if no one understood a joke it wasn't funny, and sometimes it was better to say what you meant. Louis would only answer, Yes, but in a maddeningly insincere tone. Daron would get frustrated, growing more so when Louis would innocently ask the professor if sarcasm, social niceties, and euphemism were all irony's close cousins. (Louis sideways: If it helps you understand better, Daron, think of them as kissing cousins.) The professor agreed. Maybe so, but Daron didn't think that sarcasm, social niceties, and euphemism could be mistaken for hate speech.

They'd read about this in class, how stereotypes distorted, affected, reflected reality. Asians were peaceful. Gays were nonviolent. As were women. Blacks (and sometimes Mexicans) were rarely accused of hate crimes for a number of reasons, but the underlying logic was that they were naturally predisposed to violence and mischief, and so seldom was any attack on whites motivated by hate. Contrarily, it was extremely easy to claim, and prove, that a white perpetrated a hate crime. In fact, popular opinion among the liberals was that conservatives were motivated by hate in everything they did wrong: hiring practices, legal negotiations, and any criminal activity affecting blacks, Mexicans, or gays. If Denver decided that Daron had intended to send a message of terror, then Daron's every denial must have sounded like an attempt to protect his co-conspirators.

But he honestly knew nothing about any militia. Or about #Zom-bieDickSlap, and neither did Charlie when he texted him. Candice, even though she had used it for one photo, didn't respond.

Sheriff ended the interview looking as frustrated as he began it. I just can't figure why, D'aron. I just can't figure why.

Chapter Thirteen

Why?[1, 2, 3]

---

[1] Por que?

[2] Mengapa?

[3] Why? Evolution, Bitches! Because. She eats two breakfasts. Gotta put a dick to it. Because she's your mom. Because she not. Because she's your due. Because she not. Because the morning after the Halloween hi-fi you find a shark's tooth lounging on the toilet bolt, fanned (someone forgot their tweezers and missed the target), swollen red at edge, an exploded view of your ignorance (you panic, Who cut themselves?). Because you didn't. Because not a neighbor would say not a word if this parade filled the bowl at the end of road. Because no one else is copping tickets to this circus. Because you're not even sure how to spell Ki-ya (Ginzu and watermelon?). Because it's natural. Because it's not. Because they grouse and grumble, knees nickeled, backs aspasm with jealousy. Because her legs start yesterday, end tomorrow, straddle unending night. Because she pass cell phone test. Because she drinks beer with a straw. Because she native. Because at dim sum she humored by your fake translation: small portions; and the dumpling drivers yield like Il Junior is in the house. Likening! Embranquecimento! Because she's no Luna; that slick bitch borrows her light, as do you and YOU. Because you gotta put a dick to epicanthic folds. Because father would go zombie, but mother, well, she did say that thing that one time, she did say you were free to live your own life, but she did cry that one time, so you knew what she meant . . . Because you gotta put a dick to accents. Because that no wig! Because those colors can't bleed; that spirit not bottled. Because you could fix her; she, you. Because you never had a passport, green card, papers. Because her cassolette would lure a minotaur out of the maze. Because she's the best chance your kids got, and you ain't even kissed yet, though every silent, holy night she barebacks YOUR dreams.

Chapter Twenty-1

A week after the Incident, it looked like Sheriff was correct in his prediction that matters would be well right settled. During their last meeting, he told Daron, I'll tell you how the inquest's gonna go: The cause of death is asphyxiation. One person will testify that he climbed up there voluntarily. About twenty-plus witnesses will testify that the young man was not moving when they arrived and that they attempted to render aid, but it was too late. Sadly. The EMTs will corroborate this. One person will claim that the deceased was alive until the men arrived, and that he was whipped. The coroner will testify that there were no marks to indicate that he was struck by a whip, and it will be ruled an accidental death and the Chans—Changs, I mean—can bury their boy. The only thing left will be for the Feds to call their play. That was how it went.

It had been a long week. Terror-stricken by the prospect of being charged with Louis's murder, Daron considered running away, and might have, had not the attorney his father hired finally convinced him that the inquest was intended to determine the cause of death, and that he, Daron, would not actually be on trial. Without his friends around, his father made it plain that he thought Daron was an idiot for putting his dick in this blender, of all the blenders in the free world. Worse yet, Daron was instructed to cease contact with his friends, especially in public, because, Everything you do will be deemed conspiratorial—and public means online.

(Ceasing contact had felt like one of those errant instructions adults barked to fill space when they didn't have a legitimate answer. Daron would not have believed that a conspiratorial stink was so easily raised, but there was that couple celebrating their twenty-fifth anniversary in Waffle House who asked the waitress to take their photo. She of-course-honeyed and pushed the magic button once their sausage mustaches were arranged. In the background of this festive scene Daron and his friends hunched over their menus. It's a moment he remembers clearly because Louis is counting on his thumbs as he liked to, listing the different ways hash browns could be served. When this photo made its way to TV, print, and Web, the caption was, The Comanches Plot. Rush Limbaugh called it a modern Indian massacre, an assault on tradition and family values. After that, Daron knew he would find no solace in common sense.)

He had never before ceased contact with anyone. He had never ceased anything. The embattled ceased. The Jews and Palestinians ceased. But after receiving that text message from Candice, after two days of pining, he felt better, overcome by a mood he could never have predicted—relief. Relieved to no longer worry about Candice liking Charlie, or Charlie liking Candice, or Candice being comfortable, or Candice finding something to eat that isn't fried, or that everything his mom did was countrified. Knowing he was not on trial, he was relieved when the inquest arrived to, Right settle matters, as Sheriff promised it would.

The deputies controlling access to the side parking lot waved Daron and his parents through. His father circled twice in search of the spot with the best shade, while Daron hunkered in the backseat enraged by his preoccupation with so mundane a matter. Finally his mom gave out, Just park already, hon. The building's not going to get any further away. His father's answer: To circle the lot a third and fourth time, which he did unopposed, finally parking not far from a gray sedan marked FBI. The walk from the lot to the side entrance ran along a chain-link fence that creaked against the crush of reporters snapping photos, jabbing microphones through the fence like cattle prods, elbowing each other like aggressive panhandlers.

Due to budget constraints, the county had temporarily closed the older buildings that were more expensive to heat and cool. The proceedings were held in a school board building that normally served as the meeting space for an afterschool program, a fact that the judge found distressing and for which she apologized profusely. Before beginning the proceedings, she instructed the bailiff to remove the cartoon drawings hanging around the room. There was one benefit to this location: with all the interested parties lined up to testify, there wasn't room to accommodate more than a few reporters. The rest were gathered in the sterile hall, and a few unlucky ones outside under the portico.

Were Charlie and Candice already inside? He hadn't heard from Charlie since asking about #ZombieDickSlap. It was as if Charlie'd committed e-suicide. From Candice he received one text from a strange number explaining that she was forbidden to have contact with him or Charlie until further notice—Much further notice, to be painfully precise. He didn't expect this much press, but otherwise Sheriff's predictions were accurate. He'd called it more reliably than Sheriff's wife called marriages, with one significant exception: Daron wasn't prepared for the questions the press asked. He'd received, and ignored, e-mails, phone calls, letters, visitors (greeted by his father, armed), but here, ignoring them didn't stop them from asking: Why? Would he do it again? What did he tell the Changs? And the kicker: Whose side are you on?

Whose side was he on? That was a question he'd never before had to answer.

Blue. Gray. Blue. Gray. Blue. Gray. Daron knew that during the second American revolution, Nana did say, One side—those damned yank Jehus—had strutted like Joseph, their benjamins brassed near up to their minds like Hisself had cut their coat from clear blue above, hotnosing like circus-trained dogs teetering at the table, their juniors bounced tight as a Jew's on Christmas. One side? One side meant at least two. But who was the other? he'd never insulted to ask. At just the sound of fat crackling, Nana did say, them'll stake their souls on your bet, them'll rise up on them hindmost parts an' walk beside you—yes, they will—for long enough to fool you both, Nana did say, Oh yeah, them can walk beside you, still them can't take a proper seat but in they's teeth. But just who were thems? Who was the other side? YANKS? BLACKS? GAYS? he'd never offended to ask, not even now, during the inquisition, as the coroner Frank Gist named it, regretful in tone and bearing as he had been when calling to give Daron the time and place of the hearing, regretful as he was even this morning for, The in-vi-ron-ment being in-con-ven-ient as it was to all sides involved.

All sides? There looked to be only two sides: The Changs sat opposite the Chelseas (Candice now wearing two fracture boots and a wrist brace—Bless her soul!); Changs on the bride's side, Chelseas on the groom's. The Changs with their blond sunglassed lawyer, the Chelseas unescorted. Everyone else was a midnight scramble. Sheriff behind the Chelseas, his two deputies behind the Changs. The first responding paramedic behind the Chelseas, the E.R. physician behind the Changs. When Daron asked to sit on the Changs' side, his father explained that it was the defense's side, and, Plain mean luck. It still looked more like a stew to Daron, everyone everywhere. He wanted to point this out to his father, but daren't disturb him. He hadn't moved since they took their seats in the back, was only this quiet when hunting, rooted like a fox in a duck blind. Nana must have told him, as she'd told Daron, about dealing with the law, In sooth, Court is capitalized like you or me. I don't understand. You will, Nana did say, just hope not before too late. Then tell me now. If I explain, Nana did say, you'll rightly never know. He suspected he would soon have his answer when it was announced that every witness was to give name, civilian title and rank, and then title and rank on the occasion of the circumstances under consideration. That's what they called it: Circumstances under consideration.

No one said reenactment. No one said war, and no one said civil, just like he'd always been taught. Even witnesses with tongues knobbly as old Miss Keen's famous northernmost limb listed their particulars almost rehearsed, as if those facts combined was the secret password to a secret clubhouse of which they all were night members. They might as well have been. Sheriff may as well have been straddling the building pulling the strings, or at the window, one large eye surveying his shadowbox, gaveling the walls with those blunt fingers while planning where to glue down the next toy soldier.

If he wasn't it was only because Sheriff was first to testify: One Henry-Frank-Lucian-Braggsville-police-chief-Confederate-captain swore as instructed and was granted entry to the witness stand—a folding chair padded with a coffee-stained plaid cushion. Between the low stage, where the judge sat behind a gunmetal desk, and the folding tables where the attorneys sat, someone had placed an aluminum easel holding a mounted map of the battlefield. On it, a hand-drawn red circle, bottom heavy, marked the location of the tree. Along the left of the board was a column reserved for witnesses not present at the Incident but sharing testimony nonetheless. Into this column was placed a quarter-sized magnet with Sheriff's name printed on it in green letters. He had not been at Old Man Donner's, but he had received the first call, and so could share with all assembled in the court the concern he immediately felt, and the concern he sensed in the voices of the men he talked to that day, You work with a man awhile, you know what they're feeling, and they were feeling none too good, not a one. By the time I got out there, you couldn't get a noise out iffen you rubbed two together.

One after another, familiar faces climbed into the witness box and testified as Sheriff said they would. None of them remembered a man with a cross tattoo. Worse yet, every single man, and the married ones, too, was clean shaven, even men who had worn beards since Daron's father sidled up to Daron's mother in Dougy's Bar & BBQ, stepped right into the hot flush of the jukebox, whiskey-licked her neck, rasped, I figure you for at least a Gemini. Every-damn-one that day was clean shaven (even the judge, known to the protectors-and-servers unaffectionately as Miss Hairlip).

One by one, Blue and Gray alike, they took to the folding chair and attested to the tragic perplexity of the heretofore unimaginable circumstances hereunder under consideration. Blue and Gray alike found their tessitura. Blue and Gray alike sang a chorus of sympathy for the Changs. Blue and Gray alike sang a chorus of sympathy for Charlie, who they reckoned must have been terrified by the very proposition, but who was not present, his mother having decided that, Surviving a shark attack didn't make anyone a better, or luckier, swimmer. Blue and Gray alike sang a chorus of sympathy to Candice, a few rows ahead of Daron, Candice who didn't testify, didn't need to, because she had, Already been through enough; because she had, Cooperated enthusiastically—um, well—*thoroughly* with Sheriff and the coroner; and because she had, Already given a complete statement, which the judge reviewed along with Charlie's statement. Besides, She has already been through enough. Besides, It's a right hot kettle for any young lady to pour. Blue and Gray alike were equally appalled.

But only Blue, and Blue only, would and could speak to the Incident at length, would and could plumb the circumstance without being circumspect, because, as the magnets and the lines filling the board like flight plans made clear, Blue approaches that old poplar from the low Donner wood. Blue each year steps first foot in that shaded loam. Blue was all that saw all of what was to see of importance. And as far as Blue could calculate, the victim was dead when they arrived. In the confusion, The girl run off. The whip no one right recollected, fixed as they was [pause] on cutting down the poor boy. The Changs were stoic, as expected, but Candice scrutable, stricken by a condition, her shame-sounding half-swallowed ceaseless sobs steady as that old black fan up in the corner, its waving reprimand near enough to drown out her quiet crying.

Gray had their own proclamation. Blue, Daron noticed, were floormen, pitmen, linemen, all in the figure eight of his high school, middle school years, all outsiders, the ones whose parents moved to Braggsville when the mill expanded and the office needed new sleeves, the ones whose fathers came from 'cross the state and married in, the ones whose parents were too poor to work at the mill because their grandparents crossed the wrong street a long time ago. Some were third generation but wore Blue because it took four to call Braggsville home. The Gray, big G, were supervisors, firewatchers (as the engineers called themselves), law enforcement. Parents. Two linemen from his graduating class. And the pride and relief Daron hadn't known he'd felt until then at each witness not being Jo-Jo diminished at the thought that maybe Jo-Jo just didn't want to play Union but couldn't yet be Confederate. Still he was surprised when Jo-Jo's father sang in the stand with the others. According to a Facebook post a few months back, Jo-Jo had been promoted at the mill. He should have been with the Gray. After hearing Gray out, Daron was glad he wasn't.

Yes, Gray had their own proclamation. Paramedics were Gray, as was the soldier who performed CPR, as was the soldier who propped Chang up on his hood to meet the ambulance instead of waiting for it to take the hill, as was the soldier who dialed emergency services, risking his good name because the cell phone prohibition was lifted only for soldiers whose wives were nearing delivery, and only for that reason alone could calls be made or received, but he knew, It was only right because the boy was a guest in our town. Yes, Gray had spoken without speaking. No one said reenactment. No one said war. No one said civil. No one said lynching.

The inquest, the hearing, wasn't so much a listening as a telling, and Court didn't need to say aloud what everyone knew by the time the last Confederate soldier clambered off the stand and slapped boot back into the gallery, The boy was dead when he got up in that harness. The girl panicked and run off, but not before trying to help. (As one witness said, nodding at her parents, Poor child was prob'ly scared for her life.) The young man from Chicago had the good sense not to go. Court didn't need to say aloud, Though they are to be commended for valiant attempts, for noble conduct, for disciplined grace in the face of slander, no soldier on that battlefield, not a one, could have saved that poor victim's life. (Except maybe the victim himself through a change of plans.) His death was accidental. And so this inquest rules it to be. But that does not leave aside the question of why he was there. No, Court didn't need to say it aloud, not as Daron sat there sweating until his underarms smelled like old tacos, but Court said it anyway, leaving Town to think, If no one is guilty, what was the boy a victim of, D'aron? What have you made us kin to?

As Blue and Gray departed, Daron remained seated, averting his eyes, as he had at the end of that sixth-grade swim meet after which they'd started calling him Dim Ding-Dong. That afternoon, he was too fearful to venture far enough into the dank, cavernous locker room, the endless rows of gray louvered doors the interior of an alien spacecraft. After he changed into his street clothes and returned to the bleachers, his mother said, with a laugh, that he had mooned everybody. He didn't think it funny, and wanted to wait for everyone to leave then, too. His mother refused his request. Back then, Mrs. Goman winked at him and Mr. Clark smiled and Mrs. Houston

called him cutie pie, and he felt a secret thrill, saw himself anew in
their eyes, his nudity a celebrity. Today, while waiting for the sound
of shambling feet to die out, he cut peeks at Candice as she rustled
her belongings together, rising with her father holding one elbow, her
mother the other. (Crutches Louis would have called polio crutches.
This thought was an indignity, he was certain. Why did he keep
thinking of Louis only as a funny person, and why did that make it
hurt all the more?) Her black dress covered her from fracture bootie
to neck. The day after the Incident, he'd heard his mother tell Candice, Dear, in Iowa don't you put the Jell-Os in the molds before you
take them out for a stroll? Since then Candice wore a bra faithfully.
For some reason, that turned him on more than when she let them
march free. What would he have thought if he first met her today,
without a dot, without a prepared speech on Native American rights,
in mourning? Without catching her gaze, he couldn't know.

And so he forced himself to stand, to look up, even though he
was afraid to see what was reflected in the Town's eyes, afraid to
know what he would think of himself in the mirror of their faces. No
one looked back. They all avoided him, except Candice, who gulped
when he stood, who looked back in desperation as her father pulled
her along like a stubborn child, his own head down, his other arm
wrapped tight around his wife. His wife and Candice were the same
height. At the exit he pulled them close, tight as booster rockets, and
they turned sideways to fit through the door as if they were a single
apparatus. Candice looked once more, and Daron thought he saw on
her face the same fear and confusion and desire burning his. He had
let her down.

When Daron's parents rose to leave, the only people remaining
in the room were the Changs and their attorney. On the wall near
where they sat was posted one drawing someone had missed, perhaps
because it was lower on the wall. It hung crooked, as if the child had
taped it there himself. A self-portrait in red, yellow, and green, the

little boy was skateboarding past a red house with smoke curling from the roof in broad yellow corkscrews mottled as crayon often is when applied over a rough surface, but as Daron noticed only after a second and third glance, there was no chimney on the home. Operation Confederation raised Cain instead of Abel, as Nana always warned him not to.

Tentatively, Daron approached the Changs, walking along the center aisle swinging wide to avoid surprising them. He looked back at his parents. His father shook his head, but his mother urged him on. As he came to the end of their row, he could see that their attorney was sorting cigarettes that had fallen loose in her purse. Mr. Chang appeared to be praying. He wore in his lapel one red flower, which leaned a little to the left.

Daron wanted to adjust it. Believed that if he could summon the power to do so, all would be forgiven. But he could barely walk. As a wall they stood, Mr. Chang and the blond attorney, who, as Daron approached, pushed up her sunglasses like a visor. It was Mrs. Chang, her face tilted and open. He faltered. Christ, it was hot! Why hadn't he defied his father and sat beside them? At least in the same row. At least on the same side. Wasn't his luck plain mean enough already? Was it the privilege of not having to do something that made it a privilege at all? When he was within a few feet of them, close enough to see the deep lines around her eyes, Mrs. Chang extended one finger to shush him and drew her sunglasses back down with the finality of a judge's sentence, worse yet, another inquest, and this time it was Daron's death being investigated, and she had found the cause. Like Court, the Changs did not need to say it aloud, either, and they didn't. So he did. I don't know why I didn't say, No. No. No. To all of it. The dots. Ishi. The Veil of Ignorance. This trip. I don't know why.

I do, replied Mrs. Chang. But, before you ask, it do you no good to hear it from me.

Mrs. Chang, I—

—Daron, I give you advice. Avoid my mother. Avoid the color blue in dreams. Avoid the shade of young trees. Louis's wishes, not mine.

They retreat, like in a dream because he is powerless to stop or follow. He can only wait to wake up. Once back outside, he is ashamed of how happy he is that his father parked in the shade.

Hirschfield had warned them that there could be a civil suit, though it would take at least a year to build. So Daron assumed the inquest being over meant that things would calm down. But the news coverage increased. Daron had put B-ville on the map all right: every national network devoted at least three minutes daily to summarizing the Incident at Braggsville while showing electronic stills of Daron's house, or Lou's Cash-n-Carry Bait Shop and Copy Center (they got a laugh out of that one), or the crowd at the giant poplar, their faces underlit by candles, cheeks glistening, eyes veiled. One station ran a fifteen-minute special on Billie Holiday's rendition of Abel Meeropol's poem *Strange Fruit,* ending the segment with a picture of Old Man Donner's field, the tree the only spot of color in an otherwise black-and-white image. People even talked to Otis Hunter, mayor of the Gully, whom Sheriff had said he wanted Daron to meet. What Otis had to do with anything Daron couldn't understand, but several Atlanta stations interviewed him. Otis said only that it was a sad occasion for everyone, that he didn't blame the children for being born into this world, and that anything he had to say about young Mr. Davenport he would say to his face. Other stations devoted airtime to Louis's Twitter and Instagram feeds, at least those tweets and Instagram photos marked #ZombieDickSlap. The vigils at the site of the Incident grew in direct proportion to Braggs-ville's notoriety. And Braggsville's notoriety grew.

What was a #ZombieDickSlap? No one knew. Plenty asked, but no one knew. #BraggsvilleDickSlap was another matter. Ask any earthling with Internet access. A legal row over New York's stop-and-frisk ordinance targeting black and brown teens? A North Caro-lina sports bar requires minority patrons, and minority patrons only, to purchase memberships? A white woman throws acid on her own face and then files a police report in which she claims to have been attacked by a black woman? James Byrd Jr.? Oscar Grant? A pizza order sent to a black fraternity in care of Toggaf Reggin? Officer Andrew Blomberg acquitted of beating Chad Holley, despite video evidence? #BraggsvilleDickSlap. Unarmed and seated student pro-testers pepper-sprayed by Berkeley campus police? Tony Arambula? Jose Guerena? Kelly Thomas? John J. McKenna? Kenneth Chamber-lain Sr.? Vang Thao? #BraggsvilleDickSlap. Trayvon Martin? Dillon Taylor? Michael Brown?

Photos, too. First a decorated vet with a purple sickle under his eye and a crusty gash in the middle of his lower lip, naked from his jeaned waist, his torso a calico patchwork of tender bruises as numer-ous as his medals. Next was the woman with a knot on her temple where the arresting officer kicked her in the head (seizures for life). Then the autopsy photos. Then a photo of Louis retouched, and a beret added, so that he resembled the iconic image of Che.

#ZombieDickSlap? Open sesame. Abracadabra. Shave-and-a-haircut-two-bits. Sure, he'd read about police brutality, racism, in-justice, written papers, punished classmates with PowerPoints, but at the end of each semester, he'd forgotten all, literally and figuratively. Forgotten, as he'd forgotten about his father being on active duty, forgotten about Quint when he was locked up. Forgetting being just another way of keeping his hands off hot pots. He'd never visited Quint in vo-tech. During the early sprees, he'd been too young. Later, secretly (and foolishly, he knew), Daron feared being trapped inside, due to a riot or a case of mistaken identity. *North by Northwest, The Big Lebowski, Galaxy Quest:* mistaken identity was the trope in his father's favorite films. It was in Daron's mind all too possible to call on Quint as an alien and end up a resident. And that was how he felt now, that he had become an unwitting citizen of a foreign country where human rights atrocities flourished unchecked. What pricked most when he saw that image of Louis—Che Chang!—was not that someone whose username was Gonomad and whose avatar was a vampiric beaver had hijacked his friend's likeness, but that there were so many others who hadn't, who had posted pictures and mementos of their own friends. How could there be so many Louis Changs in the world?

Chapter Twenty-3

They remain late into the summer night, parked under the stars on Gearheart, the new Lover's Lane. The Davenports watch from their living room window, Mr. Davenport timing his morning departures with the changing of the guard, that moment when one reporter is packed up, but the next not yet unpacked. The culture vultures soon catch on and schedule reporters and cameramen on overlapping shifts. It was two days after the inquest, not even two weeks after the Incident, and a carnival had planted stakes in the street in front of their house.

Call the police? Never. The news vans with their lights, antennae, and fresh faces were a relief, an oasis, an outpost of civilization in the deepest recess of a dangerous wilderness, now encroaching from both sides. Understand, please, that the Nubians arrived first—during screen door season, mind you—drumming with the dusk the morning after the inquest. Sunup an hour away, a black school bus with the eye of Horus emblazoned in gold on its sides and the glittering slogan THE SUN RISES IN AFRICA along the back awakened the Davenports when it came to a halt opposite their driveway, amid the cacophony of crunching brakes and backfiring engine and groaning transmission, and disgorged seventeen men dressed in black robes with gold trim and matching fezzes, men who promptly formed a diamond and performed their sun drum ritual.

Can't say much about protesters when it ain't federal land, now can we, mused Sheriff, calling from the car after executing a twenty-point turn. Maybe you should talk to Otis.

The attic armory was opened for the first time since Katrina. From then on, Daron's father insisted everyone carry a firearm at all times, just in case the Nubian threat of reprisals came to fruition, in case divine retribution took a secular turn as it so often did in the South. At the arrival of the news vans, though, the Nubians tempered themselves, being too shrewd to waste airtime, their suddenly sober behavior giving them the appearance and bearing of jilted grooms.

The brides, then, arrived next, their long, flowing white robes raised daintily to the ankles as they descended from the bed of the extended cab dually pickup, each pair taking a position on either side of the tailgate, extending a hand to help the others down, until lined before the Davenport residence, like vestal virgins in their pure white robes, these truly bleached to blind, were twenty-three Klansmen.

Who'dve ever thought I'd be happy to see these assholes? Let's just hope they don't start a gunfight, or a fire, was heard to be said around the block on several occasions, but no one knows by whom.

Finally, as was their way, as Daron had learned in Berzerkeley, a group of miscellaneous white people arrived to involve themselves in affairs none of their concern. This particular group was a brightly colored rainbow coalition (in dress only), complete with rainbow posters and matching rainbow shirts—So cute, said his mom—and the chanting of slogans such as, Equal Rights for All, Abolish Reenactments, and States' Rights = Slaves, Right?

Daron watched from the living room window, his mother at his side, his father refusing to pay it any mind (though he freely expressed irritation at the absence of a cross breeze, which they suffered without, now that the front door was always closed and locked).

Daron, though, found it fascinating. The Nubians and the Klan had said nothing to each other for two days, the camps remained huddled in separate groups, the Nubians with posters reading NEVER FORGET and the Klan with posters reading SOUTHERN PRIDE IS NOT A SIN, their backs more often than not turned to each other like a couple in an argument whose provenance has long been forgotten. Their relationship was soon to be consummated. (In the wake of such moral turpitude, the makeup sex isn't long coming.)

Within the hour of the Rainbow Coalition's arrival, the younger Klan members were pushing the gays, poking them with their sticks. The gays ignored the taunts. They weren't necessarily effeminate or slight, and one blond in particular looked like he worked out a lot. In fact he resembled Arnold Schwarzenegger, the Governator, during his days as the Terminator.

When the Klan grew frustrated because they could not get a rise out of the gays (who were white, remember), the Nubians teased the Klan and finally entered the fray to prove that they, the Nubians, could get a rise out of the gays. But they couldn't, either. (Throughout this, no one poked the Gay-benator.) (As no one would have poked Charlie, who wouldn't have been there in the first place.) It was clear from the expressions, though, that the gays expected harassment from the Klan but were somewhat surprised by the aggression from the Nubians. Throughout the day, they had gradually moved farther from the Klan and closer to the camp of black robes.

Finally, they joined forces: the Klan and the Nubians assaulted the gays, taunting, teasing, calling them faggots and AIDS maggots and HIV magnets, and, when that didn't provoke them, launching rocks and sticks, threatening greater violence yet to come.

His mom said gays were too passive for their own good, but Daron believed they were simply nonviolent. They didn't shrink away from the prods and pokes and name-calling, they merely ignored it, refusing to be roused to anger, and it was this presence of mind, this composure that drove the other two groups mad and started all the trouble. It was in the middle of such a skirmish that Daron risked a dash to the mailbox.

When the news featured a photo of Daron checking the mail with his shotgun, flashing VIGILANTE underneath, the front door vanished in his eyes as surely as the mystical portals of his childhood fantasies.

WHEN HE DID GO OUT, through the back door, no one in town stared. They didn't look at him at all. At Lou's they didn't even greet him when he entered. He was overnight an invisible man, a sensation so eerie he stopped going outside during the day. (Was this what Ellison meant?) On the local radio, a few people even accused him of being in cahoots with Otis, that uppity nigger. When the host chastised a caller for using that word, the caller laughed.

They're the whole problem. Fellow got dressed up like a nineteenth-century nigger. If you do that and you hang from a tree like a nineteenth-century nigger, you're fixin' to die like a nineteenth-century nigger. That's a pretty sure recipe, just like Jim and PBR make a perfect boilermaker.

Sir, that jazz language is uncalled for.

I ain't the one caused all this trouble.

But, sir, don't you understand—the host adopted a mock-lecturing tone—there's no equivalent word for white people?

I know, and it angers me. Been like that since Wilma had Bamm-Bamm. Who wants to say niggered and dimed all the time? I feel kind of left out, but as soon as we get a nigger word for white people, I'll use it. I'll use it like salt, I will. Want to hear a joke?

As long as it doesn't include the word quote-unquote nigger.

This doesn't. A black guy, a white girl, a Chinese guy, and a white guy get into college. Why don't they graduate? First day, they tell the Chinese guy to bring the school supplies. But he ain't there that morning, they're waitin' and waitin', and finally he jumps out of a closet and yells, Supplies!

Daron turned off the radio. He had heard that joke before. Used it like salt, too. Jo-Jo's father used to say that a lot. (Also favored asking the air, What's gonna happen when the jumping beans are run plumb out of Dodge? They'll climb into a Ford and drive that into the ground, too.) A few evenings, Daron had driven to Jo-Jo's house, but he was never home, at least that's what his parents said. They also never invited him in. The third time, they asked him to stop coming back.

He didn't think much of it until he saw Jo-Jo's Facebook page. The old photos of Jo-Jo drinking were all removed. He was reborn and every new photo featured a clean-shaven, innocent-looking lad that Daron would have scarcely recognized were it not for that distinctive short brow. When he frowned, his widow's peak nearly poked the bridge of his nose. In several recent photos, he held a Bible, and in others his fingers intersected like crosses, and in one Daron could clearly see a cross tattoo at the base of his thumb. He remembered Jo-Jo posting to Facebook that he was born again, and he was getting a tattoo to make it permanent, To remind me ev'ry time I yank a beer, but never had this possibility crossed Daron's mind. The same Jo-Jo who once held a beer tab between his thumb and index finger and declared, This is the only ring you'll see on my finger. The same Jo-Jo who posted a photo of himself suited up Gray on the morning of the reenactment, and hadn't made another post in the ten days since. The possibility that someone from Jo-Jo's church knew better than Candice what had really happened at Old Man Donner's nagged Daron. He drove to Jo-Jo's house that night. No one answered the door.

Still, when Agent Denver next stopped by, to again ask if he knew anything about a militia, to again ask if he was being threatened, to again ask if he was protecting anyone, Daron responded, No, comfortable, that was an honest response. There was no way that Jo-Jo would whip anyone. Besides, he'd hung with everybody back in high school. Daron also still doubted Candice's story. It's not that she'd lied, it's just that she was so frantic she might have been confused about some things. She never told the story the same way twice. There was no way that Jo-Jo would whip anyone, even though Daron had to wonder if there was a good chance he knew who did. When he asked his father's opinion, he was told, You can't take back a fart, son. No need to stink things up more than they are. Isn't there someone else Sheriff says you're supposed to call?

However this be, it is plain to a demonstration, that hot countries cannot be cultivated without negroes. What a flourishing country might Georgia have been, had the use of them been permitted years ago? How many white people have been destroyed for want of them, and how many thousands of pounds spent to no purpose at all?

—Anglican preacher George Whitefield, 1751

Wild Bill Hickok toured with a troop of up to one hundred. Three survivors traveled to Little Bighorn every year until they died. Mormons trek the pioneer trail. Gettysburg attracts scores of visitors daily and Washington's Christmas Crossing celebration continues to draw record numbers. Every Yuletide a thousand windows and lawns are illuminated with nativity scenes. The reenactment is not a Southern creation. We may do it better than most, but it is not a Southern creation. It has always played a key role in Braggsville history. After the Civil War, Congress visited town to witness a reenactment of the Battle of Braggsville as part of a campaign to bring the capital here from Milledgeville. Since then, it has continued as a peaceful event, until now, intoned the newscaster, though Braggsville, you may recall, first came to national attention two years ago when local students protested the two-prom system. I have in the studio with me Otis Hunter, mayor of the Gully, and Daron Davenport, the Braggsville native whom many hold responsible for the recent tragedy.

Daron cringed when she said tragedy. Everybody knows better. The first fact they learned in his course on Greek theater (or in any introductory lit theory class) was that a tragedy arose when one faced two competing claims of equal magnitude. Hence, when Antigone is faced with either abandoning her brother Polynices's rotting corpse to cook the air in accordance with Creon's dictates *or* burying her sibling in accordance with family duty, she faces tragedy. When a drunken idiot falls asleep at the wheel or knob or whatever it is and the subway crashes, that is not tragedy. When the term was first explained, Daron appreciated the certainty of the definition and the commitment to exactitude the professor's lecture symbolized, making possible the surety that had so long eluded him. The scales had fallen from his back, as had the fin. From that day forward, whenever he heard the word tragedy, he could tell a lot about a person. The only catch was that he himself did not believe in tragedy. He doubted one would ever face two claims of equal importance. Fuck Creon, Antigone buried Polynices. Family first. Abraham was hands up, slim blade winking, when the Lord stayed his arm. God first.

Take this interview, Daron thought, as yet another example that tragedy is a myth. Exhibit A: Sheriff instructs Daron to win the city back over, but Daron has given up on that. Pride is all he has left; however, when his father says it would be a show of good faith to appear with Otis, Daron agrees. He may be swallowing his pride, but it's important, as his father says, to let Otis know that he wasn't racist, isn't racist, to let the world know that Braggsville is not a racist town. His family is more important than his pride. There was no tragedy. There never could be. No two claims upon the self could be equal. Daron couldn't care less about Sheriff or Otis.

Moreover, before Sheriff made him do the interview, Daron hadn't known that the Gully had its own mayor, and wondered if Otis was the real mayor, or the so-called mayor, in the same way everyone called Sheriff either The sheriff or plain Sheriff, even though he was only the chief of the local police and entrusted with no county-wide authority. None of this had bothered him before, much as he'd always accepted that they called it a mill even though it was a hot air factory.

In all previous appearances, Otis had quietly insisted that he was

reserving his comments about young Mr. Davenport for the day they
met in person. Now they were together, in this makeshift studio
that NBS Charlie-rigged in the newly constructed room at Lou's.
Cameras and lights were mounted on tripods and dark quilted fabric
draped the walls. Their set consisted solely of three chairs grouped
around a central table. The newscaster sat in the middle and her
guests to either side. (Rheanne was only yards away, probably reading
a teen-dream magazine. Would she watch this, the stringy-maned,
guitar-headed bitch? She better. It was live and soon as Daron was
given the chance to speak, he'd tell about sorry all right. He'd tell
them how sorry they were for lying about him at Lou's and the Awful
Waffle. He'd tell them all. Give them lots to holler 'bout.)

Otis looked fifty, his neatly cut hair and mustache both given
over to gray. He wore a blue suit and a yellow tie. Cal colors, thought
Daron. The most notable thing about Otis, though, was his expression. He smiled at Daron from the moment he sat down until the
moment the newscaster completed the introductions, at which point
he rose, walked around the table and gestured for Daron to rise to
his feet, which Daron did only after a moment's delay. He didn't
relish being struck on live television, but perhaps that would be the
best thing that could happen to him now. A little victimhood would
definitely sweeten the stew. Instead, Otis embraced him warmly and
kissed him wetly on each cheek.

Young man, my condolences for the loss of your friend. He made
the greatest sacrifice, and I want to thank you, and—he rustled open
a sheet of paper—Louis Chang, Charles Roger Cole, and Candice
Marianne Chelsea for what you have done. The children are indeed
the future and you young folk have changed the future because you
had the courage to do what none of us have ever done, but always
wanted to do.

Otis turned to the camera as if to a long-lost friend and withdrew
from his inside breast pocket a second sheet of paper. He glanced

at the newscaster, who nodded, before he unfolded it and began to speak.

In the winter of 1864, Braggsville was the last supply stop before the Confederate forces began the steady climb to Atlanta. The troops were wore out something wicked, spiny and sharp with hunger. In Braggsville they were troughed and shod, and their numbers and confidence bolstered when Bragg himself sent his three young sons along. The men of the Gully had been conscripted for months. Atlanta burned, and within three months of sending off his sons, all three were killed in valiant action, we are told.

Bragg never forgave Lee for surrendering at Appomattox and swore that if it was the last thing he did, he'd see the capital moved to a city with some backbone, a town with heart, the true South, the real center of Georgia: Braggsville. Bragg also complained about the deserters amongst the Atlanta upper set, a show of cowardice that only furthered his conviction that Braggsville should be the new capital of Georgia.

First, John B. always said, this here is the peach pit. It's right damn near the center of the state, far closer to the actual center than Atlanta. That vice pit sits up there all smug like it's natural for us to journey nearly to South Cakalacky to see to our own affairs. Second, we's all here. Every single one of us, born and reared or transplanted to this town is still here. Ain't been no deserters. But that weren't true.

In sooth, one farmer-now-soldier turned coat and fled west, beyond the U.S. borders. They said he was originally a northerner, and that type of behavior was to be expected of them because they just couldn't shirk their crude and dishonorable ways. The extreme weather and crowded city life made them cold, untrustworthy, prone to illness, and plumb without honor, not to mention poor cooks. But that weren't true neither.

When Bragg passed, they erected a statue in his honor right

beside the watchtower—underneath which his wife is buried—in the turnabout in the center of town. Over three meters tall, they reckoned if he was alive he could nearly see Atlanta. As it is, he's certainly pointed in that direction. They'd meant for it to signify that he was challenging the citizenry, pointing out their town's future as the one true capital of Georgia, but, unfortunately, it looked like he was kindly indicating the direction to some wayward traveler who had inquired as to the quickest route to Atlanta, and when I-75 was later built he seemed to be pointing to it, and, sadly, it seemed that every year more and more youngsters took his advice and moved to the city for the manufacturing jobs on the Southside and the domestic work on the Northside (that which wasn't reserved for the blacks).

To celebrate the town's ninetieth anniversary in 1920, the city held a pageant complete with a buffet and staged a reading of Bragg's *Declaration of War on the U.S. Traitors* and even had three little boys in gray soldier's uniforms with wings. It was received with all the reverence of the Pope, and for that weekend everyone came together and forgot their side spats and pickle spitting and celebrated their visionary founder. But the next year, the crowd thinned, and it declined even more the year after that. Meanwhile the cities close to Atlanta, like Newnan and Tyrone and Peachtree City, grew into prosperous suburbs in their own right, so in 1960 Braggsville filed another petition, and eventually restarted the reenactments. Attendance shot up, no doubt helped by the growing civil rights movement. In fact, the first modern Braggsville Historical Preservation and Dissemination Society reenactment took place a week after King delivered his *I Have a Dream* speech on the steps of the Lincoln Memorial in the nation's capital.

From 1861 to 1865, the Confederate flag flew all across Georgia. In 1955, the state raised it once more, to protest federally mandated integration. But, funny thing is, they'd never stopped flying Old Dixie here in Braggsville. It wasn't about slavery, they said. It was about the Northern presumption about one man thinking he had the right to tell another man what to do. And what to think. And what to believe.

We in the Gully said nothing. No more.

What no one is telling you is that the so-called deserter was one of Bragg's sons. He died later, because he was found out and put back to gun on the front line. But for three months he hid out in the Gully, where no one would think to look. Only Bragg himself, his son, and one general knew this, and that general went on to become a legislator and sat on the Milledgeville committee that Bragg invited to view this town. That's why over the years the petitions have not been successful for the Olympic equestrian events, the state games, and even the Special Olympics. But we got Walmart in the Gully.

Finished, he took his hand off Daron's shoulder.

Oh, that slick nigger! Daron thought. Was this how Mike Myers felt during that telethon? Daron guessed it was when Quint later told him, You got straight Kanye'ed.

AND WE WERE AFRAID YOU WOULD COME BACK singing *Dancing Queen,* his father declared, trying to make a joke of it later that night. He was alone in his laughter. His mother stood with her arms crossed as though plotting. Elsewhere anger announced itself more vigorously: there was a fire in the Gully, and later a brick thrown through the Davenports' garage window. The next morning, the FBI stationed a man across the street. As Denver explained it, you'll talk when you're ready. I just want you to live until then. He wanted to station the agent in the front yard, but Mr. Davenport refused the offer, even after being assured that his taxes paid for it, instead insisting that very fact gave him the right to respectfully, but forcefully, decline. I don't need no outsiders to protect me in my own town from my own people.

Chapter Twenty-5

Daron was plotting his escape from Braggsville, and finally saw his chance. After the inquest, Louis's family flew his body directly to Malaysia, so his San Francisco remembrance celebration was scheduled almost a full two weeks after his death. Daron discovered the date by reading the school paper online, an act undertaken with trepidation, avoiding the editorials, op-eds, and columns, summoning a discipline quite unlike his usual forays into cyberspace. When he told his parents about the memorial service, they agreed that he needed closure, closure being the only shrink-speak spoken at home. (Can we get some closure on that back door? the refrigerator? your mouth? *Lost?*) Daron packed two days early, picking out his clothes for this four-day trip with even more care than he did when first leaving for college.

He and Candice had not shared a word since the morning her parents picked her up. He'd not seen her since the inquest, making this the longest period of time since they had met that they had gone without contact. The longest week of his life. No IMs, texts, or Facebook messages. No Instagrams or tweets. Simply put, no direct communication, as the lawyers advised, for fear it would be intercepted or misinterpreted, or both, intentionally. Charlie changed his privacy settings because of the endless threats posted to his Facebook wall, and closed his account altogether after he was doxed, and the death threats began to be accompanied by the GPS location of his home or his face pasted over an image of a dangling Saddam Hussein. It was as if the Indians had committed cybersuicide, as if Candice's final post, the four of them at his mom's backyard barbecue, had been a picture of the Last Supper. As it was, Daron didn't remember her asking anyone to take it, which only added to the vertigo he felt when he first saw it: he, Candice, and Charlie flanking Louis, who still stood on his stage, that white plastic chair. Their heads staggered in space reminded him of Olympians on the rostrum: Louis, the victorious gold medal recipient; Charlie, silver; Candice, bronze; Daron, a runner-up, even with a hometown advantage. He was giddy and anxious at the thought of being with Charlie and Candice again, and after learning that he would not see his friends, he suffered a deep dismay at life's caprice, felt bridled by a broad stroke of well-black despair even more suffocating than the Easter Sunday despondency that strangled the eight-year-old D'aron—bka Faggot—when his stripper cousin cautioned him: Yes! Christ can rise from the dead; it's professional wrestling that's staged. Could we have nothing for ourselves in this world?

It was the day before Louis's memorial service, and when his mom called him to the phone, Daron sprinted to the kitchen, breathless as he greeted Charlie, who had only bad news. He had spoken to Mrs. Chang, and they were not welcome to attend.

Is that what she said?

May as well. She said it might cause too much commotion. She said it might, uh, Distract from purpose. So, yes.

Charlie must have been mad to mock Mrs. Chang. Are you going anyway?

D, I can't go to the bathroom without closing the door. That's not a joke, D. It's a report from the field.

Does Candice know?

Yeah.

Have you seen her?

No.

You've talked to her?

Once.

About what?

Everything. Charlie paused. What else is there to talk about?

What did she say about me?

Charlie paused even longer this time. Nothing.

Did you tell your mom?

About what? She already knows everything.

About the memorial? About us being distractions?

Nope.

Did Candice?

Probably not. It doesn't apply to her.

Daron had been excited to hear his friend's voice, and upon learning that they were not welcome attendees, first felt the comradeship of the wrongfully persecuted. That agreeable sensation evaporated, recondensed caustic. At hearing that Candice was permitted to appear at the memorial, Daron wondered if this was how she'd felt about the morgue. Had Candice felt this angry, this betrayed, at learning that Daron and Charlie had seen Louis, but she could not? Even as part of him felt it deserved, that her attending the memorial service from which they were barred neatly repaid a debt he'd considered unfairly incurred, he felt a sting of resentment and tried telling himself that it was not her fault any more than the morgue decision was his.

More than ready to escape the claustrophobia of home, Daron didn't tell his parents, either. If he could make it back to Berzerkeley, he might not return to Braggsville. Three printed tickets to San Francisco hung on the fridge door. Printed because his parents didn't trust e-tickets. Three because Daron's mother refused to let him travel to California alone, worried as she was about reprisals. Malaysian people have gangs, too.

Daron shrugged off that comment, as he did their going catty-wonked at the airline counter in Atlanta, their civility war with the flight attendant, their kerfuffle at baggage claim in San Francisco, their muttering match with the hotel clerk, and that they made him carry all the luggage, all the way, all the time, right up to the room, his father saying, You're young, you don't need a baggage cart. He shrugged it all off. They had been tense lately, and he knew they would be angry enough to swallow vinegar after he told them that he wasn't wanted at the service. Surprisingly, they weren't. His father continued to unpack as if he had not heard Daron, each piece of clothing folded as neatly as a U.S. flag and conveyed from suitcase to dresser with two hands. His mother, though, muttered, Good, before she caught herself. Are you sure? Daron nodded. She unloosed a long whistle as she flounced back onto the threadbare floral bedspread, her arms out like it was an exercise in trust. What are we going to do here?

Get Daron's stuff together.

He can pack himself.

This isn't summer camp.

That's my point.

Roger that. His father closed the drawer with his hip and set his mother's suitcases on the ribbed luggage stand beside the dresser. The drawer action was smooth, as quiet as the rubber clap of a refrigerator door, and he looked back to be sure it had closed. Sightsee? Treat it like a vacation? It costs as much.

May as well make a stay of it. His mother smiled wryly, as often happened when she approved of an idea but intended to put up an argument anyway. She must have changed her mind, because after a moment she agreed, This trip to El Cerrito did cost as much as a trip to El Mexico. She snorted and pointed to the trundle bed on which

Daron sat. His father had wanted to stay in Fisherman's Wharf, his mother near Union Square, but after hours online, they settled for this suburb north of Berzerkeley.

What does El Cerrito mean? mused his mother. Well? She repeated her question.

I don't know.

Then I'm not sure why we're paying for that smartphone.

Methuselah! Three days of this, thought Daron, tapping out his search. A moment later he muttered, Little hill.

Thank you, D-dear.

That evening Daron said he wanted to go for a walk and made his way to the El Cerrito del Norte BART station to catch the train to campus, sunglasses on and a hat pulled over his ears for the ten-minute ride. At every stop he regarded oncoming passengers with apprehension, and when the train reached Berzerkeley, he exited one stop before campus and walked the rest of the way. One of the blue bulletin boards on Sproul Plaza had been dedicated to Louis and was covered with photos, notes, cards, letters, candles. Daron could not bring himself to go close enough to read the notes or inspect the photos. Instead he walked to Candice's dorm, moving always with a crowd. She was not in her room. The roommate's eyes flitted about as if afraid to be seen talking to him. Are you sure? With a deliberate step, the roommate pushed into the hall before opening the door wide enough to grant full view of the posters, the books, and the folded sheets stacked on Candice's stripped bed, the bare desk. I could be mistaken. Asked when she last saw her, the roommate's voice said, The night before your trip; but her tone, her tone—the pitch and enunciation were those usually reserved for eyewitnesses in missing persons cases on shows like *CSI Miami*—her tone said, I last saw Candice when she climbed into the car with you. Those eyes again, as if calling for help. If she calls, ask her to call me, please. The way the roommate nodded, Daron knew she wouldn't keep her promise any more than a Capulet. After the roommate's facial expression and tone gutted Daron, the familiarity of Telegraph warmed his bones with its patchouli-hawking hippies and the exotic scents of the restaurants, until he was on that strip of sidewalk lined with vendors, beggars, and gutter punks, all of whom Louis would have had a joke for. By the time he was at People's Park, he knew it was too soon, too soon.

The next morning, after a few hours of his father's horrid night sounds, Daron awoke to find his parents at the desk, his mother in the chair, his father seated next to her on the luggage stand. His mother was studying a map. She occasionally flipped it over to read the legend before marking another destination. His father took notes and read the landmark descriptions aloud, his voice dramatic when describing Muir Woods or the Golden Gate, and less enthusiastic about the Union Square Shopping District, Coit Tower, and the Mission, though there was at all times a tenderness in his tone, an affection that Daron had understood at last in tenth grade as the reason why they had two cars but so frequently drove everywhere together, his mother dropping his father off even when her Saturday A.M. errands ran in the opposite direction.

Daron had heard that Europeans frequently landed on these shores laboring under the enthusiasm of ignorance and impossible itineraries, unaware of the magnitude of the United States of America, into which every EU country could fit twice and still leave room for most of Mexico to rest its head, leastways those who weren't already doing so. California was no different: the Davenports in the New World. His parents eyed L.A. and the Redwood National Park with equal ardor when both were at least a day's drive away, in opposite directions. He'd expected to play the tour guide, but this morning, knowing more than his parents about anything, even regional geography, frightened him, left him feeling exposed.

You coming?

Let the boy hang out with his friends.

I have to meet a few professors.

Or that.

Want us to come?

It's college, Mom. I kinda have to go alone.

His mother tilted her head as if she needed to do that to take him all in. Are you okay with this memorial? Do you want to go later or earlier, after the crowd? We can go with you. Your father can go in and see if Mrs. Chang is there. Or gone yet, if we go after.

Thanks, Mom, but I don't need to go. I'll find another way.

That day there were three events honoring Louis. After the Changs' San Francisco service, the university was hosting a colloquium and poetry reading on race and liberty (*The Body Linguistic: Syntax, Sexicons and Civil Rights*, bait he wouldn't fall for under any circumstance, having learned the hard way that a sexicon was not a sexy-ass icon, but a lexicon inhabited by big-ass words, and that any course with a title such as Sexing the Victorian was about the lack thereof). There was also a memorial remembrance sit-in at the university student center. Daron wondered what would be said at the colloquium and sit-in, what vitriol they would spray about the South. He wasn't curious enough to attend in person. He wouldn't have considered subjecting his parents to that. Not that anyone would recognize his parents, but they would be forced to witness Daron's humiliation, so those events he mentioned not at all.

As he watched his mother bite her pencil between circling Jack London Square and Alcatraz, and his father begin to memorize the major thoroughfares as he did before driving through any new city, drawing his finger along the streets while reciting street names, Daron felt an unexpected burst of respect and appreciation. They were willing to make a go of it for him, and that emotion harrowed him, provoking Daron to imagine them lost, or worse. He ignored it, but after they left, each kissing him on the head and telling him they loved him, and all that remained was the scent of his mother's hair spray and his father's Brut, he locked himself in the bathroom and cried, overcome by the fear that he would never see them again. After drying his face, he found that they had left him two twenties and a ten beside the alarm clock, and he cried again because he felt, somehow, that he had never seen them before. What else had he missed?

When Daron was sure the tears had stopped—for good . . . finally . . . at last—he again caught the train to campus, arriving a couple hours before the colloquium. He decided against meeting with his professors and instead walked through Memorial Glade and up to the base of the Campanile to watch the waves: both the nearby students and the distant bay. Freshman year he'd often lunched here and wondered vaguely when the campus would feel like home. By the time the 4 Little Indians went to Braggsville, campus felt familiar, like a roommate who plays too many video games much too late at night but is otherwise reliable. The regional peculiarities were now badges. He knew what biodiesel was. He carried his own bag to the farmer's market. He went to the farmer's market! When it was time for the colloquium to begin, he visited Mrs. Brooks. He knocked on her open door, and she perked up at seeing him as no one had in weeks. After guiding him by the arm to a chair, she closed the door, her face as soft as Nana's.

Daron, Daron, Daron. Poor baby. How are you?

Daron picked at the seam of his pants. Mrs. Brooks sat patiently, holding the space, no fiddling with her phone or computer. When the mail alert sounded, she turned off her speaker and waited without complaint. How did she do it? After a long, long silence, he admitted, I don't know what to say. Sorry.

Don't be. Take all the time you want. All the time you need. I'm honored that you came to see me.

How long did you have to live in California before you learned to say things like that without sounding stupid? Without sounding like you were practicing for an appearance on *Oprah*? How long did you have to live in California before you could hear things like that and believe them? Mrs. Brooks, there's an apostrophe in my name.

I know. Your name's been all over the news.

I'm sorry I lied to you, Mrs. Brooks.

Is that a lie, Daron? Can finding a personal truth ever be a lie? What if Chuck is a Chelsey inside? If a young person named Sheryl feels in her heart that she should identify as an Errol, is that a lie?

Daron rolled one shoulder. Chuck and Chelsey? Sheryl to Errol?

Or Saul to Paul. Malcolm X. George Eliot. You have the right to be who you say you are. But you also have that responsibility. You can be Da'ron, D'aron, Daron, or Chuck. But whoever you decide to be, be!

I tried being, he wanted to say. I found a like-minded group, he wanted to say. And look at what happened! he wanted to say. Daron felt his eyes welling. He stood. I have to go.

Wait a minute, Daron. Have you talked to any of your professors?

Don't matter. I'm not staying. The trip. Louis. I missed too much time.

These are extremely unusual circumstances. Try talking to them. Just try. Okay? We can even meet them here if you want to. But you must be willing to try.

Yes, ma'am.

Speak your piece even if your voice cracks.

Yes, ma'am. That advice appeared on many bumper stickers around town—mostly old Mercedeses converted to run on French fry grease, and Priuses. (Prii?) Daron had never shined to the saying. He always imagined a tree nut in ankle bells and tie-dye complaining faintly about global warming. Now, thinking about what it meant, he liked it even less.

And Daron, have you talked to any of the grief counselors? Any counselor?

No, ma'am. Sorry, I have to go. Now he really did.

She handed him a card for student mental health services. And hugged him. Hugged him and he tensed. And hugged him and he melted into it. And hugged him and he hoped—knew it wouldn't happen, but hoped—that maybe he could convince his parents to let him stay. What would his friends at home say? Perhaps his entire high school graduating class would jeer—Turd Nerd!—if they saw him sniveling in this black lady's office, but right now that didn't matter. Were they ever friends, or only fellow inmates?

COULD HE STAY when people only knew bits and pieces of the story, sawdust really, rumors and hearsay gathered from student blogs, Tumblrs, the news, Facebook, patched together into a self-contradictory account—though every news outlet agreed on two points: (1) It was D'aron's idea; (2) D'aron had abandoned his friends. Professor Pearlstein officially said otherwise, but that didn't matter. Hirschfield had been right. Solely by virtue of being from Braggsville, Daron was assumed to be the diabolical mastermind who lured his roommate into a cruel trap. Surprised? At least one of James Byrd Jr.'s assailants knew him, and they still chained him to that truck, stated Francis Mohammed, leader of the Nubians, in one YouTube sermon.

Could he stay when part of him blamed the university for everything that had happened? Almost all of his professors offered to allow him to take incompletes, or submit work late and without penalty, except math class. They all seemed to sympathize, even the math prof, and he couldn't decide how he felt about that because he couldn't decide whether or not to leverage it, whether or not he wanted it, whether or not he deserved it; he was still in a state where solicitude only inflamed guilt.

But could he stay after he talked to the monocled history professor? After that professor suggested making his class project into an honors thesis? No. A repulsive suggestion. It was precisely the perverse type of academic thinking that caused the mess in the first place. It was as though academics thought the entire world was some kind of ant farm constructed for their pleasure and enjoyment and strained observations. He had no place in an institution that suggested personal loss be re-wrought, re-vised, re-fashioned as intellectual palaver, as a paper. Not even for honors.

WHILE DARON WAS WITH MRS. BROOKS, there was no parking on the city side of the Golden Gate Bridge, Coit Tower was closed for repairs, and the fog sabotaged the elder Davenports' afternoon Alcatraz trip. His mother proclaimed there would be no more museums, no libraries, no self-guided tours, no historical sites. When Braggsville was founded, this wasn't even a state yet. No guidebooks, no cultural stops, no on-off bus, no night tour of the bay, no zoo. No Japanese Tea Garden, no Botanical Gardens, no Cliff House. No stores that charge for bags—I didn't charge for travel to get there, nor can I deduct for trunk space utilized to transport said purchases home. (Utilized! Said purchases?) Gesturing around the room, she declared, This is not how I intended to spend this year's vacation, in a land where I can't even get saccharine—with a wink—in a city where April is too cold for capris.

So, for the last day, let's hit the bars and shops. The promise of spontaneity kicked in, and his parents' mood noticeably improved after that decision. Daron's worsened. When he was home, he'd wanted to come back to Berzerkeley. When he was on campus alone, he wanted to go back to Braggsville. When he was with his parents at the highest point in the Presidio, listening to his father whistle his appreciation for the view, Daron wanted to stay in California.

Then when he was back on campus with his father, he couldn't wait to leave. The night before they were scheduled to fly home, Daron's father drove him to the dorm to pack. The door to the room he and Louis had shared was laden with photos, cards, and dollar bills taped in the shape of a heart, but they might as well have spelled C-O-R-O-N-E-R. This time, Daron couldn't enter, couldn't open that door, nor could he be made to.

After his father placed the boxes and bags in the car, he sat on the trunk with his feet on the bumper, as he'd always told Daron not to do, and motioned for his son to sit beside him. Daron hesitated. Come on, son. We've got full coverage.

Daron joined him, both pleased to be asked and aghast at the possibility of being seen. From where they were parked, he could see where Hearst Ave appeared to come to a sudden end, but Daron knew it simply dropped into steep decline, and that decline was the hill the Indians had all tackled when trooping from the other direction after the infamous Salon de Chat.

Don't tell your mother I did this. She already hawks about me spoiling you worse than chocolate-covered bacon. He handed Daron an index card. This was taped to the back of the door. I thought you might want it. He was a funny fellow, a good kid.

Spoiled him? Daron didn't bother asking, How?, when all his father would ever say is, Like now. He inspected the paper. Text was written on one side of the card; the outline of a fish on the other side. Louis divided his sets into fish, bird, and human. Fish meant that a joke worked early in a set; bird, middle; human, late. This piece was among Daron's favorites because he had witnessed its evolution, starting as it did in a conversation. Daron once asked Louis why he didn't date Asian women. Daron did not mention subservience, but Louis called him out on it, guessing with alarming accuracy, as he often did, what Daron's thoughts were before they were apparent to Daron. Later, the joke became:

People always ask me why I prefer black girls, who are all rowdy, or white girls, who are self-righteous, to Asian girls, who are demure, subservient, and obsequious, and make very few sexual or social demands. Well, I always say, if I want a pet, I'll get a dog. Then when I get bored with it, I can eat it if I want, and it won't complain if I don't.

Chapter Twenty-6

When the Davenports returned to Braggsville, their beloved Gearheart Lane was no longer blustering like a three-truck carnival on the set of a doomed B movie. The Nubians and the Klan had pulled up stakes. Only the rainbow coalition remained, and Daron hadn't yet decided if they were against him or not. After a week, most of them—four out of five colors, to be impossibly precise—jumped tent, too, relocating to the park across the street from the courthouse, where once again they were sandwiched between the odd couple. After that, only the occasional busybody set up camp, never staying more than a few hours, Katy-catch-ups like the International Association to Prevent Bullying or Mothers Against Hazing or some tree-rights watchdog NGO investigating the potentially crippling girdling wounds (rope burns) that the giant poplar sustained from the pulley and harness rig, khaki arborists taking tree pulses and earing tree stethoscopes. Daron was relieved to have the front yard back, but disappointed that only three weeks after Louis's death, it felt he was mostly forgotten. Charlie felt the same way.

Daron and he talked a few days after SF. Charlie had seen the Otis interview on YouTube and wanted to thank Daron for trying, even though, You got straight Mike Myered. More importantly,

Charlie wanted to—and did—apologize for letting Daron run off with a gun, for not preventing him from undertaking a fool's task that could have been a life-changing event. Daron felt himself grow cold when he imagined what might have happened if he had found his way to the Gully, and grow colder still—a chill so cold as to feel wet—at this thought, new to him, that Charlie should have stopped him. A knot of silence welted tender while he mulled this over, swelling as certainly as the space between him and his friend. After a moment, the conversation turned to the news, how Charlie was glad to see the coverage fade, as much as he wanted to see Louis remembered, and Daron understood anew what Louis meant when he said that a conversation could have an astral body. When Daron hung up and looked at the picture on his phone, Charlie at Muir Woods, he looked a stranger. This would have upset him greatly had he not already started to doubt everything he knew. On his last drive through town, he'd not seen The Charlies in a single yard. The Hobarts' bumper wore a new saying: I DON'T LIKE HIS WHITE HALF EITHER was replaced with ELECT JESUS TO LEAD YOUR LIFE. Even the Welcome to Braggsville sign was made over like for a morning talk show, and now sported a rainbow heart. The transformation felt a conspiracy, and almost sparked him to reconsider Candice's account of the Incident, until he remembered that he'd asked his mom to hide everything offensive, and that made him guilty of nothing but discretion.

Only now did it occur to Daron that they'd struck out each day, all 4 Little Indians, with the same intention. Candice reading up on Georgia botany and football, Charlie sifting his memory for his own nana's tales of the South, whispered as if specters could be spoken into the room, and Louis's constant efforts to, Keep it real, which translated into assiduous affirmations of all Daron and Charlie said and did. And Charlie, had he really wanted to watch all that Sex-Tube?

In retrospect, Daron understood that he had actively courted his friends, becoming a mirror to their ambitions. By Daron being what they needed, Berzerkeley became less foreign and he more Californian. For Louis, he was the real American, from the original heartland, Clan Davenport staking their claim in the wilderness when the Spaniards were still building missions out of mud and straw; the Davenports fighting the Civil War while Louis's great-great-grandfather stowed away on the SS *Westhall II,* praying Buddha would deliver him anywhere but back to Ceylon. To Candice he was the liberal she thought herself to be in Iowa. Despite his rainy-night accent, an accent that bespoke a region staggering yet under the duress of history, a political microclimate where the past was alive and itching like a hive to be heard, his two best friends were of two different races, opposites, if one could imagine such a thing: He made Louis and Charlie a complete set, a triumvirate.

But Charlie was different, at turns chatty and taciturn within the same conversation, always profound, like wading into a lake in which one knew a sudden drop-off existed, but not where. As he did at Berkeley, Charlie had collected many acquaintances in high school, but few friends. He was the scholarship kid that Daron later became, and he tried to show Daron the keys to success, to school him literally: plenty of face time with the instructors, submit all assignments early for review, request extra credit even when unnecessary, in short modeling a work ethic of twice as good to be equal, but they could only be partners in anxiety because Daron couldn't apply himself that much. Only dumb kids studied, or so he'd thought until meeting Charlie. Besides, D'aron was a black name, Charlie always joked.

But hadn't they shared the same practical attitude about many things—vegetarianism, for example, began for both as a moral stance held with fundamental certainty. They preferred interracial porn only when their own race was doing the penetrating, and they harbored lurid fantasies featuring the young TAs, and neither understood at heart what it was feminists were in such a row about. In every hall were woman professors and woman administrators and some departments, like English, were nearly all female.

Thinking back, was Charlie only looking at the penises? (There were an awful lot of penises in straight porn. In fact, when he didn't think about it, the mortar/pestle ratio was more ghoulish than piquant.) Daron wanted to ask but knew he never would. He had been excited to have a black friend, and now felt a little let down that Charlie was gay. That simply didn't count as much, like if Daron was gay, his being friendly with Charlie wouldn't count as much. You didn't have to be Methuselah to know that gay people were friendlier than the Devil on Sunday morning. (As Slater Jones from 4-H once said, How else you reckon the name?)

But hadn't all three of them swayed after the stats instructor like seamen ashore for the first time in months. The boys weren't hunting MILF, as some crudely put it, but hadn't all three of them felt the spike of a strong and willful attraction operating independently of reason while in office hours with the stats professor. Nearly fifty she was if a day, but that mattered not, because in their eyes three ages defined humans: their own, grad students, and everybody else. Hadn't they all disagreed about whether the photos on her desk were of children or grandchildren. Hadn't they all fidgeted in that backless chair, smitten by her voice, the soft German accent, gray feathered wings, ripe fruit scent, feigning confusion over problems, leaving with their book bags covering their laps, ashamed that she who possessed this allure was so matronly, and yet even more sensuous because of that fact. Through her window in winter the hills of Tilden Park, flush with snow, glowed like full, pale breasts. Hadn't they all made a point to avoid mentioning Freud because, You can't trust every diagnosis to some old dusty tome.

At end, it was Candice he wanted, and Charlie he missed, at least the Charlie he thought he knew, and Daron considered his education complete, for he had learned the most important lesson: Nothing was as it seemed.

With them he was the opposite of what he was with high school friends like Jo-Jo, with whom he watched *Baywatch* and, later, porn, beheaded mailboxes and knighted possums, skipped rocks and classes. Jo-Jo? Did he ever like *BSG* as much as he claimed? Probably not. He certainly never wore the *BSG* T-shirt Daron gave him for his sixteenth birthday.

No. Nothing was as it seemed.

Virtue, e.g., exempli gratia, for example, he always thought meant: a good thing, a positive quality or characteristic; he did not think it to mean simulated as opposed to actual. A few days after SF, he received from school a notice hand-addressed to Daron Davenport. His mother blew her whistle. Ignoring her complaint, brushing the spelling off as a typo, Daron ripped open the letter to discover that he was being summoned to a Faculty and Student Review Board for a disciplinary hearing regarding his role in recent unfortunate incidents. The letter quoted some code of conduct he allegedly *endorsed by virtue of enrolling*.

No, nothing was as it seemed. Words were different, definitions ramifying until a profusion of meanings rendered them meaningless. Review meant investigation, just as religious meant superstitious, life of the party meant insecure, and standing up for oneself, macho. Holding a door for a woman? Chauvinistic. Words he'd long thought he understood grew to unwieldy dimensions, taking on new connotations and denotations both, over the last couple of years. Currency, for example, also meant recency (which wasn't in many dictionaries), as well as whether or not an object possessed value at certain times and in particular circumstances, like the day he tried to use Braggsbills a few miles over in Vickstown. Of course there was also recent, of recent-unfortunate-incidents fame, recent meaning, in this case, that Louis's death was three weeks past, but still felt to Daron like that morning, every morning. And the lesson to be learned from it escaped him.

He didn't understand how different his education had been, how profound his deficit, until arriving at Berkeley, where he learned that being valedictorian in a small segregated high school was about as honored as Confederate dollars. Likewise, what he learned in Berkeley was a grossly inflated currency with zulu value at home, as his parents unintentionally demonstrated when they reviewed his transcripts during a brainstorming session, as his mother termed family meetings.

What! D'aron broke curfew? D'aron let Marci copy off his test? D'aron was caught shoplifting? We'll have a little brainstorming session at home. It was a term borrowed from the younger teachers, the ones who also said that, Everyone is a winner, No one is a loser, and Every effort is worth an A. To storm the brain. Like a fort! Like a hurricane! The term had a cosmopolitan air that excited his mom, who read parenting magazines with a keen appreciation for her geographical isolation, but disgusted his father, who said, If a picture is worth a thousand words, I reckon a kick in the ass must be worth at least a million, and I'm one damned generous Christian dictionary.

But D'aron was too old for corporal punishment. Depositing him across the knees conjured new connotations, as his mother discovered the hard way when one of the young teachers walked in on her punishing D'aron for skipping a week of ninth grade math and spending the afternoons at Pickett Rock pokering with Jo-Jo. The next twelve weeks of mandated Wednesday counseling sessions ate up work hours and raised issues that Mrs. Davenport was well prepared to keep buried away her entire life as opposed to exhuming in a windowless office furnished like a regional airport hotel. As she explained during the last and final psychological suppository session, walking out instead of responding to yet another question conflating her father and sex, This is worse than coffin birth. I'm perfectly happy being unhappy if this is what it takes to be happy.

And when his father, mad as a wet cat, last raised the hickory switch to tan D'aron's hide—in tenth grade—the boy run off and spent the night at Quint's, avoiding his old man for a week.

Daron, for his part, thought talking was the worst possible thing to do with his parents. He had never gotten along better with them than during those months in Berkeley when they communicated primarily through texts and e-mails, when Reach Out and Touch Someone became Reach Down and Type Something, but if he texted his mom while she was in the same room, a common practice with his friends, she made a horse face that broke his heart.

Brainstorming, therefore, had at last taken root in popular opinion throughout the household. In this session, they were to come up with job possibilities. Daron wanted to take a one-year leave of absence from school. His father knew Daron didn't want to enter the hotbox even as a visitor. The house rule, though, had always been, School or work! (Also often intoned in the manner of Robert Duvall in *Apocalypse Now* and followed by a humming of *Ride of the Valkyries*.)

But after reviewing their son's record of completed courses, and hearing a brief summary of each, they were flabbergasted. Math and science, yes, but [Novel, Nov-ooo, Nove-o, Noo-voo?] Russian Cinema, The People's History, Introduction to Ethnic Studies: The Native Today? It was as if these classes existed only to prove that they could. His father rose from the kitchen table, bearing his weight with his knuckles, leaning over Daron. These are like gonzo porn.

At least they get paid for that, don't they? asked his mom.

With a hairy, calloused hand, his father picked a syllabus out of the pile and read a course description: This class will prepare students to recognize and become knowledgeable of people's biases based on

race, ethnicity, culture, political ideology, sexual orientation, age, religion, social and economic status, and disability. Students will also
learn to recognize how dominant culture influences marginalized
groups. She-it. God-der-damn-it. What about hair and eye color? Or
foot size? I could have saved you, no, me, a bunch of money. At least
for what this class costs.

It's not all critical theory. We learn about the world differently
now. You didn't . . . you know.

His father stood behind him and placed a hand on Daron's shoulder. His mom following suit, Honey, please.

His father took several deep breaths, squeezing Daron's shoulders
tight enough to send a warning to his neck. Critical theory, you say?
Named assly, all right.

Can you explain that better, dear?

School's different now. (Daron stands at the free-throw line,
gathering his energy. No bouncing, no lead-in, folks, he just shoots
and . . .) I know it might seem strange, but I'm honored that you
share your feelings with me. (. . . brick.)

Frowning, his mother blinked as though momentarily blinded.

Are you going to feel honored when I knock you into next week?
I will. His father cracked his knuckles as he picked up another syllabus. Listen to this one. He snapped the paper in the air. Don't
believe everything you think. His father pondered that a moment.
Ain't that the truth. That professor's a real genius. I don't need to go
to college for this stuff. I woulda told you this, son: People generally aren't too fond of people who are different. No one can warm
to everybody. That ain't never gonna change. Only thing'll change
is what counts as different, from time to time. So, try to take 'em as
individuals. Know you can't fix the world. Get rid of niggers, you
got coloreds. Get rid of coloreds, you got blacks. Get rid of blacks,
you got African-Americans. It's all the same if you don't like 'em.
See, 'cause if you don't like 'em, you'll make some new shit that's too

clever for them to know all fuck what's happening. Like Ed down in purchasing, he calls 'em Mondays. You think that changes what's in the man's heart? You think a different word confuses his emotions? No. Why Mondays? Why? Why? Nobody likes Mondays. Do I agree with Ed? No. He's funny, a real cut, but I don't agree with him. I woulda guessed you didn't either and that I didn't have to pay for my son D'aron Little May Davenport to take a class to tell him to act right and treat people goddamned fairly. It's a damned insult to your mother and me. It would be like if we went out and rented ourselves a kid to come live here on the holidays. Analyze stable and dynamic inequities? Analyze heterogeneous interactions? Analyze class markers in language? Professor, there is another word in analyze that oughta put you on the scent of how this smells to me. He turned away from Daron, skimming the rest of the list as he paced, Diversity and Social Justice, Urban Fieldwork, the New Democracy.

What the hell are those, he demanded to know, besides the titles of angry speeches? And what the hell, both parents demanded to know as they left the kitchen, did he have any right to be angry about?

For one, Daron was angry about the review board. When he e-mailed his professor to inquire about it, the professor promptly replied, and when Daron wrote him again, he again promptly replied, and so the exchanges proliferated without ever clarifying, to Daron's satisfaction, the particulars of the Faculty and Student Review Board:

> Dear Daron,
>   Again, let me share how saddened I was to hear about the tragedy that occurred in the wake of your heartfelt attempt to cast light on the gross hypocrisies of reenactments as a commemoration of states' rights. Most distressing is the ensuing media windstorm and the events you experienced in town following Louis Chang's passing.
>   The most anyone can hope for in this country, whether they

know it or not, is to never be made aware, to never know—
definitively, undeniably, with religious certainty—how the
accident of race has charted their life, for better or for worse.
Though realizations of that sort, facing that monster, are good
for the soul, they rob us of the illusion of autonomy, liberty,
free will, agency, and replace those oft noble, always necessary
hallucinations with fate, chance, and providence, reminding
us of the effect that others, capricious or willful, may have on
our lives. The enormity of this realization can be crushing,
especially to a sensitive soul.

In truth, we earn little of what we take.

You have wavered between pride and prejudice on the
South. Do not idolize California, we have our share of prob-
lems and have become a prison state in the last twenty years.
Our institutions eerily resemble post-Reconstruction chain
gangs, but without the chains. The machinery of this cepha-
lopod operates a three-card monte, but the chips always end
up in jail, which here means being thrown in solitary for even
possessing ethnic literature.

I hope that you will return to UC Berkeley next fall. You
would find the distance invigorating, and should you choose
to continue this project as a reflective essay, a documentary,
or, as I suggested at our meeting, a novel, consider my full
support extended.

Yours in truth and freedom
until justice rolls and freedom rains,
Professor P.

For kicks, Daron replied, Can it be a graphic novel? To which
the professor replied, Certainly, still with no mention of the review
board.

He was also angry about Candice. Just that morning he found a black footie with orange piping and an orange toe box, and imagined sorting it into her pile while she hummed along elsewhere in the house, tickled to have a boyfriend who embraced housework in that clumsy puppy way, but that was not to be.

For reasons inarticulate he knew it could not happen, not with Candice's professor parents, originally from New York, oh the mysteries of that city—Woody Allen; mafiosi; bearded Jewish diamond dealers; *Warriors,* come out to play—could not happen any more than a cop could say, Sorry, could not happen any more than D'aron could wing a Gull. In fact, back in high school, when Jean, a Gull, asked D'aron to prom with his sister, D'aron said he'd be out of town, or rather, he agreed as such when Jean suggested it. He wasn't lying. Jean said it first. No. Nothing was as it seemed.

No. Nothing was (exactly) as it seemed. But neither was it always the opposite.

When Jean asked D-nice to prom with his sister, D-nice said he'd be out of town, or rather, he agreed as such when Jean suggested it. He wasn't exactly lying. Jean said it first. And, boy was D-nice relieved when Jean suggested it. Hell, D-nice pocketed that idea quicker than found money. Jean was more Jo-Jo's friend anyway. Like everyone else who made varsity by their sophomore year, Jo-Jo had a friend in the Gully. D-nice knew they practiced together or worked out sometimes, but he didn't know how good of friends Jean and Jo-Jo were—or how good of friends Jean thought they were—until Jean asked Jo-Jo to prom with his sister. Jo-Jo claimed he'd be on front counter that night. None of them said anything for a moment. Just stood there behind the visitors' bleachers taking long draws on the Pall Malls Jo-Jo stole from Mrs. Lee's General & Feed.

When Jo-Jo said, Front counter, D-nice didn't ask how Jo-Jo knew his schedule that far in advance when he couldn't remember which jersey to wear on game day. After Jo-Jo said, Front counter, Jean turned to D-nice, cocking his own coffee bean as he did so, offered more than asked, Bet you got work or something going on out of town, too, don't you, D-nice? Elseways you could stand for Jo-Jo. D-nice nodded. What else was D-nice to do? What else was D-nice to say if Jean didn't comprende that some white people earned points for attending the Gully's Bruiser prom, and others anted them up, and among his friends were only anteers, could only be anteers? Among his friends were the muscle in the big brick hotbox, not the shirtsleeves in the rib. Later, when D-nice mentioned this, and winked like he knew Jo-Jo wasn't really working, Jo-Jo tossed him a thrashing glance the likes of which he'd never before given him.

When prom night pranced up, the one night when cummerbunds were as plentiful as belly button rings, Jean straight vultured Main Street slow as cold butter, times three he did, before squeaking sneaker into Mrs. Lee's General & Feed, first pacing around his Ford LTD a few times like to get his horns sharpened, his shoulders winged out like he was rearing for confrontation. D-nice watched the whole thing from across the street, stayed safely inside Lou Davis's—waiting, waiting, waiting, it felt—waiting so long that Rheanne accepted a date he didn't offer, waiting for Jean to come out grinning like a crow just how he did not five minutes later, nipping at a cone he most certainly didn't break a bill on.

At that sight D-nice felt a deliberate relief slip right up next to him close as a crowded pocket. Jo-Jo and Jean hadn't shared a word between them or practiced passing for even a handful of the three weeks and five days until prom night. Jo-Jo would act himself again, as he had not done for the three weeks and five days he and Jean were incommunicado, twenty-six days Jo-Jo had enumerated with dramatic gnashing, counting them off like a prisoner, bellyaching until a grist-biting envy grabbed piercing hold of D-nice's left ear and nearly drove him to find Jean and tell him something Nana did say:

Just for a reverend is in the Lord's house don't make it his sermon, or his sheep. Was it true? In sooth, D-nice didn't know.

But he knew that he wanted to scream those three-and-some-odd weeks Jo-Jo was off his squash, punch something and scream, yell about it all, the two proms, the anteers and the antees. Punch the proms, the anteers, the antees, kick them all in the ben-was. Then the next year come 'round, Jo-Jo surprised them all and went to the Bruiser prom with Jean's sister.

ALL JO-JO SAID WAS, It ain't free, D, it ain't free. And it ain't what it looks, either.

When Jo-Jo was in fifth grade, his parents worked the night shift, leaving him in the care of his fat-cracklin' half sister, whom Quint was stuck on sticky as blackstrap molasses. Whenever he four-wheeled out to see Jo-Jo's sister, Quint dragged D'aron along, his rationale being that it was lonely pups most likely to piss on the sofa. While Quint and Jo-Jo's sister made cow sounds in the back room, Jo-Jo and D'aron played *Madden NFL* on Xbox, camped on the couch, slouching, the one football position at which D'aron excelled.

However he meant it, Jo-Jo was right when he insisted, It ain't free. After Jo-Jo, who never missed a day of school or work, took off for Bruiser prom, he was fired, and coach benched him for a month, even though it cost the team three games, and Jo-Jo missed playing for the scouts. He didn't complain a minute. Just smiled and said he was always running late and it finally caught up with him. D'aron nodded, wanting to believe him, all the while thinking everything was exactly as it fucking seemed, people just preferred to pretend otherwise.

Nothing fires up the disco balls like sexual assault. When you want to get the cops out quickly, lights all the way, you don't report a murder. Fun's over. You don't report a mugging unless you're witnessing it. After a mugging, they'll take a report over the phone if you let them. And burglary? Depending on where you live, those barely get house calls these days. If you want the police to come out quickly, ASAP, you report a rape. They fly to a rape, some for the wrong reasons, but they fly. They go code blue-and-white all the way. They might get to be a hero. And unlike bank robberies, no officer has ever died investigating a rape or been shot after walking in on a rape. The other thing about reporting a rape is that it involves lots of people. Needs cops, counselors, investigators, an ambulance, rape kits, EMTs, emergency room doctors. It's more than just taking a report and driving off. You only got two EMTs. So that's your message to me. I'm still not sure what you're trying to say. But you called for help and no one came. I'm here now. You can tell me. 'Cause the thing is, D'aron, I think you knew all this already.

Daron mouthed a noncommittal O.

They were in the crowded lot of the big cold box, where even the parking spaces were bigger than in Berzerkeley. Daron had taken to frequenting stores that allowed him anonymous interactions, not that he needed to shop. His parents bought everything, but there were some items he didn't want to ask them for, purchases that he'd rather make himself. With their money, of course. He didn't need his mother commenting on his penchant for gourmet chips or his father hawking about him spending five burritos on a teakettle catalogue, as he called fashion magazines. Not that his father didn't have a point about the cost, but since coming home, Daron sought out *Details* or *Esquire* or *GQ,* one per week, an exercise in secrecy he now understood to be rivaled only by his clandestine acquisition of dick slappers during his younger years. The exhilaration of those moonlit sorties to the trash bin had withered not one bit the winter night he ventured into the backyard too early and found his father carefully wrapping three girlie mags in a plastic bag before tossing them. *GQ* and *Esquire* and *Details*? How could he explain that he read these like they held the key to his future as surely as those *Playboy*s? And so he snuck out, but apparently wasn't sneaky enough because today Denver's shadow had fallen over him before he could unlock the trunk, and the agent launched into his speech on rape without so much as a hello.

Families ambled past, some with two shopping carts—each loaded like Santa's sleigh. Daron felt a moment of superiority, like an expat come to the village market to procure specialty items undervalued by the natives. In fact, the only time he had seen anyone else perusing one of those three magazines, a rivet of jealousy pinched him right in the belly button until the tourist—and he was clearly a tourist, in that green felt Peterbilt hat—walked off empty-handed. Daron survived that, but perhaps not this. He was embarrassed to be seen here, and the fact of his embarrassment embarrassed him even more. There was a big box every two towns, so he'd find another, not that he expected to be in Braggsville much longer. He wanted to be away from all of it, FBI included.

A gust of wind swept Denver's windbreaker up under his arms. He smoothed it out and buttoned it, while scanning passersby as if to see if anyone had noticed. Why don't we get in? After Daron paused, he added, Your car.

No. Yours.

The usual laptop and electronics were installed, though the FBI cruiser was more luxurious than expected. The seats were leather, the dash all digital. But it was cluttered like a bachelor pad with newspapers, Barq's cans, and fast food wrappers on the floorboards. Plus the agent used those beaded seat covers usually seen in cabs. Denver buckled himself in, registered the alarm on Daron's face, and unbuckled. Habit. He settled back into his seat. Cal, they call it, right? Top public school in the world. So, I don't know how much of this is new to you. None I think. Why the call?

It was what I thought. Daron leaned back and struck the metal grate partitioning the backseat. At least he wasn't back there. Was this a strategy? Invite suspects into the front seat, and let the backseat silently threaten with its presence alone? (Good seat, bad seat?)

You want to take a drive? Afraid of being seen?

No.

Denver placed his phone on the console between them and scrolled through it with an awkward pawing motion before turning it toward Daron with an almost regretful look. Listen:

The voice was uneven, the tone carved by a black urgency, the cadence staggering, almost serrated, the words tumbling over themselves like racing piglets as the 911 operator repeated his questions, his attitude even and professional, as the caller howled that there had been a rape! Someone else had reported it, too? But who? Daron thought he recognized the edge of dread, could imagine the pacing, hear the slogging steps, the hand slapping the counter or wall or table—Listen!—picture the jolting arms, the winding jaw, the thumping that punctuated each repetition, the mantled face, which at last he knew as his own.

Well?

Well?

Who wouldn't come after that call? Who would have the heart? Only someone who already knew there wasn't any rape. I've spoken to Miss Chelsea. I'm convinced she's not hiding anything. She says she wasn't raped. You said she was. Usually it's the other way around, women making accusations, men denying them. How would they all know that she wasn't raped? They were all there. And you wanted to make sure someone knew it, that I knew it, or whoever would eventually come from the outside world would know it. Why? And you knew that after this fiasco, someone was coming from outside Braggsville, whether it was the GBI, FBI, or the real county sheriff. So, why?

You should have seen her.

I have. I've seen the photos. She was dressed like a slave.

I was confused. And I hadn't seen the outfit.

But you knew she was dressed as a slave. You dropped her off that morning.

They changed into their slave outfits after we dropped them off.

Charlie called too, but he didn't report a rape. Sounds like something else happened between those two calls, like you figured out what really happened back there and knew you couldn't report it because you'd be calling the cops to report the cops, so you blamed it on the Gully, knowing the cops wouldn't investigate because they knew damn well where every player on the field was, every one of them. Everyone. You didn't say a kidnapping, which is more what appeared to have happened, with Louis still missing, as far as you knew. Candice was fine but you reported her raped. At that point, Louis was in trouble. Even Charlie says that in his call, says something in the background, repeats it, says they took Louis. But you don't mention Louis at all. I think you realized that they knew where Louis was. Couldn't sound an alarm about that. It sounds like you

WELCOME TO BRAGGSVILLE

249

were trying to raise a lynch mob, except they all had a previous engagement.

Daron uh-huhed and mm-hmmed.

Is there a chance anyone had it out for you, thought that it was you hanging up there?

No. Daron laughed. That might be true now.

What's in the Holler?

Nothing.

You have to travel through the Holler to get to the Gully, don't you? You know that. First you say Holler, then you say Gully. You add that like a slap to the side of a TV. Then you start to use them interchangeably. Why?

Daron thought about it. Had he? Even though he wasn't sure he believed it, he didn't want to listen to the call again. He blew his cheeks out like bellows. That was a mistake.

What's back there?

Daron shrugged.

Everyone's heard the urban legends about the murder victim whose last act is to scrawl his assailant's name on the floor in blood. Sounds like that's happening here.

Maybe. But I can't right figure what that means, Agent Denver.

Still playing it close to the chest? Okay. That's not the real reason I'm here. How about Vallejo, California? Six Flags? He paused to appreciate the surprise on Daron's face. You have done this before, but this time was different. Things went wrong in Braggsville. But not how you expected. So what are you trying to tell me? Tell me about that. Six Flags tells me you are a political agitator, not one to antagonize. There were protests almost every semester you were at Cal, that your thing?

No. Daron rubbed his face wearily.

What were you trying to reveal here? What were you trying to tell me? At least tell me about Six Flags, and maybe I can figure out the rest. How about that?

A belch escaped him unexpected.

Denver fanned the air. I won't offer to buy you a cheeseburger for lunch.

Daron laughed. He shifted and the seat cover clacked. Why would anyone want to sit on an abacus? He felt tight inside, like his ribs were poking his lungs. [What had he thought when Candice came stumbling into the backyard? The only sensible thing. If Louis was haranguing people and wearing blackface and Candice was dressed as a slave, of course the Gulls might retaliate, like when your parents offered to *really* give you something to *really* cry about.] He recalled that child's drawing from the inquest, the one hanging on the wall behind the Changs, the one with the yellow coils of smoke hazing the roof. That was what the 4 Little Indians had done, stoked a blaze in a house without a fireplace or chimney, and his head felt too much like that house.

Chapter Twenty-8

How had they discovered Ishi anyway? A play, wasn't it? Yes, a play. Candice had wanted to go. Was it really her idea? You aren't sure. Louis was cramming for an exam and backed out. Charlie went along, though, and liked it. You were angry. She was angry. Charlie was a Saints fan, as he described it, about all things race. Best advice my father ever gave me: When you know your team can't win, you hope, pray, and cheer, but don't bet, curse, or get in anyways angry when they lose. That's how you live without your heart drawing up into your ass.

You kicked the wall after that show. Shucked your throat to work up enough phlegm to dot every light post in the plaza. Candice, too. *Ishi: Last of the Yahi,* a *play,* had done nothing for your evening plans: *play,* eat, smoke, drink, PlayStation. It was Wednesday, that semester's Friday. Lower Sproul Plaza, UC Berkeley—California even—all rifling indifferent through your every illusion, all cutting a profile like Lyle Grant when you found him neck-deep in your locker. It stung the same after, too, always throwing chin over the shoulder, shading the combination (his was next to yours) and window-shopping every opportunity for revenge. Lyle, everyone knew, was stubborn enough to argue with a sign and would just as soon kill himself to avoid caring about another person, an oak toad done up as a bullfrog.

But California, once plural, that LL's going back to, the Mamas and Papas' dream, Cali whose Wiki page you memorized that summer before freshman fall, the thirty-first state, named after a fictional paradise peopled by black women ruled by Calafia the warrior queen, thought for hundreds of years by the Spaniards to be an island, was part of the same mass, another undigested pea in a big pile of shit.

(Maybe that Salon de Chat prof had a reason for giving YOU an unofficial tour of campus and its unregistered residents: the man under his bicycle like an upturned turtle, the tai chi practitioner in court jester shoes, the man who wore many hats like a Dr. Seuss character.)

And you should have known you couldn't escape Braggsville. Not even when your debate coach and eleventh-grade English Lit warden, Mr. Buchanan, the mayor's brother, called you—Hey Ron-Ron!—into his lounge, one of the few single-occupancy offices, one of the fewer even with a couch, and beckoned you sit closer and closer, until your knees were nearly touching, until you could smell Old Spice and cold fries, took you in with his eyes, and said more than asked, Your parents didn't go to school?

You tensed, recalling that fifth-grade workshop about how some kinds of people preyed on the weak and poor, about stranger danger not being all strangers, which was why you couldn't always spot the dangers. The teacher had posted pictures on the wall of cab drivers and policemen. The entire class had acted it out even. Don't get scared. L.A.F.! Loudness. Acceleration. Focus. Yell loud for help, and loud for them to stop. Run as fast as you can to the nearest authority all the while imagining yourself accelerating like the fastest car in the world. Focus on recalling the details so you can be a helpful witness.

Instead you W.I.S.H. Want. Imagine. Solicit. Hope.

Behind you a door. May as well be closed. You know what's in those halls. Before you are holidays at Mr. Buchanan's home with

Mrs. Buchanan's pearls flashing and the gaudy jewelry tinkling at her neck. Mr. and Mrs. B, as they preferred to be known, seated at opposite ends of their hand-carved oak table, long as tomorrow, the edge traveled by the same Victorian scroll that adorned the dining room wainscoting in the family's English estate house all those generations ago. (Same as the Braggs, for the Braggs and Buchanans were cousins.) Before you is the side table (nothing but dining on the dining room table), where they stack the wrapped books they individually selected for every Gully student at Christmas, and a few lucky white ones, too. And everyone knew Mr. Buchanan had friends, special students, apprentices, those whose potential deserved prodding and whose prospects deserved probing, and you—for the first time since tenth grade, when you learned that more degrees meant more money, and a bigger vocabulary meant a bigger paycheck—were not ashamed to admit that neither of your parents went to school, withholding that your father was doing something online with economics. Yes, you wanted more.

If you want to get out of here, I've found a way.

And you scooted a little closer. Waiting.

Waiting.

With two hands he presented you a folder scaled in Post-its, a suitcase of brochures, explained what *first-generation college student* meant, sent you on your way. Not before saying, Berkeley, they're all good, but Berkeley is special. You can be whoever you want there. They won't mind you not hunting. A wink. Then, he sent you on your way. No Christmas invitation. No wrapped books on the side table. No follow-up meetings. Oh the elation upon learning he'd been fired. Was to be tried. For embezzlement. Not even romantic. The elation. The relief.

Jo-Jo told you about it when you were home for Christmas vacation, how the local editorials defended him and condemned the school board for fiscal mismanagement, how he denied all allegations of wrongdoing, how he still trooped through town like a sergeant inspecting the barracks. How everyone acted like that was okay.

You would be different. Why? ¿Por qué? To prove that you were. After *Ishi: Last of the Yahi,* the play, you watched Candice simmer outside the theater, pace between the worn wooden benches, black and pitted as old piers in an abandoned port. She walked with short steps, nearly scampering when excited, always with the steady seesaw swish of women who stepped from the heel and not the toe. When she was drunk or angry, the small heavy bag she appeared to always imagine herself carrying became a large light one as her right arm swung wider and higher, as it did then. Your seats had been in the back. Student seating allowed for last in, first out. By the time the auditorium emptied, Candice had calmed down and taken a seat on one of the worn benches, still breathing heavily. We need to do something! More people should know about this.

Charlie gestured to the crowd around them, thinning as patrons wound their way past the crumbling student learning center, where Mrs. Brooks's office was located, to catch the train downtown, or mounted the wide steps to the fountain on Upper Sproul Plaza, or veered to grab joe at the MLK Student Union, under renovation, or forked like a school of fish around Eshleman Hall, in the process of being demolished.

That's not enough. (What had Nana always said? The good Lord speaks with fire on tongue but man heeds man's advice only if spoken softly, almost hummed.) If I were a Native American, I'd be pissed. Spoken slowly, almost sung, one eye on Candice to be sure she heard.

She had.

And so YOU had ended up at Six Flags, contesting a history that no one knew or cared about anyway. Daron told Denver as much as he could recall about the ashes, their plan, the park director letting them go with a warning. Those details were fuzzy now. What he now remembered most, but didn't share, was Louis conducting interviews while they waited in line, all four Indians leaning like fishing poles on the crab, with backs arched and necks craned to avoid the sun, their bums against the railing, the smooth wrought-iron banister pressed into Candice's butt like a barbell across a mattress. In that position and dressed to scrum, with her bowed back and vaulted front, Candice resembled a ship figurehead, her own prows making it impossible for Daron to look at her. Daron's eyes everywhere but her and that padded bra. Charlie nonchalant as always, like that was his game. Not Louis.

Louis had decided that each bra cup had its own gravitational field, its own personality, and they were indeed different—the left one larger and boxy; the right one smaller and bubbly. He named them Mary-Kate and Ashley.

Tell me, Ashley, what's life like in Kate's shadow?

Daron laughed. It was hard not to smile at that one.

Mary-Kate was shy, unaccustomed to attention. Ashley was perkier and more outgoing. Mary-Kate ate carefully but was known to binge. Ashley ate whatever the hell she wanted and never gained a pound. Mary-Kate was a baritone, Ashley a soprano. Mary-Kate liked to be pinched; Ashley, sucked. Mary-Kate liked the sun, Ashley avoided it. Daron knew this because Louis was the voice of Mary-Kate, and Candice, miraculously, that of Ashley, and neither one of them, to hear the two tell it, could wait to ride Medusa and set Ishi free.

When they were slow to answer, Louis tapped them with his pen and made a noise like that of drumming a live microphone. And all Candice did was laugh an encouraging laugh. Back in their room later that night, Daron had expressed his shock that Candice let Louis get away with that.

Why not? One piece of advice my uncle gave me and made me swear never to share is the secret to women. Try this: Talk to them like they are regular people, prime the pump with a question or something, and then shut up and listen.

That's it?

Yeah.

And first class isn't going to L.A., either.

Okay, maybe there's more.

Well?

Like I said, it's a secret. He made me promise not to share it with anyone.

Screw you.

First class wasn't going to L.A.: their code for secrets not worth keeping, but kept nonetheless. Or, for lies of necessity. It was from a joke Louis had admittedly stolen:

How's the pilot get the stubborn Southerner who crashed first class to go back to coach?

What?

A Southerner on a flight from Lower Alabama to Los Angeles sees an extra seat in first class and cops it. The seatmate warns him off, the flight attendant gives him the old bartender's last-call line: you don't have to go home but . . . , the head flight attendant leans into him pretty hard. He stays put. You know. Southern pride or whatever. They call the pilot, who whispers something to the passenger that makes him pop up hotter than burned toast and sprint back to coach. What does he whisper?

What does he whisper?

First class isn't going to Los Angeles.

Daron had laughed at the time, and probably would again. He'd laughed at every joke Louis told, even if it was two days later and the chortling erupted while he was in line at Togo's or taking notes or on BART. If Louis could make that joke again, he would change Southern pride to something like These Colors Don't Run or another one of the bumper stickers he had tweeted. Daron, though, wasn't sure that he would find it as funny. First class was going to L.A., or New York, or Atlanta, or San Francisco, or wherever coach was going. The Southerner would end up in the same queue as everybody else, whether he knew it or not, whether they wanted to or not, peanuts in the same pod.

Chapter Twenty-9

The summer before ninth grade was the sweet spot. Nervous as he was, D'aron nevertheless expected the best. High school could not possibly be worse than middle school. Ninth grade would mean AP electives, competitive academic teams, and more choices at lunch. He would be allowed to set his own schedules, so he would be liberated from the lockstep of banality and mediocrity. Like many kids, he had often fantasized that his real parents would arrive and whisk him away to another planet where his unique skills would be in high demand, most notably his power to restore the undead, or destroy them if needed. That fantasy was over, but there was still high school. That life would be better demanded little proof, he need look no farther than that summer before ninth grade.

It was well before his cousin's first extended stay at hotel vo-tech. That May, Quint had been, Fuckin' finally released from thirteenth grade for good behavior. He had time to spare. Until then, Quint had paid him scant attention, but that summer they hung daily, jouncing along the former county line road in Quint's B210, Black Sabbath in the backseat compliments of a speaker he'd liberated from the cafeteria. Afternoons at Little Gorge, under shadow of spruce, watching girls stretch their limbs across the water, hoping, praying, imploring the gods to whisper into Krystal Rae Foldercap's bejeweled ear:

Backstroke. Quint occasionally inquiring about an unfamiliar doe in
D'aron's class, Quint's friends stopping by to enjoy the view, and no
one saying a single unkind word to D'aron all summer.

Marking noon with a formal twist of wrist, Quint would tip a
grill lighter up to knight his pipe and intone wisdoms like, Imagine if
everyone was your dentist's hygienist. And if you didn't immediately
Eureka! he'd accuse you of poor imagining, doing his best impersonation of the Captain in *Cool Hand Luke,* What we've got here is
failure to imaginate.

It was like that again now, Quint four-wheeling over after dark,
taking the back ways, and toting Daron out to his place to ice bour-
bon, or watch *American Idol,* or sit on the porch and count crickets.
Quint also took him to Rock-n-Bowl 2-fer-Tuesday, some distance
from home, fifty miles to be precise, still a few people did a double
take while they were in line exchanging their sneakers for the
brightly colored shoes everyone wore as if they were all part of the
same team (except the cook, Jose, according to his name tag). One
night between sets, Daron told his cousin that the Faculty and Student Review Board had met without him. He could return in the fall,
on provisional status. Provided he took no further action to discredit
himself or the university, he would be restored to normal status after
one semester.

Quint congratulated him, but looked doubtful. He pulled at
the frayed hem of his T-shirt, which read I DIDN'T MEAN TO PISS
YOU OFF—THAT WAS A BONUS! It's good news if you wanna go back.
But it sounds like they want you to behave better than you do, like
they'll be watching you. Besides, don't you restore things like cars
and houses? He laughed. I wouldn't last a week. As soon as someone
says they're watching me, I figure I got an audience, so it's time to
perform. Your cellie was like that. That was one funny Chinese dude.
I know—he was mad-Asian. He laughed again, louder, a big bellyful
of chuckle competing with the strikes and spares, drawing the brief

attention of the bowlers in the nearby lanes. No one said anything. A look at Quint and a look away.

Even in Braggsville, no one fucked with Quint. He always said it was because he looked out for Sheriff's son when they were both away at vo-tech, in the penalty box, as Sheriff Jr. described it. But the wariness, the caution, was more than quid pro quo, or reciprocation. Everyone somehow knew Quint was as he'd described Louis, shook up. His first year at Berkeley, Daron finally felt like he was one up on Quint. But what if Quint had gone to Berkeley? He would have been a king.

After the bowling alley, they relaxed on Quint's narrow porch under a fitted sheet awning. The nylon-webbing lawn furniture was black and gold, Yellow Jacket colors. The sun was set but it was still sticky humid and every few minutes they adjusted their necks and arms to find the cool spots on the chairs' metal frames. Gnats swarmed under the porch light, so Maylene, his old lady, lit a home-made citronella torch constructed of a wick and a whiskey bottle, in the process complaining that it was amazing what all people paid for now. Soon there'll be a surcharge for someone to chew your food. Like a bird.

Daron laughed.

Yeah, that's right, she continued, like a bird. Maylene took a seat in the lawn chair farthest from the rest, avoiding Quint's eye. Quint and Maylene had been together since high school. When they first met, Quint had referred to her as one sweet lick. Within a few months he started to spit whenever he said her name, like it started with a B. It was then that they'd moved in together. They'd broken up more times than Daron could count, usually after Quint broke the law, but they always ended up back together.

She sat with them for a few minutes, letting her nails dry. Q's playing it cool 'cause you're here, but he loves a pedicure and manicure. I give him one each year on his birthday, and whenever he walks away from a fight. And, as a treat for a few other special favors. When I rub his feet, his tongue hangs out like a hot dog's. She winked.

Daron laughed again, this time more at Quint's expression. Embarrassed, was it? But why? It must be nice to have a woman rub your feet. Why Quint would need it at his age, Daron didn't know, but it should be nice. And Daron had never before noticed, but Quint's fingernails did look buffed and shaped with professional polish.

C'mon, Lee-Lee, leave it alone now, or I'ma have to put something in your mouth. It was his usual joke, but there was an edge to his voice. Maylene had already apologized thirty-hundred-and-one times for missing Daron's welcome home barbecue on account of work. The third time, Quint snapped, He ain't deaf. And you don't have to apologize for working.

If she was working second shift, thought Daron, at least that meant more money. When he was in high school, D'aron had crushed hard on Maylene, the sharp jaw and pockmarks offset by an ample chest the perfect height for hugging. She cursed a lot and was quick tempered, but always had a kind word for D'aron and so seemed like the kind of woman that could protect you, a hard woman who melted into embraces. Like Quint said, You want a pit in the pit, and a puppy in the bed. She had also worked out of town for a spell, acquiring an exotic air. Now, she seemed coarse and gauche, which made Daron feel even more tenderly toward her as his former affection became pity. He wondered if she could sense that, because every time he had seen her lately, she went out of her way to appear ladylike. This evening she wore a skirt, which she usually only bothered about for church, and her hair was bunched in a bun with a few tendrils pulled down on either side to frame her face.

Maylene asked Daron about a Berkeley science professor who had a new theory about dinosaurs as herd animals and a business professor who won a Nobel in Economics. He didn't know either.

Quint sucked his teeth.

Maylene bit her bottom lip, thin, so thin, but tonight embellished with overdrawn lipstick.

Go on, then. Quint fanned the air as if after a bad odor. Tell D about your dinosaur theory.

She stumbled through an attempt at explaining how dinosaurs were more like humans than we thought, how each new theory was different in that way. First, scientists thought dinosaurs abandoned their eggs, but now they've learned they're good mothers. Thing is we're more alike than we know. She repeated that a few more times, like a mantra. Yep, she added, we're all more alike than we know.

She could start a fan club with that back in Berkeley, but it was hard to follow the overall argument. Her word choice was vague and therefore confusing, reminding Daron of one professor's choice advice: Be a word herder. The powerful intellect leashed by an impoverished vocabulary is a myth. Without a vocabulary, a language, the intellect cannot develop.

Quint stared at his feet the entire time she talked. When she went back inside, the smell of polish lingered, and for as long as it did, Daron said nothing, thinking of Candice.

Quint chucked his can. Some people shouldn't read. All it does is confuse them.

I don't think I'm going back.

Here'll drive you flat shit bat. Next thing you know, you'll be Chinese.

But there drove him crazy, too. Ever feel like you just don't fit in? Daron asked.

Nope.

They enjoyed the silence for a few minutes before Daron asked, You seen Jo-Jo lately?

Quint shrugged.

Know where his church is?

Quint grunted. Ever saw me in church? That don't even sound

right. I'll go to a goddamned gay bar first. At least they admit they're trying to screw you.

Know if they rebuilt that one back up in the Holler?

I don't keep up after that fool, snapped Quint, so Daron decided to leave it alone.

Quint lived at the very edge of town. His father built the house right before he went off to Operation Desert Storm with Daron's father. Good thing too, because he never came back. It was a covenant broken. Forty-two soldiers from Braggsville fought in Vietnam. After the war, forty-three soldiers returned to Braggsville. Frank Enders married an army nurse he met over there. As long as they volunteered, they'd considered themselves immune. Everyone asked, How can anyone take what you give? After Desert Storm, everyone in town asked, How could a war with almost no casualties happen to take one of our sons? No one had an answer. They just added Quint's daddy's name to the plaque mounted on the watchtower. They gave D'aron's father the hairy eyeball until confirming that he was stationed nowhere near his brother-in-law. It was during that period D'aron came to understand what other folks meant when they said Braggsville was a town where every wrong turn was a dead end.

Through the thin copse behind Quint's house, light glowed faint like hanging lanterns were suspended from the trees. Daron always forgot how close the Gully was.

Quint saw him looking. You wanna walk over there?

I been wondering about Otis. About what he said. He had a whole different history for Braggsville.

You were swatting at the same beehive back when you was writing those school letters, belching all about your mom's interference, kicking more racket than a drunk wingnut in a metal bucket, clicking about how you didn't remember her stories. Seems like you got in. She must have did something right. Quint raised an eyebrow. I'll tell you same thing I said then. History's personal. People are better off keeping some things to themselves, like when they last went to the bathroom or to visit the ass doctor.

Daron chuckled. There was no point in telling Quint that he'd written a new letter, trashed the one his mother wrote. After another patch of silence, a rough one he didn't enjoy as much, Daron ventured to ask, You know anything about a militia? This Denver guy, the FBI guy, keeps asking me about the Holler.

Quint eyed him like he was a predator circling, looking for the easiest angle of attack. You ain't got no business in the Holler. Not now. I'll gamble this much for you, D, ain't no Bat-Signal for the Joker. Sort them screws. Now, what about the Gully? You wanna walk back there?

Is it safe? Daron asked. He hadn't been in years, had only a faint memory. Spice. Wood. Snatches of bronze.

I do it all the time.

Is it safe?

Quint laughed.

From inside, Maylene shouted, Why don't you leave them people alone? You act like you don't get fed over here. I see 'em looking at me all funny when I take labels down to shipping.

They're admiring your nails is all. He slapped Daron on the knee and set off toward the tree line, their backs cooling where the nylon webbing had cut wet lines.

The sweet-smelling wood, the soft pine needles underfoot soon gave way to a path born more of use than planning, a gravel lane worn nearly to dirt and hugged by elms choked in bramble, which they followed until it forked, downhill to the left and uphill to the right. On the right was a collection of mailboxes, maybe twenty, several of which Daron had met in a previous life with an aluminum Louisville slugger, as well as several blue boxes labeled COUNTY EXAMINER, a few of which had not recovered from their own interrogations, that local version of the great American pastime. D'aron, much to his credit, he'd once thought, was only blowing off steam, and never once—not even one time—cracked lip when the others asked, Who writes Gulls anyway, and when they get a letter, who reads it to them? He now wondered how much of his fear about coming back here was actually guilt, and how much of the guilt was fear—nothing was as it seemed.

That way's the river. Quint pointed uphill. This way's the Gully.

They walked toward the Gully, the gravel sometimes glowing hazy in the moonlight, other times only a sound or a sharp stinging in the sole. The houses were far apart, not as far apart as they were on his street, but they felt similarly distant because there was no light in between them. No streetlights, just the gravel road and a cabin or shotgun home or saddlebag house every two hundred yards or so, set back at various distances from the road, road cut by use and not design. The first house they passed that was close to the street was in the style known locally as a dogtrot. Single story, the home had only two rooms, one to the left and one to the right, and the hallway between ran straight though the house from front to back, So as like the dogs can trot through without messing nothing, as Nana once explained. The side of the home was scabbed by fire.

A little black girl, six or seven, her hair in three thick braids, waved at them from the porch. Evening-steven, Mr. Quint, how you?

Fine, Ingrid, fine. Evening-steven to you, too. How are you tonight, dear? And your momma?

We's all good.

An older woman, probably the mother, poked her head out and waved, too.

Quint waved back. Hi, Miss Irene. It was like that at most houses they passed. Quint knew them by name, and they him.

How you know all these people?

I been walking through here for years. Half of 'em work at the mill anyway. And Gully shine is the next best thing to . . . you know.

Daron had always associated it with vo-tech, but now he wondered where Quint had learned his rock-in-the-flip-flop walk.

A mile into the Gully, the houses were made of cinder block,
like his own, but still were no larger than the cabins they'd passed
earlier. Unlike these, the Davenports' home was clad in vinyl and
neatly trimmed. At one of the cinder-block houses, painted white,
the old lady on the porch huffed as they passed. I see Ms. Maylene
not speaking today?

No, ma'am, this here's my cousin.

Really now? Bring him close for me to see.

She was a large woman, the arms of her metal rocking chair cut
deeply into her hips. She took Daron's hand and held it to her cheek.
I pray for your friend. Every night. You did a fine thing, son. It was
right fine. Over her shoulder she yelled, Reggie! Octavia! Ernie!
Tyrone! Get out here.

Windows lit up. They now stood in what appeared to be a courtyard centered in a cluster of square cinder-block homes, all in a similar style, huddled together as if to protect themselves from the night.
Now Gulls emerged from these houses in twos and threes, sometimes singly, all shuffling sleepily like the undead. An old man in
a thin housecoat, hands out, as if copping a feel through the dark.
Two little boys rubbing their eyes with their arms. A girl clutching a
cat to her chest as if to ward off a bad dream. (For one salty, thrilling
moment, it was zombie-apocalypse-esque.)

They smiled and touched him, some shaking his hand, some
kissing him on the cheek, others fingering the hem of his garment.
As they crowded 'round Daron, an unspeakable fear rose in him.
He would have lashed out and run had he not at that moment
heard the familiar voice of Otis. Give the boy some space, now.
Give him some air.

Tables were set up and a hog slaughtered. Fiddlers weaved a fine
tune and eventually an upright bass took a place between them. At

the tables, some plastic and metal, others merely planks across bar-
rels and sawhorses, preserves and breads and cobbler were all laid
out, and it was as if every house donated the best of what they had.
Through the night they ate and drank, and Daron had so many
questions. How long had they lived there? Why didn't they move to
the other side? Did it still flood? But it would have been impolite to
voice them aloud.

They looked as if they had questions as well. Why'd you do it?
How'd you come up with the idea? How are they treating you now?
But those would have been impolite as well. It felt like a reunion
after an embarrassing absence. The affection and appreciation were
earnest, but things had changed so much no one knew what to say.

Then he asked about the fire he'd heard rumor of. They fell silent.
Nothing major, said someone. Ain't nothing but a thang, said another. The way they said it, though, the sneer and dismissal, shutting
him out, as if Daron were the arsonist and they refused to acknowledge him, to give him the benefit of knowing he had inconvenienced
them.

During that lull in the conversation, Quint asked if anyone
wanted to hear a joke. Of course they did, thought Daron, irked. No
one would ever say, No, I don't want to hear a joke. I hate to laugh.
Funny makes me runny. He could only pray it wouldn't be one of
Louis's jokes.

Quint cleared his throat and rolled his shoulders. All right. Y'all
know I wrecked the old ATV a few weeks back down by the bank.
So I went to the emergency room, and it was crowded as church the
A-and-M after junior prom. Felt a little chilly, put my green hat on,
and I'll be damned if everyone didn't clear out and I got next. Went
down to the DMV, and the same thing happened. Got right up to
the front. Happened at the laundry mat too. Know what the hat said?

Daron thought, Please don't say, Pit bull with AIDS, which
couldn't possibly be a hat, but with Quint, who knew?

Quint felt around his cargo pockets for a moment before waving like a bronco buster, brandishing a green cap that his hair had never stopped wearing. He'd had it on earlier, but Daron hadn't noticed that it said BORDER AND IMMIGRATION CONTROL. Quint continued, Just don't wear it at McDonald's, they'll arriba-arriba right out the back afore you get your Big Mac. He kissed two fingers and touched them to his heart in the manner of a boy scout. One of my amigos invited me to his kid's baptism. The church was cold so I had to put the hat on, but I'll be George Washington if half his fam didn't take off before the priest finished waterboarding the baby.

Daron smiled weakly when Quint poked him in the ribs. He didn't think it was funny, and didn't know why the residents of the Gully would, either. Weren't people always complaining that Mexicans were just new niggers? Taking away all the shit jobs and driving down wages? He'd heard that half the blacks were laid off when the Mexicans moved into the area, but a lot of the whites got raises. He heard that's when some of the Gulls moved to Doeville for a spell, but soon came home. Yet he watched them laugh to a man, including Otis, and the children as well, mimicking the adults.

A few minutes later, unbidden, Otis apologized if he'd caused Daron any trouble.

Having only moments before witnessed a man allowing his daughter to stick her finger in his mug of shine, Daron was at the height of his disgust. Trouble? he asked Otis. Trouble? Not at all, not at all.

You sure now? I'm retired, but I remember what it was like. I'd hate to see you or your folks getting the squeeze. Short hours. Cemetery shifts. Hairy eyes. I know how it can be over there.

How's that? How is it over there?

Otis took a small step back. I didn't aim to offend, Mr. Davenport, especially not after what you've done. I was just hoping we didn't cause you any trouble back in the Holler.

Daron didn't know what the Holler had to do with it, but he

nodded lavish reassurance. Like he once overheard his father say, No nigger'll ever get the satisfaction of thinking they can cause me some trouble.

Well, we appreciate what you did.

I didn't do it for you.

I never thought you did, Mr. Davenport, it just turned out mighty fine for us. If you will excuse me, I'll dance with my wife. Otis snapped his fingers and the band picked up the tempo.

The song he vaguely recognized as John Lee Hooker. Or B.B. King. Or Albert King. One of them. Definitely. Otis's wife was a head taller, the perfect height for Otis to rest his head on her bosom and go dreamy-eyed. She was dark, darker than Otis by far, but her high cheekbones and almond eyes gave her a regal look. Daron couldn't tell if she had been beautiful as a young woman, but even in her sixties she was by far the most put-together of the Gully women who were out that night. Otis and the missus danced that song and the next, Otis at one point catching Daron's eye and winking.

Still more food came out, and shine, and before he knew it, dawn crept through the brush. At sunup, a little girl gave him a bouquet while Otis oversaw from the sidelines, nodding his approval from several feet away. She then handed Daron a locket. You are an honorary citizen of the Gully. Our doors are always open to you.

They were open before, but this is an official invitation, yelled someone from the shadow of the tree line, sparking riotous, carnivorous laughter.

On the way home, Quint clapped Daron's shoulder and offered, Maybe you done a good thing and we can't see it yet. They always say that in the vo-tech circle-jerks. It didn't work none inside, and I don't much believe it works out here. Sure don't work none inside. That's my problem there, D. I always been a rough cub. I couldn't never keep the two straight. My thing is I do what my rules say no matter where I am. Sometimes it works, sometimes it don't. I ain't no restaurant Tabasco. But I ain't changing, see. The world is. I'm just me. Seems like you got the same problem, in a way. He paused. But, for the opposite. Quint took a toke off his pipe and held his breath for several paces, exhaling as he sang, Some days it feels like my body is a cage. You know what I mean, Li'l D?

Daron waited for the punch line, but none came, and so he relished for some long moment that warm blanket of belonging he felt when his cousin called him Li'l D, the Li'l symbolizing for Daron his position as one to be protected. Quint spun his hat around backward. Immigration Control! It wasn't a Louis joke, but it would have been funny if it had been. Instead all it did was make Daron uncomfortable, and feel, frankly, disappointed in the Gulls. Six A.M. and two smokers plus a grill were going. And a band. Pork and chicken piled across the table, steaming bowls of yams and greens, and theyselves all laughing and joking and feeding their faces. A kid in cutoffs with a rack of ribs larger than his own. The heavyset lady with her plate resting on her tits like they were a TV tray. Any excuse for a shindig. That's why they couldn't get anywhere. Partying all night, of course they wouldn't be able to keep a job. A crisis was going on right now and the blacks were celebrating. Here, so deep in the woods no cars go, Negro fiddled. He bet it was quiet as church over in Ridgetown where the Mexicans lived.

VEXED. VEXED, HIS FATHER WAS. Very. He arrived home at about the same time Daron did, and had already heard tell at the mill about a midnight party, a pig slaughtered, shine, dinner by wick and wax. They can't afford to slaughter a pig like that, but you obligated them by visiting. Worse yet, word's out making it sound like you's in cahoots with them. Gave you a damned hero's feast. A welcome for a prodigal son. Shit, D'aron. Everyone knows it's bad luck to eat in the Gully after dark. I never paid much attention to that. But it looks like it's true in your case. Don't go back up in there until this is done. Daron thought it was done. It was, wasn't it? But he didn't object or ask for clarification. His father had been cranky and edgy lately. Daron attributed it to fatigue. He'd spent the last few weeks on the night shift.

Chapter Thirty-0

Through the phone Daron feels her strawberry breath at tear, so that he can yield and not buckle, a kind of warning, her kindness of announcing his every emotion only moments before he perceives it, her throat making new shapes, the miracle of blowing electronic bubbles through the tower—crackling—through the layer cake atmosphere above where they glisten enigmatic in the uppermost dark like shy stars before the satellite cups gently these lovely trophies—can't begrudge such loyal lonely an earful—then sending them on their way with a hush back to earth, back to Daron, who receives gratefully these divine meteors, paying for each with his tears, until his face below eye is a bandit's mask of sorrow, drawing tight his own voice until even to murmur sears like sudden loss and he can only nod, only nod, nod heavy against the stubble, when she calls for response, only nod when her gifts burn, when the meteorite singes his heart, when she tells him, They used us all. Don't you see? You think they were protecting you by not making you testify because you weren't there? By not making me testify to, Save me the horror. It's like rolling dice under river water, ma'am, trying to get facts straight, ma'am, they said, under those lights, in front of all those people. To relive it all. To make the poor boy's family relive it all.

For your folks to hear you say what you told me? Miss, save the people you care about the horror of seeing you take that stand. *Take,* miss. They say take for a reason, young miss—take— because it's somethin' you'll always carry with you. Are you there? [Nod. God, hope she hears.] They're laughing, and I can hear it all the way from there to here, hear it here in Iowa. I thought the inquest was to find the truth, not to write it. Are you there? [Nod. God, hope she hears the phone graze his chin, each pass hungrier.] They made me feel safe, like one of them. One of us, they said, one of us. They spoke with arms open wide as wishes. Like one of them. I didn't believe it. One of us, they said. I wanted to, to belong, but I didn't believe it. My parents believed it, but I didn't believe. I was wrong not to testify. Just like backing down with Vandenburg. Are you there? [God, hope she hears my heart.] I believe it, now. They made me believe. I believe. [Was this how Siddhartha felt when he left the palace?]

Residual Affect:
Race, Micro-aggressions, Micro-inequities, (Autophagy)
& BBQ
in the Contemporary Southern Imagination
at Six Flags

Daron L. M. Davenport
U.C. Berzerkeley
I.DØ.A5.IT.I5

Abstract

Scholars (Elise, Mahiri, Sims, Costarides, Johnson 2012) argue that barbecue's popularity in the South evidences its unique ontological position as both method and apparatus, a duality that accurately represents otherwise nonrepresentational aspects of Southern culture (Johnson 2012). In this paper, I argue that barbecue embodies both the nongendered and the gendered performative aspects of ritualistic social intercourse in three ways: (1) It enables heterogeneous interactions among hot dogs and hamburgers, as it does among humans; (2) Unexpected exposure to high heat fortifies flavor while allowing the meat to remain tender, just like sudden and intense exposure to stress does for humans; and (3) Everyone can afford a barbecue grill, so skill is the great equalizer, just like it is in the workplace for humans. In my field observation of a spontaneous barbecue among nomadic elders of the meridional United States, I observed prosocial behavior among disparate parties at a major U.S. theme park, suggesting that indeed we can all get along.

Research Question

PRIMARY RESEARCH QUESTION:

- Is a barbecue a social event, cooking apparatus, or a culinary method?

SECONDARY RESEARCH QUESTIONS:

- Is a barbecue what Michel de Certeau would call a strategy or a tactic?
- Is barbecue real or imagined?
- Is barbecue a noun or verb or metaphor?
- Is barbecue spelled barbecue, barbeque, bar-b-q, or BBQ?

Methods
Informants—Design—Procedures—Measures & Methodology

- The informants include nomadic elders originally from the meridional United States, and 4 Little Indians, each representing a unique tribe.
- Guidelines for grounded research have been followed.
- Names have been changed to protect the identity of the innocent.
- Nothing is staged.
- The occasion is analyzed using both eyewitness accounts and the original text as source material. So the evidence is both direct and indirect (Dehaan 1999).

Literature review

- Old Hitch, who built Lou Davis's smoker, is said to have left behind a journal of tips and recipes called *Cooking by Heartlight*. Those who have read it are rumored to have gnawed their tongues unclean off.

SIX FLAGS PART ONE: INTERNMENT AND INTERROGATION

One of us? Who is us?

As above, so below, Nana liked to say, daubing juniper oil on D'amon's forehead and chin. She'd then draw her thumbs across the upper ridge of his cheekbones and massage his temples, while reminding him that his eyes would reckon his appetites, and his appetites would be the hatch between the two worlds. By appetites she meant, Dogs don't eat on listing boats. By two worlds she meant, Ussens, and what's hid behind even that preacherman, like the Moon and the Sun, one is light while the other onliest pretend. Damon imagined the two worlds as the celestial and the earthly, as a kingdom of delights atop a realm of pedestrian bureaucracy, but he hadn't the words to express this at the time. It's like dinner and dessert, you silly goat, Nana explained, which he took to mean that he had to do right by one before getting to the other, but two such separate worlds he'd never seen before, until Six Flags.

The alleys, underground offices, and subterranean corridors our 4 Little Indians were marched through must have covered the entire kingdom, for the journey ended at red double doors on the other side of the park, far from where they had, Unceremoniously, Park Director Vandenburg insisted, released Ishi. It was as if the people in the other world, the basement offices and black alleys, the dark city, were being punished, while the people up above were, were . . . Vandenberg sipped his OJ . . . sun kissed. The contrast between the two worlds was as starkly unsettling as the social divide explored in the film *Metropolis,* which Damon's film professor called the first honest cinematic coverage of the laboring class, the first film to illustrate the gross and lamentable existential gap between white collar and blue collar, a gap Damon would not have otherwise believed existed in such varied dimensions: All the boots at the mill ever said was, Shirtsleeves are for sissies.

Vandenburg, with his superhero silver sideburns, spent most of the conversation with his right hand on the phone, tapping it with his trigger finger to express displeasure whenever he didn't like the sound of their story. They had been led first to a supervisor, then a security chief, and at last to Vandenburg, after the security chief picked at the cardboard urn with a pencil and saw that among the remains were numerous page numbers.

Vandenburg softened the more Caitlin spoke, until he finally swiveled to his computer, fingered his fancy silver keyboard, turned his screen toward Caitlin and instructed her to read aloud the entire Wikipedia entry on Vallejo. Then the one on Six Flags. When she finished, he leaned back in his chair as though exhausted, sipped his juice, fanned himself. Hot stuff, huh? Ishi's not from here, his tribe isn't even from here, his tribe should not have been the victims of overzealous retaliation, but none of it has anything to do with Six Flags. As he talked, Caitlin said nothing, which surprised Damon. Leading them to the door, Vandenburg smiled, That's why it's called Six Flags Discovery Kingdom, you learn something new every day.

The guard who drove them back to their car was the same one who'd checked Caitlin's bag at the ticket gate, the same one who was so bewitched by her rugby jersey, a fact Damon was not derring-do enough to point out. Had they not all that afternoon been blinded by reverie of one type or another? The guard looked neither right nor left, turning wide and slow, acknowledging Caitlin's whispered directions with a clipped nod, as if wearing a neck brace. Even Lee was quiet. Kain's right leg bounced like it did as he laced for runs. The guard dropped them off at Caitlin's old Corolla, then circled the aisle and returned, the whine of the golf cart catching their attention. Hey, he called, I was at the gate when you came in wearing the padded bra. There are some things you shouldn't lie about. My mom had breast cancer and she had to use prosthetics for real (Johnson 2015, p. 279).

Initial findings

Maybe those Marxists were right about class divides, but what most frightened Damon that morning was the guard. It was as if the guard himself had cancer. Cancer isn't contagious, but it is mighty bad luck, and that is highly contagious.

SIX FLAGS PART TWO: ESCAPE

In the car, Caitlin apologized. Who would have thought that fake breasts could offend people, that her excess would cast a shadow reminding others of a painful deprivation? To Damon, she gifted two fingers to his elbow and her thanks that he took a knee to acknowledge the significance of the occasion.

There was standing room only, offered Kain, who had called shotgun. The kids will think about what they heard. They'll be more reverent.

That's nice, Kain. Thanks.

Does anyone else appreciate that they gave us a standing ovation? Lee's enthusiasm was not contagious, though Damon did snort with relief when Lee whispered, What the fuck was up with Tweety Bird? Was that a plushie blowjob dream or what?

I need the lady's room.

Woo hoo! Finally! Lee held his hands over his head when they were jolted violently forward and to the right as Caitlin jerked into a spot in the overnight lot, skittering across the gravel and coming to a stop between two RVs. Engine running, she slammed the door and walked off, her arms swinging wide as she disappeared behind the campers.

I have to piss, too. Lee walked off.

Not the best idea, huh? Kain turned to face Damon, squeaking in the seat. I'm glad it's your party and not mine.

Not the worst either. Damon had kind of enjoyed the attention.

When Lee returned, he sat with the door open until the incessant dinging of the warning light prompted Kain to lean over the console and remove the keys from the ignition, at which point he saw Caitlin's phone on the dash, and asked, Who's going to go look for her (Johnson 2015, p. 280)?

Initial findings

Damon took a knee for personal reasons, but what good could come of telling a hungry person you cracked their last egg while they worked? That was like igniting the burner under an empty pot.

SIX FLAGS PART THREE: TO BE, OR TO BBQ (THAT IS THE QUEST, SON)

There were acres of RV. In every direction stretched rows of white-and-tan campers lined up like a model town, the shared spaces between them too neat and orderly for it to be a trailer park. At each corner Damon stopped and looked all four ways, waving when necessary, which was often. RVers were irritatingly friendly. He both wanted to find her and not. In D'amonville (There is no ideal world or perfect world, so let's be honest and call it your fantasy, or D'amonville, his parents decided the year D'amon read the *Economist* for class and introduced his every suggestion with, In an ideal world . . .), so, in D'amonville, he would not find her, at least not in despair, he decided. He would meet her just before she returned to the car, missing the crying episode but having enough time to fall into a meaningful conversation they could continue as they walked back and pick up later when alone again. He might hug her, would let her compose herself, could allow her grief to be a private thing, a secret between them.

When at last he heard her in conversation, though, Caitlin sounded happy, or at least her normal self. He followed the sound of her voice and saw her some yards away, thanking an elderly couple for letting her use the toilet. They stooped over her like concerned grandparents. Maybe that was why grandparents always appeared concerned, because they stooped over you like you were the center of the world and they had to hear everything you said, like you were the only source of heat in the cave. Had Nana stooped over him like that? Had Nana stooped at all? Caitlin waved at Damon over their shoulders, a quick motion, like rubbing the head of a child she didn't like. When he waited, she waved again, calling him over with her hands, where he met Colonel and Mrs. Richard Sanders, whom she had interrupted making, Ironically, they knew, fried chicken, and who not only had been nice enough to let her use the bathroom, but were insisting that all four of them stay for dinner.

Damon refrained from correcting that misuse of irony. The Sanderses' twang struck chords of home. Besides, You never correct your elders.

We have plenty, oh plenty of food. Mrs. Sanders smiled broadly (as if to prove that she still had her teeth, Caitlin later said). But this is not charity, we need a favor from you in return, we were hoping you good young people could help us with our Internet.

While Damon texted Lee and Kain, the Colonel added, In exchange for your . . . technical support, y'all'll dine on the best blessed fried chicken this side of the Mississippi. He was a slim, elegant Southern gentleman who stood tall, always scanning the horizon, who wore his T-shirt tucked into his dungarees, both pressed like dress blues. He was, as he described it, The best kind of bald— completely so. No comb-overs, no sprays, no hair clubs whose presidents are also members, just a good old-fashioned smooth pate. Too much testosterone, he explained, with a wink at the wife. It might happen to you, if you're lucky, son.

The Sanderses' Airstream was brand new, appointed with, More damned bells and whistles than General Schwarzkopf, the Colonel proudly claimed while giving them a tour.

Were they a little surprised by Kain when he and Lee joined them? Damon couldn't be sure. Mrs. Sanders called Kain a big boy and squeezed his biceps before letting her tiny paws drift down to his wrist, bringing to mind a Little Leaguer straining to heft a regulation slugger. The Colonel asked Kain what sports he played, and he took it all in stride.

And why not? Indeed, it was real Southern cooking, their brag no boast. Tasted so fine made you want to chew your tongue. The best cluck-cluck Damon had tucked away since home. Under the retractable awning, Junior Brown playing in the background, they ate food so finger-lickin' good Lee didn't even make a single joke about Kentucky Fried Chicken, or about how he and Kain sat on the RV's iron stairs because there weren't enough chairs. Mrs. Sanders had also prepared mashed potatoes and gravy, green beans, mac-n-cheese, and grilled corn. She said that her Colonel demanded colorful meals, that her Colonel swore that was the best way to get all the good nutrients.

The Colonel winked at Kain. Not bad. Not bad, right? She's got a little soul, right? Gesturing with his hands, he added, Well, a big one, but you know what I mean.

Mrs. Sanders giggled.

The Colonel winked at Kain once more.

Kain agreed, and the Colonel laughed—a laugh like a rusty pump—seeming not to notice that Kain had cut his chicken, but not actually eaten any. Maybe, thought Damon, Kain was not taking it all in stride. He never ate red meat, but when asked about chicken said, That's the craziest shit you've ever asked me. I'm only vegetarian when I don't like the food or the company. Damon looked at Kain's plate again and hoped that night would see no hot weevil about the misappropriation of soul food. Thomas Jefferson invented mac-n-cheese, and the Scots invented fried chicken.

Mrs. Sanders wiggled in her chair like she was settling in for a long spell. She did it again before Damon understood that she was dancing to demonstrate her soul. (Lee later said, I thought she was going to throw her back out. Kain later said, Maybe she was expressing joy, like when you wriggle and say, hmm-mm.)

The Colonel hummed a few bars of the song then playing. Lee joined in, having learned the hook: You're wanted by the police and my wife thinks you're dead. Damon rocked rhythmically in his chair.

Caitlin, who sat across from Damon at the folding table, ate in silence with prim bites. She wore two burns from the grill, buff pink welts a cryptic brand, a cracked nail on her ring finger, a scar on the back of her hand that she sucked at between cool sips of sweet tea, a stubbed toe, and that bee sting on her elbow. He wanted badly to kiss each one. He had inventoried her injuries earlier in the day, when her temporary augmentation prevented him from regarding her directly. Without the ashes stashed, she was approachable and cute in ways he hadn't before considered. With the fake breasts she had stood straighter, almost in challenge. Without them, she again slumped a little, cupping her shoulders as if to protect her real ones. As Quint always said, Can't hold more than a handful or suck more than a mouthful. She appeared uncertain, as she had the night of the dot party. At the time he thought she was a blubberer. Damon liked this contemplative, almost shy Caitlin.

Damon!, rushed the Colonel. Your girlfriend's pouring her own water.

Caitlin's happy hands went still.

In a faux sérieux tone, he added, You know us Southern gentlemen cannot allow such things.

Caitlin licked her fork and placed it beside her plate with the care one shows when setting the table for a first date and gave Damon an angry smile. He wanted to correct the Colonel, and probably would have if Caitlin hadn't smiled at him like that. It made him feel that they shared a secret, and he was powerless to voluntarily dispel the illusion.

We're not dating. We're just friends, Caitlin said.

Oh. The Colonel pointed at Kain, and then Lee, each time asking the same question by jabbing the air with his dirty fork. When Caitlin shook her head both times, he pointed to the three guys. Is you fellas . . . by any chance . . . not that I care.

No, they all said.

One of us, okay. The Colonel dug back into his plate, looking, even to Damon, a tiny bit relieved. To Damon, he explained, You could have won big if you bet us. We woulda wagered it, y'all seeming so compatible and all.

Where are you from again, Colonel? Caitlin asked.

L.A. Lower Alabama. Dothan to be particular.

Not far from Georgia?

Oh, no, young miss. Close. Very close. My nana was born there, in fact. She used to say, Drink enough beer and you could water their peaches, but for the fact that we were in a dry county.

Lee and Kain grunted politely.

Somehow Caitlin and Damon had become the spokespersons, even though Colonel Sanders knew a lot of Chinese in the army and none of them had accents either, and he served awhile under a negro, Called them colored back then. Wouldn't no one mess with Spike. Spike Green. Cross him and get nailed. He let me get away with about all, had a soft spot for me—just between us. The Colonel again sounded his rusty pump.

When the Sanderses asked what coasters they rode that day, Caitlin muttered, All of them. Lee told them all, Plus a special back lot tour.

The Colonel turned back to Caitlin, A back lot tour? Where do you sign up for that?

It's invitation only, Lee squeezed out between mouthfuls, now eating as if afraid he'd be at any moment banished from the stoop.

Secrets, huh? The Colonel stirred his Arnold Palmer as he walked to his wife's side of the table. Got to have something to hold on to. Sometimes secrets is all you have. He grabbed his wife's butt, and a few other things (Johnson 2015, p. 285).

Initial findings

Irony is a bastard. A special kind: mother unknown.

Final findings

Informant Caitlin uses persuasive rhetoric selectively—with minorities more than with mainstream contacts. She used it in Spanish with the Latino guards at the cemetery and the campus cop, but never with director Vandenberg or attendant Pearl (Medusa's gatekeeper), who are native English speakers.

Informants Lee and Kain may not have wanted to seat themselves on the periphery, but by willingly doing so, they were complicit in their own segregation. Informants Lee and Kain exhibited "selective perception" (Griffin 2009, p. 259). In other words, informants Lee's and Kain's preexisting prejudices about Southerners prevented them from seeing the Sanderses as generous. Instead, informants Lee and Kain assumed the Sanderses were being charitable out of pity. Informants Lee and Kain also later expressed displeasure about the Sanderses' questions about their athleticism and sexual orientation, even though no one ever asks short, dumpy, fat men if they play football, or horrible-looking people if they are gay.

The Sanderses might've exhibited selective perception when they asked if informants Damon and Caitlin were romantically involved, but their conclusions were based on easily observable facts. Informants Damon and Caitlin arrived at the Sanderses' RV before informants Lee and Kain. And, while informants Lee and Kain sat on the periphery, informants Damon and Caitlin sat at the table. When the Sanderses asked if they were dating, informant Caitlin smiled at informant Damon, which could have been easily interpreted as confirmation.

At the time, informant Damon thought the smile was a connection, perhaps proof of the likelihood and desirability of a relationship between the two informants. Upon further investigation, this researcher concludes that Caitlin's smile wasn't a confirmation of affection. It was an indictment of the Sanderses, and a question: *Who is us?* Upon further research, this researcher has determined that US varies.

Informant Damon complained extensively about the greeting habits of the RVers. Upon further investigation, this researcher determined that informant Damon felt welcomed and that the series of waves he received and returned reassured him of his place and made him feel at home, which he did without considering that his friends might not feel the same. He hadn't thought about how this was their first contact with the South, and how that made him an unwitting ambassador.

Informant Damon's nana was correct. There are two worlds, though they are not as simply defined as above and below. This is not the Fritz Lang film *Metropolis* in which the world is divided into only two groups: (1) rich capitalist industrialists, and (2) the laboring class who live and work underground. *Metropolis* could be interpreted as a metaphor for how different people experience the world. The informants were all at the same literal barbecue, but their imaginary BBQs were all personal and idiosyncratic, and had little more in common than the streets projecting from a traffic circle.

A significant finding pertains to Certeau's distinction between strategies and tactics. According to him, organized power structures use strategies, and the subjugated or disempowered use tactics. In other words, "governments make maps and pedestrians make shortcuts" (Davenport 2015). This debate is rendered moot at the communal well of fire affectionately referred to as "the grill." They might use coal or lava rocks, pecan chips or gas and hickory, lighter fluid or matches or electronic ignition, they might cook chicken and salmon, ribs and burgers, tempeh and portabellas, they might serve beer, pop, whiskey, or rye, they might listen to Drake, Buffett, Sade, Bey, or Bee, regardless, everyone says in some manner, and always with a smile, Light the grill. If they do not say Light, they say Spark!, or the technically minded say Ignite!, or the nature enthusiasts say Kindle! *In all times and places, the command to start the grill is a request for illumination* (that will be shared?).

The final observation pertains [*sic*] the Indian informants' tactical strategies, which are always indirect. Even Damon had only reacted, not acted. They never directly addressed the problem. Even on the ride home, their critique was indirect. All they said in the car was:

Damon, your boyfriend is hitting me; Damon, your boyfriend farted; Damon, your boyfriend's feet stink. Damon, your girlfriend is hitting me; Damon, your girlfriend is driving her own car; Damon, your girlfriend is having her own thoughts.[4]

---

4 See appendix for works cited

Chapter Thirty-1

During the ride home from Six Flags, while Louis and Charlie called Candice his girlfriend, Daron side-eyed her, on the lookout for a pull at the brow, a snort, a pop of the gum she so vigorously chomped. He saw no signs that she warmed to the idea, but saw none neither that she chilled at the thought. And when she gave him that peck on the cheek the morning she left Braggsville, her lips but a kiss away, so close he couldn't see them, could only imagine them, hope raised high a flag. Yet, now, several weeks after the Incident, when they were once more able to talk—so to speak—on a regular basis, Candice and Daron's secret phone calls only made him doubt that they'd ever be more than friends. The Chelseas and the Davenports were as similar as chimpanzees and humans; as NASCAR and NASA; as MIA (soldier) and M.I.A. (singer). (Can't duck truth! The Devil is not in the details; the details are the Devil's cock ring. Are not those details, those distinguishing features, those damned rigid particulars, precisely the attributes that enable the eternal dick slapping? Sincerely, Louis.) Yes, Daron winced listening to the Chelseas' professorial tones and terse barks of laughter, the mother's condescension always unholstered, winced as he had in that conversation with Mr. Buchanan when he was told more than asked about his own parents' education. Mr. Buchanan.

The Chelseas. Candice's phone calls. Those conversations, can they be considered conversations when one person does all the talking?

Understand, please, that she calls him . . . she calls him not . . . she calls him. This is what he has learned: (1) Fridays at 8:45 P.M. the Chelseas *dinner* at O'Malley's (The Irish and Arabic love their apostrophes. Sincerely, Louis); (2) Her father orders *tuna-tenderloin-rare-as-the-day-it-was-born-no-sides;* (3) her mother orders *my-usual-Raúl-the-spinach-salad-hold-the-bacon-as-far-away-as-possible-because-to-even-lust-in-one's-heart-after-such-delectable-fat-is-to-dangerously-excite-adipose-tissue;* (4) Candy-Pandy orders *yes-another-black-bean-burger-double-swiss-add-thousand-island-yes-I-know-this-is-the-best-steakhouse-in-central-Iowa;* (5) Candice is *Candy-Pandy, Candy Bear, Can-Can,* and, when the parental units are inflamed, *Marianne;* (6) Her mother responds to most of her father's statements with, *That notwithstanding, dear, have you considered* . . . ; (7) When the parental units ask what *Candy-Pandy* is listening to on her—all giggles—*meepthree player,* a trendy performer of her own generation earns an earbud exchange, but any band more than twenty years old does not, so on the fifteen-minute drive to the best steakhouse in central Iowa she often claims Nirvana or R.E.M. in ear, usually the former because Cobain polishes her mother's voice brighter than Uncle Roy's nose and triggers her father's warm sense of generational proprietorship: *Don't you millennial hucksters have your own rebels?* All of this Daron learns not because she calls him. She calls him not. They remain officially incommunicado. Her derrière, though, has different ideas, and dials him up one evening, establishing a tradition, and for three weeks continues to ring Daron from the backseat of the Chelseas' hybrid SUV every Friday at 8:25 P.M.

How does he know it's a booty call, a derrière dial in that literal sense, that literally innocuous sense, that innocuous and damned disappointing sense? The first time, hearing only scuffling fabric within reach and New York accents at dreamy remove, in the most solemn of whispers he asks: Is this a butt dial? Her answer: Cough-cough. Again sober of tone, he asks: Does two coughs mean yes? Her answer: Cough-cough. Her mother asks: *Do you need a lozenge, a Ricola throat drop, Candy-Pandy?* Her answer: No. He asks: What's the code for no? Her answer: a *throat drop* crashing into teeth, the wet *zysk* of cheeks pinched by citrus. She clears her throat. It's settled: two coughs for yes, one throat clearing for no, accompanied by Nirvana. The first two words in their private language!

But what to tell her? What is a tell? An unconscious self-betrayal? An acknowledgment of one's pole position? The rollover that offers the vulnerable underbelly? (By Louis's count.) An archeological site built up over centuries of cyclical human occupation and abandonment? (Daron's favorite.) Is it to reveal? Confess? Surrender? Does the *tell* require a listener? He is not sure. And so while imagining *Candy-Pandy* seated behind her mother, earbuds at ready, soft gaze ignoring the light spraying across the window, wearing a white tracksuit and flip-flops with pink roses buttoned atop the thongs, he tells her . . . he tells her . . . not.

He tells her . . . about his life now . . . about how it recalls the tedium of summers after he stopped hunting and before he learned to drive, except there is no job to which he need be ferried. He tells her there are only two hunts he still enjoys: the raspy Braille of old book covers and the whisper of vinyl drawn from sleeves. But no more. The record stores, video stores, bookstores, those temples of wisdom whose employees he'd so envied were extinct, themselves now *tells*. Those clerks who could name the third track on *Nevermind* or tell you that *Breed* was originally titled *Imodium*—without quite sneering—are gone the way of the dodo bird or sliced bread in Berzerkeley.

All the jobs he wants are *POOF*, and it's his fault. Killed, <DE-LETED>, he knows, by him and his generation, and all their online shopping and file sharing. What remains are a paltry assortment that rouses indignation, a long dozen of those very occupations that he's always feared most. What fun! Oh, he applies at each, and more. His father sees to that, in truth oversees, watching him complete and submit the applications for the adventure of a lifetime: cashiering at the big cold box, stocking at Pilot, burgering at McD's, as the manager called it. Cheering squads at the big cold box, employee appreciation parking lot picnics every first Friday at Pilot, community service opportunities at McD's. Each of the businesses self-identifies as a three-sun solar system, as employee-centered, community-centered, and customer-centered. These are occupations in the martial sense of the word, takeovers by invading forces. Every organization, every single one, Daron worries himself, orchestrates a silent competition with the church; they want not employees, but practitioners, apostles, acolytes—not workers, but worshippers. Between this observation and his reflections on school, he concludes that everyone advertises for the mind but expects you to bring the soul.

He tells her . . . that reporters occasionally stalk about, that Agent Denver has stopped by a couple more times, always in his signature blue windbreaker, the arrival of his black sedan marked by thin smiles and his departure by rock salt, but that he, Daron, remained distant, even after Denver suggested that his father's transfer to the night shift wasn't voluntary. That was no extraordinary prescience by Daron's mind. Charlie and Hirschfield had both said it might happen, and he had not believed them either, even though he knew Charlie to be wise beyond his years.

He tells her . . . not . . . that when he was in the garage this morning, he tripped over a stack of unfamiliar boxes, inside of which were enough econ and finance textbooks to choke Warren Buffett. As he was sorting through them, his mother came from behind without warning, scaring the Big Blue Jesus out of him, asked why he was cold-nosing around the garage. He'd no answer. It was as though he was slapped awake after blacking out, and couldn't piece together his reason for being out there or even how he'd arrived. He asked about the textbooks, and she replied, Think you're the only one who reads?

Yeah. Maybe. No. But textbooks, Mom? And these books, he'd noticed with discomfort, were very well read: highlighter marks, underlining, exclamation points, question marks, lots and lots of big question marks as if the reader were preparing to cross-examine the author, blatant interrobangs, and more dog-ears than Iditarod, or better yet, the San Francisco SPCA, which was a no-kill shelter.

He tells her . . . not . . . that his mother then admitted to being in school online, and wanted to surprise him.

With what? That's weird. You're too old to get a new job. What do you need school for?

Same as you.

You have a job.

That's not why you go to school.

Then why?

To learn?

What? What have you learned?

That's the point, D-D, she snapped twice, that's the point.

He tells her . . . he tells her . . . not . . . about how his mother faced him, leaned against the pressure-treated four-by-four support as if it were comfortable, crossed, then uncrossed her arms and legs, another holdover from those counseling sessions. Open body, open heart, open mind, Dr. Ventura always advised. Don't you remember that rhubarb with your father? You nearly came to blows. He fixed you for June and July at the mill, but you howled louder than a drunk monkey about summer camp. He said you needed to make money. She pointed at him. You said you needed skills. He said you needed work. But you said you should learn, needed to learn, that you wanted a job you couldn't figure out how to do just by showing up. Remember that? You wanted a job you had to think about. You even used his own advice against him: Never be the first one to ask her to the prom. That went over like a poke in the eye, burned him worse than a chow-chow in June. Remember?

He didn't. Not only did he not remember, he didn't believe it had happened. Just like he hadn't remembered half the things his mother made him write in his college admissions letters. He was of late suspicious of the longstanding wild divergences in the family's accounts of history, of the entire town's, really, of wrongheaded answers to unasked questions, of the subjectivity of it all. Subjectivity. An angel poking a hole in the plastic bag pulled tight as air over your head. A finger in the sky pointing not to some promised land, some high school fantasy, but to your heart, affirming that what you feel is true. A message from God. As real as a strawberry, and just as magical. Christ! Of course Nietzsche grew a burl. Daron felt his own knar growing, grubbing, fingering his being like a pimp, saw that this subjectivity had not been the dance it felt that morning in class—him being set free—but more like him being let go, or worse yet, him letting go without realizing it. So that as his mother spoke—this woman who he had always thought did not understand him—he feared, as he listened, that *he* in fact did not understand her, and the latter was more frightening. So that now, as she spoke, arms at her side, blond hair kinked and corkscrewed (when had that begun?), shoulders down, confessional in all ways, he worried that he had never understood a thing. So that as she spoke, he listened anew.

Remember what you said? Why learn to do a job? Why commit your brain to making someone else rich? Remember? Her speech blossomed into sermon. You were out back with me, it was the year we planted the pears, it was the first summer you could have worked in their little apprentice program at the hotbox. It was the last summer you worked in the yard with me. You were thirteen. You won the debate championship. You refused to hunt. I was so proud. I didn't think I could be any prouder of you until the moment you spoke up about that job. That's why your father went back to school. Of course he'll never admit that. Don't you remember? She wasn't asking. She was insisting. Remember?

Except for being called Buttercup after some kids from school saw him gardening, he didn't remember, but he uncrossed his own arms, willing to believe, damned desperate to remember it, desperate as a man stranded at sea struggling to get his bearings when he's only energy enough to swim to a shore unseen. Then he noticed the lock.

He tells her . . . that when he was in the garage talking to his mom this morning, the loft door was mysteriously padlocked, a security measure typically instituted only during that secretive season between Black Friday and Christmas, a month during which he scaled the support beams daily, ticktacking between two columns as if climbing in a chimney, inching his way along a four-foot crossbeam while hanging by his hands only, and hoisting himself at last over the loft knee wall with a grunt of pride and a soft, singing ache in the arms. He'd had imagination enough to make the climb at eight, limbs long enough at ten, hands strong enough at twelve. In addition to the pride that accompanied the exertion, the climb was one secret he didn't think his parents had ever sussed out. That was reason enough to continue the tradition.

He tells her . . . that tonight he announced his early retirement at the dinner table, soliciting both a welcome smile and a lingering look of concern—neither from whom he'd expected them—and retreated to his room, where he sat in the closet until he heard his parents leave, first the hum of the garage door retracting, followed by the Bronco easing out and dipping its toes in the dirt, patient as a sated retiree on a postmeal constitutional. He waited ten minutes after the whine of the tires was muzzled by safe distance to make his way to the garage. If his parents had not returned by then, as his mother always joked, Anything left behind has missed the ark.

He tells her . . . not . . . about why he had the house to himself for a couple of hours of essential isolation. Mother was going to make groceries, as of late always at night, always one town over because, Queuing ain't cool; Produce is restocked second shift; Sun's so much milder after sunset. (Throat clearing? Sun after sunset? Cough-cough? She means humidity.) On her way to the big cold box, she would drop his father off, To go factoring, as he used to say. He hadn't said that for over a decade, not since eight-year-old D'aron, aka Mr. Hanky, bka Faggot, begged his father to visit his social studies class on Parents' Day. His father pinched his left nostril to clear the right, said no one wanted to hear about factoring, yanked his waxy brogan laces tight as a tourniquet. Back then, when D'aron was in third grade, both parents worked nights, which he understood to mean that they worked in a graveyard. He had prided himself on this fact, on his parents' valor and wisdom, their necessary intimacy with night rangers and the Holler's other bedizened denizens, their familiarity with the many charms and amulets certainly required to hold at bay the mad ether, just as guns, germs, and steel held at uneasy remove societal collapse. He imagined them as characters in Nana's favorite cartoon, one where a Saint Bernard and a coyote spent the day tormenting each other with pranks and insults only to clock out at dinner time and clap hands like rival ballers after a game, and then walk home shoulder to shoulder, their steps and smiles as steady, and their laughter as companionable, as those of brothers-in-arms. And those nights when his father sat on the back porch playing Tool and staring into the Holler, the Holler stared back with an equal measure of affinity. Everybody knew their place, and felt not shackled but swaddled. In those days the narrow garage storage loft was a kingdom of treasures.

Tonight, though, tonight in the garage, after he scaled the support beams to the loft, Daron found a peculiar trove, he found, in a manner of speaking, Jo-Jo, and all else he had hidden, or asked his parents to hide, as well as dozens of small items he had not thought to ask them to tuck away, which explained Old Hitch's General Lee

flyswatter, the Confederate place mats, the picture of Bugs Bunny
from *Southern Fried Rabbit*. Of these, neither his mother's under-
cover education nor

    the garage menagerie, he tells her . . . not. And of the conclusion drawn

        standing in the loft—breath spooked by shock and not exertion,

            arms singing a soft ache, of the conclusion

                he draws he thinks not to tell her

                    . . .

The night before a big test, he slept with his head away from the door so that when morning came he could rise on the right side of the bed; he never sharpened more than three pencils at a time; and he always used the same door to enter the testing hall, the middle one, not the ones on the ends. Charlie had his lucky pencil, Candice her knit Rastafarian hat, Louis his entire family. The uncles would rather lose than play the four card in Uno. Mrs. Chang collected pineapples the way Daron's mom collected pigs, but Daron's mom didn't believe that pigs were good luck.

Maybe it was only OCD.

His father turning the dead bolt back and forth twice before locking it. His mother shaking the coffee can before throwing it away, and if she saw it atop the garbage later, shaking it again. Both of them always lining up the spout opposite the seam on their coffee cups. Considering how many times his father had scratched his car on The Charlies, it would make sense to back into the driveway. Then in the mornings dark and groggy the headlights would usher his exit. But his father only pulls into the garage and backs out of it, even stepping half backward across the doorsill when exiting it. Over the last few days, Daron noticed that they did this often, backed out of rooms as if to ensure they were not being followed. Maybe he hadn't thought about it because they only did it while closing doors. Subtle to be sure. They could pass it off as checking the locks. It wasn't like they moonwalked from the kitchen to the hall. But it was strange nonetheless.

Like the sign at Lou's, Daron had noticed—hadn't he?—but never thought about why things were as they were. Never pondered, deliberated, considered, ruminated, cogitated. There was truth to the saying you look with your eyes but see with your brain. Look-see-think. Think-see-look. If he had done that, he would have known the answer all along. Or would he? Read the signs, the cook at the Awful Waffle had said. Read the signs. What signs?

What about the rabbit's feet, and the horseshoes over every entry door? What about hoppin' john, greens, cornbread, and a man first across the threshold on New Year's? Why is the odd-point stag's head burned? He had laughed at Candice's harvest dolls, Louis with his crazy feng shui–zee, Charlie's old-time religion. But watching his parents, Daron found himself facing an indecipherable hieroglyphic of rituals.

And there were more. Why do so many around Braggsville leave and enter the house by the same door, even after wheeling the trash bin from the back stoop to the front curb? Why do they sit with the dead for twenty-four hours before releasing kin to the authorities? Why do they stop the clocks and wave a candle over the body three times when a child passes? Why is it forbidden to sweep before breakfast? Why are doves' eggs bad luck, but partridges' eggs fortuitous? Why touch your nose when passing a slaughtered animal? Why spit on a restless grave to appease thirsty spirits? Why was it bad luck to eat in the Gully after dark? Why did his mother sprinkle rock salt on the porch after every visit by the Great Agent Denver, as she called him?

Hmmph! Ain't working anyway, he keeps coming right back, she complained. They were sitting in the kitchen, Daron peeling potatoes, she chopping them. The sun had turned in, and his father slept the last few hours he could before heading to the mill.

Where's that come from?

She shrugged. Methuselah knows.

For the first time, though, Daron did not understand whether she meant that everybody knew or only Methuselah knew. He didn't even know, he admitted to himself with a snort, who Methuselah was.

Don't look at me funny, I know your friends have superstitions, especially the Chinese one, God bless him.

He didn't bother correcting her. Both parents made that mistake occasionally. For weeks he reminded them that Louis was Malaysian, not Chinese, from an island, not a continent. She would only remind him that when Daron first called about his new roommate, he himself said Louis was Chinese, and when Louis did his backyard stand-up routine, even Louis said he was Chinese. Touché.

When you were little—she made a fist—you used to snatch at the air in front of my mouth whenever I sang. Her speech again blossomed into sermon. It's like you thought you could grab the song right out of the sky. She smiled sweetly, as though that explained it all. He now saw that it might could account for everything.

Chapter Thirty-3

Only twice-cut trees stay down. Birds don't sky before dusk. Where wolves walk upright, their curled tails question marks. Wily wind slips silent through soft Georgia pine, upsetting without a sound. Low moon's cloudy; high moon hangs behind the ridge. Spring babes won't taste winter stew. Moss grows on the wrong side, and if tracked into the house, mutts stop eating and soon die. Cats soon die, but not before eating their young. It's where preachers hold court at branching streams divining with serpents. Feudal clans retain witches and consult wizened sages said to have seen Bragg himself consort with night itself to console his interminable grief. Beavers build dams with the bones of fallen men. Had Abel been laid here, Cain 'a nev' been found out. According to his nana.

To the Holler's edge she took eight-year-old D'aron, to see her last chance, he who read life in the spine. Preacher swathed in rags, chained to anchor, length taut, swaying on unseen waves, like a swimming dog straining at the lead. Anchor and chain scraping up the steps, clumping, clanging on each one, tearing wood and stone, grinding, as if they were eating their way in, as if all the earth's anger was set to devour the church. D'aron dreamed of it for years, hearing it in every scraping midnight step on the front porch, darting awake, breathless, like Nana's final days.

Nana's remission everyone knew would be a black lunch, short-lived. Face gray as a catfish, she'd arranged a premature release. Hearing Nana coo and mutter (she could salt the air 'til it burned your eyes), her cracked lips intoning long-forgotten chants, the nurse—who knew a curse when she heard one—blanched to match her uniform and wheeled that patient right out the alley exit. When the ward caught fire a year later, that nurse was the only survivor. Glick was her name. Glick. She was from 'round the Holler.

In flashes, the memory of the church returned to Daron. Others said the blacks were just superstitious, but being amid those Gulls cauterized by faith was the closest he'd come to a true religious experience. The floor shaking and vibrating like the porch had collapsed. The smell of bodies pressed together. Kerosene. Wood varnish fumes rising from the pews, as if heated by anxious rubbing, turning every time again the floorboards shake, the doors bow as if the Devil himself is ramming, nostrils aflame, hooves driving down, searing the dirt. Murmuring as they slyly glance at their watches, women fan themselves and slap the wrists of fidgety children while the men nod, the oldest tapping chin to chest before jerking upright and glancing about rheumy-eyed. D'aron sighs loudly, wincing when Nana pinches his ear tight as a tick. He is tempted to peer over his shoulder, to see if anyone saw, before remembering there are few whites here, mostly elderly women and a few of their grandkids. So what does it matter? He looks around anyway, and sure enough, Giselle Goman is giggling. He would have died of embarrassment but for the doors swinging open at that moment, flung apart with enough force to rattle their frame and shake the floor. Deacon Woodbridge stands on the sill, sweating in force and fury, in his usual three-piece suit and holding before him, between his legs, a thick, silver chain draped in his hands like a spent penis. The men nearest him rise to their feet, but the deacon waves them away.

No man, he says, can carry another man's cross. You may think you can, but you only delay their journey. If God has deemed that you must walk three days and three nights to reach your destination, but you try to hitchhike, the car will break down. Try he pronounces as trah. Will he pronounces as wheel. You'll find your goal is farther than you thought.

Listen to the deacon. You all hear him now? croons the reverend. Let him do his piece.

The deacon turns his back to the crowd, wraps the chain around his wrist, and begins heaving like a longshoreman, breathing in, leaning on the right foot as he pulls, exhaling on the left as he bends forward and feeds more chain through his palms. The womenfolk tap their menfolk big and little. The deacon waves them back each time, stopping only when a four-year-old boy pulls on his jacket.

Son, I know your momma raised you right, and she might not have even been the one to send you out here. You maybe came on your own, but for once and all—he scanned the room, giving each an eyeful—leave me to my work. Mrs. Patterson, I don't come downtown and make your pies, good thing, I know. Brother Hal, I don't till your field. He looked back at the kid, And, Ricky Foldercap, young man, I don't draw in your coloring book. Okay?

You can, says Ricky, and everyone laughs.

You'll know when it's time. Lord, bless this boy. The deacon scans the room. He already has, has he not? He is merciful, is he not?

D'aron feels the Amen! in his chest, it could shake the barnacles loose.

Run on back to your momma. The deacon winks at little Ricky and says, Thank you for the break.

The congregation laughs again, so loud, rushing out the sound of the chain against the steps. Woodbridge is barely ten feet into the hall, and has another ten to reach the pulpit when the anchor comes buckling through the doorway. It is rusty and flaking, encrusted with a colony of oddities collected during its obviously long sojourn, and

packs a sneaky reek, too, bearing in tow the briny odor of Port Savannah and a smidge of the rotten smell, that sickly sweet tang of decay
haunting Tollenridge marsh, and lastly, a sniff of haint not unlike the
Oconee eddies, those brown swirls downriver from the mill, where
the refuse and metal filings caught in the whorl stain the sides of
algae-slick rocks. It smells like all those places D'aron hates, and the
deacon's shortened strides—out of exhaustion, or wary of knocking
over the pulpit, he doesn't know—make it appear an unseemly act,
one to be performed under cover of night.

The anchor an offering before the pulpit, deacon and preacher
both lay hands on it and murmur, eyes closed, one even making the
gestures reserved for rebuking demons, fingers spread, palm thrust
forward. After a few moments they appear satisfied. The preacher
returns to the dais and fans himself.

Deacon Woodbridge clears his throat. Is it a coincidence that the
anchor figures a cross? Take a look. Look through the dirt and the
grime, the barnacles and rust. See what it was and what it can do.
He motions with his hand as if cleaning a window—small—Look
through the aging and see it as God sees you. Can you see it now?
Can you see how the anchor figures a cross? He points to the cross on
the wall and everyone nods.

Is that a coincidence? I see some of you nodding. Do you believe
in coincidence? He is whispering now. Then you are in the wrong
place. Louder, he is now. I believe in God, and God don't make coin-
cidences. Coincidence! Louder yet. That's what we say when we don't
want to give Him on High credit, or we need to deny the truths that
face us, when the writing is on the wall and we do not want to read
it. It is a coincidence, we say. But no. This is no coincidence that the
anchor figures the cross. Too many of you think that God is like that
energy drink everyone is drinking in the cities. He points around the
room with an index knotted by arthritis. Gives you wings, you think.
You see these angels and want to fly. But you're not for that in this

life. In this life, Jesus is like this anchor, he grounds you. See, you've been thinking, I'll fly over and do this and that, and fly back over to church on Sunday for a refill. It's not like that.

He pulls a bag from behind the pulpit and dumps it on the floor. Cigarettes, a fifth of dark liquor, and what appears to be a men's magazine, judging from the cover, fall at his feet. Gulps and gasps from menfolk as the little ones' eyes are covered and the big ones' slack jaws are smacked. He snaps his fingers, and little Ricky places one of the items in each far corner of the church, out of the deacon's reach. The deacon walks first in one direction, then the other, stopped each time by the chain.

Your battle is with yourself. That's why you need Him. There was no Cain and Abel.

A ripple of confusion passes across the congregation, flurries and snatches of protest take flight like startled pheasants.

Listen! Not, listen, but Listen! Once only. The voice cannot, will not, be denied. Even the preacher touches his heart and crosses himself. The deacon speaks, but is no longer the speaker, is no more a speaker than a speaker is a record, than that record is a musician, than that musician is any more than a speaker for Him than whom none greater can be imagined.

They were one man, Cain and Abel. One man. That's called symbol, allegory, metaphor. Metaphor means to carry. Like we each carry in us Cain and Abel, Jacob and Esau. Abel speaks for Jesus. He is this anchor, keeps us on track and out of harm's way, keeps us sane and safe. And what do we want to do with that anchor? What do we want to do come Sunday night, or Monday night, or Tuesday night, or for you all with long memories, last Saturday night at Bobby Ray Johnston's? That is right, we cut it loose. That's right! We cut it loose, the way Cain laid out Abel. But it is Cain who has to die. Hear that. Cain must die for us to live forever. Problem is Cain is just too much fun. Never yet heard of some fellas running out Friday night to raise some Abel.

Laughter.

Oh yes, laugh. When you do, I know you heard. This week, head out there and raise some Abel.

Following the sermon, a procession to the river, the preacher in the lead, trailed by flowing white robes, a pageant of bellflowers to be submerged one by one and anointed, as John did for Jesus, as someone certainly did for John. Gentle, so gentle they are, cradling Nana's head like two clumsy children entrusted with a precious egg. She stands, her eyes sparkle, and D'aron is possessed by a rush, a true possession it feels—Alleluia!—as he scurries toward her, halting as she clears the water. The eyes aglow, yes, but her body is the same, and as she struggles to pilot it ashore, he wants to look away—but cannot—from the new sheer skin she wears, from the low orbs at midrib—staring at the wild tangle beneath. In her grasp, in her clutches, she smells still sickly, only now wet on top of it, and her hands frisk him, playing along his spine as if in search of the songs of youth. And after the baptism a ritual he was not allowed to witness but imagined all the more, knowing as he did the sounds of slaughter and recognizing, even at that pitch, Nana's voice.

He didn't sleep well for three days afterward. When he complained of it, Nana blessed him with juniper oil and warned him to never go back there alone.

Toward the end his nana suffered olfactory illusions, the doctors had a word for that, but it made her sound mentally deranged. (Maybe Candice wasn't so wrong to challenge Hirschfield for referring to Louis as the deceased.) Nana was always smelling things that weren't there—fire, and charred wood, and burning grass, and blood. Clouds, she once claimed. For years, D'aron admitted it to no one, but he thought that if kids and old people truly were closer to the Lord, maybe she did smell something. He mentioned it to no one except Charlie early the morning of the Incident, expecting him to understand, but he only shrugged. Why are you telling me now? Daron shrugged back. He'd been smelling something burning since dawn, but didn't say it. Later there was smoke on the horizon and he figured that was it, someone burning trash.

As one professor would have said, It's just the mind playing tricks on us to rationalize what it can't explain. It's how religion started.

It was all a trick of the mind. Of course. He couldn't be remembering it right.

Couldn't be.

Couldn't be.

All that chatter rattling about the Holler was hearsay, not a lick true, but as he climbed Mosby Ridge and descended south into the shallow vale, he would have preferred anything to what he was facing, setting off in the opposite direction of the meadow he'd run as a child and over the rise that separated Smiths from Houstons, town to the west clear as day, the scattered trailers to the east obscured as always by the obstinate thicket that brooked not even wind, then bearing due north to descend into the Holler.

Nope, none of the chatter was true, but he plumbed his memory nonetheless, sounding the words out until the rhythm rang right, and he knew for certain it was two steps back and one to the right before entering the Holler at night.

Chapter Thirty-4

Through a photo-encrusted hall, through a large industrial kitchen, shiny and serrated, through silver double doors smudged with fingerprints, and at last into a smaller kitchen, like the kitchen in someone's home, a kitchen appointed with a car key hook fashioned from burned wood, those clay trivets every fifth grader made for Mother's Day, and needlepoint samplers on the wall: GOD BLESS THIS HOME over the mantel and sink, A WAIST IS A TERRIBLE THING TO MIND over the window, HAPPINESS IS HOMEMADE over the swinging doors, and on the refrigerator a mosaic of magnets advertising local businesses, as well as Lou's Luscious News & Animal Calendar, featuring game in various stages of dress. It was as if Daron had sat in this kitchen all his life, and in a way he had, had he not? Daron, D'aron, Donut Hole, dat Wigga D, Turd Nerd: every few minutes a familiar face passed through, rifled the fridge or the cabinets, grabbed a cookie or a glass of milk, gave him a wave, and called him by a not-so-long-forgotten nickname. Oh, the cookies! How had he forgotten the cookies? He probably could have smelled them from the Holler. If he had, he would have imagined, precisely as it appeared, this kitchen.

ON HIS TREK INTO THE HOLLER, he had worried he was walking in circles until one faint trail, a line of broken shadow, ended at an unpaved safety-pin turn in a rough road, a hard-cocked elbow of packed and rutted dirt, no normal road because in one direction it stopped short of the last rise before the highway as if it didn't connect to any other roads, and in the other direction it ended at a gate marked PRIVATE DRIVE. He could see both from where he stood in the crook of that elbow. At the end of Private Drive, no church. No squat, wooden single-pen building with a simple cross carved into the door. No deacon at anchor. A congregation, though? Yes.

A windmill and a few sheds, a pump house and a short silo, a grain closet and an old dairy, and a soaring barn, majestic even in decay, all facing a broad low hunting lodge with a porch wrapping three-quarters around, and between them a courtyard with a single pole in the center. He vaguely recognized the man who answered the door, but couldn't recall his name. Was it Rob? Whoever it was knew him because he sighed, Finally. Postmaster's got an earache all over for you. Come on in, D'aron.

He was led to a room immediately inside the front door, a room with a desk and a few rows of government-issue metal chairs, and a TV/VCR combo on a wheeled cart like the ones they had in the elementary school media center. In fact, the blackboards on three walls, desk chairs, and flag in the corner made it feel very much like a classroom. Along the walls above the blackboards hung photos of the U.S. presidents, ending with G.W. Bush.

Behind him, a voice said, Why no 'Bama? I know you're thinking it, and I'll tell you it ain't got nothing to do with his race. It's his nationality. He wasn't born here. That's why the Terminator had to get out of politics. There was nowhere left for him to go.

Daron went knock-kneed. Postmaster? What kind of code name was Postmaster? Or so he'd wondered until hearing the man speak.

Harry Jones was indeed the local postmaster. Should he turn around? Pretend he didn't recognize the voice? Make a run for it?

The postmaster placed a kind hand on Daron's shoulder and gently spun him around. Let's talk, Little D.

He motioned for Daron to follow him down the hall, past photos of locals shaking hands and sharing beers with David Duke, Railton Loy, Hal Turner, Tony Perkins, John Tanton, Senator Russell Pearce, Terry Jones, and others. On the hall bookshelf, *The Bell Curve, Who Are We?, Freakonomics, Darwin on Trial, Illegal Is Not a Race—It's a Crime,* Jon Entine's *Taboo,* tracts by James Watson and Charles Murray and a few others. Below that, rows and rows of photo albums. They passed through an industrial kitchen into this smaller one, and now sat at an old oak table under needlepoint samplers and Lou's calendar, a plate of oatmeal raisin cookies between them.

Sure you won't have one? Eatin' one ain't gone doom you to stay here forever. Sure, they all say, Don't eat in the Holler or Gully after dark, but this here's different. These Reebah's.

Daron selected a cookie from the side of the plate closest to Harry and took a small bite. They were as good as he remembered from grade school when Little Harry brought them to class every Valentine's Day. The cinnamon warmed his cheeks and the raisins tickled his tongue.

Harry smiled. The world is changing, D'aron. All we want to do is be prepared. As he explained it, voice quiet and unassuming as when explaining the particulars of certified mail, the majority of crimes were still committed by blacks, with Mexicans a close second, interracial marriage was on the rise, and, as they have already figured out in Arizona, the white race would be a minority by 2020. Michael Hethmon said it best. We're fixing to be a minority-majority country, and there ain't a single example in history of that kind of shit storm ending well. Mind you now, the South was ten-to-one black back in the day, but we didn't have half the problems. Don't mean that we want to bring back slavery, but we shouldn't be ashamed to say that things are what they are.

When Daron was a child, this man delivered his comics and sea monkeys, drank tea with the family, sat on the porch and pushed back his hat to let breathe that red crease D'aron always took as a mark of manhood. It was D'aron who greeted him when expecting birthday cards, hurtling across the yard at full speed while the postman cheered, Run, Forrest! Run! It was this man who placed in his hand the big envelope from Berkeley, who clapped his shoulders in celebration and said, Make us proud. It was D'aron who each Christmas handed him the envelope prepared by his parents. A solemn duty it was, his father explained. Never think you're buying respect. Respect, like honor, you must earn, because both are eternal currencies. This here is only showing appreciation. Daron doesn't want to be, but he is soothed, calmed.

Counting on his fingers, the postmaster explained, There's the patriots, the sovereigns, the fools who say the sun revolves around the earth, the black separatists, nativists, the Klan, the ham-headed hammer skins—talk about standing out, might as well take a Christmas tree hunting—the True Church of Israel, and whatnot. But we're not like that. When the cuz visited you last year, he was out there as our envoy to the State of California Northern Militia Action Group. We know you've been brainwashed, we know that Berkeley's knitting with only one needle and Columbus Day was renamed Indigenous People's Day and everyone gets free parking. How can you name a day after the people that were saved? That would be like naming veteran's day Vietnam Day or France Day.

Harry was confused, he must have been. Quint had never visited Daron in California, and he said so.

Harry looked at him for a long moment while he licked the raisin off a cookie, which was terribly unsettling. You're safe here. He opened a brochure. This is our code of conduct. Here is a list of words you'll never hear any of us use: You hear nigger, nigger this and nigger that, that ain't us calling no one nigger. Or Spic, Chink, Porch Monkey, Spade, Piss-Easter, Spear Chucker, Rice Eyes, Wetback, Beaner, Beano, Bluegum, Camel Jockey, Ching-Chong, Chinky, Coolie, Coon, Cunt Eye, Darkie Dink, Dog Zombie, Dune Coon, Eightball, Gook, Hajji, Heed, Jap, Jigger, Jungle Bunny, Kike, Nidge, Niglet [a warm chuckle], Nzumbi, Pancake Face, Pickaninny, Porch Monkey, Prairie Nigger, Raghead, Sambo, Sand Nigger, Schvartze, Sheeny, Shine, Slanteye, Slope, Slurpy Slinger, Sooty, Spade, Spearchucker, Spick, Spook, Squaw, Sucker Fish, Tar Baby, Timber Nigger, Towel Head, Uncle Tom, Wetback, Zipperhead. Hear any of that, ain't one of us, not even on a Monday. I don't mean to be a double-speak, or even double-double-speak, by listing so many. I just want you to give full considerate attentions to the multitude. There's a lot of crap floating around ain't from our asses. We didn't make it up. Hear any of that, and you know it ain't one of us.

One of us what? Daron finally asked, recalling Denver's questions and what Candice had said on the phone. And the Colonel. Hadn't Colonel Sanders said something similar?

A member of the collective.

What's the collective?

All of us here who are members of the hunting lodge.

You mean a militia?

The postmaster rubbed his face. A deputy rooting through the refrigerator at that moment laughed. Oh, no, not that word.

The postmaster cupped his hands. Let's talk about the M-word. We're not a threat, a fringe group, or crazy. We're the legacy the forefathers fought to build. We're not antigovernment, we're prociti-zenship. We're not antigovernment, we're anticorruption. We're not antigovernment, we're pro-self-sufficiency. We're not separatists or racists, we're constitutionalists. We judge a man by his actions, not his skin color. The Bill of Rights tells us that all men are created equal. We know our history and we revere it. We are citizens. We are your neighbors. We represent all the county—all the surrounding town. We are your anchor in this rough sea.

Daron didn't dare ask why no one was there representing the Gully. How long?

How long what?

How long has this been here?

The postmaster laughed, the deputy joining him. How do we beat the chaos back? How did we install order in the middle of nowhere? How'd we get rid of those injuns? You may as well ask how long the Gully's been here, or the town, or the Holler. It's all there's ever been. Forever.

But how could he not have known? He had known there was a hunting lodge back here, one you couldn't join until eighteen, but he'd given up hunting long before then. How had Denver and Candice known more about his town than he did? He cursed his idiocy. I didn't know there was a militia.

Again, it ain't a militia. It's a hunting lodge and we're a collective, like those co-ops out west. We never burned no crosses or lynched no one here in Braggsville proper, least not until you came along. Let me show you something. He led Daron back to the classroom, which was, he now understood, also a recruitment office. They played him a couple of videos, handling the VCR cassettes with two hands, like relics.

Watch this.

Images of wounded U.S. soldiers and natural disasters in America, and local citizens' brigades providing support services.

Now this.

People, mostly men, training for military action and taking an oath in front of a flag. The voice-over:

From many different cultures, and every country of the earth.

Forged by only one common bond: the Constitution. The greatest enemies: domestic. Every culture, every color, one country. We do solemnly swear to the best of our abilities, to preserve, protect, and defend the Constitution of the United States of America.

That's all we are, D'aron, citizens. Everybody knows that this nanny state can't last. Everybody knows that and about the *Bell Curve* and Dr. Watson, but all we're saying is be prepared. He handed Daron a photo album. In it were daguerreotypes and old photos of the town founders posing in front of the hunting lodge. Some of the photos, though, were death shots. He recognized Bragg and one of his sons and several town elders from the replicas in the funeral home foyer.

Now this one.

The next album was mostly in color, and he saw his parents staring back at him, his father posing in front of the lodge in a Confederate uniform, his mother at the Green Egg in the backyard. There were also photos of the local intramural playoffs, like the softball match between Lou Davis's Cash-n-Carry and Howard's Hide Park, the bitterest of rivals. He recalled seeing posted in local restaurants photos of youth league teams thanking the various businesses that provided support, and the hallway in the lodge was lined with them. In fact, now that he thought of it, he had seen the lodge mentioned in photos mounted elsewhere.

On each page of the album, a surprise or pleasant memory. There was Rheanne dressed as Lady Gaga. That was the Halloween he kissed Joyce Templeton on the neck. There was his first and last football game. The debate championship in Macon. The Belle Ball, where the adults get all gussied up. It was well past sundown by the time he finished the albums.

I'm glad you finally visited. Saves us the embarrassment. The postmaster looked outside. You don't want to walk home now. Everybody knows that, even Methuselah. Besides, now that you have

finally arrived, we can have our trial. The tribunal will meet tomorrow first thing, which at least one someone should be glad to hear.

Trial? I'm being—

—Whoa, boxer. Acts one-seven. It is not for you to know times
or seasons that the Father has fixed by his own authority. Your arrival is not a coincidence. He has spoken. All your questions will be
answered in the morning. The postmaster again looked outside. You
sure don't want to walk home now. But we've dressed a bed for you.

As was often the case for youth in the South, invitation meant
instruction. Daron spent the night locked in a bedroom. At least
it may as well have been locked. Where could he go at midnight in
the middle of the Holler? It was a small room with no window and
scarcely space enough for the tube-frame twin bed. The floors were
bare wood, dark from years of wear, and the walls oak faded to ash.
It could have been a backdrop for an Abercrombie & Fitch ad, if it
weren't for the propaganda. With no cell phone service, there was
nothing to do but read. Brochures stacked neatly on the side table.
A Gideon's Bible camped out in the nightstand drawer with *The Bell
Curve*. The code of conduct, posted on the back of the door, where
the rack rates would be:

1. Good citizens make no contact with media unless first
   cleared.
2. Good citizens don't proselytize or openly recruit.
3. Good citizens make no actions representing or claiming
   to represent the collective.
4. Good citizens do not behave in ways that could harm the
   collective's public image.
5. Good citizens don't practice foul language or behavior.
6. Good citizens practice gun safety at all times.
7. Good citizens replace what they eat.

He sat on the edge of the bed most of the night, in a fugue, feeling, when he felt anything, self-disgust. How could he not be scared or angry? Why did he feel empowered, like he had stumbled into the base of Mount Olympus and they'd thrown down a rope? He fell asleep pondering the postman's final words.

What about the Gully? Daron had finally asked.

They got their own thing.

I thought this was for everyone.

Don't be a waterlog, Little D, warned the postmaster, plucking a cookie crumb off his mustache. They get work, they don't get hassled. Don't make that turned-up face like a stranger pinched a biscuit in your toilet. Look at all we do for other countries when our own house isn't in order. What if we rebuilt and gave jobs to the Fort Runner folks two towns over when people right here in Braggsville, like your father, need jobs? That wouldn't be right, would it? If your father didn't have a job right here in our community and someone over the county line did? Someone across the river? All these special interest groups. What if we didn't look out for our own? Who would? Who will?

Chapter Thirty-5

In the morning, oatmeal. Alone. No cinnamon or sugar. From the kitchen, Daron heard laughter often abruptly interrupted by uncanny silence, and he was glad to have feigned belly mites, to have begged off attending the liturgy and the pancake breakfast that followed it. At sunup he was led out to the barn, where men congregated by age. Under the hayloft sat Oliver Williams, Mayor K. (the previous mayor), Robert Butch Buchanan, Jim Stark, Justin Stark, and other elders. Near them stood Mark Lance, Tony Foldercap, and others from his father's generation. Nearest the door were Josh Turner, Kevin Dole, and several of Daron's former classmates. At the back of the barn was a long table behind which were three empty chairs, and facing the table, with his back to the crowd, stood Jo-Jo. As he was positioned, Daron could not see his hand.

Jo-Jo was a hulk, always had been, man-sized since middle school, one of the few moons rugged enough to roll with the shines. Here now, all that was gone. With his hair tangled and dread-dirty, Reeboks caked with red clay, head dog down, Jo-Jo had vanished, and the man before him was someone Daron didn't know. Certainly, though, everyone knew that back in high school, Jo-Jo hung like handcuffs with not only Jean, but also Trayvon, a lethal Gull linebacker known as the Brown Bruiser. (He was originally the Black Bruiser because the Gull team was known for a time as the Blackjacks—as in they would knock you the fuck out—but that wasn't well received at away games.) Certainly everyone knew that Bruiser and Jo-Jo had been as tight, as Jo-Jo's father liked to honk, as a Jew and his shekels. Certainly everyone knew that Jo-Jo escorted Jean's sister to the Bruiser prom, where he'd danced shamelessly according to reports, and even posed for photos, like the generous celebrity he was for that night, an eminence apparently greater even than being first string on the football team. And certainly everyone knew that he'd lost his job over that, and more. Were they still punishing him for that? He surely would not have whipped Louis.

Lou Davis entered from the back door, dressed in forest BDUs with a red patch on his shoulder and a gavel in hand. He called the hearing to order with one outstretched arm. This *collective*—he stressed the word—goes back to Bragg hisself. When the Northerners came, we fought for our country. We sent men off to every conflict big and little the U.S. has been involved in. Already receiving training here, they done us proud. We've had Rangers, Green Berets, drill sergeants, Marine Force Recon officers, plus two you-know-whos doing you-know-what. We fended off the Indian invaders and the French trappers that ventured too far north—Or south!, someone yelled—we fought off the redcoats and the Spanish, and we are still fighting for our country—this U.S. of A.—at this moment, in Afghanistan, Iraq, Somalia, Bosnia [AND PLACES WE CANNOT MENTION]. In this hearing, it is that history and honor that guides our bearing and purpose. He dropped his arm and gaveled three times. Three judges in white robes, white hoods with veils over the eyelets, and white gloves entered through the back door and were seated behind the long table. Under the dim light, they were a ghostly snowcapped range against an angry sky.

Lou read from a printout:

John-John Kelly VI, known familiarly as Jo-Jo, is hereby charged with violating the official code of conduct dated 1830, updated in 1863 and 1965, and also in 1912 and 1992, specifically Codes one-point-three, two, and ten-A, said codes respectively barring members from participating in outright violent behavior or even public pantomime of said behavior unless in self-defense, from publicly pronouncing racial epithets, or from undertaking any deed which could cast the collective in a bad light. You have also committed activities considered treasonous, including reckless endangerment, being loose of tongue, and possessing questionable moral dispositions. Like a railroad stake being driven to ground, Jo-Jo's head ratcheted down a notch with every accusation. The audience groaned at the fall of that final hammer, groaned worse than when Jo-Jo fumbled in that game against Vickstown.

Have you seen the charges?

Jo-Jo nodded. Yes, sir.

How do you plead?

Guilty, sir. I submit to the mercy and wisdom of the tribunal.

And you waive your right to meet with a senior member to discuss your plea and statement?

Yes, sir.

Lou turned to the tribunal, who conferred for a moment before flashing a hand signal. Daron had identified three so far: palm out for Stop, palm on table for Proceed, and straight hand waving, palm to the side, for Repeat. They also wrote notes, which they shared with each other.

Lou turned back to Jo-Jo. Your plea is accepted. Before sentence is delivered, you have the right to make a statement. Would you like to make a statement?

Yes, sir. Jo-Jo swallowed loudly.

Lou nodded.

Well, sir, and Your Honors, sirs. On the question of the morning, when we reached the rise up there at Old Man Donner's—

—Old Man Donner is not being reviewed.

Yes, sir. I—

Lou held up a hand motioning for Jo-Jo to stop. Several people turned their attention to the corner of the room, where, of all things, Lee Anne was fiddling with a small green machine that resembled a miniature cash register. When she finished inserting a new roll of paper, and began typing again, Lou nodded to Jo-Jo.

Yes, sir. Well, sir, when we reached the rise, I seen the man hanging there, like did Captain Williams, who pointed first that—

—Captain Williams is not being reviewed.

Daron was reminded of middle school English. Jo-Jo was always cut off there, too. By high school he'd stopped trying, picked the pigskin over paperwork, which now made sense to Daron, though at the time he'd thought Jo-Jo just needed to try harder.

Yes, sir. I seen the man hanging there and I thought it was a joke because I knew D'aron was back in town and—

—D'aron who?

D'aron Davenport. So, I thought it was him doing—

—Why would you think that?

—He had that wig, and we'd dressed like that in middle school. And like the Jackson Five for senior prom. He paused, waiting to see if that explanation was sufficient.

Lou nodded for him to continue.

I didn't mean it. It all seemed in fun. I thought it was part of the show. He's got the makeup on and all. I even thought maybe it was a test of some sort. His girl was there. She was the one holding the whip. Candy.

Miss Chelsea is not being reviewed.

Daron almost couldn't stand under the weight of shame. Candice had never stopped insisting that the man with the tattoo had delight in his eyes. He should have corrected Jo-Jo when he'd asked about the juniors and all. And if only Candice wasn't always so fucking zealous, getting as toothsome, hot, and gorged over her playacting as a fly locked in an outhouse.

Jo-Jo continued. And Cand— his girl was standing right there, saying, How do you like this? How do you like this? How do you like this? Almost like I was supposed to be angry, like we'd finally caught him. Now to mention it, I think she said, We finally caught him. Then she handed me the whip and I just cracked it in the air. I was only playing and didn't try to hit him, of course, but I think it might have grazed him, or I thought so 'cause he got to fidgeting and jerking and kicking his legs about, but he wasn't saying nothing or reaching for his throat. It was only later I learned that his hands was tied behind his back. Poor fella. Jo-Jo's heavy shoulders heaved once. Little guy didn't have a chance. I had done swung it only once a few times, but this other guy he looked real close, must've knew right away that it was that Chinese fellow; he went to town, lashing and lashing—

—Some other guy is not being reviewed.

Yes, sir. Jo-Jo cleared his throat. So, I took the whip voluntarily, yes, sir, yes, sir, I did, just planning to give D'aron a scare and get in on the joke, but then I saw it wasn't him. I thought, I'll be damned if it's not a Mongoloid-looking fella. Then I knew it was a joke. I just cracked the whip once or twice, but we was just having some fun, for Methuselah's sake. That's my statement.

The judges handed a piece of paper to Lou, who read it aloud. So, you didn't strike the man with the whip?

Well, no, sir. Of course not. I thought it was D'aron at first.

Daron's stomach spiked again.

You did not whip the man.

No, sir.

Anything else?

No, sir.

Louis would have called them sexy Afghanis. But when they huddled, the judges looked like Mount Rushmore, except Daron knew that underneath the white they were Gray. They must have already made up their minds because they consulted each other and a note-book for less than a minute before motioning to Lou, who motioned Jo-Jo over. You may step to the bench. Go ahead, son. Go on.

Jo-Jo approached the table for the sentence, which was delivered in a whisper. Jo-Jo looked back at Daron once and nodded yes, and looked back at him again and nodded again. Jo-Jo was led away. Daron was called to the front, where he stood before the jurors. There were gasps as he passed. There were also more than a few cross tattoos.

They couldn't get away with this, thought Daron. The compound. The trial. Mount Rushmore. A constitution. A stenographer. A stenographer? Fuck! They weren't getting away with jack rabbit shit. They'd already done it. He recalled again the lesson on Nagasaki, how the swimmer surfaced to find a harsh new world. Did he hold his breath to the last minute, as Daron did? Did he relent because he had to know? Were his doubtless brief remaining years irrevocably corroded by the ironic end of that now eternal kicking to the surface, the unexpected outcome of pedaling liquid in his ascent back to life? Did he even recognize his friends' shadows? Or were they warped, autonomous silhouettes? Can a shadow be ill-fitting? What does it mean when the shadow does not suit the man? Does the man change? Or does the shadow?

You won't get away with this. Even as he said this, though, Daron feared that he was wrong, that maybe the collective had, and were, getting away with nothing, that maybe Postmaster was right. This was simply what had been, what was, what would be. Forever. You won't get away with this, he repeated weakly.

Mocking falsettos echoed. Someone yelled, Cut! Take one. That's a wrap. Say it with gumption next time, son.

My father knows where I am!

Of course he does, young Davenport, of course he does, crooned Lou. We're sovereign, you see. You tell the officer who gives you the speeding ticket, You won't get away with it? He tells you to tell it to the judge. It's the same thing here. You can plead your own case before the tribunal. We can provide you a counselor to familiarize you with the process and the bylaws, and even sit beside you at the hearing, but you got to plead on your own—his voice dropped to a whisper—believe me, son, it's best you plead on your own.

My father knows where I am, Daron whispered.

Of course he does, son, of course he does. Lou draped a warm, paternal arm around him, his rough hand hanging over Daron's shoulder, his scabbed knobbly knuckles reminding Daron of the fox stole eyeing him at Hartsfield Airport in Atlanta.

I'm not guilty of anything.

You got to plead on your own, young Davenport.

I'm not guilty of anything. He muttered, unable to rouse conviction, chilled as he was after Lou again called him young Davenport, as had Otis. Chilled because he liked it, and knew he shouldn't. And once again, that cold feeling—so cold as to feel wet—at the thought, new to him, that Lou was right: Of course he was, son, of course he was.

Lou patted Daron on the back and turned to face the audience. You, young man, are guilty of just about everything. If I didn't know better, I'd think you set out with a plan to destroy our fine little town here. But we're assuming you were more foolish than anything else, and led astray by all those leftists. Do you want to make a statement? Do you want a senior member to guide you?

I didn't do nothing wrong but not be there for my friend.

That you'll have to reckon with your maker. I take it you don't have a statement and won't enter a plea, so we will proceed. D'aron Little May Davenport is charged with treason, moral turpitude, and egregious actions against the state.

I'm not a member of this militia. Daron's voice splintered. You can't try me.

He could see Jo-Jo though a crack in the door, his head hanging low, his fingers playing his thighs, pacing back and forth and forth, more agitated with each passing, the smoke trailing behind him from a cigarette he looked to have forgotten as it hung from his split lips.

You appear rightly scared, and contrite, so we accept Jo-Jo's bargain. Your sentence is twofold. You are banished from the Holler and the town, allowed back only for holidays and funerals.

A hand motion from Mount Rushmore. A quick conference.

Okay. So you can come back for weddings. We're not stalling.

Another whispered conference with Rushmore.

Okay. We're not Stalinists, so weddings are in. You are also to deliver Jo-Jo's punishment. This is his wish.

It was only seven A.M. Daron was reminded of an old joke. How did it go? We do more before eight A.M. than most people do all day. That was true at the lodge. At Berzerkeley, at this hour, he'd usually be sleeping. Sometimes he would get up early for the pleasure of being among the first in the dining hall, when the breakfast bar is fresh and steaming and really does look like the photos. Then, return to the dorm and sleep for a few more hours. Here, he had already eaten oatmeal, witnessed a trial, been tried himself, and now stood behind the barn, watching two yellow rails play tag, all bright bulging buff breasts in the brush, dark wings spotted white in flight. A tree not far away had been felled by lightning, and from the stump new shoots pushed skyward, and under its crumbling trunk, tiered shrooms sprouted from wicked moss. He examined the grounds, wondering who cut the grass, recited the Greek alphabet, and visualized the periodic chart, anything to take his mind off Jo-Jo, who was at that moment being lashed to a pole centered in a ten-foot dirt circle bordered by blue painted rocks, Jo-Jo who was calling to him, Be quick now, when it starts, just be quick.

I can't do it, whispered Daron.

You gotta. Think about it, D. The poor fella was all made up in blackface and that wig and I thought it was you up there. It wasn't until he was kicking and choking and sweating off the makeup. It was too late by then. I could tell he was Mongoloid Chinese or had that syndrome or something. But it was your girl. And it was your wig.

That was middle school. And just one night in high school.

And? And? Jo-Jo's speech was swallowed by sobbing.

No, you don't, warned Lou, pointing.

Daron had moved closer to Jo-Jo while talking. Two men-at-arms repositioned him a few paces farther away, the distance stepped out by Lou.

The bailiff read the decree. According to statute, for his behavior during the Patriot Days Festival, John-John could be stripped of his rank, but in lieu of that he elects hereby to receive twenty yards of leather, or twenty lashes. This sentence of flogging was unanimously rendered by the tribunal and unopposed by the brethren. Said flagellation is to be delivered by one D'aron Little May Davenport, who delivers said lashes as part of his punishment, said sentence which includes conditional banishment.

Flagellation, Candice liked to say. Oh, yes she did.

Someone pressed the whip into Daron's hand. The handle was heavy braided leather, eight feet later the tip tapering into little more than a shoestring. All it needed was an aglet, he mused, to make me believe we can tie this all together. I won't do it. Daron dropped the whip. It coiled at his feet like a dead snake—dead, but daring him to tread on it nonetheless, like the T-shirt popular with soldiers, like the motto on the first U.S. Navy maritime flag. The hashtags mashed. #ZombieDickSlap and #BraggsvilleDickSlap at last came together.

You gotta do it, D, you got to. It's twenty from you or fifty from them, Jo-Jo whispered. And my rank.

Someone pressed the whip back into his palm, closing his hand around Daron's. That someone stood close behind, close quartered, close as he'd once wished Kaya would, and then Candice. That someone said, You gotta own this one. That someone said, I ain't much for philosophy, especially other men's, but as the Boss said once, You got to learn to live with what you can't rise above. That someone sounded so much like Quint, so much that Daron couldn't turn around.

Shaking, he delivered the first lash.

The bailiff walked out to John-John, poked at his back. Not even so much as a welt. Try again.

Harder, yelled John-John, harder goddammit, D, harder please.

The next one cuts. Jo-Jo, shaking and shivering, says, I'm okay. Candice had said, Delight in his eyes. Daron imagined John-John Kelly whipping Louis—Lenny Bruce Lee, swinging harder each time, the whip unfurling like an extension of his arm, starting the strikes at the wrist, but soon swinging from the shoulder, then the hips, leaning into each blow like Michael Jackson in *Smooth Criminal,* his self-reproach diminishing by the yard, every lick a neat slice, the skin parting like broad petals. By the ninth, John-John Kelly passed out, his back torn like an old sail, the waist of his stonewashed jeans pink with sweat and blood, one sneaker, the clay kicked clean, upside down a few yards away, in the shadow of that stump. Candice said he had delight in his eyes. Daron felt the nettling in his chest that had plagued him on the drive from the morgue finally begin to unwind.

The bailiff nodded and two men wheeled out a cart bearing a coffin with iron bars in place of the hinge lips. The satin bedding was ripped out and replaced with slimy river rocks and black snakes. The men-at-arms lifted Pvt. John-John Kelly VI's limp figure, and sympathy and repulsion assailed Daron in equal measure as he watched Pvt. Kelly's body droop, and he saw the hand with the cross tattoo dangle, and he saw Pvt. Kelly's head loll like Christ carried down from the cross, and he heard the liquid sloshing in Pvt. Kelly's stomach as they tossed him into the coffin and locked a metal gate across the top. About five minutes later, muffled screams could be heard from everywhere, it seemed. Daron heard them even from the gate, when he was being driven back into town, the gray, aged wood of the hunting lodge fading in the side mirror to his right, his cousin whistling in the seat to his left.

Flagellation, Candice loved to say. Oh, yes she did. Flagellation. It sounds so much like sexiness.

FOR LUNCH, HIS FAVORITE: meatloaf with sweet onions, jalapeños, and extra ketchup, and his mother even remembered to fry apples on the side. Kissing him on the head every time she passed his chair was only the beginning. For dinner, Out! Out? Out! Hell yeah! Outside the house? Outside the backyard, even. An early dinner, when it's still broad, bright, cave-man naked daylight?

And why not? his father asked. Not even those second-string Katy-catch-ups are across from City Hall anymore, and there's an antijournalism barricade up the way.

Daron hadn't noticed.

At the end of their street, Sheriff had now stationed a deputy, who waved them through, giving Daron, he could have sworn, a conspiratorial nod. Didn't he? On the ride through town, Young Tanner, David First, Greg Keen, Ellen Ray. All at their windows or porches, all waving for a parade. His father drove at a leisurely clip, in no rush tonight, no longer on graveyards.

At Lou's they were greeted with smiles. Rheanne gave him a little wink, and there was even extra whipped cream on his pie that he didn't ask for. After dinner his father pushed back from the table and rubbed his stomach, drawing his middle finger in a circle around his belly button. His mom burped once, demurely. Excuse me, she giggled.

I told you about being flirtatious in public. His dad winked.

His mother placed one hand on his father's forearm. With the other, she tightly clasped Daron's fingers. Eyes watering, she said, My men, my men. My little piggies. What would I do without you?

I wonder that myself, agreed his father.

She sniffed and sank a foot deeper into her sentimental abyss.

No. I mean that's a good question. What would you do without me? asked his father.

I don't know, but I know what you won't do with me. She reached across the table and took his father's cake. I shouldn't have let you order this. No one over twenty needs a second dessert.

When his father objected, she explained, You'll thank me for this one day.

That was what Quint had said on the way home. Those were in fact the only words they had exchanged, or ever would again.

Chapter Next

Agent Denver had warned them that it wasn't over, though they tried to live otherwise. It was twelve months after Louis's death and the Incident at Braggsville. D'aron had transferred to Loyola University of New Orleans to be with Candice, and both were on track to graduate with honors. Charlie was living at home, attending Northwestern. The Incident at Braggsville had been too much for his mother to bear, though she did let him travel (by train only) to Nola to visit his friends (for a weekend only). The occasional laugh sounded, but when the 3 Little Indians bid adieu at the station Sunday night, tears couldn't mask their relief. Charlie promised, via text, to be back, He!!a soon!!! All three agreed that would be, S+upendous!!! Daron was therefore shocked when, some thin months later, Candice skipped in clapping and singing about Charlie spring breaking in Nola.

Since that visit, Daron had entertained very few thoughts of Charlie. Fewer than few, he had to admit, turning his mind over and finding himself to have been agitated by only one query. Idée fixe. This constancy of theme was of no solace. No, not at all, not when it traveled brothers-in-arms with a rabid and merciless frequency, tugging at his hems, cuffs, collars like a child with a limited vocabulary who will have his chocolate bar or, oxygen be damned, return to the

womb. (That's crazy, D!) Likewise, erudition be damned, so D'aron's
mind assaulted him with this artless inquiry. And explanation be
damned, he ignored the incessant reiterations, attributing them to—
horror!!—ego!!. ego!!? [And that horror paled, appalled as it was by
guilt of C/catholic—yes, both majuscule and minuscule—guilt of
C/catholic dimensions (with apologies to Louis ten-times-hella-ten-
times over. For we were to shed Freud like diapers, were we not? For
we were to transcend the institution's attendant psychic impositions,
were we not? For we were to walk upright, were we not? Or we were
to be slapped straight up in the dick with this hefty textbook, to,
Give us something to motherfucking crouch about!) LeggoMyego!!,
No!!, EgoLeggoMe!!, LeggoMe!!, dammit!]

Certainly, it was ego!!, which, like yet another awful waffle, was
mostly empty space inexplicably generously outfitted with fluffy deep
pockets for your favorite toppings—misinterpretations and defense
mechanisms and neuroses, inherited and congenital. In his case, Daron
mused, a double dose of contradiction. For how else could D'aron come
to ask Daron if Charlie ever had a crush on him? How else could he
have come to house such anguish and alarm when imagining Charlie
laughing at that inquiry? And what if he said no? Would D'aron be
relieved or offended? When Maylene's boyfriend had claimed that
Charlie was a three-way-caller, Daron had dismissed said claim, said
implications, said sentence as neatly as . . . as . . . as Lou enacting his
role as sergeant-at-arms. Oh, no, he'd said to himself, Charlie's sexuality is NOT BEING REVIEWED. When Charlie had admitted it
himself, Daron still hadn't believed it. Oh, no, he'd said to himself,
A surreptitious-smooch-shared-amid-middle-schoolers-at-summer-
camp-in-a-split-second-of-adolescent-uncertainty-to-alleviate-
a-hormonal-headache-exacerbated-exotic-by-de-facto-segregation
was NOT FUCKING BEING REVIEWED! Not to mention that
(don't worry, he won't) D'aron had once touched his own cinnamon
bun—as Nana called it—while shooting his goobers to the moon—as

Nana called it; Daron had admitted, sober, that Bruno Mars was an aw-ite-looking fellow; Daron had taken an interest in matching clothes; and knew none of that made him a three-penny nickel. Despite this, Daron watched in amazement as D'aron reminded Candice that it wasn't spring break for everyone, and that he was carrying an exceptionally ambitious course load in anticipation of early graduation, and that they'd promised themselves a romantic weekend in Gulfport, Mississippi (We're open for business and geared for a good time!). Finally, he prepared the doomsday device: Our spring breaks don't end well! Fortunately, before tearing into the launch codes for that one, the spirit of curiosity possessed him because Candice added, And guess what? He's bringing his new boyfriend!

As Charlie's arrival neared, regret plagued Daron. Charlie and his beau—D'aron preferred beau over boyfriend—would sleep in the living room, making D'aron a detainee, and indeed the first night of Charlie's visit D'aron remained trapped in the bedroom, a political prisoner in his own home, thirsty and anxious to piss, mourning the wee-wee hours of the morning but afraid to walk in on, as Maylene's boyfriend described a scene in vo-tech, Two wet bears in a wrestling match.

Surprisingly, though, he mostly liked Frederick. The only thing gay about him—and it took Daron far more than a gander to gather even this—was that he smelled nice, as D'aron imagined French cologne would smell. (Don't worry. Candice lectured him about that.) Frederick was half-Tunisian, half-Vietnamese, wore a Bruno Mars pompadour, and donned a blazer daily. His open face and wide-set cow eyes provoked and projected sympathy. Freddie— that's *I* and *E,* please—as he liked to be called, was slimmer than Charlie, but also graced with enviable athletic definition. That's not why Daron liked him, though. Frederick's parents had guessed his sexuality when he was young (The now legendary King Holiday fifth-grade dress-up day fiasco, was all he would say), and enrolled him immediately in karate classes, Not to change you, to protect you, and he'd gone on to earn a black belt. That's not why D'aron didn't like him, though. He had an intense stare, more intense than Louis's had been, and he played cards, drank everything that could be poured, complained the moment too much air invaded his glass, cursed, and talked about growing up in a rough Bronx neighborhood where fathering a kid in high school was a badge of honor and where men tossed about *Faggot!* like confetti (some, he added, more like dollars to fire up skank strippers), where he had to fight every day, and did so successfully and not entirely regretfully. By the time he was fifteen, his roundhouse kick kept the teasing to side talk, and those who didn't know him would back off once he quietly issued the standard warning: Your sorry tail is about to slither home and confess that RuPaul kicked your ass. That's not why Daron liked him, though.

Why was Charlie with a mixed guy instead of a black dude; who was the man in the relationship? He could draw no conclusions based on observation. They shared duties as he and Candice did, still Daron found it hard to picture himself one-half of a two-pants partnership. Quelle différence?

Charlie sat the same, erect, but an air of relaxation had settled over him. He ran each morning at a pace that accommodated Candice and Frederick, and his legs no longer bounced as he laced his shoes, and when waiting for his nuked burritos, he didn't pace. A few days into his visit, they ran out of vodka (okay, really it was day two, more specifically the first morning—but it was Nola, prudence be damned) and Candice dragged Frederick along to the store to buy more, leaving Charlie and Daron alone. On Charlie's first visit, whenever Candice had announced an errand, Daron offered to go, or suggested that all three travel together and treat it like a tourist excursion, which was not hard: even making groceries was an adventure in Nola. Candice had always relented. This time, though—Operation Vodka—she and Frederick tweeted their departure from the park-

ing lot, leaving Daron flush with sympathy for his mom, who threw
a fit blacker than a striped hat if she received an electronic message
from anyone within shouting range: No texting in shouting distance.
Birds are real! Tweets are real! Twitters are not! had echoed through
the house often enough that he couldn't be angry at Candice, even
though he suspected she'd planned it.

Nice apartment. Charlie looked around.

Thanks. That was nice of him, because it wasn't all that great an
apartment, another tenement in the undergrad ghetto, Daron first
thought. Actually, that's weird, Daron second thought. Is this what
they would do now? Should he compliment Charlie's new skids—
custom double-tongue Converse with a black cap—or would that be
a snide swipe, a cat slap?

I like that you have a picture of Louis up. I do, too. Freddie was
jealous. Jay-lous! He laughed. Do you love Candice?

Uh . . . I don't know. I think so, but I don't know. The spo-
radic insomnia he'd suffered following the visit to the morgue, which
worsened something awful after the inquest and went downright
feral after the trial, had abated since they'd moved in together, but he
didn't know if that meant they were in full-on love finer than frog's
hair. Do you love Freddie?

I think so, shifting in his seat, letting his hand flop over his knee
like a rag.

They compared notes, for the hundred-and-seventh time, on the
differences between their new schools and Berzerkeley. They were
loath to admit as much, but the latter won out. Diversity, weather,
alien technology: chillation nation. All the while, Daron found
himself studying Charlie. Had his carriage, his facial expressions
changed? As D'aron watched, Daron was aware of the observer's
paradox. Daron was aware that Charlie might be monitoring his behavior because he was aware that D'aron was watching him. Daron
was aware that he might see only what he was looking for. To top

that pyramid of gothic cheerleaders, D'aron was hyperaware that, as Maylene's boyfriend did say, Those theories and shit can zap your bug, scramble your egg real bad, make it hard for you to connect to people.

They reminisced about Louis. Charlie had assured Daron that his mother did not hate Daron. Daron had assured Charlie that his mom did not hate Charlie. Neither could assure the other of anything regarding the Changs. In the twelve months since Louis's death, he and Candice had mentioned Louis only seldom, but for the first few days of this trip, talking about the absent was easier than talking about the present. At least for Daron.

Again, he was curious. When the skin of masculinity was shed, as one professor put it, the psychic constrictor evaded, as another professor put it, the full humanity of all beings embraced, as another professor put it, what was left but equality? Daron had cracked his walnut on that idea. He knew it meant that somewhere out there existed a freestanding entity, an island called Equality that was obscured by a fog of prejudice that was slowly burning off, being licked clean by light, being evaporated—as it were—by the rising sun of enlightenment and social justice, as one professor put it. As Daron thought of it, though, it was as if someone cut an East Coast massive fart, and until it cleared no one could smell the roses. Or, maybe it was like eating a hamburger in a bus station bathroom. By his reckoning, if there was that much damn fog, how did anyone know that the fog wasn't real and that the island wasn't an illusion, that the fog wouldn't burn off to reveal yet more fog? (No one liked Mondays!)

How do people treat you now?

Now what?

You know.

I do? An uncertain smile bit Charlie's lips. How do people treat Charlie? Or how do people treat Charlie the Gay Man?

Charlie.

The same.

And the other?

The other?

A bubble of lunch belched. When they find out you're gay, said Daron.

Thank you for finally saying it, Daron. The same but different. Used to be blacks weren't bothered when I was around; everyone else was more likely to be. It's reversed.

(What could he say to that? That he understood because it was how he would have described his feelings about Braggsville, his family, the Gulls? But where was one to go after claiming that kind of kinship? Would Charlie even accept it? Maybe it wasn't that bad because Charlie had acceded to a seat in high society and Daron to fringe authority, at least not bad for Charlie. There were an awful lot more whites than blacks. There were also an awful lot more people who weren't from Braggsville. He hoped Charlie thought he'd made the right decision. To his own mind, Daron never had a choice. On a third, unrelated hand, was that why Charlie seemed blacker? Didn't he? Sported his own rock-in-the-flip-flop walk? Daron once asked why Charlie didn't swagger or dip with the choreographed stride of theyselves. Charlie said he had. One time. And his mother threw her shoe at him, which he caught just in time to be unable to deflect the smack that followed. He'd shared several similar stories: Crouching Mother, Hidden Dragon.)

Again, he was curious. Didn't it smell funny? Didn't it hurt like a motherfucking fatherfucker? Who was the boss? Still he wondered, had Charlie liked him? He had not known if he would be offended or relieved, but looking at Charlie that afternoon, Daron knew that even though he would never, ever, ever, under any circumstances have sex with Charlie—the thought terrified him, good heavens, even trying to not imagine Charlie's cock terrified him [he didn't like the slap-fight sound of that idea running naked through his head]—he would be offended if this Charlie, this poised Charlie with the sculpted lips, didn't like him at least a little bit. That didn't make Daron gay. He was sure of it. (He had thought it through, even though following his own logic was a bit like tracking a shadow through a tunnel, he was never sure the idea he was tailing at the exit was the same idea he had been following at the entrance.) Yes, Daron was sure that didn't make him gay, nor did it make him gay to ask, What's it like?

What?

It. You know. What's the stuff like, when you do it?

Stuff? When you do it? It? Charlie blubbed his lips, and, as he did so, gave a sharp inhale and long exhale. A look of peace came over his face, his eyebrows lengthened. Now we're talking. That's the Daron I love. Louis said what shouldn't be said. You ask what shouldn't be asked.

So, does it hurt?

Does it hurt when you put your finger in your ass?

No. Who said that? Who said I put my finger in my ass? Did Candice—

Charlie waved him down, his arms scissoring big as a swimmer calling for help. Then he held his thumb and index finger about zero inches apart. That's your asshole.

So it does hurt. (Fuck! Why'd he say that? Of course it hurt, even taking a Thanksgiving kerplupple was no bear's walk in the woods.)

Initially, yeah. But it's like sex with a woman. You have to get aroused first. Men don't secrete anything, but it still helps to get aroused first. It's all about the introduction, the first impression.

Daron hmm-mmed studiously.

Ha! Charlie again blubbed his sculpted lips, wiggled his foot, and regarded Daron. It was a look Daron recognized but could not name. He'd last seen it the crisp November morning he and his father took Chamber, their German shepherd, out for the long walk. D'aron had already finished digging the swallow, and was climbing out of the ditch when his father crouched before Chamber as if to tell him something. Chamber raised his gray forepaw to shake, his happy tongue hanging down like a hungry Christmas stocking. His father held on for a long moment, until D'aron, embarrassed, looked away. Finally, his father said, I'll be damned if this paw hasn't healed up right nicely. We'll head back. You best fill that hazard. And don't forget the rifle.

Daron again hmm-mmed studiously, this time holding Charlie's eyes as he did so.

Okay. I'll tell you. Charlie leaned in. You have this feeling, this undefined longing that rattles around like the pellet in those ball bearing mazes, and stuff pulls at it. But you don't know why or even what's pulling at it. Then when you finally have sex, this longing is given shape, texture, scent, sound, taste, until it can only be itself— like being beamed up to the USS *Enterprise*. So, when it happens, if it's supposed to happen, no matter how it hurts, or pleases, or disappoints, it feels right, and that's how you know. That's what it's like. It's like when cells specialize, said Charlie.

Daron flushed with unexpected joy, and hoped that the occasion when Charlie's cells first specialized was as thrilling as his first time with Candice, excepting her baseball trick, which raised not the joy of the specialized but the specter of the metastasized. He wheeled his hands like a steamboat paddle. What about? You know? Up or down?

Charlie described what it was like to penetrate someone, that odd interplay of affection and aggression. Daron found that similar to what he'd experienced his first time with Candice, except for the baseball. During the act itself, he had felt like he was piloting his body but not inhabiting it, that it was a drone, and for one unexpected and frightful moment was caught in a shockingly direct connection to Candice. This was followed by pure puzzlement at how she could find it enjoyable, but he did—So oh well, he thought—and let slip away the question of how one person could let another person into their body, perceiving only at the moment of ejaculation exactly what Candice had done for him. How to say that the body could be a gift?

Charlie shared that, too, described what it was like to be penetrated, to invite another into your body, a voluntary possession, how different it was face-to-face versus from behind or the side, how top didn't always mean boss. How after the first time, he'd felt relief then shame then guilt. But thirty minutes later, by the end of round two, that storm had passed, and he nested into the guy's embrace like he'd finally arrived where he should be. It was sort of how I felt when we all met. It clicked.

Was that when you knew you were in love?

No, dude. That was Tracey, this other guy. A real jerk. He dumped me a week later. Turned out he was a test pilot.

The doorbell. Daron, disappointed that Candice and Freddie were back so soon, slammed the door with relief on the Mormons littering his porch.

That's solid C-O-two.

You know what's solid C-O-two? They go around asking people to join a made-up religion with a metaphysical glass ceiling. That's cold. Besides, it's not even a real religion. I've been to real church.

Oh, have you?

Yeah. A black one back in the Holler.

A black one is a real one? There's some essentializing I can let slide.

He wanted Charlie to continue, but the mood had passed, and the ensuing bantering was not the gift horse to kick in the balls. Besides, he had heard what he needed to hear: The act is different. The feeling is not. (The act still scared the shit out of him.)

Daron laughed. Again, louder.

What?

Etymology.

What?

Anus means ring, as in, With this I thee wed.

Charlie cut up, then asked, Why are you reading about anuses?

I'm gonna be a college grad. I gotta know what shit means.

WHEN THEY LEANED OVER the coarse wooden railing of their balcony—how he loves her leaning, sprite's hope gracing her face—the entire Loyola campus opened up, Holy Name cathedral their favorite, the parapet walk atop the tower high enough, she insisted, To see the future. Predictably, the first night they crept up those 162 steps, fueled by spirits, laughing through their noses, the sky was a blue-black bisque. They couldn't see their building, let alone tomorrow. They could smell the sour dishwater odor of the cafeteria, a nearby bakery, the mournful river. They could hear an ambulance, a siren of sorority pledges, car starters barking far too loudly for the hour. The night they climbed those 162 steps with Charlie and Freddie was a clear night, laughter wafted from open windows like home cooking, and somewhere downriver a foghorn refused to stand on ceremony. Daron took that as a sign. The moon'll tell you, Nana always said. You might not like it, but it'll tell you.

This time at the station, as if to give Daron and Charlie time alone, Candice and Freddie fell behind (that's why he liked him—confirmed when Candice later admitted that Operation Vodka was his idea). When their train was called, Freddie pulled his hair under a knit cap, and when he turned to wave, he resembled Lenny Bruce Lee, and Daron squeezed Candice's hand so hard that she snatched it to her chest with a short bark. After the whistle sounded, she and Daron ran alongside the train, Daron timing his strides with the clanking side rods. When they could follow no more, Charlie and Freddie stuck their heads through the window, and Daron felt like they were seeing him off. How strange and wonderful, he thought, it was to have friends.

LATER THAT EVENING after Charlie and Freddie left, Daron walked in on Candice in the bathroom, I just need the Vaseline. She was brushing her teeth, and waved him by with a winging elbow, grunting her okay, he'd thought. It was the scene he'd imagined so long ago at home in B-ville, couples sharing small spaces while attending to separate tasks, carpooling through life in defiance of physics. After a time, they hardly noticed each other. But he would never grow weary of watching Candice. Each day a gift of observation or revelation, or both. Two coughs and one throat clearing were only the beginning. Each day their lexicon would grow, their shorthandoffs to the heart: slang, ironic advertising slogans, winks, fingers grazing earlobes, book titles, film quotes, conspicuous lyrics, a tidal wave of desire surfing a wisp of a glance, their private language a suprasemiotic domain, a code not even Turing could crack. But when she slapped the Vaseline into his palm, spit a tangle of pink foam, and shouldered by him without wiping her chin, the enigma was his alone.

She'd been acting oddly ever since Charlie left. Was she raking because she wasn't baking, as Nana said? Candy-Anne? he called. Candy-Bear, what's wrong?

The bedroom door slammed in response. Stomping. I'll study at the library, she called, that punctuated by banging the only other door worth slamming, the front door, shut with force sufficient that the windowpanes rattled in their mullions and the whole apartment felt to cough with embarrassment. When she returned later, sans books, it was not to watch the shows he'd DVRed and dutifully waited to view. And later, when he thought he heard her crying in the bathroom and tapped on the door—What's wrong, Candy?—only a flush in answer.

Promotion politics! That's what it had to be.

His father had warned this happened eventually with all women. Cohabitation, engagement, marriage, kids—not necessarily in that order these days, but each one is a rank, and the higher the rank, the more they demand and the less they explain. Your girlfriend is a private, your fiancée a captain, your live-in a lieutenant, your wife an admiral, your old lady a drill sergeant. Trick is to grant them privileges without promoting them. That's the trick, all right.

They'd had this conversation in the garage when D'aron was in middle school, his father scooting around on his favorite creeper, inspecting the muffler and the CV joints under Maylene's pickup. Her boyfriend was away at school: vocational training. As they conversed, D'aron watched his father's Red Wings tap out the tempo of his speech.

How do you do that trick? he asked.

D'aron grinned when, before answering, his father dug his heels in and rolled out from under the car for emphasis, which meant hearing French. His father believed you had to look a man in the eye when you spoke French. (French was of course known about town as the Dirty Italian at that time because all things French were on the No Fly List.)

His father thought about it a moment. No damned idea, son. If I could figure that I wouldn't be in the hotbox.

You'd be in the rib with the sleeves?

His father laughed every bit of air out of his lungs, as he had when an even younger D'aron asked how they knew it was French kissing if no one was actually talking. It was not a laugh of encouragement, no matter how many times his father apologized, said, I'm not laughing at you, boy, I'm laughing with you, only in advance of you gettin' the joke. And so, with a keen awareness of his naiveté at hand, an awareness spiny and febrile in feeling and effect, Daron had always expected his initiation into the mysteries of intimacy to be a somber affair, but after that first flailing cocktail of sweat and desire, after they lay stuporous in an afterburn longer than the flight itself, only energy enough to inch over to the dry spot—her giggling, he in drunken delight at having a bedful of her—after walking his fingers across her sweet rise of thigh and into that acreage where legs swell with envy, after wondering if there was a name for that kiss of a crease under her ass, after recovering from his astonishment that the actual could be greater than or equal to the imagined, and while attempting to predict his refractory period, she yelped and nearly tripped over the sheets scampering to the bathroom, Bam! A minute later, she returned wearing his robe—Excuse me, but it says Hilton, Daron, Hilton! She stood with her fists clutched to her stomach, moaning, Something's wrong, something's wrong. Did the condom slip off?

What?

Look!

She guided his trembling hands to her navel. Through the terry cloth he felt a lump the size of a fist and hard as a skull. His first thought was C/cancer! (Ridiculous, he knew even at the time, but Big C was the guest star in every waiting room brochure and on every other TV show, not to mention all those pink ribbons. And everything caused cancer: balsamic vinegar, underwire bras, barbecue. Secrets even.) So his first thought was, C/cancer!, until the node started to move, to roll. He jerked his hands away, cracking one of Candice's nails in the process. She retreated to French: Ooh la la, Daron, relax, tranquille. Meanwhile, the lump—too large to be benign—rustled and moled down the folds of the robe. A baseball landed between her feet, the red stitches looking for the first time just that. She withdrew from the pocket two walnuts, smiling. We didn't have marbles. We didn't have a frozen chicken or hot dogs, either.

[As this happened, he had noticed that her chipped golden toenail polish highlighted a thread pattern in the carpet, a short weave called Berber, and he wondered why carpet, that most stationary of furnishings, would be named after a nomadic people. He'd also noticed that her fingernails did not match her toenails, or the Berber. He'd also noticed that the first image that stomped into his head without knocking or wiping its feet was Louis on the gurney in the morgue, and he feared for the first time that he and Candice could not be together, that the past few splendid months had been a period of tentative remission, a long kiss good night, and fate plotted in the wings to claim them all. {What if D'aron had not been Ron-Ron, had not been Philadelphia Freedom? Faggot? What if Daron had met her in the party, on the parquet, and asked her to dance? But . . . would they still be here?} Was Agent Denver right in ways Daron had not considered? When all four of them—Charlie, Candice, Daron, and Denver—had last met, Denver ended the session by announcing, It's not over yet, but soon enough we'll be able to go our separate ways. Daron said to himself at the time, Please go your own fucking way as soon as you fucking can, but us, we're not separating for shit. Then this. God, what was going to happen to them? Nana would have known what to do.]

It was the first and only time Daron hawked Candice. She was never, he demanded, neh-vah to do something like that.

I wasn't making fun of you, she sputtered, hand to neck, like the night they met at the dot party. I thought the sex ed story about the frozen chicken, baseball, and hot dog was cute, the way Quint told it.

Daron skipped a breath, winced his shoulders as he calmed himself, I shouldn't have raised my voice. I mean scare me, said Daron. He explained what he'd thought, foolish as he knew it sounded.

The kiss that followed would take another book to describe. Their first time had gradually faded in his memory, and he hadn't thought much about it until the night Charlie and Freddie departed, when he awoke to Candice's face only inches from his own, her breath heavy on his chin. They lay head to head, her staring. Staring. Staring. Staring. When did she begin sleeping with her eyes open? Using a finger, then a hand, he windshield-wipered the air before her face. She muttered a word of which he heard only the end. Was it dammit? Frederick? Sheriff? Certainly not Sheriff.

How's that?

This is serious, isn't it, Daron.

How's that?

Us.

Us?

You. Me. Us. Living together. This city. New Orleans, for Christ's sake. We say Nola, but it's not. It's fucking New Orleans. I have a goddamned fleur-de-lis tattooed on my ankle. When my parents got mad because I cut my hair, I grew it back out, but dreaded it in retaliation. How fucked is that? When we gave Charlie and Freddie that tour, you pontificated on the differences between Louisiana and Red Rooster hot sauces. The same goddamned company makes both of them. It's not our city. After everything. This is real, said Candice. She drew a long breath, nuzzled deeper into her pillow. This is real.

Very, very. Daron nodded and rapped the headboard: a section of wall six feet long and two feet high, edged with ribbon and painted gray to match the lamps.

You don't understand.

The neighbor knocked back.

He laughed.

She sat up. You don't understand. It's like the night we did it the first time. You got mad at me, thought I was sick. No one gets mad at me, not like that.

I'm sorry, Candy. I didn't mean it like that, Candy. You know I was only scared. Candice. Please. Candice.

It's the same way you looked after the morgue. I saw it today when you looked at Freddie. She lay back down and rolled away from him, sobbed. Daron placed one hand on her arm, where it lay still, a trespasser afraid to be discovered.

I'm scared. It's real, and Louis is dead, said Candice. And the last thing I said to him was, Shut up! Those might have been the last words he heard. Sheriff knew that. She wailed like a newborn.

And Daron joined her.

◆ ◆ ◆

MAYBE THAT WAS CANDICE'S BURDEN. Daron heard: We got your back, Joan of Arc! What they'd really said was: Show daddy what you made in school. No one took her seriously, and so she had to take everything seriously. The guard at the Mt. Olivet cemetery and Officer Hernandez. Vandenburg. The professors. Even Sheriff and the coroner. It wasn't Candice's fault that everyone listened to her, believed her, assumed she was next in line.

Maybe there was such a thing as tragedy. He had thought she had a power, but recalling how cautiously the flower vendor at their Saturday market twohanded over her bouquets as if she were the frail one, as if delicate, vital petals sprouted from her heart; how Sheriff & Co. talked her out of testifying; how they all wanted to protect her. Even he, Daron, had claimed her idea as his own, to save her blame. Maybe she felt caught between two worlds, too. Maybe she knew how often she was denied direct experience because she looked like someone who had to be protected. Maybe she'd sensed all their big blonde spots, could pass them no more than a starving man an abandoned picnic, a gator a baby. Had she taken everything, or given everything?

[sniff]

Yes. A body could be—No!—was a gift. If the body was a gift, what was Louis's death? Was it a gift only if accepted, and could it be accepted only if change ensued? It wasn't ironic, it wasn't a waste, it wasn't tragedy, was it? Maybe it was ironic if he died pretending to be black in order to raise awareness about how reenactments lionize racist traditions. It was also ironic if he died trying to be ironic and, fucked up as that was, he and Charlie reached that conclusion separately, sharing it the last night of Charlie's visit, which, he remembered with a shudder against that chill of time, was only hours past.

[sniff]

He'd also heard Charlie's mom's take on things:

The Incident at Braggsville had been too much for Charlie's mother to bear. It would not have been the first time a Chicago boy made his way South and fell into trouble from which he was dredged, taking second class down and the sleeper back, at least most of him. History always takes her piece, so that the Devil can find his way home.

No, that wouldn't be the first time, and true we needed progress and people needed to stand up for what was right, and we needed to speak our minds even if our voices cracked, but this was a sacrifice of biblical proportions, and only God himself had the foresight, courage, and well-for-all to sentence his offspring to such a fate, to sacrifice his child for the good of all mankind (God herself, we say sometimes, but rubbing, holding her son's head to her breast, No, No, No, she hums, never would a mother do or ask such a thing).

But God also had the advantage of being able to resurrect his son, to return upright what the wicked world laid to ground, to breathe into him what light drove the first bird to venture off its safe limbs, the first fish to flounder and struggle ashore, the first single-celled organism to divide, to decide two was better than one, that then there was at least the possibility of love. God had it like that. That's how God rolled. Not us. Metaphysically: hooptie-ville. Besides, as Dad always said, Racism is the white man's problem. He started it, and he needs to fix it.

It was too subtle, he knew, they all knew, quite the serpent it was, not unlike the notorious reptile, the so-called demon in Eden, but this one says, Eat of this fruit of the knowledge of race and know thyself to be master of all. Only they who do not eat the fruit bear its painful seed.

[Louis's cousin had been on a talk show, and was right when he said: Every day that you continue your deceit and your imperialism and your exploitation. Your nepotism. Every time you lie to protect your friends and circle the wagons you are making a choice. Who could blame Louis's cousin for being angry at what he'd described as a murderous academic exercise? That had cut Daron, who had thought the university the center of the world and learned it was only a part, a smaller part than one imagined, certainly less than advertised. Not all people warm much to others, and nothing the school said or wrote would change that. Uprooted from the soil of lived truth, none of their theories, French philosophers, or social justice creeds amounted to a hill of beans, and wouldn't grow a beanstalk if they did.]

Daron wants to tell Candice, in sooth . . . yet tells her not . . . that he reread his college application letters, then reread his letters. He was right about wanting out. The best thing would be to never return home because you can't escape after you're 'let' in.

[sniff]

He wants to tell her that their professor had lied, lied, outright lied when she described white privilege as a kind of heliotropism, plants nodding at your passing, plants bent willy-nilly at your passing. It had made sense at the time, but it was a lie. Race wasn't a natural system and didn't follow natural laws any more than it followed rational ones, and shouldn't be compared to natural laws.

Young D'aron had walked the midnight garden flashlight in hand, scanning azaleas, probing morning glories, even inserting a pen light into a crocus. (Sixty-sixty, as Louis would say, 60 = 10.) (Nycti-nasty? Louis would say, You know what's up with that.) When his father, rifle at hand, found his son thus engaged, he'd chuckled until he choked, but for the first time, D'aron sensed envy and sadness in his father's laughter, and as they walked back to the house, the Holler behind them, D'aron, who usually felt safe with his father's heavy arm warming his neck against the fall chill, with the fine hairs teasing his clean jaw, had the uncanny sense that his father wanted to tell him something but couldn't or didn't know how, or, worse even, didn't yet know that he needed to, felt it as surely as the prickling that arose when one entered the Holler, that ghostly presence that announced itself only after you were too far beyond that rank of elfinwood to turn back.

[pause]

He wants to tell her . . . in sooth . . . yet tells her not . . . that God did Adam and Eve a favor, as his father had done him. No one could live well knowing that much about someone they loved. So he had to turn them out and be alone. Maybe that, and only that, was tragedy.

Maybe Louis's cousin was right, Daron thought, maybe we lied to ourselves as the postmaster and my parents lied to me. Or maybe this is what the Greeks meant by tragedy, not that there were two equal claims, but that your heart so wishes them to be twinned that it's torn asunder by desire deeper than love.

(¿Por qué? Because because because nonetheless understandably.)

He wanted to tell her . . . in sooth . . . yet tells her not . . . cannot . . . about the collective, née militia, how his father later that night—after John-John, dinner, desert—had cried, because D'aron wasn't Irish; because D'aron Andrew Jackson from Detroit was his father's best friend in the Gulf, a real American, African-American at that, saved his father's life twice, and even stayed with them a spell after he lost his own son in Goddamn Saddam, the Sequel; because his parents could never sell their Braggsville home, nonetheless Daron wanted to—really, truly wanted to—call Agent Denver, even wrote a letter telling him, Drop a net on the whole town, the butcher, the baker, the candlestick maker (and the postmaster), in short, everyone in the Hot Air factory, then tore it up, understandably. How could you blame them for working together, for looking after their own? Besides, as his father said, the collective weren't really a threat. None was. Black people weren't no more interested in starting a race war than making mayonnaise. And in regards to population, the Mexicans were just outfucking us; it's plain and simple ándele, arriba, arriba under the covers. But most importantly, as his father said, You can't not be white. So there's no good use chewing yourself rough as a cob about it. He wanted to tell Candice all, but it wouldn't bring Louis back. [sigh] He swallows this serrated ache—because because because nonetheless understandably—it would only break her heart.

(Besides, wouldn't he be blaming them for mysteries beyond their comprehension? His certainty that Candice had been raped, his suspicion that Charlie didn't want to seek vengeance because he was black, his anger when the residents of the Gully [Candice forbade him to use Gulls] apologized for inconveniencing him. Where had that come from? All that smoke in his head, and yet he'd never so much as wanted to light a match at a black person, never hoped any ill on them. The N-word. Nigger. Where had that come from? He'd never said the word aloud, though it had pop-locked into his mind, beatboxing unbidden. Didn't *the N-word* mean the same thing? How would it feel if someone pointed to Charlie and yelled, Hey, you N-word! How would it feel? It? How would he feel? He? How would I feel?

How did anyone, anyone, any-damn-one, in this country, for Methuselah's sake, rise above the mire? Bootstraps? How did anyone live without salt or pepper, speak plain and easy, not want to taste *fucking* instead of sex or carnal knowledge, *ass* instead of buttocks or juniors, *nigger* instead of negro or colored. F-U-C-K-I-N-G-N-I-G-G-E-R-A-S-S-E-S. The cosseted spelling out, and, when not allotted a letter at a time, the highfalutin way they said it all—carnal knowledge, buttocks, negro—said it in that tone which was first cousin to that patronizing timbre used to announce the choo-choo train entering the tunnel when babies were fed. Even then you knew, even the babies knew, that the real good shit was on the table for the adults to nosh.)

He tells her . . . about the afternoon he scaled the support beams and found himself . . . found himself . . . found himself confused . . . no . . . confronted . . . no . . . found himself staring down the international menagerie in the garage loft: The Charlies, the mammies from New Orleans, Salt and Pepper Climb on Cucumber, as well as the Bibinba, Zwarte Pieten, and Hajji Firuz dolls his cousins picked up while stationed abroad, not to mention the Blackface Soap and Watermelon Whistler tins, and that strange guy wearing only a loincloth, turban, and a skeleton's grin. Cloistered in the dark, arranged as if guarding the steaming furnace, the fire of accusation in all eyes. When he was young they had both intimidated and empowered him. When he was young, after being threatened, D'aron-aka-Brainiac-aka-Sissy-bka-Faggot shadowboxed with the Moor in the loincloth and, when teased, he, Hippie!, kicked The Charlies. One Tom's scalp was pocked along the left, jagged laps and plastic gashes of exposed skull a visible testimony, a reminder of the day that happy hickory stick licked some pits into its head—after yet another rhubarb with Rheanne. When he was young, they were talismans giving him a measure of control over the world. As an adult, they were curses, provoking him to think that as much as he loved Charlie, it would be easier if there were no black people at all. If only there could only be people. (He'll feel this sensation again during a study abroad outing to the Vatican museum, when the docent explains that among the garden sculptures crowding one seemingly forgotten small, sideways gallery are pagan idols, that a closer look reveals amid the doe and stag statues of Mithra and Gayomard and other decommissioned gods, and his guilt is replaced by the terror he feels for us all. This he will dare to speak, but that only breaks her heart, too.[   ]

Chapter Latest

Good morning, sir. I am Candice Marianne Chelsea. I am a junior at Loyola. I am pre-law, with a minor in public health. My date of birth is July third, 1992.

You don't need to call me sir, Candice.

Yes, sir, Agent Denver.

My name is D'aron Little May Davenport. I was born November thirtieth, 1992, in Braggsville, Georgia. I am a student at Loyola. I'm a general studies major.

I'm Charles Roger Cole . . . Chicago-Bronzeville . . . Jan. fifteenth, 1994 . . . Northwestern University . . . Junior . . . My major is sociology and my minor is social justice, though I still don't understand why you need that information. At school I write for *The Protest,* so know that if we veer dangerously from protocol, the public will be informed . . . What? . . . My friends can tell you their own names. They can talk; believe me . . . Yes. I did use a semicolon in speech . . . No . . . right there. That should be a semicolon.

No, sir, not as far as I know. There wasn't any intention or suspicion there would be any danger. If we thought there was, Louis and I wouldn't have gone.

Who in Braggsville would have threatened us? Threatened me?

The town's not that kind of place. No, we were never threatened in any way.

Suspicious of what? Tampered with the harness? . . . That question does not even make sense.

Daron? Secret societies? No, sir! [laughter] No, we never went past the backyard.

I never seen anything back there 'cept that old church.

Daron in a militia? . . . How long are we going to be here?

We thought it was a good idea at the time, sir. Maybe Charlie and Daron never really liked the plan, but Louis and I always did. States' rights is not a convincing argument. If we say the Civil War was not about slavery, next we will say that slavery was not about race. Even if we get generous and say it wasn't about race—at first—what else could it become about? How else could you live with that cruelty? If we deny that, then we'll say that it was actually a beneficent institution, an early model for the welfare state. The Holocaust goes next, starting with the argument that it was also about handicapped people and the Roma, too. Where does the self-deception end? And who pays for it? We do as much as them! It's like all those crazy right wingers . . . Yes. We hoped to get news coverage, but not because of the reasons we did, sir.

No. I never thought it was a good idea, but I didn't think it was a dangerous one, either.

If you can't see how this could have been effective had things gone differently, no explanation will make sense to you anyway.

Only those letters I showed you, sir. The marriage proposals from the prisoners.

When do all these interview records—the paperwork and recordings and all—become available to the public? All the fan mail I told you about is just between us, right? You promised that, right?

That's not me. My social media accounts are still closed. I'm strictly IRL—In Real Life. I haven't been on Facebook or Twitter or Instagram or Tumblr in months. The barbed and articulated Glenn Beck anal plug was the most civilized of the threats.

The blackface was a surprise to me, sir. The wig, not really. I mean it wasn't surprising, knowing how . . . Louis [pause] Louis was. But seeing it was a surprise . . . I thought I saw a tattoo. A cross tattoo right here at the bottom of the thumb. I should have brought my phone, sir.

I wasn't there.

You know I wasn't there.

Yes, sir. I realize you might still have a hard time believing or understanding how or why four Berkeley students thought this would be a good idea. We never would have done it in Iowa.

I don't know why we thought it was a good idea.

Of course you don't understand. Look at you. You guys still wear windbreakers.

It was my idea, sir.

It was my idea.

It was my idea.

Mine, sir.

Mine.

I already told you.

Why not, sir?

Why not?

I already told you.

Says who, sir?

Says who?

I already, already told you.

Yes, sir. It was foolish to fake a hate crime to make the opposite point. But we weren't faking a hate crime. We were reenacting American history.

We shouldn't have done it. It hasn't made anything better.

It was collaboration, a collective effort. Dress in period costume and ask about slavery. Questions such as: If you could have slaves, would you be happy? Would you still drool over pro bowls? Would you stop reliving this moment like it was the last of the glory days, a decisive fourth-quarter ninety-nine-yard run ending in a fumble? Would you ease up on the fucking zombie movies? Maybe I'd tell them not to get so red under the collar about Obama, an aberration not soon to be repeated, that a rising tide lifts all boats, but a yacht is still a yacht and a dinghy is still dingy. Maybe I'd ask them why they're so damn restless. Why so impatient? Slow-acting poison yet kills. Maybe I'd ask why they can't just be happy, or at least satisfied. That's the question. Yes! Why can't they be satisfied with our fractional existence as bequeathed by Article One, Section Two, Paragraph Three of the United States Constitution? Why can't they be satisfied that three-fifths is the only real number with an irrational tail, its endowment an enduring quotient, a problem never solved. That is the only question: Why can't you just be satisfied that thirty-five percent of black children grades seven through twelve are suspended or expelled during their school careers compared to fifteen percent of whites; that the *Diagnostic and Statistical Manual of Mental Disorders* continually refines Oppositional Defiant Disorder and that each revision accelerates the process of coding, tracking, and incarcerating black children; that only sixty percent of blacks attend high schools that support and prepare them for graduation, compared to nearly eighty percent of whites? Why can't you just be satisfied that blacks are three times more likely to be searched and four times more likely to experience use of force when stopped by the police; that when mandatory minimum sentencing laws for crack fell under judiciary review, mandatory minimum sentencing was instituted for juveniles, grew straightaway long in shadow, is applied disproportionately to black youth; that blacks comprise only twelve percent of monthly drug users, but constitute thirty-two percent of persons arrested for drug possession; that blacks comprise twelve percent of the gross U.S. population but forty-three percent of the incarcerated population; that wages grow slower, twenty percent slower, for former black inmates once released from prison? Why can't you just be satisfied that the black unemployment rate is roughly thirteen percent while the national average is roughly seven percent? Why can't you be satisfied that blacks represent approximately twelve percent of the population but account for over forty percent of new HIV infections? Why can't you just be satisfied that blacks have the highest mortality rate for all cancers combined? I demand not that you be happy about this, only satisfied. Are those numbers not sufficient cause for your quiet celebration? Can you not simply enjoy the conflagration, warm hands at those bodies burning eternal, Roman candles illuminating your feast of angels? Why can't you allow this crime to continue, this auspicious advent of the slow crime movement, to continue victimful but assailantless? Why can't we have a hands-off instead of a handout? Why must you dress for the party? Why must you dance around the swallow dug so generously as to mock natural phenomena? Why can't you let us die in peace? Why can't you look at this Medusa: history in its myriad inversions, loops, whorls, coils, corkscrews, spirals; from slavery to Jim Crow to the Carceral State; this Medusa: the Möbius trip; the helix that stitches the U.S. of A.'s social DNA; yes, coach goes to New York, but never disembarks; this Medusa: upon whom to gaze turns only heart to stone, for how else could a people suffer so unless born of inherent deficiency or willed by God? Why can't we bear our Curse of Ham in the privacy of dignified silence? Why can't you sit back, crack a cold one, and let America in toto enact its collective reenactment? That's what I would ask, but I wasn't there. So, would I do it again? Yes, but this time I would attend. That's what I would do differently. Only that.

Never funny. No, sir. Not funny in that way, sir. By joke I didn't mean inconsequential. I meant a critique, like a political cartoon.

Of course not. Never. I knew it wouldn't be funny. You might be able to laugh at it a lot, but it wouldn't be funny. No way.

Richard Pryor funny? Paul Mooney funny? Eddie Murphy funny? Louis CK funny? Funny like your windbreaker? Bill Cosby funny? Maybe more like George Bush was a two-term president funny.

No, sir. Never again.

No.

Next time I'll only hang an effigy.

No, sir. I'm just glad it's over. It's like I barely escaped a burning building.

If I could be there to make sure it went okay . . . but not in my hometown again . . . Well, actually, no, nowhere, in no one's hometown.

I plan to! My answer won't change regardless of how many ways you ask the question.

No, sir. I don't know of any militia. I never saw any militia activity in Braggsville. Daron has never mentioned any militia to me. If I may ask a question, sir, when will . . . I don't want anyone to know about those proposals . . . I would hate for the others to know about those letters . . . I wish I hadn't read them . . .

There is none that I know of, and I've lived there all my life. That's why you didn't find anything when you combed the wood or the Holler. There is no militia or hate group in Braggsville. It's the center, the heart of Georgia, the city that love built.

You mean the reenactors, the entire town, the state of Georgia, the South, or the entire United States of 'Merica?

GO AHEAD, MR. CHANG:

In the words of Ice-T, O.G., Eat a dick.

Please, Mr. Chang:

[PAUSE]

Blood is thicker than water, but you can stab a motherfucker to death with an icicle!

[DRAMATIC SIGH]

I'm reminded of this joke:

A very, very white kid walks into the kitchen where his mother is baking and rubs chocolate all over his face, and says, "Look, Mom, I'm black!" . . . No. Fuck that . . . An Asian kid walks into a kitchen. A handsome Asian kid. Real handsome. So you know he's Malaysian. Smart, too. Smart as shit. In case you didn't know he was Malaysian. (And shit is smart, smart is shit, who carries whom?) Walks into a kitchen where his mother is baking. He rubs chocolate on his face. He turns to his mother and says, "Look, Ibu, I'm a rapper!" His mother smacks his head, bends him over and spanks him, and says, "No. You're going to law school! Go tell your uncles what you told me!" The boy finds one uncle and says, "Look, Pak Long, I'm a rapper!" His uncle bends him over, spanks him. Then tells him to go show his other uncle what he did. The boy runs out to the backyard, where his other uncle is medicating Cali-style. "Look, Pak Ngah! I'm a rapper." His uncle laughs, reaches out to pluck him, but being heavily medicated, pokes him in the eye with his roach clip. The little boy—the smart, handsome little boy, that is—runs back into the kitchen and cries into his mother's apron. What have you learned? she asks. The boy yells, "I've only been a rapper for five minutes and I already hate you Chinese people!"

See, as they say around Little D's way, I ain't no restaurant Tabasco. You heard my man, Big-C, fool! It's gigantomachy, fool! Like Big-C, I still say it was a good idea. We're activists. Activists are always ahead of their time.

And we never die—in peace or otherwise!

I've freed thousands of slaves,
and
I could have freed thousands more
had they known they were slaves.

—Harriet Tubman,
FOR REAL

Appendix 1

Sexicon
(The Glossary for the Rest of Us)

Alien technology—See **Incredible edibles**.

Bingo wings—Aka triceps tacos, the bag of skin hanging inelegant from the triceps of many an arm. Most commonly seen when waving.

Braggsville—see **U.S. of A**.

Civil War—(1) Polite disagreement. (2) When people of the same race argue over what to do with people of another race. (3) Divide and conquer taken to the extreme.

Crumb catchers—Snake charmers.

Cultural relativity—We're okay, they're okay.

Curse of Ham—Genesis 9:24–25.

> 9:24—And Noah awoke from his wine, and knew what his younger son [Ham] had done unto him.

> 9:25—And he said, Cursed be Canaan; a servant of servants shall he be unto his brethren.

> Also known as the Curse of Canaan, Ham's son. For centuries apologists quoted this verse to justify slavery. During the Enlightenment, religion was supplemented with scientific justification such as phrenology (the measuring of skulls). In modern times,

both justifications have been supplanted by standardized testing
and speech patterns.

~~D-Nice~~

Digital literacy event—See chapters 16 and 22.

Dropping it like it's hot— ███████████████████

██████████████ Maybach ████████

██████████ make it rain ████████████

███████████████████████████

███████████████████████████

██████████ pole █████████████ tea party

██████████

Essentialize/essentialism—Essentialize lives next door to stereotype. They have been dating for some time now, and they frequently appear together on Fox News and at conservative events.

Ewoks—(1) Mammal-like bipeds native to the forest moon of
Endor. Made famous by the Star Wars movies. (2) Tree huggers
from the wilds of Berkeley.

Freud—Nineteenth-century cocaine enthusiast. "Woe to you, my
Princess, when I come I will kiss you quite red and feed you till
you are plump— you shall see who is stronger, a gentle little girl
who doesn't eat enough or a big wild man who has cocaine in his
body. In my last severe depression I took coca again and a small
dose lifted me to the heights in a wonderful fashion . . ." [from an
1884 letter to his fiancée Martha Bernays].

Hermetic irony—(1) Aesthetic productions delivered without the
metadiscursive features traditionally relied upon to decode them.
(2) The joke you don't recognize as such. (3) Laurel and Hardy.
Abbott and Costello. Amos and Andy. Laverne and Shirley. For
years popular comedy and irony have depended on a clear separa-
tion of powers. A comedic duo has a straight man and a comic.
The comic delivers the punch lines, and the straight man acts
as the audience's surrogate, expressing rage, frustration, aplomb,

whatever the appropriate emotion may be, freeing the audience to laugh and assuring them that the joke is not on them, that it's safe to be amused and not outraged. Many new media such as online videos or mock websites are self-contained. In other words, the audience has no windsock, no surrogate, and no laugh track, nothing to indicate where the joke begins and ends—hence, hermetic irony. When Louis method tweets the bumper sticker slogans, he thinks it's funny because he knows he is joking. As Sheriff points out, and demonstrates, no one unfamiliar with Louis or the immediate scenario is guaranteed to come to the same conclusion.

Holler—A small valley or hollow.

Incredible edibles—See **alien technology.**

Institutionalization—The spiritual and emotional ossification of higher education's long-term inmates.

Institutionalized racism—Structural racism.

Internet—The bisexual digital incubus.

Irony—The use of metal where wood is expected.

Ishi—Man.

Johnny Appleseed—Semen.

The Juniors—(1) Euphemism for buttocks. (2) Littler versions of yourself.

Kerana—Because.

Ku Klux Klan—Social club dating back to mid-nineteenth-century America. Bringing a Message of Hope and Deliverance to White Christian America! A Message of Love NOT Hate!

Likening—(1) Industrious folk climb the ladder of success, others take the escalator (to paraphrase the great Biggie Smalls, RIP). Likening is your pass to the escalator. (2) See Michael Jackson. (3) See Beyoncé.

Lynching—(1) Ceremonial purification and sacrifice featuring a piñata stuffed with sweetbreads instead of sweetmeats. (2) Ritual offering to the New World gods of honor and justice.

Mengapa tidak—Why not?

Methuselah—You'll have to ask him.

Micro-aggression—The plastic gun of racism; you can sneak this one through security most of the time because it is comprised of nonracist ways of being racist, nonsexist ways of being sexist, and the like. E.g., You're not like other BLANK people, or, You speak English very well.

Mondays—Be honest. Who likes them? *You* can be honest with *me*.

Oppression porn—(1) The depiction of poverty, oppression, and/ or despair with the intent of provoking moral arousal. Frequently appears as digital media, literature, and pseudo-immersive favela tours. The most common side effect is a dangerously inflated sense of national and/or cultural superiority. (Fortunately this form of priapism does not require lancing, an icepack, ligation, or aspiration.) As with Internet porn, desensitization is a risk. See also favela tours. See also Sally Struthers.

Pen mawashi—That pen-spinning trick you wish you could do.

Performance—That time you expressed great thanks for the toe socks, lavishly praised a lackluster meal, or thanked your boss for the "feedback."

Performative intervention—(1) Activism through acting. (2) Acting through activism.

Porque/¿Por qué?—Don't know a Spanish speaker? Treat this as an invitation to meet one. Say hello to a busboy or a nanny or a Supreme Court Justice.

Reenactment—(1) See reenactor. (2) See **Braggsville**.

Residual affect—When colonial echoes haunt the station.

Sexicon—(1) A sexy-ass lexicon. (2) The practice of using big words where small would do.

Siddhartha—Like Bruno Mars, Lady Gaga, and Biggie Smalls, Buddha had a birth name.

Slavery—Employment by another name.

Solid CO_2—Dry ice. The magic engine of smoke machines. Metal-heads, ravers, *Wicked* fans, salute!

So-Me—Social media.

Split in the bib—If you know what a bib is . . . and where a bib is worn . . . and what it covers . . . join us in this celebration of cleavage!

Suprasemiotic domain—The constellation of meaning-making practices engaged in when people communicate face-to-face, including speech, writing, gesture, and dance. The suprasemiotic domain is the communicative field within which people naturally function. Speech is more than words. Body talk.

University—(1) Colonialism's most exquisite distillation. (2) The birthplace of spring break.

Uppity-Plessy—Portmanteau combining *uppity* and *Homer Plessy,* the plaintiff in the United States Supreme Court decision that upheld the states' rights to segregate under the doctrine "separate but equal."

U.S. of A.—See **Braggsville.**

Veil of Ignorance—The golden rule gussied up as a fancy theory.

Wormhole—(1) A shortcut through the space-time of virginity, the journey through which leaves the driver exalted and vehicle unde-filed. (2) The dirty virgin superhighway.

Appendix 2

Works Cited

Adorno, T. (1985). On the fetish-character in music and the regression of listening. In A. Arato & E. Gebhardt (Eds.), *The Essential Frankfurt School Reader* (pp. 270–99). New York, NY: Continuum.

Butler, J. (2000). *Everything*. New York, NY: Various Press.

Certeau, M. (1984). *The Practice of Everyday Life*. (S. Rendall, Trans.). Berkeley, CA: University of California Press.

———. (1986). *Heterologies: Discourse on the Other*. (B. Massumi, Trans.). Minneapolis, MN: University of Minnesota Press.

———. (1988). *The Writing of History*. (T. Conley, Trans.). New York, NY: Columbia University Press.

Cowan, E. R. (2015). *16 Voices*. Atlanta, GA: WXP.

Davenport, D. (2015). Residual affect: Race, micro-aggressions, micro-inequities, (autophagy) & BBQ in the contemporary Southern imagination at Six Flags. In T. G. Johnson (Ed.), *Welcome to Braggsville*. New York, NY: William Morrow.

De Haan, F. (1999). Evidentiality and epistemic modality: Setting boundaries. *Southwest Journal of Linguistics, 18*, 83–101.

Fairclough, N. (2001). *Language and Power.* (2nd ed.). Upper Saddle River, NJ: Pearson.

Griffin, R. (2009). *Fundamentals of Management.* Mason, OH: Cengage Learning.

Johnson, T. G. (2010). Birth of a notion (From the great divide to the digital divide: Consilience in literacy studies during the age of the supra-semiotic domain). Unpublished MA thesis, UC Berkeley.

———. (2011). Death of the straight man: New media literacies, aesthetic education and ambiguity in the ironic age. Unpublished proposal, UC Berkeley.

———. (2012). *Hold It 'Til It Hurts.* Minneapolis, MN: Coffee House Press.

———. (2015). *Welcome to Braggsville.* New York, NY: William Morrow.

Mahiri, J. (Forthcoming). Deconstructing race: Micro-cultures shifting the multicultural paradigm.

Ochs, E. (1996). Linguistic resources for socializing humanity. In J. J. Gumperz and S. C. Levinson (Eds.), *Rethinking Linguistic Relativity* (pp. 407–37). Cambridge, UK: Cambridge University Press.

Old Hitch (1825–1999). *Cooking by Heartlight.* Braggsville, GA: Handheld.

Acknowledgments

Welcome to Braggsville, aka Braggsville, aka BRAGGZ, aka B-Ville, aka WTB is indebted to many a literary Sherpa: Eleanor "I'll Be the Judge of What's Hard to Sell" Jackson, aka agent extraordinaire, who found a home for "this peculiar little book that I can't quite describe"; Jessica "Make Them Say No" Williams, editor deluxe at William Morrow and sister by another mister; Katy "Clear-Eyed" Whitehead at HarperCollins UK/4th Estate; Jaimy "Libretto" Gordon; Sam "The Architect" Chang, quiet revolutionary; Connie "The Guru" Brothers; Karen "The Linguistinator" Russell; and Wiley "First Responder" Cash; and early readers Kate "Volte-Face" Sachs, Richard "Scorpio Rising" Katrovas, Jennifer "Mixmaster" Dubois, and Shane "Reed" Book.

Without saying—well, almost but not quite: U. C. "Fiat Lux" Berkeley; that beautiful woman who looks good in everything she wears; the Braggsville novel commission; LaCherriere, French polyglot factory; Vltava, both minor planet and river; Sheryl "Town Crier" Johnston; Saturn; Kelly "Eagle Eye" Farber; the tribe at HarperCollins/William Morrow, most notably Team BRAGGZ—Candice Carty-Williams, Mandy Kain, Lynn Grady, Kaitlin Harri, Jennifer Hart, Doug Jones, Morwenna Loughman, Tobly McSmith, Jonathan Pelham, Mary Ann Petyak, Clare Reihill, Kelly Rudolph, Liate Stehlik, Mary Beth Thomas; and the home teams at Iowa y WMU y OSUC y Berzerkeley y Atl y Nola.

And of course: my mom, Irene "The Matron Saint" English-Johnson; my dad, Tyrone "Esquire" Johnson; my sister, Ingrid "A Cappella Queen" Johnson-Lucuron; mon beau friere, Pierre "Waffle House" Johnson-Lucuron; the neph, Little Geronimo, for being a model of tenacity; Elizabeth "Tour de France" Cowan; and the old school ATL krewe (Click, Costarides, Dixon, Hazim, Mclean, O'Ree, Prieto, Price, Wages). Masquerades! Know that your contribution is not forgotten, even if you are not listed here.

About the Civil War, Sigmund Freud, Ishi, and "protecting and serving," there is little left to say, except that half a haircut is no haircut at all.

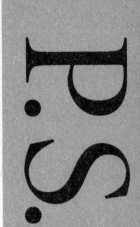

About the author

About the book

Insights,
Interviews
& More . . .

Read on

Meet
T. Geronimo Johnson

Elizabeth R. Cowan

BORN AND RAISED in New Orleans,
T. Geronimo Johnson is the bestselling
author of *Welcome to Braggsville* and
Hold It 'Til It Hurts, a finalist for the
2013 PEN/Faulkner Award for fiction.
He received his M.F.A. from the Iowa
Writers' Workshop and his M.A.
in language, literacy, and culture
from the University of California,
Berkeley. He has taught writing
and held fellowships—including a
Stegner Fellowship and an Iowa Arts
Fellowship—at Arizona State University,
the University of Iowa, UC Berkeley,
Western Michigan University, and
Stanford University. He lives in
Berkeley, California.

Behind the Book

AM I *THE* MAIN CHARACTER? In other words: Am I the model for Achilles Holden Conroy? Readers of my first novel often ask that question. I hope to field similar inquiries about D'aron Davenport, the main character of *Welcome to Braggsville*—even though he is white and I am not.

That wasn't the original plan. When I was scratching out snatches of dialogue and notes to self on napkins and scraps of paper, Daron was black, and not because I am, but because of my abiding interest in how we form identities in hostile environments. More specifically: I am interested in how racism, sexism, or any other jerkoff-ism alters our internal landscapes (our self-confidence, our range of aspirations) and our social landscapes (friendships and amorous engagements). Even more specifically: After living in the lower right-hand corner, the left side, and the middle of the contiguous United States, I became fascinated by how varied are the experiences of being a black male. Being black in Columbia, Maryland, or Berkeley, California, is not the same as being black in New Orleans or Atlanta (neither is being white).

But when I began writing *Braggsville*, the impulse to lead with a black protagonist was derailed. First, faking a lynching requires a critical—and in this case, comedic—distance. Fear and stress tend to collapse that distance. I had a hard time imagining a black ▶

3

Behind the Book *(continued)*

kid from the South returning home
to protest a Civil War reenactment by
staging a death by hanging. Second,
research revealed that militias had
grown exponentially since Obama's
inauguration. Those militias had a very
specific membership profile, one that
would not surprise a black kid from
the South but might disturb a white
kid from the South. One rule novelists
could live by: Don't send characters on
journeys to discover what they already
know. Last, while moving around the
country I learned that white people who
are not racist tend to underestimate the
vitriolic nature and enmity of those who
are—perhaps blacks overestimate the
same—and everyone tends to exaggerate
the ills of the South, as if it's the bad
sibling in whose company you can't help
but shine, that relative you relish calling
a "character."

But am I *this* character? The details
diverge, but like D'aron/Daron, I live/
lived in *at least* two worlds that don't
always speak the same language or hold
the same values: Columbia, Maryland, a
planned community, and New Orleans,
planned chaos. I also spent chunks
of adulthood in two distinct locales:
Atlanta and Berzerkeley, which, like
Braggsville and the Gully, are on
opposite sides of the sun, separated
by far more than simple geography.

My Columbia school smelled like
wet paint, and boasted an experimental
open-space plan with small classes
grouped in pods. My New Orleans

high school had chipping paint and chattering radiators, a higher student-teacher ratio. Street names in Columbia are inspired by Robert Frost poems, Tolkien's *The Hobbit*, and other literary touchstones. My subdivision, Bryant Woods, was named after the poet William Cullen Bryant. Only upon writing this essay did I discover that my village in Columbia—Wilde Lake—was built around a former slave plantation.

When I moved to New Orleans in tenth grade, one of the first things I noticed was that streets were named after military heroes, such as General Lee (*Mom, wasn't he on the other side?*). My taste buds blew a fuse, too, as did my concept of confinement. I was thirteen and a half years old, and as far as I could recall, it was my first time in classrooms with doors. The small library, wedged into a corner, was barely a quarter of the size of Columbia's, even though both schools had equal numbers of students. The school didn't have discipline problems, or drug problems, or metal detectors. The school had a waiting list. Yet my tenth-grade peers were being taught civics lessons that I had learned in sixth grade.

My biggest lesson: *I talk white.* I learned this in my Nola Spanish class, of all places, where they teased me for sounding white. Not for sounding American when speaking Spanish, but for *sounding white when speaking* ▶

Behind the Book *(continued)*

English! Yes! I was denounced as a *proper talker.* I say "they," but I mean one particular person, the guy who started it by condemning me, then mocking me until I cursed: *Fuck you! My nemesis's response: You even cuss white.*

None of this occurred to me until a job interview years later when the interviewer pontificated about how the United States is a country where a kid from urban New Orleans public schools can attend Stanford. I was confused until I realized he'd assumed I spent my entire life there, and I thought back to that civics lesson and how most of the kids I met while *at Stanford as a Stegner Fellow, not a student,* were from yet another world—one where the high schools teach two languages plus Greek or Latin (*Mom, how does a language die?*).

But after that interview, when the full weight of my fortune clicked on like neon, I felt survivor's guilt, and sorely divided between who I am and who people think me to be, and just damned lucky, and possessed by a new appreciation for education, and anger at how unprepared my Nola classmates were, and what can I do with that, except write?

Did I tell you that the kid—Mark, I remember his name now—who teased me for *talking white* later bonded with me over skateboarding? Did I tell you that Mark, who mocked me for not sounding black enough, *was white*, a fact that made zero impression on me at the time? It didn't occur to me until I wrote this essay. Why think about it now? Maybe he was Daron/D'aron, too. ✺

Questions for Discussion

1. The main settings are Berkeley, California, and Braggsville, Georgia. What are the primary characteristics of these towns, and why does the author juxtapose them? Is there significance to the nickname "Berzerkeley"? What about Braggsville's town motto, "The city that love built"?

2. The main character is introduced as D'aron, but he drops the apostrophe when he reaches college. What do you think this signifies about his changing self-identity? What is the implication later in the book when both spellings are used in his internal monologue? Do you think these two parts of his identity are reconcilable?

3. What does the story of Ishi, the Native American who lived in a museum exhibit, symbolize for Candice? Can you think of a historical figure or event that has had a profound influence on your worldview?

4. At Berkeley, the students are encouraged to utilize "performative intervention" to shock onlookers into engaging with uncomfortable topics they might otherwise ignore. Do you think this type of political performance is a worthwhile and eye-opening approach, or is it too avant-garde to ever be useful?

5. In the beginning of the book, D'aron views his parents as uneducated and unworldly, but later his perception of their worldview seems to evolve. Do you think the author intended the reader to like or dislike them? Can they and the other Braggsvillians be categorized as simply "good" or "bad"?

6. Compare and contrast D'aron's personality with his cousin Quint. Have you ever had a friend or relative with a wildly different worldview? Were you able to make your relationship work in spite of your differences?

7. Louis's brand of humor frequently makes light of issues around race and culture, but he isn't characterized as a racist. What differentiates his jokes from Quint's? Does his stand-up routine help him get along with D'aron's family? Under what circumstances do you think it's "okay" to joke about race?

8. After the staged lynching, when Candice returns to the Davenports' home in torn clothes from the direction of the black neighborhood, D'aron assumes she was raped and picks up a gun to retaliate, even though she never states this herself. What do these actions suggest about D'aron's internalized prejudice? How do his prejudices affect his behavior toward Charlie when Charlie later makes a personal revelation? ▶

9. In the aftermath of the "Incident at Braggsville," the Davenports come under scrutiny, and it's suggested that D'aron may have masterminded the entire event. Does this warped interpretation of the facts parallel the way real news is reported through media channels today? Can you think of a news story that you felt misrepresented or omitted information to serve the agenda of the author or reporting agency?

10. The militia touts itself as a well-meaning group of concerned citizens, but their stronghold on the city is extreme, as evidenced by the abrupt shift in the way the Davenports are treated after D'aron visits the hunting lodge. Have you ever belonged to a group in which the majority's viewpoints were so strong you felt you could not disagree with them? Did you choose to leave the group, if you could?

11. Jo-Jo and D'aron are forced into a startling and severe punishment ritual by the militia. Is this a "performative intervention" of its own kind? Between Jo-Jo's physical castigation and D'aron's banishment from the town, which do you think is more severe and why?

12. In the "Sexicon," the author defines Braggsville as "U.S. of A," and vice versa. Do you think Braggsville is a microcosm of the United States? In

which ways do you perceive it to be similar to or different from the country as a whole? Is Berkeley depicted as an ideal environment, or is it criticized for its own shortcomings? ∾

Have You Read?
More by T. Geronimo Johnson

HOLD IT 'TIL IT HURTS

"*Hold It 'Til It Hurts* is a novel that defies categorization. It is at once a mystery, a meditation, a modern-day myth, an indictment of war and an ode to love. But this much is clear: This masterfully written book, filled with trenchant observations and unafraid of tenderness, marks Johnson as a writer to watch."
—*San Francisco Chronicle*

"The magnificence of *Hold It 'Til It Hurts* is not only in the prose and the story but also in the book's great big beating heart. These complex and compelling characters and the wizardry of Johnson's storytelling will dazzle and move you from first page to last. Novels don't teach us how to live but *Hold It 'Til It Hurts* will make you hush and wonder."
—Anthony Swofford, *New York Times* bestseller author of *Jarhead*

"*Hold It 'Til It Hurts* is the kind of impressive debut that marks its author, T. Geronimo Johnson, as a writer with a career that bears watching."
—Stuart Dybek, award-winning author of *Paper Lantern: Love Stories*